the secret of rainy days

the secret of rainy days

Leslie Hooton

Keylight Books
An imprint of Turner Publishing Company
Nashville, Tennessee
www.turnerpublishing.com | www. keylightbooks.com

Cover design: Emily Mahon
Text design by Karen Sheets de Gracia in the Archer and Soin Sans Neue typefaces

Library of Congress Cataloging-in-Publication Data
Names: Hooton, Leslie, author.
Title: The secret of rainy days / Leslie Hooton.
Description: 1st Edition. | Nashville : Turner Publishing Company, 2021. |
Identifiers: LCCN 2021021834 (print) | LCCN 2021021835 (ebook) |
ISBN 9781684427048 (paperback) | ISBN 9781684427055 (hardcover) |
ISBN 9781684427062 (ebook)
Subjects: LCSH: Women—United States—Biography. | Best friends—
United States—Biography. | Families—United States—Biography.
Classification: LCC HQ1421 .H66 2021 (print) | LCC HQ1421 (ebook) |
DDC 305.4/092/273 [B]—dc23
LC record available at https://lccn.loc.gov/2021021834
LC ebook record available at https://lccn.loc.gov/2021021835

PRINTED IN THE UNITED STATES OF AMERICA
21 22 23 24 25 10 9 8 7 6 5 4 3 2 1

For

My Beloved Village,

The MMOPS, and

Sandy.

MY Life would not be possible

YOU are my lucky dust

xo

Each friend represents a world in us,
a world possibly not born until they arrive,
and it is only by this meeting that a new world is born.

—Anaïs Nin

Let us be grateful to the people who make us happy;
they are the charming gardeners
who make our souls blossom.

—Marcel Proust

prologue

Her name was Nina Barnes Enloe. She was my grandmother. I was born in 1988 and named after her.

My parents did this for two reasons. The first was because my grandmother was mean. If Ebenezer Scrooge and the Wicked Witch of the West produced a love child, the result would have been my grandmother. "Biggie," as we called her, was controlling and cheap, and her laugh had an uncanny resemblance to that of the Wicked Witch. In their disillusionment, my parents thought that maybe having a namesake would negate all of that, would lead her to become doting and grandmotherly, but they were wrong.

The second reason I was tagged with my grandmother's name was simply because she informed my parents it was what they ought to do. And they acquiesced. But she didn't stop there. I was forever saddled with an infuriating nickname, counter to hers; one that showcased her dominance and my deference to her. They called me Little Bit, and my slight stature only secured Biggie's justification. She was the grand imposing mansion, and I was the tiny outhouse tucked behind her. She was big-boned, and Mama said I looked like a toothpick with two chocolate chips on either side of my face—brown eyes so large they could take in an entire room in one blink.

I dragged that stubborn moniker around until I crossed over the Mason-Dixon Line and dumped it outside Manhattan. But it's funny how those things shadow us even when we think we've left them behind.

I suspect the real reason my parents named me after Biggie was in the hope she might leave her piles of unspent money to me. Well, one of three ain't bad, and let me say this, as the old brokerage ad goes, "I earned it."

In the beginning, my best friend was Winifred Woodwiss Baxter. I think the gods gave her a lifetime supply of what I call "lucky dust." I, by merely being in her presence, sometimes got a sprinkling of it myself, but it never stuck like it did on her. We called her Win. And "win" she did. At everything. Her whole damn life.

Lucky dust is an intangible thing. You either have it or you don't. Like charisma. Or confidence. When it's knitted together with beauty, intelligence, and wealth, the tapestry of your life is just easier and prettier than anyone else's. Hardship is blunted or simply nonexistent.

Yes, Win had lucky dust. Good fortune is vibrant and alive; even now, it continues to trail and puddle behind her wherever she goes. She wears a uniform of splendor, and no doubt she'll be draped in it all the days of her life. I've watched this from the beginning. I had a front row seat, cloaked in an unremarkable uniform of envy and awe.

I don't know when Win became my best friend. She was just always there. Like air or water. Or memory. Win was my only friend, except for Carter and Haines, until Avery came along and moved in down the street just before my thirteenth birthday. Haines is my older brother, and his best friend Carter was like a brother, so neither one of them really counts. Plus, Win and I didn't really play with those boys. They only wanted to build forts or play basketball, and neither Win nor I were into roughing it outdoors, especially in the summer in Alabama. My curly brunette hair would have been one giant frizz ball.

It didn't always thrill me to hang around Win and all her lucky dust. We haven't always liked each other, she and I. It's hard to say why we stayed friends, because there were times when I refused to even talk to her. But maybe like a weathered marriage, it's about loyalty and hanging on when there's nothing but a collective history, which, in our case, turned out to be everything.

No, our friendship hasn't always been easy, and it doesn't just include us. It also includes Avery. Avery, who always took my side when I battled with my grandmother. Avery, who accepted me just the way I was, flaws and all. Avery, who called me Nina the first day she met me, never limiting me to "Little Bit." Avery, who taught me about life and love and sacrifice and that home was more than bricks and mortar and a place to lay my head at night.

Win was my best friend by default. Avery was the best friend I chose.

part one

one

"Come home," Haines said.

My reflexes responded for me. "I can't," I said into the phone. He waited, something he had gotten good at doing. "Cy's big Christmas party is tonight," I started to explain, "and I have to go."

"I didn't think Cy Weinberg had Christmas parties," Haines said, pronouncing Cy's last name with a whine—something else he had gotten good at doing.

"You know what I mean, Haines. He's the managing partner and my boss." I cradled the phone in my ear and cut the tags off yet another little black dress. "It's a holiday thing. Besides, you know that George will close five deals before the night is over, and I need to be there." I also knew where this conversation was headed.

"Biggie is dying, Bit," Haines said. "For real this time."

My doctor brother, for all of his education and stature back in our hometown of Erob, Alabama, would never understand our grandmother. But I had gotten good at playing her kind of game: cold and unsentimental.

"Haines," I said, "Biggie has been dying for two decades now. She goes into the hospital to die twice a year like most of us go to the dentist for cleanings." When it came to Biggie, my lawyer skills easily trumped my doctor brother's prowess.

"Bit," Haines persisted, "she wants to talk to you. She says she *needs* to talk to you."

I sighed. Biggie always needed to tell me something, and I had gotten used to that, too, over the years—her underhanded manipulation, that is. I gathered up all the loose dress tags on my bed. Did I really pay that much for a simple black dress? Indeed, my threshold for "sticker shock" had risen since moving to New York City almost five years ago, but occasionally I still questioned my purchases. After hiring personal shoppers at Saks, Bloomingdale's, and Bergdorf's—where this little number came from—my wardrobe had improved even though my pocketbook suffered. Ah, the New York singles' way of life.

Of course, I was only putting off the decision I was about to make. I plopped into my old club chair, a Biggie cast-off, as was the rest of the furniture in my apartment. But admittedly, her cast-off furniture suited me, unlike "Little Bit" or "Bit," the hand-me-down nicknames I still tried so desperately to shake. I replaced nude heels with black, a decidedly easier task than responding, to go with my dress for tonight. No more avoiding the issue; it was concession time.

"Listen, Haines, I'll talk with you about all of this tomorrow. In the meantime, I'll see what I can do."

"I can tell you're in a hurry," Haines said, "but need I remind you, Bit? Who is your family, anyway?"

There it was. The sting. The indictment. The truth.

I stood up and reached for my jewelry box, eager to conclude our business.

"I hear you. I'll check in tomorrow." We both knew he had landed the ultimate blow.

"Bye, Little Bit," he said, severing my connection to him and to the childhood nickname that everyone in Erob, Alabama, still used, except for Avery.

I slipped on my dress and my New York moniker—Nina

Barnes Enloe. I was the only one in the Metro NYC area. There was no Biggie. I was not a sequel here.

As I brushed on lip gloss, the doorbell rang. Even without opening the door, I knew it was George, arriving early, as usual, to take me to Cy's holiday party. Someday, when I made partner, I'd have an apartment like George's with a doorman, an intercom system, and an awning.

And there he was, George Taber, my boyfriend, comfortably handsome and tall. I looked up at him, and his kind eyes smiled down into mine.

"Hi, Shorty. You look beautiful," he said, standing 6'4" to my 5'1." The nickname fit, and while not much better than the one I left behind in Erob, coming from him, it was certainly tolerable. I figured he was allowed one minor shortcoming anyway—no pun intended.

He wore a tobacco-colored cashmere sports coat, gray slacks, and cuff links. No one wore cuff links in Erob except to weddings and maybe funerals. George leaned into my neck. "Happy anniversary," he noted, zipping up my dress the rest of the way. I smiled. He remembered. It was true—we had met exactly two years earlier at Cy's annual party and had been dating exclusively pretty much ever since. We laughed together now at the memory, an unspoken version replaying itself in happy silence.

He was a man generous with his compliments. When Cy, prompted by his loving and feisty wife, Olga, thrust George in front of me at that party two years ago, I had immediately respected his looks and his job at Goldman Sachs, but it was George's kindness, his generosity, and his self-deprecation that won the day and, eventually, won me.

"So, this is the talent I've heard so much about and have been anxious to meet," George had said, reaching down and enveloping my outstretched hand in his own. Safe, warm, and kind. "I admit to being a little intimidated," he'd added. "Cy likes me, but you're in a completely different league in his eyes!"

As if Cy was as adroit at love connections as he was at mergers and acquisitions, he then excused himself, pleading hosting duties and leaving George and me comfortably alone. But when I opened my mouth to speak, trouble ensued. Biggie's garden and her years of tutelage popped into my head, and in my best Southern accent, still not tamed by life in the city, I gushed, "George Taber! Did you know that you share a name with a lavender flower? An azalea named 'George Taber'?" What self-respecting person "gushes" in New York City?

He had looked at me in a bemused way and then asked if he could get me a drink. When I declined, he walked away but looked back several times, in my mind, clearly unsure as to what he had just been introduced to. I remember thinking, *Way to go, Bit. Way to chase that one away. But then again, that's my talent. Keeping good men at arm's length. All guys love being compared to lavender flowers. He'll never call.* And he didn't, not right away. And then he did, inviting me to lunch. Several lunches turned into a dinner here and there, each of us arriving and leaving in separate cabs until one glorious night when, after dinner, we shared a ride back to his apartment on the Upper West Side.

"Nina, stop daydreaming. We're going to be late," George said now, jolting me back to reality.

"It's a good memory," I murmured.

"Did you get to the best part?" George teased. He pulled me close. How did he know me so well?

"Save it for later," I laughed, gently pushing him away. In truth, I stored up our memories like vintage clothes in an old trunk and studied them through the lens of time. They brought me pleasure, and I did this often.

My phone buzzed as I gathered my coat and purse, and I glanced down at the number. Win. Nothing good could come from answering that.

"Do you need to get that?" George asked as we moved toward the door.

I hit the "off" button on my cell phone, knowing she'd try to text next.

"No way," I said. "We'll be late. Let's go."

A uniformed attendant whisked our coats away and another thrust a tray of hot hors d'oeuvres in front of us. I declined, as I had long made it a practice to dull my taste buds with wine before consuming any of those garish pre-made treats, regardless of how swanky the party. I downed my glass so quickly that George whispered, "Slow down, Nina—we've got all night."

After the gentle reprimand, he pushed a fugitive strand of hair away from my face. "Do you mind if I go and talk with some of the guys?" he asked. I answered by shooing his hand away from my head and directing him toward a circle of similarly dressed partners.

On nights like these, Cy's apartment always seemed grand. People were clustered in small groups in every corner, and yet the place graciously expanded to accommodate the masses. Like they'd been dropped into the United Nations, Cy's guests used these affairs to conduct business—seemingly speaking the same yet different language from normal social conversation, as each moved around the room jockeying for better positions, fancier offices, and raises. They laughed almost too loudly at Cy's pathetic jokes, hoping the good impression at the party would extend to the office the following week. As a last resort, they often accosted Olga, Cy's greatest asset. She helped him by remembering the important things like the names of each guest's children, their children's colleges, and any recent changes in health or marital status. I envied that about her. But her sincerity and compassion were her finest qualities.

On other nights when it was just the four of us—Cy, Olga, George, and me—the apartment transformed itself again and struck me as cozy. The warm-beige brocades draping the massive windows cocooned us in comfort. Olga's choice of muted browns and creams, not unlike those in Biggie's living room and bedroom, were settling; yet also like Biggie's, Olga's heavy drapes couldn't completely protect anyone living inside from family drama and squabbles. Each one of us, in our own way, knew that no barricade, however pleasing to the eye, could keep away the pain of grief, sorrow, and regret.

I remember expecting Cy and Olga to live on Park Avenue, overlooking Central Park—so cliché. But their place, tucked away on the Upper West Side, suited them. As I refilled my wine, I saw George across the room, still deep in conversation and heading toward the study with a colleague. Cy was in another corner, seemingly desperate to extricate himself from some bore. I caught his eye, nodding appreciatively at the tie he was wearing, and he used our eye contact to excuse himself to retreat to the bar cart and freshen his drink.

Uniformed "ants" were running around, replacing and arranging food. Elsa, Cy and Olga's longtime housekeeper, stood at her post near the dining room, commandeering and inspecting all trays as they left "her" kitchen. I suspected that my own dear Agnes, tending to Biggie back in Erob, would be that diligent as well, on the slim chance that she'd even allow caterers in "her" kitchen in the first place. To my knowledge, it had happened once, and only once—when Agnes was feeling "under the weather"—and to this day, the experience remains Number One on the list of "Agnes's Sore Subjects" back home.

I walked over and hugged her. "Hi, Elsa," I said.

"Hello, Nina," she said, acknowledging the big crowd. I nodded and stood by her side; an understanding formed between us.

"Miss Olga made some tuna salad this morning and a batch of those blueberry muffins you like," she offered. "It's all in the fridge. You know where, Miss Nina." She winked at me, adding, "They're wrapped up in case you want to take a few home with you."

"Why do you think I brought my purse?" I teased, winking back.

Entering the kitchen, I took one of the clear caterer's plates and opened the refrigerator. Finding the familiar Tupperware, I spooned a heap of tuna salad on my plate, grabbed the Hellmann's mayonnaise from the bottom shelf, a fork from a drawer, and a stool from in front of the sink. Then I walked into the oversized pantry, sliding the pocket door behind me.

I loved Olga's tuna salad. Like Agnes's, she made it with lots of egg whites and bits of onion, and they popped up like pristine pearls. My only complaint was she was skimpy on the mayonnaise, so I always added more of my own.

The door slid open. "I figured I'd find you in here," Olga said, "and with extra mayonnaise, no less."

"Hi, Olga," I said. I moved aside so she could place her chair next to my stool. "You know mayonnaise constitutes one of a Southerner's basic food groups. That and butter and sugar constitute the holy trinity for Southern cooking."

She closed the door on the both of us.

"You know, darling, there's a whole table of food out there—very expensive food, I might add. Do you really prefer my tuna salad to tenderloin?"

"Sad but true, Olga," I said.

"I made a sandwich myself before everyone arrived," she confessed. I met her gaze, smiled, and took in the whole of her face. As usual, her full lips were stained with red the color of merlot wine, and her shiny, jet-black hair was pulled back into a tight, neat bun. Her eyes, deep-set and teal green, were beguiling and brilliant as ever. I had met her for the first time at this same party two years ago, gravitating toward her style and grace and warmth. Her eyes conveyed many things—kindness, amusement, vulnerability, and sadness.

In the past couple of years, we'd formed a friendship; our chats became longer and longer until we eventually met for coffee and then dinner. We discovered commonalities. There's not a pinch of salt difference sometimes between a Jewish mother and a Southern mama. Both cook. Both feed their families. But my mama was more of a "milestone cook," an "event cook," who did her best for funerals, weddings, and parties to mark special occasions, while Olga took great joy in baking for "no reason at all." Olga also took great pride in telling me about her heritage and her family, especially her daughter, Robin, who unfortunately had passed away too young.

"I guess that makes three of us who like my tuna."

I remembered and touched her hand. "Oh, Olga, is today the anniversary?"

"Monday, but I appreciate you thinking of us, darling." Without preamble or awkward change of subject, we smoothly moved from discussing tuna salad to discussing the untimely death, over ten years earlier, of Cy and Olga's only child, Robin.

A teenager when she had passed away, it had become their habit to mark the anniversary each year with a quiet evening at home. Last year they invited George and me to join them.

"Biggie's sick," I told her, sharing what had been weighing on my mind. "She's in the hospital again. Haines thinks this is it."

Soothing my worries, Olga reminded, "Doesn't your grandmother look at death rather frequently?"

I managed to laugh. It was nice to know that Olga understood.

"Yes, she does. But this time she told Haines that she wanted—no, *needed*—to talk to me. In person."

"Any clue as to what's on her mind?" Olga asked.

"No, but knowing Biggie, it could be about watering the ferns twice a week. The '*needing*' to talk to me in person is new, however."

"I'm sure it's fine, Nina. Besides, if it was truly serious, I think your friends would be phoning as well."

I nodded and finished off my second glass of wine, thinking of Win's call earlier.

"What's George doing?" I asked.

"Making money," she answered.

"Cy?"

"The same."

I smiled, knowing I could be making money, too, by billing some of my time at this party to a client, if only I would come out of the pantry and work the room. But when I stood up, I realized how unsteady I was. I decided to collect my blueberry muffins and go find George to see how much longer he wanted to stay.

My worries, scattered and uncollected, remained behind.

two

In the bleary wakening, when it's uncertain where you are and what day or time it is, I heard a phone ringing. I was hungover, which explained why, initially, Haines's message and the news he shared caused only a superficial wound.

We generally stayed at George's place, especially after a night at Cy and Olga's. I listened to Haines's message again.

"What was that all about?" George asked distractedly, moving beside me and then getting up and out of bed, presumably to bring the coffee pot to life.

"Biggie did it," I answered slowly. "She really did it this time. She called my bluff, and she up and died."

George came back in the room, took my phone off the bed, and placed it on the bedside table.

"I didn't come home, so she pulled her ace of manipulation. Haines said she went peacefully. I guess she won that bargain with God after all."

I pulled the covers tighter, and George moved in beside me, wrapping his arms around my shoulders. "Are you okay?" he asked.

"Her presence was just so enormous. I guess I just thought she would outlive us all. I can't believe she really did it. Haines said that the last thing she said to anybody who would listen was 'I don't want Bit to be mad at me. Please tell Bit not to be mad.' She kept saying it, apparently, over and over."

"I'm sorry, Nina," George said, rubbing my shoulders before leaving again for the kitchen. He returned a few minutes later with a steaming mug of java and one of Olga's muffins, and we sat on the bed, quietly sharing.

"What do you think your grandmother meant by that?" he asked.

The wound started to fester and burn and throb with a reality I couldn't have predicted. And along with the pain came a fear, a realization that I had no control over what Biggie may have meant or done.

"I need to go home," I said abruptly.

"I'll go with you."

"Absolutely not." I loved him for offering, but it would be too much to do that to him. In the two years since we'd met, I had yet to take him home to Erob, and even I wasn't sure sometimes as to why.

"I mean, George, you have to know Biggie," I explained, attempting to soothe the hurt in George's eyes. "She wants to be the center of attention, even in death." I guess I knew that if I brought him into the three-ring circus that was waiting in Erob, he might never want to see me again. I described how the hometown paper would chronicle the life and times of the elder Nina Barnes Enloe along with the inevitable comparisons to her namesake, the younger Nina Barnes Enloe, who arrived home from the big city just in time for the funeral with her handsome young suitor. Hard pass.

"George. Biggie would haunt us forever."

"Can I still be your handsome young suitor?" George asked. My heart expanded for him; in the midst of turmoil, he could still make me smile.

"Yes, but not in Erob," I said. I reached up and gently squeezed his face with my blueberry-stained fingers. "I need to do this alone."

Back in my apartment, I first bought a plane ticket and then called Haines as I packed my suitcase.

"I'll be there in four hours," I told him.

"Good," he said. "Avery will pick you up."

George drove me to the airport. And I went home to do something I thought I would never do—bury my grandmother.

The plane ride into Atlanta would take a couple of hours and the drive to Erob another hour or so beyond that. No need to rush, and delays were always welcome. It gave me the time I needed to swap one life for another. And to remember.

How is it we can't recall what we had for lunch last week, or something pressing on our "to do list," yet a memory can pierce the wall of the past and collapse itself into the present with explosive vengeance? Like a crane might demolish a condemned dwelling. How is it that the same memory ends up defining us and builds its own idea for our life? A dream house or a flimsy house, fashioned on a floodplain.

I thought about what I had told George and how true it was that Biggie craved—no, *demanded*—to be the center of attention. Like the day she'd taken over the room when Daddy died, how she'd firmly planted her feet in front of her grand piano—a reception and a receiving line of one. How it had all played out just the way she'd orchestrated it, except for the part about her only child killing himself. Yet, despite it all, with her head held high, she'd towered over me and Mama and everyone else in the room.

From funeral casseroles to flowers, everything had always come to Biggie. She was a trained manipulator. She had spent her entire life manipulating the whole town, and now, traveling back to Erob for her funeral, I wondered if she had saved her most diabolical plans for me.

"Prepare for landing," the flight attendant called out over the intercom, interrupting my thoughts. I noted the irony of her words. Given the circumstances, how could I truly prepare for what awaited me in Erob?

I was thankful that it was Avery who would be meeting me. She'd greet me with a bright, much-needed smile, unlike Win, who I knew would start giving me orders or her opinion before even saying "hello." Yes, from the time we were children, Win could always be counted on to make a bad situation just a little bit worse, and nothing was sacred—even on the day we learned my Daddy had died.

"It's like I've always said, Little Bit," she'd started in her abbreviated Win-Speak. "O.K.O.P.—Our Kind of People—just don't go off and kill themselves." Win seemed to know a lot about suicide and took the opportunity that day to enlighten me on its consequences.

No, Avery would never give me orders, or offer an opinion unless I asked for it—which I did, often, because I really did want to know what she thought.

Avery, the bright beacon of light who knocked on the back door of our house the day of my daddy's funeral, bearing a casserole and so much more. With only God's irony would that turn out to be the best day of my life had it not, up to that point, already been the worst. But I would learn, thirty years later, Daddy's death was just God's little warm-up act.

The real worst day of my life was yet to come.

three

When the plane landed in Atlanta, gone was Nina Barnes Enloe, the grown woman in control. Just like that, I was once again "Little Bit," the little girl everyone thought they knew—except for Avery, bless her—who always called me by the name I was given at birth. Waiting for her in Baggage Claim, I knew that she and I had bonded on that horrible day so long ago. I understood then, as I understood now, that I could tell her anything.

"Nina!" I heard her call. I looked up to see Avery dodging people and their luggage to reach me. We hugged, and she cried.

"Why are *you* crying?" I asked. "I'm the one who should be crying!"

"Oh, I know, but I also know how much Biggie meant to you. I'm sad because *you're* sad. Her death hurts me because I know it hurts you," she explained. "I'm so sorry, Nina." Little did she know that I had yet to shed any tears for Biggie. And wasn't sure if—or when—I would.

As we drove out of the airport toward Erob, I asked, "How's everybody?"

"Fine, Nina," Avery answered. "We're all fine here. Nothing new . . . well, except for Biggie, of course."

I nodded, then asked, "So why does she not want me to be mad at her?"

"I have no idea. I think Win may be your go-to girl on that one, but I will say it was all the buzz at the hospital. Biggie even grabbed my arm and told me to tell you that herself."

"You saw Biggie?"

"We all did. We were all there." Avery stated the obvious but was nice enough to not mention my absence.

"It all sounds very Macbeth or Lear-like, doesn't it?" I ventured. "She probably split her fortune three ways between Haines and me and his kid, and she just doesn't want me to be mad that I didn't get it all or something." I trailed off, adding, "It's probably nothing," hoping to bolster my own beliefs and squelch my rising panic.

"Your grandmother loved you, you know," Avery said. "And she wasn't as mean as you always made her out to be. Remember the Debutante Ball? And my wedding to Arush? I'll never forget her generosity."

"She had her moments, Avery, I'll give you that, but there were usually strings attached. Once I figured out how to work them, I did all right with her." It was too long ago to bother explaining to Avery about the deal we'd struck with the Debutante Ball. Too long ago to worry about now.

A comfortable silence settled between us as we drove closer to my childhood home.

"You're quiet." Avery noticed.

"Just thinking," I said. "And remembering."

"We miss you around here, you know."

"I know. With Biggie, it seems I've been here a lot in the past year, but I haven't had much time for visiting, I guess. I miss everyone. But my life is in New York now, and I'm really happy there."

"I know. There's George too," Avery said, and then, "Here we are," as we crossed into the city limits. Suddenly, I was confused about where to actually go. Out of habit, I would usually choose Biggie's house, but what to do now? Should I go to Mama's instead? To Haines's?

Avery decided for me, turning down Biggie's street and pulling up in front. Dozens of parked cars, mourners no doubt, lined both sides of the street, leaving Avery no choice but to just stop in the middle of the road.

"Listen to me, Nina." She pulled my shoulders around so I had to look at her. I anticipated an "Averyism"—hoped for, actually—one of her "pearls of wisdom" that I could treasure and mull over the next few days. I waited.

"If your grandmother wished you not to be mad at her, maybe you should listen."

"Oh, Avery, you see the good in everybody. Hell, you even see the good in me."

"And don't forget," she added, "I see the good in Win too!"

"You *are* a saint," I said, stepping out of the car and grabbing my small bag.

"I love you, Nina," Avery called after me as I moved up the driveway.

"You too," I called back, walking through the breezeway and toward the kitchen's back door.

I fought through the usual cloud of memories as I entered the kitchen. The door snapped shut behind me, announcing my arrival. I adjusted the scarf on my gray suit—"this year's black," Andrea at Bergdorf's had proclaimed—and I smiled, as I knew Biggie wouldn't care how I was dressed today as long as she was dressed better for her final send-off. It was Mama and Win I had to please.

Agnes appeared, arms opened wide. I returned her embrace.

Agnes's eyes were heavy with expectant tears. It occurred to me that of anyone, Agnes probably knew Biggie the best, unquestionably the longest, and she was one of the few who had genuinely liked my grandmother. But then again, Agnes loved us all, and of anyone, she deserved to sit in the front row at the funeral.

Agnes Prestridge started working for Biggie when I was little. She was a member of the First Methodist Church and was known for two talents: cooking, and choosing the *wrong* men. They always left. Biggie couldn't cook, nor did she care anything about it, so at first it was a way to help both of them. Neither one wanted charity. Over the years, an unlikely friendship was forged. Agnes was as tall as she was wide and had white hair that looked like a halo on her head bestowed by God himself. Somehow, her cooking gig turned into several days a week, but we loved Agnes. Mainly because she ran interference between us and Biggie.

I had watched Agnes's hands many times—in Biggie's kitchen—making our favorite: yeast rolls. She would knead the dough back and forth, and the constancy of the motion made everything bearable. Then she'd cut and shape the tiniest little balls, brushing the insides with butter. Her hands would fold them over like an oyster waiting for a pearl, and then she'd softly pat each one like it was the head of a beloved child. We'd all anxiously wait until the smell of yeast and butter wafted from the kitchen, beckoning like a loud church bell saying, "come get one 'fore Miss Nina finds out!" Taking turns with spoons, we'd dig into jars of homemade strawberry, fig, or whatever fruit preserves had been canned in generous supply, and slather it all over the freshly baked rolls.

In the years since, I'd often thought it was those rolls that held us together.

I hugged Agnes again, tighter this time.

"Bit, do you want a roll?" she asked. "I made some just this morning."

"You know I do," I answered. "You always know."

"Have one quick 'fore you see your mama," she added. "She's in the living room with the rest of the folks."

"Of course she is," I said, going to the refrigerator for some homemade jelly.

"Agnes," I asked, taking advantage of the quiet, "do you have any idea why Biggie would think I would be mad at her?"

"No, Little Bit, and I'm staying out of it. I may be old, but I'm smart enough not to get in the middle of any business involving you and your grandmother. I've learned there are no winners . . . just casualties," she said.

That was true enough.

"Well, Bit, you're home." I heard Mama's voice heading in my direction. "You look nice," she said, as we stood face to face.

"I have a matching skirt to wear to the funeral," I explained.

"Here," she said, thrusting an envelope into my hand. I recognized it immediately as being part of my grandmother's married stationery. "We've all been waiting for you. It was your grandmother's last wish for you to tend to the arrangements," she added, confirming my suspicions. The plans and proceedings had indeed been hinging on the return of the not-so-prodigal granddaughter. "It's all there, in her note. All of her instructions and requests. I suggest you get started as soon as possible."

I thought she was done talking, but there was more. "Bit, I don't know where you plan to stay, but I think it would be best if you stayed here so the house won't be empty."

With that, she passed me and moved out of the room. Mama and I had settled into a familiar place—cordial and respectful of each other, nothing more. Our eyes made contact. Nothing else. Even in times of sorrow, Mama and I wouldn't breach each other's personal space with something so intimate as a hug. Yes, we were family. Yes, we were blood. In much the same way as a detached garage is still part of a house.

In truth, Mama had always been distant; it just got worse after Daddy died. And the day I moved to New York City and left Erob behind, an even greater distance, beyond mileage, grew between us. Mama became increasingly cool, if not downright frigid at times, ceding me to her mother-in-law, to Biggie, carrying out Biggie's final instructions.

I remembered how right after Daddy's funeral, Mama had been forced to get a job. It took her days and days of phone calls and interviews, but she eventually landed a position teaching English at our school. Barely a week before, Carter broke the news to me that Biggie was rich. While Haines seemed to already know, I was shocked because I couldn't figure out why Biggie had been so stingy with presents all of these years and why now Mama had to work.

"Are you sure about this?" I pressed both he and Carter one day, demanding clarification.

"Yes," Carter had said, sounding very sure. He was the best eavesdropper in our little group, and with his daddy being a judge, he usually brought us all kinds of interesting information.

Piles of money.

At the time I figured Biggie would finesse some sort of way to take it all with her.

But now, who knew?

I took the back stairway through the kitchen up to Biggie's old bedroom—the one she'd had for years until her body betrayed her and she had to move downstairs. It remained as it always had—the ivory drapes, plush ivory bedspread, and overstuffed chair. I sat on the edge of her bed and looked down at the letter I held in my hand. "Little Bit" was all it said on the outside, written in her confident stroke. It almost matched the gray block letters engraved on the ivory stationery I knew to be inside. Gray. Always muted. Biggie had never liked much color, not in her stationery, her bedroom, anywhere in her house—or in her life, for that matter.

Footsteps creaked on the stairs, and I recognized them immediately. Slow but deliberate. Why hurry when you always know exactly where you're going?

"Hi, Bit," Carter Gideon said, appearing in the doorway. "What can I do to help?"

He sat beside me, and we embraced. I hadn't thought that I needed comfort, but his hug felt too welcome to refuse. Our feet dangled off the side of the bed, conjuring up a childhood memory of Carter, Haines, Avery, Win, and me and our five sets of feet swinging off the side of Biggie's mattress, forever trying to get to the truth of Biggie's money. Short legs, long, long, short, short—Carter and I usually bookended our little group—Haines and Win in the middle. Somehow Win, needing to accommodate her enormous adolescent crush, always managed to finagle her way next to my brother.

Often when we were in the thick of our theories, Agnes would appear in the doorway with a "yeast roll bribe," protecting my grandmother's privacy and, I also suspect, the truth.

I handed the note to Carter. "You read it," I said. As always, Carter's courage never wavered.

Dear Bit,

Please select what I am to wear. As you recall, blue is your grandfather's favorite color.

As for the flowers, this should go without saying, but as a reminder, do not choose carnations nor allow even one sprig of that wretched baby's breath to come near me.

Tend to Elrod if he needs tending to. Sober him up if necessary.

The most important thing: Agnes is to sit with the family.

Finally, Little Bit—I hope you are as content with your life as I have been with mine.

Yours,

Nina Barnes Enloe

Carter laughed, noting her disdain for carnations or baby's breath. "She's a piece of work," he said, "and she didn't even sign it with 'love' or 'Biggie.' Well, I guess it's just you now, Bit."

Finally, and I didn't feel up to the job. Not only was I out of my league with these arrangements, she'd also given me responsibility for Elrod.

Elrod wore many hats. He was primarily Biggie's yardman, house painter, and lightbulb changer—that is, when he wasn't off drinking with his brother. Then, he would end up in jail and become a whole other problem.

Seemed Elrod was always behind and owed Biggie money for something, but Biggie often ended up bailing him out. I always suspected it was less about her generosity than it was about needing Elrod to be at her beck and call. One time, she bailed Elrod out on the Friday before Easter Sunday, not because she felt he should be in church, but because she didn't want the whole of Erob talking about her unsightly lawn on Monday morning.

Suddenly Carter jumped up and went into Biggie's bathroom, closing the door behind him. From memory, I assumed my accustomed spot on the opposite side of the door. After a generous passage of time, I asked, "Are you all right, Carter?"

Everyone was struggling with this it seemed. Avery, Carter . . . everyone but me. Or was it something more? I heard the water running, then it stopped, and Carter emerged.

"I'm fine," he said. "I just have a lot on my mind right now."

I grabbed his arm, forcing his eyes to look into mine. "Like what?" I asked. "Is it Jenny? Is she okay?" Carter and his wife, Jenny, had been trying, rather unsuccessfully for several years, to have a baby. The last thing I knew, she was going in for some more tests, and I had been wondering about the outcome.

"She's fine, Bit. We're fine. It's just that Biggie was like a grandmother to me, too, I guess." I hugged him, heard and felt his breathing rise and fall. In that moment, all of the tragedies we'd shared and weathered—my daddy, his parents, and now both of our grandmothers—seemed to draw us closer together.

I let go and pointed to the blue suit draped over a chair near Biggie's bed. "I guess she didn't trust me to pick it out after all," I said. "Interestingly enough, it's one of the last things she bought and, surprisingly, one of the most expensive."

Before Carter could comment, we heard the stairs creak, impatiently this time.

"Here comes trouble," he whispered just as Win appeared. She moved across the room, kissing Carter first, and then me, on both cheeks.

"How is she?" she asked Carter.

"I'm right here, Win, and I'm fine," I said.

"Well, good. I'm here to take you to the funeral home."

I smiled, knowing how much Win enjoyed participating in every aspect of the funeral spectacle. She was already dressed head to toe in black, ready to grieve.

In truth, Win and I were best like this, doing something, on task. If we sat around with nothing to do, heaven forbid, we would actually have to talk to each other.

She collected the suit, nodding her approval, and she and I drove in her car together to the Featheringills. Sandy Featheringill had the perfect touch of empathy and efficiency.

Select a casket.

Check.

Closed or open? Closed.

Check.

Onward to Mary Sue's, the florist.

Check.

Win then called Ukalene to do Biggie's hair and makeup for her big day. "Now don't go too heavy-handed on the rouge," she instructed. "And for heaven's sake, don't paint her fingernails red like you did Virginia Weathers."

Hair and makeup.

Check.

If it had been a normal day, Win and I could have finished up in time for an early dinner. But it was not a normal day by any means, and it had been a long one for me, so she drove me back to Biggie's.

"Do you need me to help you with anything else, Bit?" she asked. She had pretty much done everything already.

"No. Good catch on the fingernails. Biggie would have a fit. Thanks, Win."

"You're welcome. I wouldn't want Biggie haunting you. I've got to get home to Rich and the children. Just remember to keep all the names straight, and after the funeral, I'll come over and help you with the thank-you notes." A past Junior League president knew a thing or two about the value of a good thesaurus and a timely written thank-you note. Win loathed a tardy thank-you note. She may drop you as a friend right then and there if you neglected to write a thank-you note. I used to laugh about it.

"I see Florence Newsom sent a poppy seed chicken casserole." I waited.

"That would be 'Flo of the No-Notes'," she said. "I am still waiting on a thank-you note for the wedding gift and party I threw her two years ago," she said with great exaggeration. "Can you believe it? She knows better. She hired all those fancy calligraphers for her wedding parties! She couldn't just keep them on staff afterward to write notes for all the wedding gifts. I mean who even knows her handwriting. That still just galls me." When she directed her venom at someone other than me, I found her quite amusing.

"Are you saying that I shouldn't write Florence a thank-you note? Should we just say 'Bless her heart' and be done with it?" I joked.

"I wonder if she would recognize a thank-you note if it bit her in her backside. But two wrongs do not make a right."

I hated to agree with Win, but when she was right, she was right. We referred to Florence as FOTNN. Now and forever. Florence of the No-Notes.

four

I didn't read at the funeral. Biggie had given that job to Haines.

When we got to the Enloe family burial plots, I saw the hole in the ground next to Biggie's husband, H.B., and just above that, Daddy's stone. I also saw finality. Biggie was really gone. The preacher said a few words and a prayer, and I whispered "thanks" to Carter for being one of Biggie's pallbearers.

Massive flower arrangements surrounded the graveside tent; my eyes landed on a particularly garish one done in yellow and red flowers. I moved closer to peek at the card. It was from the city. Figures. Judging from Biggie's long-running feud with the mayor about the bypass, they would choose her least favorite colors. But it was Win who added the perfect "color commentary," so to speak.

"Cost just enough to cross the threshold of respectability while conveying the proper amount of sympathy, don't you think?" she whispered in my ear, adding, "But you big-city folks know how to do it right."

Cy and Olga had sent the most beautiful spray of lilies and white roses. The card read, *We are thinking about you and we love you.*

I wasn't sure of the protocol, but I decided to keep the card, and tucked it into my pocket.

"Now, who are they again?" Win asked.

"Some very special people," I murmured. "Olga's like a mother to me."

"But you have a mother."

While Win would never understand the friendship that I had formed with Cy and Olga, I was decidedly less confused about it than about my ongoing relationship with Win. Or Mama.

Chewy and Jordan, Erob's resident funeral professionals, came up to us at the end of the service. There are some in every small town, and they are ours. If there's a viewing or a visitation or a burial taking place, Chewy and Jordan are in attendance, regardless of whether or not they even knew the deceased. According to Agnes, graveside services are their favorite.

Chewy has a distinctive voice. When he was young, all of his teeth rotted out and were replaced with false ones. They never quite fit, so he smacks when he talks. More of God's irony. His grandmother gave him the nickname Chewy, and he and his sidekick, Jordan, are as much a part of the funeral ritual in Erob as funeral casseroles themselves.

In the open, the duo always felt free to offer a running commentary on the preacher, speculating, "Didn't he just say the very same thing about someone else at that funeral last week?" And they always comment on the weather.

"The sun is finally coming out," Jordan opined now.

"Do you think Miss Enloe ordered it up from God Almighty herself?" Chewy asked. "Elrod, is that a new sport coat? Looking mighty snazzy."

"Well, if anyone could order up the sun, Miss Enloe could. I thought I would show proper respect. It belonged to Judge Gideon, Carter's daddy." Elrod said, sounding surprisingly alert for midday.

After the burial, we ended up back at Biggie's to receive folks we didn't see at the funeral home or earlier. When everyone left and Mama was getting ready to go back to her house, Carter came through the wrought iron gate, alone, sans Jenny. She was tired from the day was all he said. And then Avery and Win pulled into the driveway. The original five—Haines, Carter, Avery, Win, and me—together again in both happy times and sad.

Mama managed a smile as she left to go home. If anyone could appreciate the value of good friends, it was Mama. She'd certainly had, and lost, her share.

Biggie had led a good life and died in a way any of us would envy. So the first order of business was music and cocktails. Wine corks and beer tabs popped while we unearthed high school tunes, college tunes, and even some Sinatra to honor our parents and Biggie.

"Biggie would have a fit," Haines said. "Us dancing away in her living room like this."

"I don't know," I said, feeling a little tipsy. "I think she'd like it. Besides, I got everything right today. Her outfit, the hymns, the flowers, all of the arrangements. You've got to admit, I hit it out of the ballpark. Although it was a little strange sitting in that front pew again."

"Sooner or later, we all have to sit in the front pew," Win said, as if it was her very own platitude. Win was always the first to dress for bereavement and to interject some lofty commentary about death.

"We do?" Avery asked.

"Yes, Avery, we do," Win decided, adding, "and the flowers were lovely, Bit. Biggie would have indeed been proud. Too bad gardenias aren't in season, however. They always were her favorite."

"And yours too, Bit," Carter interjected, "off Mother's gardenia bush in the backyard. Do you remember that?"

"The Debutante Ball," Avery provided, giving me context I didn't need. I remembered.

"Ah, yes. The Debutante Ball," Win intervened. Her tone suggested her version of history and her obvious displeasure with me.

I looked at Carter and smiled. "Yes, I remember, Carter. I'm surprised you do," I said, unable to say they had been the prettiest flowers I had ever received. They were, even though I had told him, warned him, that I wouldn't be caught dead wearing a wretched corsage to that dreadful dance.

"Mother put three flowers together and some . . ." Carter stopped, his memory faltering.

"They were tied with a green ribbon, like a falling star," I added. "They were beautiful." I had relented and for the whole night had danced in a cloud of sweetness. At the memory, Carter only nodded back at me from across the room, embarrassed, maybe like me, to be remembering such a moment with Jenny missing from the room and the conversation. Haines filled in the silence.

"I just remember that we were all scared to death up until the last second that Bit wouldn't even go. Carter's mom, quaking in her boots, worried about the flowers, wanting to please Bit so badly. Because we all know how Little Bit can get!"

A round of "that's the truth" and "you can say that again" followed.

There it was. When did I suddenly become "Little Bit" again? Was it a crime to want something different from the rest of them? A character mutation, to defect from this weird-ass Alabama town to New York City? In my mind it made perfect sense—tantamount to choosing a gleaming penthouse over a dilapidated shanty—but it seemed I might never grow up where this group was concerned.

"Well, at least y'all didn't have to go with Geeky Newsom," Avery piped in.

For the next four hours we settled into a happy rhythm of our best selves, and after Avery had gone home, Win, Haines, and Carter stayed behind to help me clean up.

"I have Biggie's will, you know," Carter said casually, tossing an empty wine bottle into the trash.

Like his father before him, Carter had been a judge in Erob for so long now I sometimes forgot that he still practiced law. Haines and I both shrugged.

"Can you bring it over in the morning, say, around nine?" I suggested. "That should give us some time to get through it before Avery takes me to the airport in the afternoon."

"You're not staying longer?" Carter asked, boring a hole of guilt right through me. Win sidled up next to Carter and added a second helping.

"What about all the thank-you notes, Bit?"

I was not unprepared for this question. Win had a philosophy about thank-you notes: being dead is no excuse for not sending out them out.

"I have finally found the upside of having Biggie's name," I answered. "I inherited an entire wardrobe of engraved stationery with *Nina Barnes Enloe* sprawled across the top. I'm all set, Win." Biggie's expanse of paper products bearing her name was seemingly endless. The prodigious script twirled and announced the *N, B,* and *E* in gray threads of ink knitted together, standing regally on the thick paper in an uncharacteristically submissive way. "I'll just take them back to the city and write them from there."

Win looked as if she had swallowed straight moonshine rather than the last of her polite chardonnay. I wasn't sure if she was more upset that I was using a dead woman's stationery or sending notes with a New York City postmark.

"Carter," I said, "I have a job to get back to. And a life," I added.

For just a moment, awkwardness settled between us, strange in its unfamiliarity.

"I'll come by in the morning," Carter said, heading out into the night, through the breezeway and across Biggie's yard to his own house just next door. I heard the gate clank shut.

"See you bright and early, Bit," Haines said. He and Win both gave me a hug before leaving.

Leaving me alone—in Biggie's house.

The next morning began like a replay of so many others. Agnes in the kitchen fixing breakfast, the smell of yeast rolls, bacon, and fresh-brewed coffee acting in concert, nudging me out of bed. I threw on my khakis with my sleep T-shirt, aware that both Carter and Haines were already downstairs, completely at home in Biggie's kitchen. I came into the room, noting that my brother's medical jacket was fresh and starched as it always was at the beginning of the day before his patients, his sweat, and his job wrinkled it up. Carter wore a suit, but I was unsure if today was a "court day" or not. It had always been a running joke with us that his father, Judge Gideon, wore pants with holes under his robe on "court days" or no pants at all. Haines and he thought that was funny, but it had always conjured up a bad mental image for me.

"Morning, all," I said.

Carter had just started eating, sitting where I usually sat. Haines already had his seat, so after getting coffee, I was forced to sit in the spot normally reserved for Biggie. I felt uneasy as I looked down at Carter at the opposite end of the table.

"Are you ready to get this thing read and over with?" I asked.

"Got it," he said, tapping his suit pocket.

"Listen, Carter," I said, "I'm pretty sure I already know what it says, so you can just summarize if that makes it quicker. But you can bill us just the same." I smiled.

"So, you already know what it says, huh, Bit?" Carter asked.

"Yes, unless she pulled a fast one and lined her casket with money while my head was turned."

The moment of awkwardness returned, along with the rising panic.

"She pretty much left all of her investments to you and Haines," Carter said.

"Congrats, brother. You can now retire." I lifted my coffee cup in a mock toast. I was feeling smug as I, myself, had no intentions of touching one cent of my grandmother's money.

"And there's a codicil," Carter said quietly.

"Codicil?" I repeated, looking at Haines, who didn't seem at all surprised. "When did Biggie do a codicil to her will?" I asked, now looking at both of them.

"About six months before she died," Carter said. He had been family historian to Haines and me throughout our childhood, giving us "inside information" about Daddy's death and Biggie's money. Even now, apparently, he held secrets.

"Don't tell me she got all charitable in her last months and is leaving a chunk to the Methodist church."

"No, as I already mentioned," Carter said, "she split most everything evenly between you and Haines. Except for the codicil."

He paused and pulled a thick, folded document out of the pocket of his suit jacket.

"Bit, the codicil says in effect that Biggie's leaving her jewelry, her account at Citizen's Bank, and her house and all its contents outright to you. She appointed Agnes to serve as the executrix."

"What?" Agnes said. I don't know who was more surprised, Agnes or me. What kind of dirty trick was Biggie playing on me? What did she want to win this time?

"Let me see that," I said, reaching across the table and jerking the will out of Carter's hands. I leafed through it to read:

I, Nina Barnes Enloe, being of sound mind and health, wish to verify that my estate of stock and bonds and other investment monies be divided equally between my two grandchildren, Haines Benjamin Enloe III and Nina Barnes Enloe.

I want to appoint my beloved friend Agnes Prestridge as the executrix of my estate and expect her to receive the full and rightful executor fee.

I want to amend said will to clarify that all my jewelry, my account at Citizen's Bank, and my house and its contents on Magnolia Avenue be given outright and solely to my beloved granddaughter, Nina Barnes Enloe, known as Little Bit.

It is my hope that in this house she will find the love that she has given me through the years. It is my hope she will marry and raise her own children and grandchildren in the house we both loved so much. It is my last wish that she uses this inheritance to live in this house and by doing so finds her own happiness and peace.

I looked again at the document, frantically searching for dates and witnesses. Carter and Haines. Haines?

"You knew about this?" I asked my brother, almost whispering the truth. Anything louder would have made it more real.

"Yes," Haines said.

"I wouldn't have drawn it up without Haines being okay with this," Carter began. "I've seen more families squabble over money and possessions—"

"Did it ever occur to you," I interrupted, "to include *me* in this discussion?"

"Biggie didn't want me to," Carter said firmly. "Or Agnes."

"I never wanted Nina's money. She was my friend."

"You would include Haines and not me? You sure picked a fine time to get your oath of confidentiality back," I spat. "Does anyone else know about the codicil?" I caught the swift glance between the two men.

"Win," Carter said. I was having trouble wrapping my head around the codicil and Carter's disloyalty to me.

"What did she say?"

"To let her know so she could be out of town," he said, and laughed. He considered this a joke. He was one of my best friends, and he was treating my life as cavalier.

The air was thick with my steam. No one said a word. I calmed down, realizing I had overreacted. Realizing I had an ace in the hole.

"It's precatory language, Carter. It's all precatory, and you know it."

Haines, the only non-legal one of us, asked, "What's precatory language?"

"Precatory is a wish, a desire. You can put them in a will, but they are not legally binding. In other words, Biggie can't *make* me live here." I looked at Carter, challenging him. My Duke Law going up against his Duke Law.

"You're right, Bit," Carter said. "We all know Biggie can't *make* you do anything."

"Well, personally," Haines interjected, "I don't know what the big deal is. I'm happy for you. This is what Biggie wanted. Believe me, there's enough to go around. But that's why I couldn't take anything out of this house. It's all yours."

I felt another surge of anger, and with it, *that* memory came rushing back—a flash almost, yet fully formed. I was back in high school. Haines, Carter, and I were sitting in Carter's car, drinking leftover bottles of bourbon and a small jar of something brown. Haines was there, and then he wasn't. There was just enough alcohol to provide me with false courage. I had never kissed a boy before, and Carter just happened to be in the wrong place at the wrong time. We leaned into each other like two pieces of a jigsaw puzzle fitting together perfectly, and he kissed me back—like he meant it. Even then I recognized it was fleeting, so I took in his eyes, the freckles on the tip of his nose, and the taste of his mouth. "What's with the search and rescue with my tonsils?" It shocked me sober. In that moment I knew, for sure, two converging things: One, Carter was the best person I knew, and two, he stirred something in me scarier than surging hormones. It felt so natural—too natural—to kiss him, and I knew if I wasn't careful, it would settle down deep in my bones, and I couldn't let that happen. Mostly because of Biggie. It was always her fondest dream for us—Carter and me—to get together, and there was no way in hell that I would ever give in to my grandmother as long as I lived. "Friends, okay?" Because even though I was just sixteen and drunk off my ass, I knew that Carter Gideon was the kind of friend I needed. He nodded in agreement. So, I forever banished Carter's kisses to the recesses of my memory bank.

Unfortunately for him, the mixture of hooch and bourbon came pounding forth with such a force I had no place to throw up but all over the back seat. And on Carter's lap.

"Shit, Bit," Carter said, as my brother came back.

Now that pesky memory was back, out of nowhere, the way it often arrived at odd times, like in the middle of the night, and it scared me shitless. But why now? Perhaps because I was witnessing Carter's ultimate betrayal. As if he had schemed with Biggie to get me corralled back home. The word "codicil" got mixed with "conspiracy," and I was having none of it.

"So, what do you think, Bit?" Carter had the nerve to ask.

Think? I didn't know what to think. My brain had become mush, and the room had started spinning.

I stood up, spitting the first words to come into my mind. "I'll tell you what I think! If this is my goddamn house, you two can get the hell out! Now!"

Agnes had been quiet, working at the stove, her back to us, and I knew she didn't approve. But I didn't care.

How dare Biggie go and leave me practically everything! How could she? I didn't want anything from her.

I didn't need her house, and I certainly had no intention of living in it. And raising children? Finding happiness? In Erob? Please. But just how far could the bonds of friendship stretch?

This was low, even for the Big One.

part two

five

Daddy was missing—over a day and no one had heard anything from him. Looking back, none of this was new. None of this was really surprising, but somehow, this time, this day, things felt different.

We spent most of the time waiting at Biggie's house, which was also not surprising. I was thirteen, and it was summertime; Haines and I usually spent at least one weekend night at Biggie's house regardless of the season, but whenever there was trouble at home, which was often, Haines and I sought shelter at Biggie's. Summers lulled us to sleep with the sound of the cicadas, and while I don't remember much about the weather itself, I remember the steady, comforting hum of that air conditioner.

On the morning of the second day, I woke to hear Biggie downstairs, talking on the phone to the mayor of Erob. Her voice was confident and big. She was giving him "what for." I knew because that's the voice she gave everyone "what for" with.

I got out of bed and moved quietly to sit at the top of the stairs. Biggie was just below, at her little desk in the foyer, her profile to me. Her gray hair was fixed in the same gray helmet each and every day when she got up. She wore a navy dress, in case she had to run up to our church, which couldn't seem to function without her. Personally, I thought God was supposed to run the church, but evidently not Erob's First Methodist. There, Biggie was in charge.

She twirled a linen handkerchief through the belt that tried to separate her big bosom from her mighty waistline. It didn't succeed, and to my eyes, that 18-hook bra she wore never did hold her generous endowment all that well, since her bosoms swayed when she walked like the revival fans at church on a hot summer Sunday.

Today Biggie's face was serious, her glasses drooping from a chain around her neck. Her steely blue eyes were glaring at the phone as if she were holding the mayor himself in her hands. She took up space; she was a presence—tall, confident, and handsome, even in the way she sat in a chair at that little desk. Even with her only child gone missing.

"That moron!" Biggie said, hanging up the receiver. I blinked. *Moron* was her harshest put-down. That and *honey*.

"Why didn't you ask the mayor if he's seen Daddy?" I asked.

"Heavens, Little Bit," she said, noticing me. "This is a private family matter. I don't want the mayor involved. I was discussing the very idea of a bypass being built for the new Wal-Mart. It will dry up the town's business. It's a bad idea. But the mayor and his cronies are pushing it, and I need to make some calls. That bypass is a bad idea," she said again, for emphasis.

"But what if Daddy needs us?" I asked. "Don't you need to stay off the phone?"

Biggie didn't have an answer for me. It was a pretty ordinary day, waking up to hear Biggie yelling at the mayor or a council person on the phone, but when I saw that uncertainty bloom across her face, I knew this was not an ordinary day.

"Why don't you call Win to come over?" Biggie asked.

"No, thanks," I said, coming down the stairs.

Through the window I could see Elrod setting up his mower to cut Biggie's grass. Elrod always mowed on Fridays for the weekend, if he bothered to show up.

But today was Wednesday, not Friday. As his mower roared

and he started moving, I stopped to ask Biggie, "What's Elrod doing here?"

Again, she was speechless. Not once, but twice in one day, and I hadn't even had breakfast. No, this was clearly not an ordinary day at all.

Behind Elrod, I could see Harriett Gideon, my mother's best friend and Carter's mother, walking toward the breezeway. I decided to see if I could glean some information about Daddy's whereabouts from Miss Harriett and my mother.

I learned this from Mama and her friends: you can get as much from watching as from listening. Facial expressions often told more than spoken words ever could. Like when it came to Virginia, their other friend. She was sick a lot, and when they got quiet and spoke in hushed tones, like in church, and their eyebrows crunched together, they were usually talking about Virginia, and it was usually bad. The doctors had taken her lung out, and everywhere she went she carried her oxygen. She always got to ride in the front seat because of her tank.

And then there was Miss Isabel, Win's mother. She always seemed busy, but no one could readily point to what she did with her time. Many times Virginia would say that if Win had to wait until her mother went to the store and cooked a meal herself, little Win would be waiting "till you-know-where freezes over."

I had just about reached the breezeway when I heard the boys and their bouncing ball. Their basketball had bounced off the wrought iron gate that separated the two yards, and it was heading straight for Biggie's porch.

Biggie had put up the basketball hoop years ago—not so much for Haines but more to one-up the Gideons' pool. That's just how Biggie operated. Compared to Biggie's basketball hoop and court, that pool never had a shot, no pun intended.

But now that basketball was seriously impeding my ability to gather information. It hit the bricks with a thud, and they clattered along behind it. "Watch it, Carter," I said, kicking the ball across the yard in the opposite direction. I tucked myself into the patio love seat and scanned Harriett's and Mama's faces.

The look that passed between them conveyed worry and concern and the thing I couldn't identify then but can now. Resignation. Mama's shoulders slumped into Harriett's, and Harriett forced a smile my way. Mama clasped her hands tightly together as if she had no idea what to do with them.

I went over to hug Mama, but she swatted me away.

"Where is your headband, Bit?" she asked.

"I left it upstairs." She was in a white, sleeveless blouse with a khaki skirt, also a sign of seriousness. Mama always wore shorts in the summer, so her attire that day sits in my memory like an undeniable fashion line of demarcation: before and after.

"Honestly, Harriett, she's Miss Harum-Scarum! All over the place and so forgetful. That headband is the only thing that anchors her head to the rest of her body!" Mama said. I went back and sat on the love seat and tried to push the hair out of my eyes.

Harriett's kind voice matched her sympathetic green eyes. "Judge is going out to the cabin this afternoon." Daddy and Judge Gideon were best friends, too, and Daddy loved going to their cabin. We always spent the Fourth of July there, but I never much enjoyed it. Outdoors in July in Alabama plus the fact that I always had to ask Win to come along—not much of an Independence Day if you asked me.

"Psssst, Little Bit." It was Agnes through the screen door. "Quit eavesdropping! It's not nice."

We were all positioned at our respected posts—Biggie manning the phone, and Mama, with the second biggest job, guarding the front door. It seemed unimportant, really, since only strangers would use it, but I also somehow knew that it could just as easily be strangers that might find Daddy first. We had been here before, too many times to count.

Haines and Carter had the breezeway doors covered, and I, having no talent for manning anything, decided to stay close to Agnes in the kitchen. She had food, but I wasn't hungry; my stomach was churning, and my mouth felt dry. It wasn't until Elrod needed a glass of water that I left, carrying one to him. He patted my head and asked me if Agnes could *maybe rustle up something a little stronger.*

I headed back to the kitchen through the courtyard and forced myself to watch Carter and Haines shoot hoops. Then, as if to make my world complete, in strolled Win. She had on a white tennis skirt from her lesson, and somehow she still looked fresh and clean, her hair in a perfect ponytail showing off her perfect face and bone structure.

"I have B.S.," she declared. That was Win-speak for "Big Scoop." She was always doing that, coming up with her own secret codes for phrases, thinking it gave us something intimate to share. Here I was in the middle of a crisis, and Win had news. She fancied herself a miniature global informant.

"The new girl has moved in, and she plays tennis."

"Have you met her yet?"

"No, and I'll reserve my right to comment. She is from the north, you know," Win said, but before she could add any more disdain, Carter's daddy, Judge Gideon, came through the gate. We should have known from the sound the wrought iron made that this time was different, that the news wasn't good. The long, drawn-out screech climbed higher and higher until, finally, the latch caught behind him with one big, jarring clank. Much like our worry, that gate was stretched to its limits.

"Where's your mama?" Judge asked. His face looked way past grim.

Soon after, the adults marched all of us into Biggie's house and into the study. They told us together, Win, Carter, Haines, and me. We assumed our familiar position: Carter, Haines, Win, and me. Win always positioned herself next to my brother. I knew this time was different from the last time. This time had a more menacing and permanent quality.

The looks on the adults' faces were serious. I guess they figured the number of bodies in the room would diminish the loss of the one that was not there and would never be again. The information assumed almost solid form, as if no one wanted to be the first to let it touch them. Win fidgeted the whole time, unaccustomed to bad news.

Sitting beside her, I watched her twist her hands back and forth in her lap, surveying her freshly polished pink nails. I was having my life ripped apart, and she was admiring her manicure. To this day, every time I see that color, I think of perfect Win and how she stole my daddy's moment.

The details came later, from Carter. Judge Gideon had found Daddy down at the cabin on the back porch, sitting straight up in a rocking chair, overlooking the Gideons' man-made lake.

Judge could see him through the front window. At first, he thought Daddy was taking a nap or just deep in thought. He'd walked softly across the wooden planks, making as little noise as possible so as not to wake or disturb him. But that was before he got to the doorway of the porch. It was then he saw the bottle, then the blood, and finally, he saw there was a gun.

"Goddamn it to hell!" Daddy was opening and closing all of the cabinets in the kitchen and cursing under his breath. Open. "Damn!" Close. "Shit!" Open. "Where in the hell has she put it now?"

I debated. I'd seen a bottle in their closet yesterday when I was looking for my library book. I thought Mama had hidden the book to "teach me a lesson." I didn't want Daddy to drink, but I didn't want him to leave either. Mama always worried when he left.

"There's a bottle up in your closet, Daddy," I whispered.

"What's that, Bit?"

"I said, I saw a bottle up in your closet. Behind your shoe-shine kit."

Like a backdraft from a three-alarm fire, I think we both felt her coming before we saw her. Mama flew through the swinging door and into the kitchen, and her eyes bore into us.

"Go to your room, Bit," she hissed.

"But, I—"

"NOW!"

"For the love of Christ, Frances," I heard Daddy say as I ran upstairs. "She was only trying to help."

"That child can hardly keep up with her library books," Mama said. "Yet somehow she knows where her daddy keeps booze. Is there anything about that scenario that seems right to you?"

"Well, a man should be able to get a decent drink in his own goddamned house."

And so it went. Back and forth—their argument escalating until I heard the front door slam and Daddy's car start up in the driveway.

That was two days ago, and we hadn't seen him since. I should have kept my mouth shut. I shouldn't have tried to help Daddy, but he'd looked so desperate. And then Mama had gotten so mad . . .

The Judge did not go into details, but Carter overheard him later. How he found Daddy, blood running down from his mouth, and on the floor was a bottle of bourbon and a pistol. Carter said it made his dad physically sick finding his best friend like that.

Sure, I didn't pull the trigger, but I wondered if anyone would notice that it was all my fault.

six

The best thing about my friendship with Win was also the worst. We were always honest with each other. Painfully. Brutally. This was evident in the aftermath of Daddy's death. We were sitting on the breezeway on the outskirts of the bereavement spectacle but within earshot of any and all conversations. Our job was to assist Agnes in categorizing the funeral casseroles as they trickled in.

"Wow, there must have been a run on poultry and mayonnaise at the Jitney Jungle," I said to Win as I watched her line up the chicken casseroles on Agnes's kitchen counter, gleaming white Corningware like cookie-cutter houses lining a newly imagined subdivision.

"I just hope you didn't miss anybody," Win responded.

"How could I? You've double-checked everything." I noticed Win smile.

"You've actually done a pretty good job," Win said, although it was impossible for me to tell if she was offering praise or was simply surprised.

"Maybe I'm turning over a new leaf. Maybe my daddy is up in heaven right now, and he's got me changed."

This is when Win scrunched up her nose like when Mrs. Nolan used the word "hisself" instead of "himself." That kind of thing could get to Win more than when I would leave a book behind in second period.

"What is it?" I asked.

"Well, Little Bit, here's the thing." She waited. I'll give her that. "Your daddy did not go to heaven. When you die like *that,* you do not get in." She spoke as if it were some long-standing ecclesiastical rule.

"What do you mean, my daddy didn't go to heaven?" I may not have been as religious as Win, but I had attended every Bible study she had, and I'd never heard of such a thing.

She lowered her voice and brought her face close to mine. "Bit, that is why Biggie and our mothers are so upset. When you, you know, do what your daddy did, you do not get into heaven. Everybody knows that."

I just looked at her. It didn't even sound like a Methodist kind of thing. I was somewhat confident, but I admittedly deferred to Win in these sorts of matters.

"Are you saying that God categorizes the way we die? That suicide"—I lowered my voice—"is a lesser form of dying? I don't believe it, Win. I just don't."

"Yes," came the answer. "Even insurance adjusters don't consider 'that way' a form of dying correctly. That's why families sometimes don't get paid in those particular instances." She still hadn't said the word, like it was a virus and if she said it, she would be contaminated. God and insurance adjusters. When were they ever on the same side?

"Sorry, Little Bit, that's just the way it is."

I thought about it for a while longer before saying, "Well, if God runs heaven like some sort of country club clique, I don't think I want to go there either." I was beginning to hate God. I was also beginning to build up animosity toward the "best friend" sitting there beside me, presumably in the role of providing some comfort in my time of need. Yet in the moments following this revelation, I also felt a deep well of sympathy for my mother and my grandmother. It may not have lingered long, but it was there, edged out only by the feeling against God and Win that took root deep within.

It wasn't until days later that I received an ecclesiastical reprieve to Win's recently disclosed heavenly rule. It came and was, ironically, delivered by my most fervently prayed prayer.

Turns out, all funeral casseroles are not created equal. While most people came, dropped off their food, hugged Biggie, and patted my head, they left as quickly and quietly as they arrived. I guess nobody really knew what to say.

Biggie insisted that everything be held at her house. After all, Daddy was her son. The word "suicide" continued to be whispered, and only when Biggie left the room. *Suicide.* No one we knew had ever died this way. Not O.K.O.P., as Win would say.

Biggie was the center of attention—standing by the piano, the guest of honor with beautiful flower arrangements poised on both sides of her. One sent by the mayor and the city organizers and one sent by Win's family, who had the unique talent to mix understated with over-the-top. A smaller arrangement of carnations sent by Daddy's co-workers at the clinic was relegated to a table outside the living room. It's a wonder Biggie displayed them at all, since they were pink and with baby's breath to boot! In my grandmother's opinion, carnations and baby's breath were the floral equivalent to poison ivy.

The looming sadness could not diminish the power—or was it confidence?—that Biggie could command over a room. Even people who didn't like her were afraid not to show their respects. She was stoic. No emotion would dare break free of her carefully composed and powdered face. Moments like this screamed of Southern hypocrisy to me.

Her gray hair was perfectly styled, fresh from an appointment just that morning. Ukalene had made an exception to fit her in; in the South, death trumps even long-standing appointments. Occasionally, Biggie pulled out the well-starched monogrammed handkerchief she kept tucked neatly in the belt of her trusty navy skirt. Like some scene from a play, she frequently dabbed at her eyes. I wondered if this was for effect, and I wondered how she could hog all of the attention away from Daddy.

I had on my usual navy dress that made me look like a giant blue square. Win sported a new little knit black suit with gold buttons in keeping with the bereavement spectacle. She looked like a child widow.

Haines and Carter sat silent, together, out by the basketball court, the basketball quiet, too, between them. After the news, all action on the court had ceased. I couldn't say if it was out of respect or that neither one could muster the energy to shoot. There was a sad awkwardness about them that day but also a connection that didn't rely on words, and I envied their friendship.

I stayed in the living room with Mama. She thanked the few people who lingered and sat, and I felt guilty for their uneasiness. Mama's face was drawn with lines and was blotchy as if she had been out in the sun, only she hadn't. Her features were diminished, in danger of disappearing from her face, except for the crevices.

She would put her hands on my shoulders from time to time, not as a sign of affection but as a sign of imprisonment for me to stand still and listen to the adults.

"Now, Little Bit, you must remember your daddy was a nice man despite this."

I hated what the adults were saying. They smiled weakly; it felt condescending. When I finally got free, I went into the kitchen to be with Agnes, who knew a little something about condescending people.

"Don't let those folks get to you, Little Bit. They just don't know what to say."

I mean, why *wouldn't* I remember Daddy being a nice man? Despite what?

Then I saw them coming, and I heard Mama say "excuse me" and come through the kitchen. She walked down the breezeway in long single steps, the heels of her shoes clicking, clicking, clicking toward our newest visitors.

Agnes leaned in. "Your mama's a real lady, Bit."

"Come in, please," I heard her say as she opened the door.

I wasn't going to be denied, so I broke free of Agnes.

"Hi, James," I said, peeking out from behind Mama. She turned in exasperation and then hugged me—again, not with affection but with confinement.

"Well, hi there, Little Bit. Why, don't you look just like your daddy."

I was making everyone feel awkward. "I don't know what we're going to do without Dr. Ben," James said to Mama.

I came to find out that practically everyone in town "with means" had been lured from Daddy's practice to the fancy office with the fancy internist, except for Carter's parents and Win's family. Half the time Daddy still was paid in homegrown vegetables or firewood. Haines and I got a kitten when Daddy did Elrod's son's appendectomy. We joked that we should have called him "Services Rendered" instead of Beauregard. Then, after "he" had kittens in my mama's station wagon, we changed her name to Bo-Bo.

I never thought much about cats as currency; that's just the way it was. In a small town in the Deep South, doctors could still help the needy.

"Ben would be glad you came," Mama said.

As James and the others made their way out, Mama and I turned to go back inside. I tried to match her stride for stride, sensing this would make me a lady, too, but each time I fell short.

"Bit, why don't you go find your grandmother," Mama said, like I was some unwanted shadow. I lumbered off.

I spotted Biggie all alone in the dining room. At the far end. In the dark. Clutching the chair where Daddy always sat. She almost appeared diminished, as if there was a stubborn fight between her well-preserved stoicism and some buried heartbreak from failing her only child. I feared if I intruded something would break loose. Something would take the Biggie I had always known away. I left her alone. I went the long way back to the kitchen.

"Well, did you find her?" Mama asked. I stepped away to the door closest to the dining room.

"No. I couldn't find Biggie anywhere," I said, loud enough for Biggie to hear me. When it was just Agnes and me, she nodded and smiled at me.

Daddy's funeral was the first one I ever attended. If one simply observed it, the only thing different between a party and a funeral were the clothes. And most of Mama's friends wore black cocktail attire to parties too. The gaiety was tempered, but certainly not the food. The rows of casseroles were full of creamy chicken and vegetables like fresh squash out of Mrs. Casey's garden. I knew because it said so on the little masking tape labels. In the South, people fed grief.

There was also plenty of cream of mushroom soup and mayonnaise. Hellmann's, of course. I bet the soup and mayonnaise sections of the grocery store mirrored the bread aisle when the weather forecast called for snow. Agnes served cheese straws, pecan tassies, and her famous "tea punch" to, as Biggie called them, "our guests."

Agnes's tea punch started out like regular good ole Luzianne iced tea—Cinderella before she got all gussied up for the ball. Then she'd add lemonade and pineapple juice to make it swampy and sweet. When it took on the color of the sun at sunset with shades of orange and red, she garnished it with a sprig of mint. My northern pals called this the "bastardizing of iced tea," but I always defended it, saying if anyone bastardized iced tea it was the folks out on Long Island, thank you very much.

Before the funeral, people came by to pay additional respects, even though we'd just seen them last night. I spent most of my time in the study staring at the clock on the wall, a gift to Biggie from my grandfather for their anniversary. Mama had disconnected the mechanism that made it tick at the hour of Daddy's death, never to restart again. In the South, time stopped for grief.

After the funeral, most of the same people formed a grief caravan to the cemetery. Seeing a wooden box lowered into the ground was the South's idea of closure, a visible punctuation mark, a tangible ending of things. And luckily there wasn't much of a criminal element in Erob, since the entire police department took time off and volunteered to lead the procession; the remaining officers could be found directing traffic. And every car that passed stopped, because, well, in the South, cars also stopped for grief.

We rode in a borrowed limo, driven by Sandy Featheringill himself. I remember that his bald head was glowing on that hot August day. It was my first time to follow a dead body, and everyone we had ever known seemed to trail out behind us. I buried my head down deep in Haines's shoulder. I felt the weight of everyone's stares. But it didn't matter if they were friends, relatives, or folks you nodded to on the street. In the South, despite Win's proclamations, class, social status, or how one dies appeared irrelevant during grief.

We could have been a parade—Daddy's casket being the grand float. As people stood on the sidewalk and waited for us to pass, I noticed a boy leaning on his bike. I recognized him; he'd sat behind me in school the year before. He stared straight at me, stood erect and fidgeted with his cap—a cherry-red cap with *Piggly Wiggly* stitched in white letters across the brim. I saw it then. His indecision. He took it off his head and held it midway between his heart and his side, the indecision competing with the enormity of his gesture. I smiled at him as we passed by. In the South, everyone acknowledged grief.

When we arrived at the marble bearing the Enloe name, the police officers bowed as if we were foreign dignitaries, not a family they saw regularly at church. My heart softened. In the South, even if just for a moment, life, too, stopped for grief.

Later that day, I escaped up to Biggie's bedroom. These rituals had gotten to me, and I was tired. I sat at her dressing table, the big mirror reflecting a gritty image back at me.

I just couldn't shake loose of the feeling that it was all my fault. If only I'd stayed quiet that day. Helping Daddy had been a mistake. It had made Mama mad, and it had caused them to fight. That fight drove Daddy out the door and out of our lives—forever.

There was a knock on the door. I didn't want to answer it. It could be Biggie or Mama or, worse yet, Win with some more of God's exclusions. Biggie's room was serene. The beige damask draperies and bed skirt remained in repose, undisturbed by the funeral chaos. Her beige bedspread lay still across her four-poster bed. Muted colors splashed on the walls and windows as if to say *sh-sh-sh* to anyone who dared interrupt their calm reverie.

Turns out, it was a stranger, but somehow, I immediately knew who she was.

"Can I come in?" the new girl asked, plopping down on the raw silk love seat at the end of Biggie's bed. I turned from my own reflection to face her.

"I'm sorry about your daddy," she said.

"Thanks."

"My name is Avery. What's yours?" Surprisingly, I had never been asked this question before. In Erob, everyone knew who I was and who my people were. I steadied my voice and spoke out strong and loud in the way I had only done inside my head: "Nina. My name is Nina Enloe."

"Well, nice to meet you, Nina," Avery said.

"You, too, Avery." And it *was* nice.

I took her in. Amidst all of the careful beiges was this girl, my age, but bigger, in red shorts that looked just a smidge too tight, a navy shirt that I'm sure she could tuck in at one time. And red Keds. It was raining and her hair was frizzy like mine only worse. In her imperfection, she was totally perfect.

"This is a pretty room," Avery said. Her eyes were brown, also like mine, and open wide.

"It's my grandmother's. It's Biggie's room. My room is the pink one down the hall." I pointed.

"You live with your grandmother?" she asked.

I laughed. "Biggie wishes I did," I said. "But, no, I just visit mostly on weekends. I live down the street with Mama and my brother, Haines, and . . ."

"Oh, is that your brother downstairs? I saw two cute boys," Avery said.

"Cute? Well, the tall one's my brother, and I guess he's pretty cute, but he's taken. Win likes him. The other one's Carter—he lives next door."

"He's the one I noticed first."

"Carter?" I asked. I almost laughed. "He's okay, I guess. I never much thought about it." But like Jane Austen's *Emma*, wheels started turning. Avery and Carter together.

For a moment, we were quiet again.

"It's sad, Nina," she said. "I'm sorry." Then she got up, moving in my direction, and for a moment I was alarmed. She hugged me. Her arms were soft and fleshy, and they came all the way around, not out of obligation, but to comfort.

She sat back down on the love seat, facing me. More silence.

"I think I was the reason my daddy did it," I said, staring right into her eyes. A bolt of thunder crackled about that time for punctuation. The rain came down.

Avery didn't blink or shift uncomfortably. Maybe she had known another thirteen-year-old murderer back in Cincinnati where she'd moved from. Cincinnati was in the north, after all, and who knew what went on up there.

"Go on," she said.

"I tried to help my daddy, but it made Mama mad, and they got into a huge fight. He left, and that's when he did it."

Avery was quiet, and then, "No, you didn't do it," she said firmly. "I know of people who have committed suicide, and it's not anyone else's fault."

She had said it.

"Hey, Avery, can I ask you something?"

"Sure, Nina."

"Some people say you can't go to heaven if you commit suicide."

"I think that's a rule or something that only applies to Catholic people." She went to the window.

"I love rainy days. They keep our secrets safe, and if we're sad and want to cry, it is like heaven is crying along with us." She came over to me and hugged me.

I never once looked at the adults in my life as playing leading roles in the gothic tragedy Haines and I had been living in, truthfully, from the beginning. I never once blamed Daddy or Mama for their premature abandonment. I blamed my own deficiencies. How could I have known about the dangers of alcohol and depression? I'd only lived with their repercussions. Even before Daddy's suicide, chaos and secrets had drained all of the color from our ranch house on Dexter Avenue. I had sought refuge and safety at Biggie's.

seven

Avery and I bonded on that wretched day. I understood that I could tell her anything. If you can tell someone that you're a murderer and they don't run for the hills, you'd better call them a friend. One afternoon, she and I were sitting in Biggie's breezeway playing cards, but secretly we were waiting for Carter. I felt confident, if given the chance, I could pull off this "love connection." The first step was to create opportunity, so we waited. While we were waiting, I told her my discovery about Erob, the town she now called home.

"You know where you live now, don't you?" I asked with suppressed glee.

"Where?"

"You live in Erob, Alabama."

"I know that, silly," she said.

"Erob spelled *backwards* is Bore, Avery. *Bore*, Alabama. Get it?"

Instead of being horrified as I was when I first saw an ambulance coming toward me ablaze with BORE, AMABALA YCNEGREME across its front hood, Avery squealed in delight.

"Ain't that quaint?" I said. "I'm leaving this town as soon as I can. I see it as a sign."

About this time, Win stormed in.

"I didn't know we were hanging out today," she said. Okay, so maybe I forgot to invite Win.

"Nina just told me the funniest thing," Avery said.

"What?" Win asked, although I knew Win enough to know that she wouldn't see the humor in it.

"Little Bit," Win began, as expected contesting my name once again, "is always putting Erob down." Her voice, almost shrill, took all the hilarity out of my story. Even if most ambulances have words spelled backwards on the front hoods so people can read them correctly from their rearview mirrors, not all town names turned out as ironically as ours.

"So do you, Win," I responded.

"I only put down the tacky people," she said.

Avery jumped in again. "Nina, have you told Win about—"

"Oh, let me guess," Win interrupted. "Not the lucky dust thing again." Win was provoked.

"Well," Avery said, "She does make a compelling argument. Your hair, your figure, your face . . . "

"It's genes, Avery. There is no such thing as lucky dust. It's just something Little Bit here invented to make herself feel better."

Avery looked dubious as we looked at Win. "Seems like you might have it," Avery said finally.

"You can listen to that all you want to, Avery, but Bit is just making fun of me." When Win was right, she was right. "I don't like lucky dust," she finished, her tone ominous and hurt.

"You can hang out with us, Win," I found myself saying, a gravitational pull where habit and predictability reside. Because as much as I could hate her, I needed Win, as much, if not more, than I needed Avery. I only hoped I would never have to choose between them.

Win remained suspicious of Avery. Whenever the three of us found ourselves together, she would do her best to undermine her.

"She doesn't even know the Bible as well as you do, Bit," she'd say. This was a serious accusation because my knowledge was slight at best, and I preferred it that way. I knew there was an Old and New Testament, and that the "Good News" was all about Jesus, but I'd told Miss Frankie that the Jewish kids were lucky since they only had half the Bible to learn and follow.

Every Monday, after school, like a caravan or "Exodus," we would walk up to the Methodist church. One of our mothers would provide "refreshments" in the friendship hall. After our snacks, we got down to the serious business of studying the Bible. We did this from fifth grade until we graduated. Haines nicknamed it "tea parties and torture." None of us wanted to go, and though it wasn't punishment, on beautiful afternoons it felt like a serious confinement.

Miss Frankie had been Erob First Methodist's Bible teacher forever. She was as patient as one would wish a woman of God to be. Her voice was watery, and her deep blue eyes were soothing. And she called us all Precious.

"Precious, what comes after Deuteronomy?"

I had been precious to no one, so despite the school-like atmosphere, I loved Miss Frankie. She really believed that God heard us and would answer all of our prayers.

Up until Avery came along, I'd had my doubts, since I'd been praying for a real best friend and all I kept getting was Win. But now, by God, I believed.

Miss Frankie made us memorize all the books of the Bible, in order, from start to finish. I somehow felt God thought it more important to know what the books of the Bible said, not where they were. When I brought up my theory, Miss Frankie said I had a good point and allowed me to skip memorization. Unfortunately for me, Biggie found out and made me learn them anyway. Win was the first to memorize both the Old and New Testaments.

To this day you can say "Obadiah," and she'll say "Old" with the consistency of an automatic door.

Daddy always said if you want to find a bunch of hypocrites, go to the nearest church. But I never told Miss Frankie that, because I never wanted Daddy to get into trouble with her, Biggie, or God. I should have prayed harder.

On days when Win wasn't preaching to us, we'd have tea parties in the breezeway while Carter and Haines played basketball. The challenge was keeping the ball away from our china.

I used to love to watch those boys play. They were so serious. It was a thing of grace, especially Haines, even when they got off balance, threw up crazy shots, and landed smack on their fannies and said "damn" or "hell" or one of the "boy words," as Win referred to the more colorful "fuck" or "shit." I vowed to someday use "boy words" myself, when I got away—away from Erob and from Win.

I think Haines got all of the lucky dust in our family. He was tall, dark, and handsome (even a sister could see it). When his long body extended to the basket, he stretched out easy, like a rubber band. He had the darkest hair with the most perfect wave to it and the most inviting green eyes. If you looked real close, you'd see gold flecks in them. His eyes can still reel me in, a powerless minnow to his bait.

Carter, on the other hand, was short and stocky. He had sandy-colored hair that never grew too much below his ears, but his eyes made up for any imperfections he had. To this day, they are still the kindest eyes I've ever seen, and when they smile at you, life is fine again. Blue, the color of summer hydrangeas, like the ones Biggie would put on a tea table along with Queen Anne's lace; the kind of blue that makes you want to reach out and touch—the flowers and the eyes—to see if they're real.

G.G., Carter's grandmother, also thought it would be nice if her only grandson, Carter, would one day marry Biggie's only granddaughter. But children, you see, have their own ideas. In my mind it was Avery, not me, who was meant to have Carter's heart.

I'd watch the intensity with which Haines and Carter exchanged glances, the twinkle in their eyes when they were telling dirty jokes. They did that a lot. From them, I never got the notion that men didn't have good friendships. I envied them that. Their equality. With Win and me, it was always Win domineering. The more she pulled, the more I dreamed about escaping her clutches.

From the beginning, she was always on my case to *sit up straight, cross your legs, let me organize your papers for you.* There was no equality between us. I wondered if she learned those looks from my mama, or if she just knew as ladies know. But even Mama and she together couldn't turn me into a lady. That was Biggie's task. I shared her name, and by God, I was going to be a lady according to her rules.

Turning into a lady is not for the faint of heart, nor can it be done with a magic wand. It's about composure and maintaining a face that appears unfazed. It's about perspiration-free dinner parties. And endurance. Taking whatever the good Lord gives you, smiling, and never letting real emotions surface. It's about making and accepting funeral casseroles with the same grit and sense of duty. This was for Biggie and Mama and Win, but never for me. In the end, I had to turn my back on all of them and their damn rituals or else I would end up like my daddy.

So, Win turned into a lady and I, instead, turned into a lawyer.

Daddy died and might not get to heaven, and Mama had no money. Seems God and those insurance agents rejected both of them.

I heard Mama talking on the phone one morning. "I can teach English," she said, "and I really do want the job, Mr. White. I need it. I have my family to look after."

All this just didn't square with me, so I took it to the Committee, or more specifically, Haines and Carter. "I thought you said Biggie had 'truckloads,' yet I just heard Mama begging for a job." I looked directly at Carter. "Why doesn't Biggie help Mama so she doesn't have to go to work?"

Haines and Carter looked at each other.

"I know Biggie's cheap," I said, "but hell. This is serious."

"It's true," Carter explained. "Just this morning Daddy and my mother were talking, and they were both wondering about what Biggie would do with her piles of money. Mother thought she should help your mama out now that your daddy was gone. But your mama wants to get a job, even though Biggie did say she'd help out 'if things got too catastrophic.'"

I looked at my brother while thinking about all those phone calls and of the off-brand food now lining our refrigerator and cabinets.

"Seems to me we're there," I said. "I mean, the stuff Mama is using to wash our clothes doesn't even advertise on TV. Who ever heard of Suds-All anyway? It might not even be real, and who wants to eat Thrifty English peas?"

Carter laughed.

"Here's the deal, Little Bit," my big brother said. "Biggie is sending me and you to college." He paused. "As far as the rest of it? Who knows? That's between Biggie and Mama to figure out."

Indeed.

Later that afternoon I saw Biggie tending to her flowers, pulling unwanted weeds.

"Biggie," I said, approaching her, "I need some money." The word "money" always got her attention.

"What for?" she said, barely looking up.

"For Mama, so she doesn't have to beg for a job."

"Frances already got a job," she said, "teaching English at your school."

"I still need money," I continued, wanting to add *so I can run away*, but instead I said, "so we can buy real food and normal laundry detergent."

My grandmother straightened, wiped her hands on her apron, and looked at me, yet her expression remained the same. "I will give you one hundred dollars," she offered.

It sounded like a lot, but I really had no idea. Daddy used to take out tonsils for fresh vegetables; next to that, this seemed like a fortune. But with Biggie, everything came with strings attached.

"There's a revival at the church starting next week. It would be nice for you to go," she said.

There it was. "Isn't that at night?" I asked. Night church. Even Mama drew the line at that. The hymns were slow, and the minister took his watch off and didn't look at it again until he lost his voice. Only Jesus's second coming could shut him up.

"No, thanks," I decided. I'd rather eat Thrifty brand than give in to Biggie.

"Suit yourself." Biggie went back to her pruning. "But Bit, it would be easier for you if we were on the same side."

I blinked. Haines might have placated Biggie, but I would never give in to her. I vowed right then to get three things straight before trying to negotiate with my grandmother again:

1. Put my best argument first.
2. Know the true value of money. I knew that the sooner I had

my own money, the faster and farther I could get away from Erob and Biggie's clutches.

The third and final lesson I took from the master herself:

3. Never say never.

eight

These fine tenets from my childhood came back a few years later when I was choosing colleges. By then Biggie had taught me more about "wheeling and dealing" than she had about being a lady. I guess I owed her.

I dismissed the initial rumblings about my going with Win to the University of Alabama. They were Win's O.K.O.P but not mine. I had also been to UNC-Chapel Hill with Haines and Carter during March Madness and had fallen in love with the architecture. I found the diversity, and the people, refreshing. Avery's dad had gone to Chapel Hill and that's where she would go. I had gotten in, too, but hadn't told anyone. Besides, Avery had developed a deepening friendship with Carter, and he would be next door in enemy territory.

Although I still wanted to see them together more than anything, she was not my most compelling argument.

"Biggie, I've been accepted to UNC," I announced.

"Bit, that's out of state and very expensive. You can go to the university with Win."

"I know it's expensive, Biggie," I continued, seemingly on her side, "but I've applied for student loans, which will defray the cost some and make it almost the same as going to Bama." For her at least.

Biggie appeared impressed. "You've done all the work, Bit?" she asked.

"I really want to go." It was time to use my best argument.

Biggie had a small sliver of sentimentality, and I was determined to exploit it.

"Besides, Carter is planning to go to law school at Duke when he graduates next year." I paused. "I just thought it would be nice, that's all. He and I could have dinner every week, and we could ride back home together on weekends."

Biggie smiled. "Well, now that would be nice, Bit. Having someone like Carter looking after you would be nice indeed."

"I thought so too," I said, smiling.

"I'm proud of you," Biggie continued, "and Carter is the finest boy." She had made my argument for me.

"Yes, ma'am, and maybe I'll even become a lawyer too."

"Why, the two of you could go into practice together, Bit!" Biggie said, forever scheming. Agnes gave me a look from the kitchen that said *don't get too comfortable*, knowing I had beaten my grandmother in this battle, but that it would be a long war.

Avery and I were planning our dorm room décor when Carter stormed through the gate and onto the porch. He wore a serious expression, and I abandoned my notion to get Avery and Carter together just now.

"Bit," Carter said, letting the screen door slam, "can I talk to you?" He paused. "In private?"

"In private?" I asked, looking at Avery. "Sure."

I got up and followed him past Agnes. She and I exchanged bewildered glances as he and I made our way into the dining room.

His voice slightly raised, Carter began. "Don't you *ever* put me in the middle of one of your grandmother's battles again, Bit."

"What are you talking about?" I asked. I was feeling very defensive.

"Your college plans. Or should I say schemes."

Apparently, Miss Harriett had joined Biggie and G.G. in plotting our life together. I knew Miss Harriett loved me. I laughed.

"It's not funny, Bit," Carter said.

"Don't be mad at me, Carter," I said, still laughing. "Is it not a fact that you're hoping to attend Duke Law after you graduate next year?"

"Listen. I won't be a part of any machinations or schemes you have going with Biggie. Especially this one." Carter paused. It seemed to me he was trying to come up with something as devious as what I'd concocted. It took him a moment or two. Then he smiled, and it was as if he had conjured up the most clever plan. And he had.

"No, Bit, I'll not be a part of this scheme of yours." He paused again for effect. "Unless, of course, you want to make good on my mother's assumptions."

He walked up to me, embraced me, and started kissing me right there in the dining room for anyone who passed by to see. I finally caught my breath and pushed him away.

"What if Agnes walked by? Or Biggie caught us?"

"That would really cook your goose. Biggie would have you married off so fast." He laughed. Laughed! Dammit. Sure, we still fit together perfectly. His kisses were better sober than drunk. And scarier. That's all it took to find my shaky resolve.

"Carter, don't be that way," I pleaded. He couldn't be serious. If nothing else, he knew I would never betray Avery.

"Those are my terms." When I refused to answer, he said, "I thought so," and walked away.

He left me standing in a pool of what I know now was pure, unadulterated fear. He could play hardball as well as Biggie. I'd give him that.

I followed him. "Please, Carter," I tried again. He was way ahead of me, and I heard the gate slam. "Carter!" I called. "Please?" I begged. Seconds passed before he stuck his head back over the gate, a sly grin on his face.

"You were kidding?" I asked. I had begged him, after all.

"Partly," he said.

"Asshole!" I screamed, loud enough for Biggie to hear it all the way up at the church. I could also hear both Agnes and Avery laughing inside the house.

"Nice, Bit," Carter said. "That mouth of yours is going to keep getting you into trouble if you don't watch yourself. One day it might even cause you to lose. Not with me, but with Biggie. Don't put me in the middle. I'm serious."

Win had a few choice strides—stroll, saunter, and storm—and I could usually predict with stunning accuracy how our conversation would go based on how she walked into a room.

"What are you doing?" she asked.

"Working on homework and waiting for Mama to finish up with her faculty meeting."

"I have made a decision," Win announced. She always made these grand proclamations as if the Associated Press surrounded her for commentary.

"Yes?" I asked.

"I'm not going to be Homecoming Queen."

That's what it's like with lucky dust: three weeks before Homecoming and you know you're the shoo-in. Win still wore her naturally blond hair straight, she had grown to a statuesque six feet tall, and her figure remained the envy of every girl at school. She had become more beautiful than I ever could have imagined. She probably could have been Miss America if she wanted to. Win was all about her résumé, so I was intrigued.

"Win, why not? You know you'll win."

"Well, I know *that,* Bit," she said matter-of-factly. She paused so I could give her all my attention. "I just don't want to be a cliché," she declared, and I had to laugh.

"Good for you, Win."

"Valedictorian."

"What?" I questioned.

"You heard me. I'm going to be valedictorian instead."

"Geeky Newsom might have something to say about that. For that matter, so could I. I've been studying so hard my GPA is higher than Geeky."

But Win's main agenda lay ahead. You just had to hunt for it sometimes.

"In poetry maybe," she continued. "You're really going to UNC instead of Tuscaloosa? I thought we were going to be roommates." I waved my latest poetry collection at her.

"I wanted something different. Besides, you'll be busy with all that sorority stuff, and I don't care about that. I really liked it when I visited with her. And Carter will be close by at Duke."

She and I both knew that choosing Chapel Hill over Alabama was tantamount to choosing Avery over her.

nine

I was sitting with Avery in our dorm room, chatting, when she said, "Nina." It was the voice she used to deliver juicy secrets or bad news. I feared it was the latter.

"What?" I asked.

"I love you. Please don't be mad." Bad news. She continued. "You know when I get together with 'friends' to have coffee and study? It's only been one guy, Arush Bhatia. I really like him."

"Whaaaat? Why haven't you told me? How far has this gone?" She lowered her head, and the answers to my questions were pretty obvious. I didn't want to know details for once. I recognized the elephant in the room.

"I know. I didn't want to put you in the middle between me and Carter." For once, words abandoned us, not like usual when we were eagerly talking over each other. She was right.

"I want you to meet him. You will love him, and he will adore you."

"What about Carter?" If it wasn't going to be Avery, who could I set him up with?

"You know Carter and I are just friends. I wanted to tell you first. I'll probably meet his parents at Christmas when I visit my grandmother in Ohio."

"You're meeting his parents? That sounds serious."

"It is. I want to bring him to Erob. Will you come for moral support?" She began crying, and so did I. This was my best friend, and I wanted her happiness. But holy shit . . .

"Bit."

It sounded more like *Bi-ut,* so slow, like honey moving on a biscuit. In my years at UNC my campaign to move away from Bit and into Nina had been successful. With a few notable exceptions. It amazed me how anyone could stretch three letters out into two long syllables.

"Hi, Carter," I responded into the phone, having long since given up on reminding him of what I'd rather be called. "What's up?" Still hopeful, until the bitter end.

"How would you like to go to supper with a good-looking, successful lawyer?"

I smiled. A balding, bleary-eyed law *student* was more like it.

"Have you got a friend in mind?" I asked.

We decided to meet at LaRue's, a local restaurant.

He looked up at me and smiled when he saw me. I decided that the balding thing was good because it made his blue eyes stand out that much more. If Win had eyes the color of the Mediterranean Sea with splashes of blue and green, then Carter had the blue color of all the oceans in the world combined. To infinity, and beyond.

"Let's order first," Carter said, flipping through the menu, breaking eye contact.

I suspected something right off the bat. Carter wore his habits like he wore his freshly starched shirts, comfortably and consistently. He always ordered a cheeseburger—medium rare, tomato, no lettuce—fries, and sweet tea, but here he was, studying the menu like it was the bar exam.

When the waitress came, he closed his menu as if he had arrived at the ultimate epiphany—and he ordered the cheeseburger.

His eyes were busy doing everything but looking at me.

"What's up, Carter?" I asked, feeling my own sense of anxiety now.

"Oh, Bit," he said.

I gulped my tea down so hard I swallowed wrong and began to cough.

"I met someone I like a lot."

"Who is she?" I asked.

He looked surprised. I had guessed. Apparently, not so dumb either.

"Her name is Jennifer. She's from Charlotte, North Carolina."

When did I get to be Madam Confessor? I didn't want everyone's secrets. *Carter and Avery, my perfect couple . . .*

"She's sweet and kind . . . " he started.

"And she would be different from Avery just how?" Carter smiled. My loyalty was showing.

"She's a senior. I want you to meet her."

My loyal spirit was in turmoil. "Does Haines know?"

"He's my best friend, but he's a gossip. I wanted to get to you first."

I smiled. My long-held dream for an Avery Gideon had gone out like a lightning bug's yellow glow on a hot summer's night.

I hated these endings. It was like a death without the casseroles. I mourned to myself what might have been, and I was strangely reminded of my daddy. Jennifer and Arush. Who were they? They didn't know us. I sounded like Win with her suspicions about new people. Jennifer was from Charlotte and Arush from somewhere in Ohio.

"Nina, Carter is the best. But that was *your* dream. Never mine," Avery said.

There were different forms of love, and each takes the proper place in our lives to be cherished as something precious and ultimately fleeting.

"Hey, Little Bit, how're you doing? I'm just calling to check in." The confident, caring tones of the next generation of doctors in our family who still refused to drop "Little" from my name.

"Hey, Haines."

"You doing okay?"

"Yeah, it's not like anything happened to me."

"Well, maybe not directly," Haines said insightfully. His timing, as always, was impeccable. Besides being handsome, smart, and ambitious, he could also be so damn thoughtful.

It was as if this love-match business was a contagion, like the flu. Because just like that, Carter and Avery had found others. Then Win stopped crushing on my brother and within days found Richard Montgomery III at a sorority mixer. He was from Atlanta and was a first-year med student at the university.

"Yes, Richard, but we don't call him that," Win explained. "We call him Rich." And I found out later he was just that. Very rich.

Rich and Win. If that doesn't say it all, what does?

Haines, in turn, found Addison Lowry, from Mobile. Addison was a sorority sister of Win's and, according to Win, "She's perfect for Haines, and you'll like her."

It was as if there was some internal genetic magnet that drew them all to want to be "coupled." I was convinced the reason Win stayed stuck on my brother so long was because she didn't want to lose the moniker of "Dr. and Mrs." But as lucky dust would have it, she didn't have to compromise.

Arush Bhatia was handsome and tall. His voice was both

intellectual and kind. His eyes never left Avery's. He looked as in love as she did. I couldn't take my eyes off his eyelashes.

He told me all about computers and bytes. I was intimidated. And bored. But not Avery. It amazed me that someone with that computer lingo could ever get someone as colorful as Avery and, especially, could beat out Carter. I hated that I liked him.

Arush didn't keep up with sports. Alabama boasted two exports—football and beauty queens—and Arush didn't even know who Nick Saban was, for heaven's sake. Avery blushed, batted her eyes, and ignored me, sure signs that a girl was in love.

They did go well together, but if I must be honest, no one, except Carter, would ever be good enough for my Avery.

"Is he O.K.O.P.?" Win asked after she heard I'd met Avery's new boyfriend. We were both home on spring break; our schedules, like the planets, aligned to perfection.

I gave her the blow-by-blow of my encounter with Arush, and she reveled in every juicy detail. She'd been the first person besides Haines that I got into this with, and she was aglow with enthusiasm.

"Oh, that Avery just isn't clever enough to know how to choose a man. It's not entirely about love," as if she were Elizabeth Taylor.

Spewing her venom on Arush was one thing, but spilling it over to poor Avery was quite another, and I guess I did what any good lioness would do. Defend.

"Don't start with me, Win. I really like him, so you better be nice." Like rote. The mantra that shadowed our friendship. Win trying to get me to do one thing or another and me shutting her down before she could go too far. My victories, in general, were about 50/50, but when it had to do with Avery, I always won.

"Okay, Bit, I just wish he were . . . " She was looking for a word that would be acceptable to me, and I put her out of her misery.

"He's perfect for Avery," I said simply.

"We've got serious matters to discuss. Our debutante dresses."

"Don't start with me on that either."

"Listen Bit, this is important. Something to put on our résumés. We've got to get our dresses while we're home on break."

"No, Win, curing cancer is important. Being one of five debutantes of Podunkville is nothing." Besides, there was no way in hell I would splash something as embarrassing as that on my résumé.

"One of twelve," she corrected, pulling her hair back into a French chignon.

If it were possible, Win was even more beautiful now than in high school. The lankiness had turned to swanlike grace, and her shoulders rounded to hold her confident demeanor that radiated from the inside out, always the best kind. Her eyes were now greener, giving her a slight edge over those who sought to be copies. And her hair was still perfectly straight and blonde, which continued to bug the hell out of me.

Win, Avery, and I were in Wanda's Dress Works and More! Win was trying on white dresses for her debut. Wanda had gotten them on approval from a boutique in Atlanta. So far, I hadn't tried on one outfit.

When Win came out of the dressing room, it took both Avery's and my breath away. I didn't remember the dress being that pretty on the hanger, but Win made it look stunning. I couldn't take my eyes off of her. She was born to be a debutante. Or a bride.

The strapless gown was made of sheer layers of white tulle.

It came in tightly at the waist and then cascaded down, like a mound of light, fluffy whipping cream.

"Win!" I exclaimed. "You look beautiful."

"You do," Avery seconded.

"Win, that's the one. It makes you look as pretty as a bride," I said, giving her the ultimate of compliments.

"It does, Little Bit?"

And then I saw it on her face—pure rapture. This was Win's life. She knew what she wanted, when she wanted it, and getting married was the first step to getting it all started. That's the way things work in small Southern towns. Or in Jane Austen's England.

The sound of the door and the cowbell ringing up front interrupted my thought.

"Nina." It sounded like an alarm rather than a greeting. It was Biggie, who rarely called me by my proper name unless it was important or somebody had died. Being that my dignity was slowly slipping away just by being in this dress shop, it seemed justified.

"Hello, Wanda," Biggie said. "I believe my granddaughter is here. Has she tried on any dresses yet?" The formidable voice resounded back into our dressing room.

"No, ma'am," Wanda replied.

"And why not? Didn't you order any in her size, or did you just listen to Mr. Baxter?"

"I have plenty for Little Bit to try on, Mrs. Enloe."

This could take a while, so I got up to see Biggie. No use in causing a family scene at Wanda's. She talks.

"Hi, Biggie," I said, coming out from my hiding place.

"How can you try on dresses in those tennis shoes? Honestly, Nina," she admonished. Using my proper name twice in one day?

This was clearly much more important to her than I had anticipated.

"Biggie," I whispered, "do you have any idea how much these dresses cost? Mama can't afford one. Besides, I don't want to be a debutante."

"You come from a family better than any of those other girls. You will make your debut."

"Biggie, I'd rather not."

"You must do it for your family."

I hated it when she used *family*, only because it was an effective argument. I heard her breathe long, tenacious breaths, and I matched her with my own conniving ones. We were not in unison, and I sensed her growing impatience.

"On one condition," I said. "You propose Avery so she can be a debutante with us." I had seen the longing way Avery had looked at all the fancy dresses.

"It's too late," Biggie said.

"Not for you. Both of us or neither of us." I waited, neither of us capitulating.

"Avery is a nice girl. I'll make a phone call."

"You've got yourself a debutante."

An invisible bargain was struck. As Biggie walked out of the store, she turned to say something to Wanda. She had a funny smile on her face that almost looked like pride. Could it have been I had learned Southern hardball from a master, or was she just surprised that I had been paying attention?

I was waiting for him in the booth at LaRue's and smelled him before I saw him. Citrus, like a freshly peeled orange.

"Hi there, good looking," he mumbled in my ear from behind.

"Carter," I said, and smiled. "Jennifer's late."

"She has lab. Go easy on her, Bit."

"Do I have a choice?"

But his eyes had left me and focused on something in the distance. "Jenny." His eyes lit up and his voice approached reverence. As she meandered into the booth beside Carter, she looked at me, and I realized I was staring.

"Jenny, this is Bit," Carter said.

"I've heard so much about you, Little Bit," she cooed.

"Is any of it true?" I looked at Carter, but only for a second. I couldn't believe it. She could have passed for Win's sister—*oh my God, there's another one*. She was blonde and had eyes like blue silk, but her features were softer and less confident. Tan freckles glittered her cheeks from her nose to the highest point of her cheekbones. I would learn that's where the similarity ended; she was similar to Avery's calm presence. When she touched Carter's hand, there was a certain gentleness that forced me to smile. Her voice was as unobtrusive as chamomile tea. At one point Carter left us alone.

We chatted. She was from Charlotte, more specifically Myers Park, which Carter had likened to the Buckhead area of Atlanta or Mountain Brook, Alabama. It was clear from our brief time together that her family had money. She had gone to private schools and been spared the cruelties in life.

I detected the faint smell of tea leaves and felt its softness and delicacy matched Jennifer Massey perfectly. Despite my misgivings, I liked her. I had to admit that she, like Arush, was perfect for my friend, and she seemed to like me too.

As we were leaving the restaurant together, Jenny excused herself to go back inside. When she returned, she was carrying my book bag.

"Here Bit, you forgot this," she said, handing me the bag I'd left behind. I guess I hadn't given up all my harum-scarum ways.

"Don't say anything, Gideon."

There was age-old symbolism that wasn't lost on either Carter or me. As he held the door for Jenny, I whispered, "She's a keeper." And I meant it.

ten

It's a funny thing about debutante balls and escorts. You don't always get who you want. Ours was no different. There was so much changing partners that I though Ida Mae Byrd was going to have to leave the whole listing out of the Erob society page, and God knows that would have sent everyone into schisms.

It began simply enough: Win and Haines, Avery and Carter, and me with Peaches Newsom's older brother, Billy, who we had nicknamed Geeky since high school. Then, because of the Avery-Carter awkwardness, it got changed to Win and Carter, Avery and Geeky Newsom, and me and Haines. After a good look at this, it was changed again because Win was a few inches taller than Carter with heels, and that would have thrown off all the pictures, which everyone knows are the most important.

It ended up being Haines and Win, Avery and Geeky, and me and Carter. Plus the three other couples. Ida Mae was able to do her line-up for the paper, which memorialized the event, unfortunately.

I had chosen a simple dress that came in at my narrow bustline then fell straight down; nothing flossy for me. Haines and I went over to see Biggie. Carter and Win would meet us there. Biggie decided not to go out into the night air, even though it was early June and eighty degrees.

"Bit, you look just like a little doll," Biggie beamed. At almost twenty years of age, I don't know if I've ever been so mortified.

"That dress," Biggie continued, "is just perfect for you." A compliment? It scared me that she was being so nice. "Come here, Bit," she commanded.

I walked over to her, thinking my bangs needed to be brushed or my strapless bra was riding up in clear view under my arms. Neither was the case. She touched my bony little shoulders with both of her massive hands. Then she reached for the box that was on the table next to her chair and opened it.

She took out a single strand of pearls, the one with the diamond clasp that H.B. had given her on their fifth anniversary.

"Your grandfather and I would like you to wear these, Bit."

She had been doing that lately, referring to H.B. in the present tense. I often wondered if the closer you get to death, the more real the dead seem and more far away the living become.

They were beautiful. Besides her diamond watch and diamond rings, which she wore every day, these pearls were her pride and joy. I was surprised and touched she was offering to let me wear them for the night.

"I don't know what to say, Biggie. I'll take real good care of them and bring them back first thing in the morning." I turned around so she could have the honor of putting them on me. She was pleased at what she saw, and when she smiled at me it was a complete smile. It held nothing back. She hugged me then, and I wondered what had gotten into the crotchety woman on whom I had come to depend. Maybe she was playing mind games with me, or perhaps the sight of her debutante granddaughter had softened her up.

"There's no need to return them. They're yours now, Bit, but I hope you will think of me and your grandfather when you wear them."

I had no experience dealing with generosity when it came from my grandmother. Apparently, Mama hadn't either, because her eyes remained clueless except for the water that had suddenly moistened the edges.

A speechless debutante. Two things I never thought I'd be.

I reached up and touched the pearls reverently, like I was wearing rosary beads. They felt good and cold against my skin that was hot with nerves. The moment ended when Win and Carter burst through the back door.

"We're here in the living room," Haines called out.

Win glided in, despite the volume of her dress, armed with her lucky dust. She wouldn't dare trip, even in that get-up. I had to follow her, and I worried that I would fall flat on my face and pull Carter down with me.

By then, Avery had joined us, looking like a princess in a fairy tale. "Smile for pictures, everyone!" Win exclaimed.

Just what I needed—more pictures to memorialize this cultural humiliation.

Ida Mae was already lining everyone up when we arrived. Her face had expanded over the years, along with her backside. Tiny drops of perspiration dotted her forehead from a mixture of heat and large quantities of pancake makeup. I was actually thankful Win had taught me a thing or two about "doing my face" or I would have been right there with Ida Mae, sweating like a pig in front of a Hormel factory.

My eyes combed through the crowd to find Mama, who still had the smile on her face, unlike Win's parents, Mr. and Mrs. Baxter, who each had a look of suspended anxiousness. *Please*. Win would be the last to make a wrong move. Win, who could balance a book on her head, walk, talk, and serve dip at the same time.

She, of all people, would not disappoint.

"Jenny's not jealous, is she?" I asked Carter. Jenny was making her own debut at the Charlotte County Club on this same night with her brother as her escort. Similarly, Rich was committed to his medical residency but had sent Win a massive bouquet of long-stemmed roses as a stand-in.

"Nah, she knows you." Carter smiled as he extended his arm. "Listen, you'd better pick up your dress a little so you won't fall down."

"You sound like Win giving me a bunch of instructions," I admonished him before flashing the crowd a benevolent smile, camouflaging my disdain with a surprisingly natural flair.

I quickly released Carter of his duties so he could go and dance with all the other short girls. I watched Haines and Win glide about on the country club floor like they owned the place. In reality, they did—they were beautiful, and lucky dust swirled around them everywhere they went.

Avery had extricated herself from Billy's clutches after two long dances to join me over at her parents' table.

"You look just wonderful tonight," Blaine Mitchell said to me when her daughter joined us. "Doesn't she, Avery?"

"I've told Nina how pretty she is, but she doesn't believe me." Avery hugged me. She was still the most demonstrative person I'd ever met.

"Well, Avery, you look pretty great too," I said.

"If I see another grapefruit or Diet Coke," she started. "Who am I kidding? I'll be eating grapefruit and drinking Diet Coke for the rest of my life."

"Quit that, Avery. You look pretty just the way you are."

"You're partial, and thankfully Arush doesn't mind either. I feel so grown-up."

I was glad Avery was having a good time. It made me happy that she was happy. Then I heard her sigh and followed her gaze. Arush had finally made it and was standing on the sidelines, wearing a brown suit. I thought only old men wore brown suits. I noticed that many in the crowd gazed at Arush, so I followed Avery over to him. I greeted him, and Avery gave him a hug.

"We're having so much fun," Avery said.

Fun? I couldn't wait to extricate myself from this strapless bra. Overanalyzing was my specialty. I didn't feel a part of this circus, even in my expensive dress and pearls. The reluctant Southern belle was rearing her head again, making me want to escape those feelings of inadequacy and empty rituals.

"Bit, you look downright beautiful," Judge Gideon said in approval.

"As pretty as a picture," Miss Harriet concurred.

I pointed to the corsage that Miss Harriet had crafted from three gardenias in her yard. "I really do like my flowers," I said. "They're just perfect."

"Oh, I'm so glad. When Carter said you didn't want a corsage, I didn't know what to do. I know how you are."

How am I? I wanted to ask. *Wanting a corsage that didn't look like everyone else's? Wanting life on my own terms? Wanting to move away?*

"Your brother and Win make a beautiful pair," Miss Harriet said of the Kodachrome couple. "We're going to Charlotte next weekend to meet Jennifer and her parents. I hear you've met her."

"I have. You'll like her. She's perfect for Carter."

"Your approval means a lot to him, and it seems Avery has found her match as well."

"Arush is nice and perfect for Avery too," I said, lying so effortlessly that I wished Biggie could have heard me. She would have been so proud of my Southern hypocrisy.

I was talking to the Judge, Miss Harriet, and Mama, content to be outside the circle of Debutante Hell, when Tony Bennett was replaced with the unmistakable growl of the Commodores' "Brick House."

I felt a hand grab mine, and I didn't even have to guess who was summoning me. "C'mon," he said, pulling me onto the dance floor. At first, I remained still even while Carter was already moving as only he could. "You really do dance like a poor white boy," I observed, but I soon joined him. Besides, Carter was enjoying himself too much to let me interfere. He kept me out on that floor through "This Old Heart of Mine" and of course "Sweet Home Alabama."

"Enough!" I finally said. "Save it for your wedding!"

"I will," Carter said as Avery came up to us. I allowed her to cut in before saying, "See what you're missing," motioning to what-could-have-been. Tony Bennett started crooning again as Carter grabbed Avery's hand right on cue.

I looked around at all the beautiful girls dressed in white. Poise, presence, and confidence. Like the beautiful white antebellum mansions that dotted Erob's Magnolia Avenue. They weren't going anywhere. They were built to stay put and thrive. And procreate future generations.

I felt like a spec house that didn't quite belong. Still under construction, and not a can of white paint in sight.

It was way past time to get out of Erob. To build my own life. Where no one knew "who I belonged to," where no preconceptions would follow me. Where I could always be Nina. Where I could make my *own* money and live my *own* life.

Money could buy freedom. And distance. And precious independence.

Back at the table with Mama and Miss Harriett, there was a tone in their voices that I had only heard when Mama talked about her life with Daddy. A sad inevitability. The music swirled around, but it was the tenor of their remarks that kept playing in my mind, as if gaiety itself had decided to sit this one out.

While we were seemingly carefree, Mama and Miss Harriett carried their burden. For the rest of the weekend, Haines and I hung out at Biggie's while Mama and Miss Harriett sat with their friend Virginia in the hospital. They had spent a lot of time there in the past months since the cancer diagnosis, but this time was different—the term "aggressive" spoken in resigned fashion. For days now, Mama or Miss Harriett would prepare supper for Virginia's husband, Charlie, keeping it warm in the oven for him to pick up each evening.

On Sunday night, he dropped in to get the chicken loaf and cranberry salad Mama had fixed.

"Just put a dollop of mayonnaise on that salad, Charlie, before you eat it," Mama instructed like she used to talk to me when I was five years old.

"Thanks, Frances," Charlie returned, and then he began to cry. "Oh God, what am I going to do?" he asked. He was sobbing uncontrollably.

"Charlie," Mama began, with Herculean self-control, "it's going to be fine."

"I just don't know how long I can keep this up."

"Let it out, Charlie. You need to get it out so Virginia won't worry so much about you," she said as he continued crying. "It's all going to be okay. It is."

There was truth in her statement, but I didn't know how.

"You eat and get some rest, and I'll tell Virginia you'll see her tomorrow."

It would be hard to tell Virginia anything, I thought. Last I heard, she was in a coma.

"You and Harriett have been good to her," Charlie said.

Mama managed to calm him down, and his tears retreated for the moment.

Today I see it for what it was. Charlie had shown amazing courage to allow such honest emotions, and Mama had indeed been strong and unflinching in the face of it.

The next day, Carter filled both Haines and me in on the backstory.

"Well, after visiting Virginia in the hospital last night, your mama came home with my mother," he said. "And then, after Dad left the room, I heard them opening a bottle of wine."

I interrupted. "Mama? Drinking wine on a Sunday night?" I asked disbelievingly.

He nodded and continued. "It's bad, Bit," he said, as a grown man would say, waiting to see if I wanted to hear the rest.

I nodded, slowly, apprehensively.

"'All the tubes,' your mama said. 'Virginia has tubes to do everything for her. Harriett, when did we stop going to sit with Virginia and start sitting with those tubes? I don't know how much longer I can watch her suffer.'"

Carter continued. "At that point, they lifted their glasses, and my mom said, 'To Ginnie. Be at peace.' Then they were silent, and as each put their glasses down, they started crying."

Haines and I looked at each other. Mama never cried. Not even when Daddy died. The only time since then was when she and I watched *The Way We Were* on television, and she started sniffling during the scene where Hubble and Katie see each other in front of The Plaza. She donned her sunglasses for the rest of the day rather than allow the world to see her bloodshot eyes.

"Well, she and my mom were crying together. They were quiet, and I couldn't make out anything else," Carter added.

"Maybe they knew you were listening," Haines intervened. He already acted like a doctor, like he knew about inevitability.

What was said or done in that hospital room after that, we'll never know. Carter and I had our theories, but my brother would shake his head at us. All I do know is Virginia had passed away by the next afternoon, and neither Harriett nor Mama seemed surprised.

"At least y'all are in town to attend the funeral," Biggie said, "but it sure is sad to know that Virginia finally lost her battle." I could tell Mama was hurting. Virginia had been her good friend, a confidante, and now she was gone.

"Biggie," Mama began cautiously, "Virginia did not *lose* anything. She has finally gone to a place where she is whole and well and healthy. Virginia has won."

Biggie huffed. It seemed Mama realized that she'd made a stir over a simple comment, and she left to go into the kitchen to cook.

I followed her, and this is the way I remember it. She was standing in her corner of the kitchen, the place where the stove and counters converge. The can opener was grinding its teeth around a can of cream of mushroom soup. I saw the five other Campbell's soup cans lined up on the counter, and I wondered how the puttering, whizzing appliance would have the energy for all of them. Mama was making a casserole—the essence of finality and resignation.

They are innocuous enough, to be sure, and they are creamy. They bubble and ooze and have those damn Ritz cracker crumbs sprinkled with dots of butter on top. It's apropos that they are laced with chicken, since the person bringing one often leaves it with a housekeeper or a caretaker and makes a clean escape, feeling like they've done their duty without having to actually pay any respects to the grief-stricken.

But as I watched my mother dump cans, stir, and pretend not to cry, there was nothing fake about what she was doing. She was just so damn stoic—so damn *Southern*—it made me sick.

I didn't mind her making the casserole. It was the "who" she was making it for that I minded. Mama had known Virginia longer than Virginia's own husband and had loved her better than Virginia's own children. She had kept her secrets. In fact, the only time I had ever heard Virginia laugh was at my mama's table, during a game of bridge or after a glass of white wine. Yet here was my mother stirring in that chicken while folks comforted Virginia's family. She, of all the people, was the one who had standing, the one who knew Virginia the most. She was the one who needed comforting.

I tried to put my arms where the strings of the apron met and made a perfect knot together, but she swatted me away, saying I would make her spill the cracker crumbs and *wouldn't that make a mess of her clean floor*?

I moved away, hurt and confused but thinking I'd be damned if I would ever believe that a chicken casserole with buttery Ritz crackers on top could ease any kind of pain.

I wore a taupe suit to Virginia's funeral. Mama said since it was June, *a good taupe suit is as subdued as black*. Chewy and Jordan were graveside, as usual, commenting on the weather, how humid it was, and of all things, Charlie's mismatched socks. I wouldn't even have noticed if I hadn't overheard them, and it somehow made it more sad to know that he'd need more help than usual in the coming days, not just with meals, but with matching his dark greens, browns, and blues.

Virginia's death left a sadness for sure. Miss Harriet and Mama looked uneven, like they were missing something, maybe a scarf or a necklace or a favorite purse.

More than once since then we have speculated on the suffering that took place in Virginia's hospital room. I'm talking about Mama's and Miss Harriett's suffering. I've often wondered if suffering bound them in ways that love had not. All we knew was that the two of them withdrew from us for a time, and we wondered if Virginia had somehow taken them along for the ride.

eleven

"Arush and I are getting married."

"What?" I blurted out.

"At the end of the summer. After graduation. I want you to be my maid of honor."

I couldn't even be pleased to be asked to be in the wedding for being so stunned. And, to be honest, a little upset that I was not included in the deliberations.

"Why now?"

"We don't want to wait, Nina."

"What about me?" I asked, thinking how that sounded but unable to stop myself.

"You're starting to sound like Win. I mean, thinking of yourself, Nina, when you ought to be thinking about my wedding."

That "Averyism"—a phrase I'd long ago used to describe her personal brand of wisdom—now, it seemed, Arush would be with us for the rest of our lives.

"What do you say, Nina? Will you be my maid of honor?"

Her brown eyes glistened, and her face glowed with love and happiness.

Avery was asking me to be her maid of honor. As if I could ever deny her anything, and I *was* truly honored.

"There's something else. We would really like to get married at Biggie's in her backyard. I know this is a big ask. We would like to have a Hindu wedding on Friday and then a smaller wedding on Saturday. Do you think you could ask Biggie for me? Arush's mother will do all the cooking for the Hindu celebration. Her name is Jasmeet. We call her Jas, like 'jazz cellar'," Avery gushed about her future in-laws. "I know I've gained ten pounds eating Punjabi food. You'll love Jas and Amit."

I learned Arush's father, Amit, was a doctor in Ohio and his mom owned a Kumon studio, a learning center for kids.

Leave it to Avery to single-handedly lift the cloud of sadness left by Virginia's death.

Weddings change the landscape and focus to the living. It's all about dresses, flowers, parties, and of course food: wedding cakes, which included Agnes's two favorite food groups, butter and sugar. But I had to ask Biggie and negotiate with her. I didn't know how she would feel about having her backyard turned into a venue for a Hindu wedding.

I walked into the kitchen where Biggie and Agnes were chatting. I was nervous.

"I need to ask you a big favor." I looked at my grandmother. "Avery wants to have two weddings—a Hindu wedding and a traditional wedding—and she wants to have them in your beautiful backyard. You won't need to worry about the Hindu part. Arush's mother, Jas, and her sister will do all the cooking."

She wiped her hands on the dish towel.

"Let's go sit down and discuss." That was just another way to say negotiate. I was already worried that she would say no. This was a big ask. I explained to the best of my ability what a Hindu wedding would entail for Biggie. I had even printed out pictures from Arush's sister's wedding, with all the beautiful colors and flowers. I knew enough to appeal to Biggie's aesthetic. The roses and marigolds and orchids. She sat there studying the pictures, occasionally glancing at the kitchen and Agnes. After a long silence, Biggie cleared her throat and laced her fingers together.

"Well, if we have this wedding, our kitchen needs a renovation and some painting." She stared at me. By using the term "we" I was afraid she was going to ask me to pay half of the renovation budget. We sat there saying nothing. I realized I wanted this. For Avery. Unfortunately, Biggie knew it too. I started biting my fingernails.

"Stop that, Bit." Another pause. I knew this was the most serious negotiation we had ever had. "I realize you will have only been working a few months when the wedding takes place." She stopped. I knew it! She wanted me to pay for the renovation.

"Biggie," I pleaded, "I don't have that kind of money. I have saved up about two thousand dollars that I could give you for the renovation."

She leaned back in her chair, studying me, or maybe considering her next move.

"The thing about negotiation you should remember, don't ever volunteer something until the person has gone first. I wasn't going to ask you for any money. But because you have offered it, here's what I will suggest." Damn, Biggie was good. She thought a moment longer. "You said earlier that Arush is moving here to open up a computer store. Take your money and support his business. He'll need it." She took a deep breath, and I realized she was not done, nor had she said yes. "You think your name is baggage that you drag back and forth from here to New York. Your name is more than that. It means respectability and responsibility. You and I can help make it a little easier for Arush in Erob. That's what your grandfather, your dad, and even Haines are doing with their medical practice and running the clinic." I just thought people went to them because they were so cheap!

"Yes, ma'am."

"We better get busy. I will call our contractor, Craig Willingham, and Elrod. You and I have a lot of work to do." Then she got up and left. She was going to all this expense for Avery. I sat there trying to figure out what her game was. I looked to Agnes.

"Now that is the woman I know and love," Agnes said, understanding fully.

If Biggie couldn't be the center of attention, having her beloved house and yard take center stage was the next best thing. From all Biggie's lists and orders you would have thought she had more to do than the bride did.

Avery hand-delivered her wedding invitation to both me and Biggie. It was thick, with beautiful handwriting on the outside. Biggie took us into the living room to open it, as if opening it required formality. I let Biggie open hers first. The first thing we noticed was the color. It was red with gold filigree. She scanned the page and smiled. I opened mine to see where her eyes had landed. I smiled. *These events will take place at the home of Mrs. Haines Benjamin Enloe.* Tears welled up in my eyes. The invitation made it real. Sacred. I hugged Avery.

"You girls better get it together," Biggie said. "We've got not one, but two weddings to put on."

Biggie had spared no expense with the renovation. Her house had transformed and updated with ease. She invited Arush's parents to stay in her guest room downstairs. When Jas arrived, she looked like she was moving in for a month. Food, flowers, and things I couldn't readily identify. She quickly made friends with Agnes and Biggie. Her spirit was warm and joyful. She embraced them and me until I wanted her to move to Erob.

The morning before the first wedding, it was all business. Jas, her sister Sha, Agnes, Biggie, and Avery's mom rolled up their sleeves in Biggie's kitchen. Small bowls of color popped against Biggie's new white marble island—an array of reds and yellows and oranges—blended to smell like a delightful convergence of cardamom, cumin, cinnamon, onion, and tej patta, which I learned was an Indian bay leaf. The smells were rich and exotic. Everything exploded with colorful potency. The aromas coming from the kitchen dwarfed the smells of Jimmy's Chicken, which I had brought for lunch. Jimmy had moved home from Chicago and opened the Chicken Emporium, the most popular establishment in Erob.

Jas cooked dinner for us that night in place of a rehearsal dinner. When she heated up the oil, it caught both Agnes's and Biggie's attention.

"We love anything that's deep-fat-fried in the South," I said, and Jas laughed. She called the dish chicken biryani. "Indian comfort food," made up of chicken and vegetables. Later, she taught Avery how to make it. Avery would make it once a week and became a better Indian cook than a Southern one. It was yummy. I watched the women laugh and whisper as they gathered in the kitchen. I guess in many cultures, the kitchen is the heart of the family. For Jas, home was her recipes and cooking.

The night was joyful and full of love.

The day of the ceremony, I walked in on Avery getting ready.

"You look so beautiful."

"You don't think my bare midriff is too much?"

I saw the red top with gold embroidery and its corresponding full skirt.

"Who needs a white wedding dress?"

She grabbed my wrist, and I admired the henna that decorated our hands.

Before the ceremony I saw Biggie and Agnes huddled together. They were allowing Jas and Sha to apply henna to their hands. I looked at Biggie.

"When in Rome!" She smiled at me.

During the reception the following day, I took some time to inspect the inside of the house. Biggie had attended to the most miniscule details, and small vases of flowers peeked discreetly from clever pockets throughout.

As I concluded my survey, I felt Biggie's hand on my shoulder. "She's beautiful, isn't she?" she asked.

"Yes, she is." I didn't know which was scarier, that I understood completely that my grandmother was not talking about the bride or the fact that we had just personalized an inanimate object. We were talking about Biggie's one true love: her house. She gently, and with great affection, flicked a speck of dust off the piano.

"You've done a good job with this place," I said. I was never as close to Biggie as when we were discussing our mutual love of something that went beyond bricks and mortar.

"*We've* done a good job, Bit. Your drapery selections in the breakfast room and living room were perfect. I have come to appreciate the paint color you chose. It really does accentuate the molding and floors. What did you call the color again? 'Coffee Soup'?"

Win walked in then, trailed by the scent of gardenias. "That would be Café Bisque," Win offered. "Bit was lost in that paint store, but lucky for her, I've got the knack."

Biggie uncharacteristically gave me that same affectionate smile, and after a genuinely pleasant interlude, we returned to our guests.

"P.C.N.M.," Win whispered as we made our way to the refreshments. "Very traditional."

"What?" I asked, needing clarification on this new line of Win-speak.

"Punch, cake, nuts, mints," Win recited with just the smallest hint of disdain.

I stood on the sidelines listening to Win's commentary. This was, after all, the happiest day of Win's life, too, since now she had me all to herself.

Carter and Haines walked up, wondering, I'm sure, when the site of these wedding soirees would turn back into their prized basketball court.

"So, Little Bit," Carter managed, "after you pass the LSAT and make it through law school, why don't you come back home to Erob and go into practice with me?"

I breathed in the late summer afternoon full of happiness, gardenias, and future plans. "Come back to Podunkville? Not for all the love of Biggie's money," I said.

He looked as if I had crushed him like a summer mosquito.

By Christmas, everyone, except for me, was engaged. I thought about the genetic magnet again. Not only did I neglect to get the magnet that would draw me to a special someone, but I also got a "pull" to a place: New York City.

Things looked good for me. Biggie promised to foot all of my bridesmaid's dresses, a trip to Europe in May with Win as a graduation present, and an apartment to myself in the fall in case I got into law school. I asked Mama if Biggie was going senile, and she said I "shouldn't look a rare gift horse in the mouth."

Still, over the holidays, Biggie's living room could have easily been Sesame Street, where "one of these things is not like the others"—and, once again, that one thing would be me.

I couldn't help but feel like an extra wheel as I watched the eight of them together, their whole lives planned out, like an architect's blueprint for a house. My plans were vast and uncertain. Nothing *but* surprises.

One evening, feigning a headache, I excused myself from the festivities, and I sat on Biggie's stairs, just listening. Their laughter spoke of intimacy, their conversation commonality. I realized that even though their plans seemed ordinary, I appreciated them and was oddly drawn to that certitude. While I knew I didn't want their conventional blueprints, something in me longed to have their confidence.

"What are you doing sitting here all alone?" Avery whispered when she found me.

In an unguarded moment, even with Avery, I asked, "When is it going to be my turn? Not to be married, God forbid, but to have something to celebrate? Something of my own?"

She took my hand and then hugged me.

"How can it be your turn when you want so much more than the rest of us? For you it will take time. Be patient." Part of an Averyism I'd heard throughout my life: *be patient.* Patience implied idleness, waiting for the right time. In truth, it was a word heavy with sweat, determination, discipline, work, and the need to stay focused. Waiting was easy. Patience was hard.

But wanting so much more? I hadn't really thought about it that way.

To keep moving forward, I took the LSAT, and I did well enough to get into Duke Law.

Avery was right—I did want more. Lots more. Of everything. The only rule I had discovered was to keep my grades high enough to keep my options open. Maybe then I could get myself away from Erob and on to New York City.

After graduation, before all the big weddings, Win and I were given a two-week graduation trip to Europe by our grandmothers. I told Haines that this was final confirmation that Biggie had gone soft. But when she gave me a whole $20 bill to do with as I pleased on the greater continent, I knew that this was the same old crotchety woman as always, and she still had fire left in her.

Traveling, they say, is broadening for the mind. I say traveling with Win was equally as educational.

"What are all the plastic bags for?" I asked, sitting on the edge of her bed, which looked a bit like Mama's countertops at the end of summer when she canned, froze, and put up fresh vegetables like squash, tomatoes, and okra for the winter.

"Don't tell me you're not taking plastic bags, Bit?"

I didn't have the heart to tell her I didn't know for sure what she was using them for.

"You use them to pack with," she said as if reading my mind. "So your clothes won't get wrinkled? My Tri-Delt sister who travels abroad all the time says plastic bags are the way to go."

My clothes stayed in one big wrinkle. I volunteered to keep the dorm vacuum cleaner in my closet so I could throw my clothes on the handle.

"You should have seen all those plastic bags," I told Avery as soon as I could. "Win folds her clothes meticulously, and then she slides them into bags. Next, as she closes the bag, she squeezes all of the air out. She looked like she was going on some reconnaissance mission for the FBI. Get this, Avery, she packed an extra box of bags for when she buys clothes on our trip. She even gave me a box." I laughed.

"Win should have given you two boxes for when you lose the first box," Avery said, without missing a beat.

"That hurts, Avery."

"The truth often does."

"Oh, I wish you were going, Avery," I said, pulling the clothes off the back of my chair to pack.

"Me too."

It started before we even set foot in Europe. Or even on the plane.

We were staying at the Ritz Carlton-Buckhead the night before our flight, since we flew out of Atlanta's Hartsfield so early. Win took charge checking us in to the hotel.

Upon opening the door to our room, Win said, "This room simply will not do."

The bellman and I looked at each other and then at Win. I bet a bellman at the Ritz had never heard that before. What could you not like about a five-star hotel?

"I said this room will not do," Win repeated, just standing there. I surveyed the plush gold and maroon décor trying to figure out what she saw that I didn't.

"Last year, Mama, Daddy, and I stayed here in a room with happy colors that overlooked Saks."

The bellhop still didn't understand, nor did I, for that matter.

"I specifically requested a room that is done in happy colors like blue and pink, and I want it to overlook Phipps Plaza. This gold and maroon is too close to brown, and I simply cannot sleep in a brown room. I believe the room number I want is 444." She waited until the bellman went to call the front desk. I was beginning to think we were going to get thrown out.

"How can anyone sleep in a brown room?" Win asked logically as we waited. She was visibly shuddering and *not* budging. "I hate brown," she moaned for emphasis.

Finally, the bellman came back and took us to another room and opened the door. "Does this suit your color palette?" he asked Win.

She walked in and surveyed the pink and blue brocade draperies that were pulled back to reveal a clear view of the Plaza.

"Yes!" she clapped. "These are happy colors!" She gave the bellman twenty dollars for our four bags. Let it be said that Win is a good tipper. I would spend most our time in Europe trying to learn in several languages the equivalent of "Can you break a twenty?" while Win handed them out freely.

Once we were settled, Win asked, "Isn't this better, Bit? I mean, I just can't sleep in a brown room. Can you?"

Win and I returned from our little jaunt to Europe where we somehow survived each other, and even I had become a little picky about accommodations. I'm sure Win was glad she had me all to herself, although she did repack my suitcase with those plastic bags every couple of days. I reciprocated by taking pictures of Win in front of every European tourist spot so her trip would be properly documented. I got her head but missed the Eiffel Tower.

All of us had such different plans that summer. Avery was married and already pregnant with her first baby on the way. Carter's wedding to Jenny was rapidly approaching, with Haines's and Addison's to follow soon after. Win and Rich would get married when Win said so, and I was heading to law school.

"Any regrets?" I asked Avery about not going to Europe with us.

"Regrets?" Avery paused, then, "No."

I felt an Averyism coming on.

"Regrets are like potato chips," she said. "You can't stop with just one, and pretty soon the bag is empty, your life is over, and you've spent your whole life wishing you'd done things differently."

Later that spring, Avery had her baby: a boy named Dhillon—"gift of God."

"What about you, Win, when are you and Rich getting married?"

"We'll get married when I'm twenty-four, and when I'm twenty-five, we'll have our first child."

"Don't you think you ought to consult Rich about this?" I asked, knowing poor Rich didn't stand a chance if Win's mind was made up, yet I had no doubt Win's lucky dust would make it all come true.

Summer came around again, bringing another wedding season to Erob, Alabama. I split my time interning at an established New York City firm and preparing for Win's wedding. Not necessarily in that order.

"Are you trying to pass yourself off as a Yankee now?" Haines asked when he heard about Bernstein & Weinberg. I liked it there—a lot—and was hoping to be offered a permanent job as an associate someday.

"Are you still trying to pass yourself off as a doctor who doesn't care about money, Haines?" I retorted.

What Win's wedding lacked in size it made up for in grandness. I have never seen or smelled so many flowers.

Avery, who was pregnant again, and I exchanged looks, doing the mental math for this extravaganza.

Before they embarked on their honeymoon, Win shamelessly tossed her bouquet to me in a last-ditch effort to get me married off and tied to Erob. After I reluctantly caught it, Geeky Newman gave me a flirty smile and asked me if I wanted to dance. I declined. Weddings in Erob were like the Bermuda triangle—any minute you could wind up getting stuck there, cooking cubed steak every Tuesday night and watching *Wheel of Fortune* for the rest of your life.

Biggie couldn't believe her only granddaughter was working for a fancy New York City firm, and her displeasure only pleased me more.

To show how upset she really was, Biggie had a stroke.

Haines called to tell me. "Is it serious?" I asked, holding the phone in the crook of my neck while highlighting a document.

"Yes, Bit, it's a *stroke*. Her legs were affected. She may need to move downstairs and use a cane."

"Her speech?" I asked, highlighter down.

"Wasn't affected at all."

Figures, I thought.

"She wants to see you. You're all she talks about. When can you come?"

Oh, so this is her game now, I thought, but I went home anyway.

When I got to the hospital, it did look like Biggie was close to death, with all those tubes going everywhere. Then she opened her mouth, and I knew she was her old self.

"Come in, Little Bit," she commanded. Her voice seemed even more formidable wafting up from her sick bed. "I want you to help me walk down the hall. Bring me that stupid walker."

"Are you sure you're supposed to get up?" I asked. Suppose her legs were too weak to support her? "What does Haines say?"

"I don't listen to Haines. I listen to my own body, thank you, and it's telling me to get up. So hold that walker steady. You wouldn't want me to fall," she said. The burden had been shifted to me. What did Haines think? What if I got yelled at for participating? I felt the will of my grandmother like a separate appendage. I wondered where that kind of determination came from and what it had done to us and, more importantly, what it might have done to Daddy.

For a brief moment, a hint of vulnerability seeped out of her anger, and I watched as she struggled to get out of the bed while at the same time tried to keep her robe from opening. Her vulnerability clutched at me, and when I was brave enough to finally meet her eyes, there was fear in them. Was it a fear of death, or was it a fear that she was finally losing control?

Miraculously to everyone but me, Biggie made a full recovery. She was even able to go back upstairs to her bedroom.

"Biggie, you're amazing," marveled my doctor brother. But then he'd not seen it like I had seen it. The "it" factor: Biggie's will. Quietly strong, unless her legs failed to comply with the plan, but confident enough to defy medical science.

"She'll probably outlive all of us," I heard myself say too many times.

The only thing different was the locks. A new anxiety had crept in, and she had new locks put on her outside doors as well as locks placed on every door leading up to her bedroom, which she began to lock behind her every night.

"Like Fort Knox. How would we ever get to her in a fire?" Mama wondered.

Let the fire take its chances like the rest of us, I wanted to say.

But I had seen the other side of Biggie, too, and wondered if I would ever stoop so low as to use it against her. The strand of vulnerability that bobbed along the surface when she was trying to get out of the hospital bed and stand for the first time in front of me. That vulnerability and her will residing in the same place, each trying to have its way with the other.

I knew why the locks were there. Fear. Not a fear of who—a burglar—but of what: death. She was afraid of it now because she had gotten close enough. Close enough to feel it and even see it. Flippantly, I surmised, she didn't like what she saw, so it must be hell, and more specifically, there are "terms and conditions." Most people are like that really. Will we suffer? Will it be quick? Will it hurt? Will we be alone? Yes, will we be alone?

I could see Biggie wondering all of this. Hence, the locks, to give her more time to bargain with God when the time came.

What I came to know, that I would never admit then, was that I respected that about her. Her will. No one could or did stand up to her, unless you count me, the New York rebel.

It took me a while to figure out the reason she made me so angry.

I was more like her than I dared admit.

"Paging Nina Enloe," the receptionist announced to the whole firm.

In the short time I'd been with Bernstein & Weinberg, I had learned something about pages. They were almost never from a client or a senior partner. They were usually from a senior associate throwing his weight around, or it was from Haines or Win. Neither felt the least bit bad about paging me, and it could be for God only knows what. The latter was right. It was Win.

"Bit," Win asked when I picked up the phone, "are you in your office or are you out in the open?" Win had not seen my firm's offices yet.

"I'm in my office."

"Is the door closed?" she asked.

"Yes," I said, lying.

"Good," Win proceeded. What she didn't know wouldn't hurt her, I guessed.

"Bit, I think I'm going to have a baby," she began.

"Well, are you or aren't you?" I asked. Being the lawyer, I wanted some evidence.

"I googled it, and I think I may be pregnant."

"What symptoms did you google?" By now I was looking at my watch.

"Being late, swollen breasts, being irritable. Shall I go on?"

"Win," I interrupted, "you have just described signs that you're about to have your period."

"Well," Win said, seemingly confused.

"Go get a pregnancy test!" She was trying my patience.

"Good Lord, I can't just stroll into the Wal-Mart here in Erob, Bit. Everyone would talk! Dorothy Kay will check me out, and you know it will be all over the town before I even get out of the store," Win countered logically. Oh, how Win exaggerated her own importance.

"You're married!" I said, bemused. "You just don't want folks to know you and Rich have—"

"Bit," Win interrupted. "Besides, if I'm not, then Dorothy will look all sorry for me, and I just cannot deal with that." I immediately wondered where Rich bought condoms. But I showed impressive restraint.

I wasn't Biggie's granddaughter for nothing. I could see where this was headed. On my lunch break, taking time out of my busy day, I went to the nearest Duane Reade and bought one EPT test and an extra box. The good thing about living in a big city: no one knows you—plus, I didn't give a shit about my reputation like Win did. The price it cost me to send it overnight was about as much as what I paid the drugstore. But Win was grateful. And pregnant. And she didn't have to tell the ladies of Wal-Mart first either.

I had been through a labor of my own—the Alabama bar exam—and I had taken the New York bar the previous February.

Like my exams, Win scheduled her labor, and she wanted me to be her coach. She reluctantly permitted her doctor husband to help, but only after Rich promised to stay away from "down there" lest he be traumatized for the rest of their marriage.

I had no idea what to expect, so I took my cues from those around me. When the nurses said "good job," I looked Win squarely in the eye and repeated the affirmation like a foreigner picking up the language. Win, for her part, smiled back, and I found myself reaching for her hand to squeeze it. Not one to tolerate any sort of pain, Win opted for an early epidural. Rich cautioned her that it was too early, and to my surprise, I spoke up and sided with Win. She squeezed my hand back and said thanks, and we held hands until the baby girl appeared. Even though it was covered in mucus, I could tell the baby was perfect.

When the nurse observed "it must be nice to have a best friend," I neither disagreed nor cowered in fear. It was true. It was the best thing Win and I had ever done together. In that moment, I felt a rush of unbridled love for Win. Talk about a miracle! But I soon recovered.

"Do they need to paint the walls in these rooms such a wretched beige?" she asked. "I will have to speak with someone about that."

So you want to know how lucky dust works? Win said she always wanted to have her baby when she was twenty-five. She did. A girl.

Winifred Baxter Montgomery. After four hours of pain-free labor, like anyone would want.

She had planned out her whole life, and all the pieces were falling into place like a prepackaged puzzle. A beautiful life with no rough edges and no brown colors scribbled outside the lines.

Two princesses, charming the world with their mere presence, and two weeks later, Win's stomach was back to her pre-pregnancy flatness. It would be later that my theory of lucky dust would be tested.

Four months after Winnie was born, I was doing some late-night work in the firm's library when the page came.

"Nina Enloe."

"You have your first niece," my brother's ecstatic tone bounded out from the other end. "Addison Frances Enloe. We'll call her Addie."

"How's Addison doing?" I asked.

"She's great. Just as beautiful as ever. Addie looks just like her with a head full of black hair."

I could only imagine his joy and Mama's. Now she had a new little girl of her own.

"Win's here—mobilizing the troops," he said.

Childbirth and death seemed to bring women together.

Wai Wong was the first and best friend I made in New York. She had a wicked sense of humor to go along with her wicked intellect. She came into my office and closed the door.

"Cy told me to meet you. I do most of his paralegal work, and I know you're his favorite associate. I'm Wai Wong." She slung her legs over the arm of the chair like we were at a slumber party. I laughed and loved her immediately.

"I love the name Nina!"

"Believe me, it's much better than my nickname," I told her.

"What's your nickname?"

"Back home, people call me Little Bit. I was named for my grandmother, who also has a nickname, Biggie."

"Those are some weird-ass names. You *are* petite. Is your grandmother big?"

"In every way. But please don't spread that around. I'd like to be Nina."

"Your secret is safe with me . . . unless I'm buzzed." I found myself laughing again. She cussed without repudiation.

She was tall and skinny, and she could eat her weight for supper.

"Wai," I said one day when she handed me her work, "what happened to the big bowl of potato chips in the conference room and those sandwiches?"

"I was here until 4:30 in the fucking morning."

It was the first time in my whole life that I had my *own* life, my *own* identity, and my *own* money. I could be Nina here, and Nina could be anyone.

"I have found my people," I would say to Avery during our marathon phone calls, when she'd fill me in on life with Dhillon and Kiran, her new baby daughter. "Divorce, suicide, affairs—I seem pretty much near normal here."

"I'm glad. But I think you always knew who you were. You just haven't always accepted yourself."

Avery was right, of course. But it was good to be around others who lacked lucky dust, like me.

"This lucky dust," Wai said after I had let her in on my theory, "are you sure you don't have it? I mean, you have a family who loves you, friends who love you too, and Cy. You know he likes you. He's not that way with most people. I've seen him act like a real asshole."

"I pick out his ties, Wai," I said, reminding her of what I took to be my most significant assignment. "You always look pulled together. I don't have the vision thing."

"Shit, where did you come from? You can buy style with personal shoppers." Wai proceeded to tell me about Susan and Andrea, her "on commission" style gurus around the city. "If I dressed myself, I wouldn't be allowed in the building. Not after I showed up in drop crotch pants." The mental image sounded both dirty and made me want to get a pair to torment Win.

"That's expensive, isn't it? I have to feed myself. Especially if you're gonna finish all the office sandwiches."

"You think I have that kind of money? They just put clothes in the dressing room for you—let yourself be lazy for once. You still make Cy look good to the clients, and that's fucking genius."

"Well, in my next life I'll gladly turn in my smarts for a big set of hooters."

Wai, who was small, too, never seemed to be without dates or boyfriends. She also loved to indulge in that great pastime of "sleepovers," or as Win would say with her more pejorative term, "one-night stands."

"All you have to do is stay with the firm, and you'll be rich," Wai said simply.

New Yorkers are like Southerners with their idiosyncrasies, except New Yorkers are more direct. And after living in the South, it was a relief to always know where you stood. Even with my boss, managing partner Cy Weinberg.

Most of the work I did was done for him. Everything from

the professional to the personal. One minute I'd be in his office reviewing an important case and the next his private tailor would swoop in with swatches of fabric for suits and colored silks for ties and pocket squares, and he'd ask for my assistance.

"Nina, help an old man impress his wife," he would say, thrusting small pieces of fabric my way.

Thank God for Wai telling me about the ability to just "buy" style. For some reason Cy waited for and seemed to value my opinion.

"What colors does Olga like to see you wear?" I hedged.

"Gold," he'd say, fully aware of my hedge. "She thinks that golds bring out my brown eyes."

I could see that. Both Cy and Olga had dark eyes and both looked sad, too, probably a result of their pasts. Cy's family lost everything during the Depression, and Olga's family lost their lives at Dachau. And together they had lost an only daughter, suffering the ultimate blow.

"She's right," I'd concur. "The gold brightens up your face."

But here's the funny thing about Cy. He'd pay whatever price the clothier named for his suits. Then, he would dash from the office at 5:45 p.m. so he and Olga could make the Prix Fixe special at one of their favorite restaurants.

Life, I learned from Cy, is all about rationalizations.

twelve

"Paging Nina Enloe."

I was in Cy's office going over an initial purchase offer when the call came. I was hacked. Here I was in Cy God-Almighty Weinberg's office, and Win was probably calling to tell me about some Junior League drama.

But it was my brother, and he sounded far away, much further than distance.

"Bit," he said, his voice absent of expression. The fact that there was so much silence that I could hear him swallow scared me. Staying connected, it seemed, was all my brother could do for the moment.

"Haines?" I asked, to make sure he was still there. Cy tried to look busy so as not to hear all of the things that were not being communicated.

"What is it?" I asked.

Again, the awful sound of nothing, swallowing.

"Is it Biggie?"

"No," he managed.

"Mama?" I hated to ask.

Time passed, as if he were assessing the answer to my question. It finally came out in one horrible burst.

"Mama is okay, Bit, but it's the Judge and Miss Harriett. They were killed this morning by a drunk driver out on the bypass."

Funny, I first thought of what Biggie had said about something bad happening out there. *You take your life into your own hands when you pull out of Wal-Mart, the bank, or the post office. No traffic lights. Who'd ever heard of such?*

Biggie was right. A drunk driver had killed the Judge and Miss Harriett two miles from their house. Instantly, in the time it took me to blink.

"How's Carter?" I asked tentatively. I received no reply. Haines couldn't answer, and I heard the phone gently click. Nothing. I was cut off from all of them.

Silence seeped into Cy's office.

"My parents' best friends, my brother's best friend's parents . . . " I started. "They were killed in a car wreck out on our bypass. In Erob." To this day, what remains with me is how fact and memory blur together as to when I knew what. "They're like second parents to Haines and me."

"I'm so sorry, Nina," Cy said, "for all of you. It's hard to lose couple friends. You'll need to go."

Couple friends. I hadn't thought about that term in a while. True, Mama and Daddy were close to Miss Harriett and the Judge. But it had been a long time since Mama and Daddy were a couple. Now, Mama was all that was left of the original foursome.

I guess I was deep in thought in the past, because Cy continued talking. "Of course, you can take as much time as you need."

I felt far away. If I were closer, I would have been amazed at the generosity of Cy Weinberg's offer. As far as I knew, he only ever took two days, Rosh Hashanah and Yom Kippur.

"Thanks, Cy," I managed. "I'll only need a couple of days off for the funeral." I rushed the words out like I had already gone and was back at my desk.

"Are you sure?" Cy asked. "Maybe your mother needs you. Or your brother." *They have each other,* I thought.

"I'll take this registration statement with me and work on it on the plane."

"No, Nina, I can get someone to take care of that."

"No, Cy, please. I need something to do." I must have sounded convincing because he handed the documents to me. Things were moving in slow motion, but I felt comforted by his paternal presence.

"Is it the shock or the finality that is the hardest to take?" I asked him.

Cy's nostrils made a short, sweeping sound as he inhaled quickly. "Finality," he answered. "Shock wears off eventually."

I wore my new green suit and scarf.

"This year's black," Susan had proclaimed. It was like fashion was some Pantone color of the year. I wondered who decided such things. The scarf, silky and foreign, omitted the need for jewelry. Haines picked me up in baggage claim at the Atlanta airport.

I threw my bag into the back seat of his car.

"You look pretty uptown, Bit," Haines said, fingering my scarf and patting my shoulder.

I wondered if I looked too uptown for Erob. My brother, I noticed, had on his old khakis and blue blazer. The Southern man's uniform. And he looked tired. Older.

"What's the plan?" I asked, trying to be lighthearted.

"Addison has Addie and Winnie. Arush has Dhillon and Kiran. Win and Avery are over at Carter's, and Mama is in the kitchen cooking," he said.

How typical. This was one of the insane rituals that I had gladly escaped. My brother didn't elaborate. He couldn't. He was biting his lower lip.

I didn't know what was worse. Watching a grown man cry or watching a grown man fight hard not to.

Carter's house. In truth, the house still belonged to Miss Harriett and the Judge. But trading houses among family members was a Southern tradition, like funeral casseroles. It had been G.G.'s house first until Carter, her grandchild, came along, and then the trade was made to his parents. I'm sure they had been waiting on grandchildren themselves before making it official, but now it looked like Carter would get the house the old-fashioned way: through inheritance.

The smell of ham hit me first. Of course, Avery had baked a ham, the size and smell drowning out that of any casserole.

"Bit," Win exclaimed, sensing my presence even before I entered the room.

"Hi, Win." I closed the door and took inventory of who was gathered in Miss Harriet's kitchen. Me, Win, and Avery. We embraced before Win started handing out duties.

"Carter and Jennifer wanted to know when you got here. They're upstairs," Win informed me.

I was glad to have this quiet moment with Avery and Win before the crowds descended. "Goodness, Nina, you look beautiful," Avery said as she fixed a cup of coffee.

"Who designed your suit, Bit?" Win asked suspiciously.

When I told her, she said, "No wonder it looks like a million bucks. It probably cost it."

"She still looks nice," Avery said.

"Well, you would too."

I decided to leave Win alone, but I just couldn't. She was being a bitch right there in Miss Harriett's kitchen. "Don't start with me."

This time Win did not take heed.

"You wouldn't be all smug and citified if you knew what Carter had been through."

I would have let it go if it had really been about Carter, but it wasn't. She was jealous, and it made me feel utterly triumphant. I had finally pulled myself together, and it had not been Win who had done it for me.

"Quit being a bitch."

"Well, well, nice talk, Bit. Something else you've picked up in New York, no doubt."

"Nina," Avery interrupted, "we all need to be together and respect Judge and Mrs. Gideon."

I glared at Win.

"Remembering people who die is like remembering a Thanksgiving dinner," Avery continued as we held our fire. She was about to unleash another Averyism. "You can remember how good and fine the meal was or you can focus on the argument you had with your mother about what you were going to wear to the table. Let's remember the wonderful meal. Let's remember how fine Miss Harriett and the Judge were."

Avery was right, and we both knew it. It was about Miss Harriett and the Judge. And Carter.

"Carter has had a time with his relatives. They wanted the service one way and Carter another. They want nothing but scripture, and Carter wants some poetry. I guess you really need to talk with him, Nina."

I could see where this might be heading. The Judge was never a scripture kind of guy. He used Shakespeare some in rendering his opinions, proclaiming that in *his* Bible, Shakespeare followed Psalms. That's how he got the nickname the High-Brow Judge.

There was nothing left for me to do but go upstairs. I knocked on his parents' bedroom door, and Jenny opened it and embraced me. I kissed her on both cheeks, one foreigner greeting another.

"I'll let you visit with Carter," she said, leaving.

"Win, I'm sure, could use your help," I said, offering her something to do.

She gave me a dubious look, and I knew she had figured out the dynamics of Win, and it made me like her even more.

"Help him, Bit," Jenny added. This time it was I who gave a dubious look. Intimacy filled the room, like an embryonic sac protecting all emotions about to be expressed. It was warm and safe there, away from funeral arrangements and the flood of sympathy. Away from the laborious visitation filled with well-meaning people. Away from the sharp pain of grief. We were safe, if only for a moment.

"Carter," I announced myself, as if he didn't know.

"Bit."

"Carter," I repeated.

He walked the distance of the room and hugged me. He didn't cry. I was rigid with fear that he might. His grief-rimmed eyes met mine, and we stayed there a long time, long enough for me to relax.

Then I saw it. Miss Harriett's skirted bedside table, and on it, the photo album that my mother had shared with her. Inside, I knew, was a photograph of Jenny and Carter at their wedding and many honeymoon pictures from Sea Island. Next to the album, in a frame, stood the small picture of Carter and me taken at the Debutante Ball. The corsage of gardenias that Miss Harriett fashioned was pinned to my dress. The photo that was taken just three days before Virginia died.

Seeing me standing there, in frozen picture form, I forgot. Forgot who this was supposed to be about. After all, I was my father's daughter, and all of the ghosts were with us today, maybe more so than the living. It was as if with our embrace, that grief had exchanged hands, and I lost it. Lost every bit of control a Southern woman should possess.

I released him and ran into the bathroom. I closed and locked the bathroom door so Carter couldn't come in to comfort me. Poor Carter was on the other side of the door, the one needing help, but I was a failure at these rituals. Here I was adding to it with my own pain. My feelings for his parents were more apparent to me in death than they had ever been to me in life.

Carter didn't say a word, but I heard him slump down on the other side of the door. We just sat there joined by our sorrow, separated by a plank of wood. Neither one of us asking for more.

Win would have been better. Avery would have been better. Even Mama would have been better. Certainly, Carter deserved better than me.

Just where in the hell are you, God? I wondered. Carter was so good. He deserved better than my brand of reluctant sympathetic platitudes and my silence.

I finally pulled myself together. I found Jenny's makeup bag and began applying her foundation to my splotchy face. It was called Dramatically Different, and here was its chance to prove it. I also found a discarded EPT test, and I covered it up with a hand towel. I guess this would be their bathroom in their house from now on. I knew they'd been trying. For years now. Maybe there would be some good news soon.

After brushing my hair, I opened the door.

Carter's eyes met mine. A conspiracy formed.

"I have to ask you something, Bit."

"Please don't, Carter. I don't think I can."

"You're the only one of us who had a poetry book in her hand all the time. Remember *The Little Prince*?"

"When I was young, the Little Prince and Dr. Seuss kept me company."

"I don't think Seuss wants any credit for your development."

We laughed. And then we remembered. Carter was an orphan grieving here, and I was discussing *Green Eggs and Ham.* I stepped to him and touched his shoulder.

"I'll do it," I said. "I'll read a poem at the funeral."

The connection born between us that day would remain with me forever.

I escaped out the front door without having to go back through the kitchen. I walked the well-worn path of generations and opened the wrought iron gate that put me into Biggie territory.

The familiar smells greeted me, enveloping me like an old friend. Agnes was there, and she was baking. Familiarity can destroy, but it can also force you to do things you don't think you can do. Like reading a poem at a funeral because a friend has asked you to. I hugged Agnes, hoping to draw strength from her full embrace.

"Well, Lord, look at you, Bit. You look so nice."

Then, I heard my grandmother's booming voice from the adjoining room. "I mean it, Tom. I said it years ago. Something's got to be done about that deathtrap. Losing two prominent lives should distress you like it distresses me."

I wondered if prominent lives counted more than regular ones?

If I had a running conflict with "The Church," Biggie's nemesis continued to be "The City." She was always unhappy about something, and it was never-ending. I remember one time when Daddy said to her, "Mama, you've got the money. Just pay somebody to fix the crack in the sidewalk in front of your house."

"Ben," she had said, "it's the principle of the thing. The city should take care of its property."

As a lawyer, I can tell you that more bad things begin with "it's the principle of the thing." But the bypass was her biggest, most long-standing feud, and now it had taken two of our own.

I heard her bang the receiver down. "Moron," she said. Some things never change. Then, "Bit, is that you? Come in here and let me look at my granddaughter." I loved it when she accepted me as is.

"I trust you've been over at the Gideons' house."

"I saw Carter, yes."

"Are you reading scripture?" Biggie asked.

"No, I'm not, at Carter's request. But I am reading something from the Lord. Alfred Lord Tennyson," I said, playing with her. "Now, I'd better go see Mama."

"Mama," I announced, hearing the familiar sound of pots and pans clanging and catching the smell of Campbell's cream soups wafting from the kitchen.

"Little Bit," the voice replied, "in here." That was a no-brainer.

"Mama," I said again, going over to the stove to hug her.

"No, don't," she recoiled, pushing me away. "You'll ruin your suit, and you look so nice. I wouldn't want to get food on your new clothes."

I realized I still looked to her for approval on my suit and ability to accessorize.

"Mama, how are you doing?" I asked, truly wondering how she felt. Wondering how it was to be without both your best friends.

"Well, Bit, it's a blow," she said. She turned away from me then and back to her cooking.

That's as much as she would say, but the distracted way she cooked told me more. I watched her hands tremble with teaspoons and familiar ingredients. I heard her mutter a cuss word as she dropped a stick of butter. Feeling like an intruder, I retreated to my room, leaving the sad little crowd of Mama and her memories behind.

For though from out our bourne of Time and Place
The flood may bear me far,
I hope to see my Pilot face to face
When I have crossed the bar.

I lifted my eyes, meeting no one's. After such weighty words from Tennyson's "Crossing the Bar," I ad-libbed.

"And because the Judge quoted Shakespeare on every possible occasion," I managed, "I will read a favorite passage from *Julius Caesar*:"

Cowards die many times before their deaths;
The valiant never taste death but once.

I left the pulpit and sat by Mama, who seemed to have transported herself somewhere else other than Miss Harriet's funeral.

Carter was on my other side, and he reached over, found my hand, and squeezed his appreciation.

We all ended up graveside. *Have you found your peace?* I wondered, and lofted my thoughts their way. His way.

"You really should try and come home more often," Haines whispered as he moved in next to me.

"What are you, one of Biggie's minions now?"

"No, but Bit, Mama isn't getting any younger. And Biggie could use you."

"Well, Mr. Perfect, they do have you," I said, and shot my brother a well-intended smile.

Then, from somewhere off to my right, I heard the familiar banter. "Who's going to help us with our parking tickets now?" I heard Chewy ask Jordan. "Who's going to bust Elrod out of jail?"

This much thinking was enough. For me. For Mama. For all of us. And just where Mama was that day, like her feelings, remains a mystery to me, but her eyes stayed focused for a long time on the two freshly dug holes in the ground.

thirteen

Not long after I got back to New York, Rich and Win bought a beach house on the coast of Georgia. I suppose that's what the wealthy do—multiply their stuff. Win did it in her usual flamboyant fashion, with five bedrooms, no less.

"What do you, Rich, and Winnie need five bedrooms for anyway?" I asked when she called to tell me all about it. She answered as if it was I who hadn't done the math properly.

"Well, silly, there's our room, of course. And then one for Haines and Addison, another for Carter and Jennifer, one more for Avery and Arush, and we'll be putting the children in the last. Since you're single, you'll sleep on the daybed in the den connected to our room. But don't worry, the den is decorated in happy colors—and you get your own TV!" she finished with glee.

"That *is* a relief, Win. I certainly can't be sleeping in a goddamn brown bedroom."

Needless to say, for Labor Day weekend, we all took a road trip to the beach. We, the next generation, but watching Carter slip off by himself, I knew his parents were with us as well. Ghosts, it seems, pack up and follow us on vacations too.

I'll hand it to Win—she was a clever hostess. The blender kept a steady buzz concocting beach drinks—margaritas and piña coladas—all day long. For the children, we substituted ice cream for rum, per Avery's special recipe. The smell of coconut, sand, salt, and Bain de Soleil blended together to signal vacation and escape. We soaked up nostalgia like we soaked up suntan oil—carefree, while avoiding sunburn and painful memories that can sting.

Win, to her credit, knew we all needed this trip. Had she really bought the house for us? Could she then, in turn, write it off as a charitable contribution?

Walking with her one morning, picking up sand dollars, she told me that Carter and Jennifer had used the beach house not long after the funeral. She also told me that an extra key would always be under the mat, for anyone who needed to get away and use it. Anytime.

"That's nice, Win," I said. And I meant it.

"Well, duh," she replied.

I ignored her and asked, "Do you know any other news? How are Carter and Jenny doing?" I was thinking about the EPT test I saw in their bathroom several months back.

"I don't know anything for sure, Bit. I just worry about Jennifer. She's so quiet and keeps to herself. I don't think she's well. Maybe tomorrow you can take a walk with Carter," she said, but by her tone I could tell she knew a lot more than she was letting on. I wondered if our friendship now had boundaries and limits and if the hometown crowd had more loyalty with her than me. I was surprised how the prospect sent shivers down my spine.

The next morning Carter and I managed to slip away for a walk on the beach before breakfast, and before the effects of the blender had a chance to start their numbing effects for the day.

"So, how are you doing, Carter?" I asked. I dreaded a real answer. I realized I'd posed it too casually, when all you really want to hear is the one-word response: "fine." The equivalent to leaving a funeral casserole at someone's back door and calling it a day.

But Carter and I don't have that kind of relationship, so what I got was, "Not so good, Bit."

"I miss your parents too."

"It's not just my parents, you know. It's me . . . it's . . . listen, Bit, I'm sure you don't want to hear about my troubles right now. We're at the beach. On vacation . . . "

For a minute we just stopped walking. We looked at each other like we were standing in the middle of an emergency room with doctors and a dreaded diagnosis. I heard the squeals of "Marco Polo" in the distance, reminding me that, for the rest of the world, lightheartedness was a given and not a rare commodity.

I had two choices, but for some reason, that day, I couldn't take that road "less traveled." I felt too wobbly. I felt too unsteady. I felt, unfortunately, too sober.

I heard my voice say, "You're always telling me things get better, Carter. And they will. You'll see. Whatever's going on will get better." And then I began walking again, leaving things unsaid with my cowardly retreat.

Later, after dinner, wine, and putting the children to bed, beer became the favorite beverage among the men, and the blender cranked up once again.

"I've got to change rooms," Haines ribbed. "Carter and Jen are completely out of hand, and we can't get any sleep!"

"Haines," Win said. "Behave." I laughed to myself, as I had seen Carter and Jenny's pajamas, and I didn't get the sense there was a whole lot going on after the lights went down.

"Hey, Little Bit," my brother said. "What's it like sleeping next to Win?" I was about to make a joke, but when I looked over at her, she didn't look like she could take it. As much as I would have enjoyed embarrassing her, I just replied, "Oh, it's just fine. You know, I sleep like the dead," a most unfortunate turn of phrase that made the room go pale. I should have gone with my gut the first time.

At some point over the long weekend, I decided I should get home to see Mama, so I called Cy and asked for a couple of extra days off. After returning from the Judge and Harriet's funeral, Cy and I had had a long talk about work ethic, commitment, and my future with the firm. He said he was concerned about how much time I spent at the office, and he encouraged me to "take a breather" now and again. Yes, he valued commitment, he'd said, but not at the expense of family, friends, and what was truly important in life. He finished with, "I trust you to make good decisions," and I was more convinced than ever that this is where I wanted to work for the rest of my career—if he would have me.

Avery and Arush had room in their car, so I drove back with them.

After lunch, I met Avery at the church's playground. Before the children ran to the equipment, Avery caught their attention.

"Look Dhillon. Look Kiran," she said, pointing up to the tallest part of a tree where the sunlight came streaming down in pencil-like shafts of light.

I saw it too. The sun was peeking through and all around, illuminating each and every limb. It filtered through like long, singular strands of earthly particles touching the earth and those children.

"That's the hand of God reaching for you. See those long strings of light? Those are His fingers, and they are reaching down from heaven to protect you. Whenever you see the beams of sunlight shining through the trees, think of God's hand protecting you."

"Is it really God's own hand, Mama?" Kiran asked, never taking her eyes off the rays of sunlight. "God's fingers?"

I watched quietly for a long time and almost hoped that it was indeed God's hand, protecting Avery, Dhillon, Kiran, and perhaps me.

"So, Avery, what's really going on with you?" I asked, once the children had left to play.

"Not much," she began. Sometimes Avery could be downright tightlipped.

"Okay . . . " I let her continue.

"Well, Arush thinks I'm messy, disorganized."

Her quiet control and organization were the things I liked best about her. I started to protest, but she interrupted. Avery was on a roll.

"Since having the children, their toys and books are everywhere. There just isn't anywhere to put anything." She and Arush were still living in the same small "starter" house.

"Arush wants the fantasy. He wants to come home to a clean house, quiet children, some wondrous smell coming out of the kitchen, and me all dressed up and looking great. It's hard when you can't do it all." Avery's voice trailed off. Did Avery think she *should* do it all?

Did she think she needed to live up to Arush's expectations? Arush's fantasy was coming down hard on her reality. But just as quickly, Avery stopped herself.

"Listen, everybody has something. You don't need my pity party." Just like that.

"You call that a pity party? Avery, you need to talk to Arush. Make him understand that being a good mother is a full-time job." I thought about saying that I wished that I'd pushed harder to get her and Carter together a long time ago, but instead I said, "What you need is a trip to the Big Apple in the spring. My treat, and I won't take 'no' for an answer." Avery looked pleased by the idea.

As we were walking over to the children, I asked her a simple question. "Do you still love him?" I wasn't prepared for her answer, sad in its acceptance, more truthful than I wanted.

"We have children together, Nina."

And just like that, two months later, I had a car pick Avery up at LaGuardia. I couldn't believe she and I were going to spend the whole weekend together in my city. Without kids. Without Win.

I first took her around the office and watched her eyes get as big as the whole state of Alabama when she looked out at the New York City skyline. Then, I introduced her to Cy.

"He's such a nice man," Avery said as we got back to my cubbyhole of an office.

"He's always nice to prospective clients," I said.

"I'm not a prospective client," Avery countered.

"In Cy's mind, everyone's a prospective client." I laughed.

"Your office is so nice." She peered out my office window to the grayness below.

"You must be kidding. Did you see Cy's?" I asked.

"Two walls of windows," Avery said.

"Here's something that will blow your socks off," I began. "First-year partners here make one million."

"A million dollars?" Avery said so loudly I had to close my office door.

"Yep," knowing that a million dollars sounded like John D. Rockefeller to Avery. She'd stroke out if she knew what I was earning already.

"Let's go to lunch. We'll go to this little deli, but first I want to show you something."

I took her to the athletic club where I worked out early each morning on a track that was on the second floor, encircling the exercise space below. As we looked down on everyone, Avery noticed it right away, as I knew she would.

"All those women look like emaciated sticks," she said. I laughed. Their beads of sweat were the only bulges on their bodies, including breasts, which consisted of zero percent body fat. Like limber pipe cleaners in stylish black spandex.

"They're here every day. It's a clique. That class is closed. Afterward they'll splurge on lunch, usually some atrocious green juice."

"Let's eat," Avery said, and we went to my favorite deli. After, we went to FAO Schwartz to get gifts for the children.

I loved sharing my New York with Avery. I was possessive of it in the same way that Win could be of me. It was a short but special time, and I was sad to see her go when she left for the airport. A week later, she called to say that she had come down with a terrible flu bug. I always worried about Avery and those of us without lucky dust.

After a few days, I called to check on her. "It's not the flu, Nina," she said.

"Well, what was it, then?" I asked.

"I'm pregnant." There was no joy in Mudville in that statement.

"What?" That would have been my last guess. Then hearing the silence, I asked, "What's wrong, Avery?"

"Nothing," Miss Always Optimistic said.

"C'mon, Avery. It's me." I waited, letting our shared silence be as much a part of the conversation as our actual words, and then some.

"It's just that Dhillon is seven, and Kiran will be going into kindergarten."

That was her explanation, for herself. For me, I needed more.

"I wouldn't have had any more children at home. I could play tennis, go out to lunch, spend more time with you in New York—" She stopped abruptly. "God," she said, sounding suddenly mad at herself. "I'm being so selfish. Forgive me."

"Lord, Avery, I sound selfish every time I open my mouth," I said.

"No, you don't. You are so good to me." She went on to thank me again for the umpteenth time for her trip to New York. Then she was silent again. "It's just that Arush and I are better now, and then this," she said finally. I heard her crying.

"I love you, Avery. I just want you to be happy."

The dead air carried on without us, and I began to cry. Avery and Carter could always bring on the waterworks. I almost felt her sadness should be mine. Hell, I could handle loneliness and pain better. I'd had more practice. Spare Avery, God. Please. The unconscious thought broke free like a prisoner seeing daylight for the first time. I thought it again, only this time my conscious was in unison with my unconscious thoughts. Spare Avery, God, please. A short prayer made by the out-of-practice.

We stayed on the phone and in touch weekly for the next seven months, and as usual, God had other ideas. Arush seemed to come around to the idea of another baby, and eventually Avery did too. When their little girl arrived, she was healthy, and we were all overjoyed.

They called her Ruhi, meaning *a flower who touches the heart*. We nicknamed her Ruru.

fourteen

Olga and Cy were having their annual holiday party when I noticed him. I had seen him in Cy's office a few times before, and finally Cy introduced us.

"Nina, this is George Taber. George, Nina Enloe. George works for Goldman Sachs, and Nina is one of our brightest second years."

There was some exchange of pleasantries, but I barely heard any of it.

"So, this is the talent I've heard so much about and have been anxious to meet," he said, sticking out his hand to shake. His smile stole my composure, reminding me of Biggie. Right in the middle of meeting a nice man, there she was. Biggie in her garden, tending to her beloved azaleas. She loved them so well she knew each of their names, like mine or Haines's. Her favorite was an azalea that has beautiful, silky, large lavender flowers with dots of pink on the inside. They are one of the most distinctive of all azaleas, so unique I have to concede to Biggie that a color so perfect and pastel must only come from the good Lord up above. "I admit to being a little intimidated—Cy likes me, but you're in a completely different league in his eyes!" George said graciously. "But—what's so funny?" George asked.

Without thinking, I announced, "George Taber! Did you know that you share a name with a lavender flower? An azalea named 'George Taber'?" He looked a bit curiously at me and then nodded. What else could he do? I was a novice in the flirting department, and here I was trying, for the first time ever, and I found myself wishing I'd paid better attention to Win. I failed miserably, and nobody was more surprised than me that I actually cared.

When she arrived two weeks later for a visit to see the Big Apple and me, Win was subdued about my modest apartment in Murray Hill.

"I thought you would have a view of Central Park."

I rolled my eyes. "Only if I made millions of dollars and had an agreeable co-op board," I said. "Besides, Murray Hill is on the fringe of Midtown, and it's a good neighborhood for young professionals." *I'm used to living on the fringe,* I wanted to say, *just look at our house in Erob.* At least she approved of my color scheme.

I had a long white sleeper sofa with peachy pink tapestry pillows and a sage green bound carpet rug. All Biggie castoffs. My New York friends thought I had a rather nice apartment filled with antiques, but Win had seen them in Biggies's house before she gifted them to me and replaced them with finer, grander pieces.

It was an entirely different New York City than the one I had shown Avery. Instead of sitting around in our pajamas having heart-to-hearts and instead of khakis and grabbing sandwiches, Win and I were dressed up each day, lunching and having tea at the Plaza and shopping in Bergdorf's and Saks. Even in Bergdorf's, Win could commandeer a line of salespeople to help her. The two most commonly uttered phrases throughout the weekend were "excuse me" and "do you have that in my size?"

On Saturday afternoon, after a tedious day of shopping and lunching, we stopped in a local spa to get facials and massages and our hair done. I don't know what Win's bill was; she bought moisturizers and antiaging creams and products for her hair. She was a one-woman stimulus package.

She reluctantly agreed to go see my office and seemed under-impressed. Wai was there, so I introduced them, and I could tell immediately how both women felt about the other.

That night, when we were in her nightgowns, we talked. In truth, this is my favorite Win. Chill and relaxed.

"I think that Wai girl is T.T.F.W.," Win-speak for Too Tacky For Words. "Is she loose?" I wondered how Win knew. "Bit, let's call a spade a spade. Promise me you do not condone such behavior." Win used her most condemning tone.

"No, of course not." Despite a few transgressions during my college years, it was hard to escape Biggie's—and Win's—sensibility "that a lady should never wear to the breakfast table what she wore the night before."

Two New York Cities, my two friends transitioned between two worlds. Would I ever be able to live in both completely with ease? I hoped never to be in a position to have to choose between them.

"I need a glass of water to take these vitamins," Win said.

"Since when did you become such a health nut?"

"They're pregnancy vitamins."

"What?" I was stunned. Win was an only child, her mother was an only child, and I'd just assumed Winnie would be too.

"I wasn't telling anyone just yet," and in answer to my unasked question, "I was waiting until I was twelve weeks."

I wondered if Rich even knew, and I wondered if it was planned. But if I asked her, we'd have to talk about it, and I knew Win would rather die than be caught having accidental sex with her husband.

"Well, congratulations, Win," was all I said. Short and uncommitted.

"I'm happy. Yes," she said matter-of-factly.

I was still incredulous when I went to work on Monday, and I had lunch with Wai to get her impression. "I hate to say this to you, Nina," Wai began, "but that Win is a Class One Bitch."

I smiled. "Don't worry, Wai. Win has always taken great pride in that."

"I can't believe Win is pregnant," I said three months later when Haines and Carter visited me.

Haines said, "Rich was looking for any excuse to get to sleep with Win."

Carter laughed.

"Don't pick on Win," I said, finding myself in the unusual position of defending her. "She would just die if she heard us talking about her that way."

Having my boys visit me reminded me of the man I could not stop thinking about.

"Come home," was all she said, and for some reason, I didn't ask questions. Her voice was pleading yet proud, remote but resilient, secretive yet strong, and I had admittedly not heard it sounding like that before—a tone filled with wounded determination. I waited.

"It was a routine test. Until it wasn't." She paused. "They drew some amniotic fluid . . ."

"Did you go by yourself? I would've gone."

"You would've?" I surprised us both by volunteering. "They're looking for something."

"What something?"

"Down syndrome." Those words were enough. "I'll pick you up. And . . . thank you, Little Bit." It must have been hard for her to ask me and even harder for her to thank me.

"You're welcome, Win," I said.

I made plans to go to Erob in a surprisingly quick and efficient fashion. It was ironic how fast I could leave one life to go to the other. I got a double espresso coffee and spent the rest of the afternoon doing what every other attorney does: research. Except I was googling everything I could about Down syndrome children and Down syndrome mothers. Reading blogs. Making notes. I noticed raindrops on my window. They looked like silver teardrops. I remembered what Avery told me the day we met. And I hoped heaven was keeping my secrets.

My flight got into Atlanta on time, and Win was waiting. I threw my suitcase into the trunk of her car and sat beside her in the front seat. She hugged me tightly, another uncommon occurrence between Win and me.

"Thank you for coming, Little Bit."

I could feel her full weight, and the uneasiness in her voice returned. I felt the wetness on her cheeks. Silent tears and whimpers from a well-composed woman not used to a public wellspring of emotion. Uncomfortable despair from someone who lived with the motto of stoicism during life's trying situations, clashing with the same woman whose heart seemed to be coming apart in front of me.

In silence, Win began to navigate her way out of the Atlanta airport and onto the freeway. I let her drive, although she has always been more comfortable being driven than driving herself.

She started talking, and her words were deliberate, well-chosen and well-rehearsed, like an actor delivering a pivotal soliloquy.

"Little Bit," she began, as if to awaken a closeness between us. "The doctors think the chances are pretty high for Down syndrome."

That, she knew, would be enough to last another few miles . . . But in that moment, in that car, with those words, Winifred Baxter Montgomery and I, whether we wanted to or not, became adults together.

Her words began to sputter out like a car engine trying to get started on a frigid winter morning.

"They did prenatal genetic testing and we're waiting for the results . . ." Her voice trailed off. "The results will come back next week to give me choices."

Choices? Choices? Choices.

"What does Rich say?"

"He'll support me in whatever decision I make." For once I didn't think Win wanted the whole decision to be on her.

"Have you talked to a sorority sister who knows a specialist?"

"They're not my friends. You are."

"Bit," she said suddenly, "Would God do this to me just because I didn't want another baby?"

I remained silent. No use in teaming up against God. He knew where I lived. I thought of my mother. Were there moments like this between Mama, Virginia, and Miss Harriett? Secrets shared over time with one another that they alone knew, moments when they finally let their guard down? Those secrets, like blood, bound them together and gave their friendship an ease and their life a richness not even their families could breach.

"Maybe I shouldn't pray for a healthy child. Maybe that's too selfish," she said.

"I think you can pray for a healthy child, Win."

"Look at me, Bit. I've had a good life. Maybe this is just another part. What kind of a person am I to be having these thoughts just because the baby might not be perfect?"

I grappled with what to say next. I reached over and touched her shoulder, and to my surprise she didn't flinch. "He knows how fiercely protective you are about the people you love, whether they deserve it or not," I said, thinking of myself.

"Is it too much for me to want another healthy child? Look at poor Carter. He and Jennifer can't get pregnant to save their lives. Who knows what kind of toll it's taking on their marriage? Maybe God is teaching me a lesson," she said again.

I knew Carter and Jenny were having trouble having a baby, but the rest of it? The marriage? Carter, God bless him, had tried to talk to me.

In lieu of the radio, a symphony of ethical and moral dilemmas tuned high. These were not superficial questions, and this was not a superficial woman. I felt completely inadequate and ashamed.

"You're human, Win," I said. "Let me drive the rest of the way," I offered. She didn't argue as she unhooked her seatbelt to switch places.

It was pouring rain. When we got back in the car, I looked like a drowned rat and Win glistened as if she had been protected by an invisible umbrella. We began driving again, and she looked out the window as if something held her in rapt fascination.

"You know, Win, now's the time if you want to yell or scream or cry," I said, feeling the car and the rain would provide her a safe refuge. I could tell she was trying to unleash the tears, but her years of training prevented it from happening. Suddenly, she began to cry uncontrollably.

I had not counted on this when I came up with my theory of lucky dust. I had always thought those with lucky dust had a problem-free life, that lucky dust protected them from anything too sad or terrible. "If God is trying to teach me a lesson, I wish he had just gone ahead and burned down the doctor's office with me in it." She screamed.

Today I was the witness. Today I was the secret keeper. Today I was the friend she chose. Today I was there when Win lost. Today Win ran out of lucky dust. Today Win fell down and broke apart. Today the odd couple of emotion, sorrow and privilege, wound around my heart and took root.

It made me utterly sad.

Biggie greeted us as we pulled up to her house.

"I've already spoken to your mother, Bit. You'll stay with me in your pink room," Biggie said as she watched me get out of the car. I instantly regretted that I'd let them know I was coming. It gave Biggie time to plan.

Win hugged me, then touched my hair and said, "You should really get your hair trimmed. That length makes your face look way too narrow." Our equilibrium, old and familiar, restored.

"She can get it cut when she takes me to get my hair fixed tomorrow," Biggie joined in. I was trapped between Win and Biggie. I didn't want my hair cut by Ukalene at The Clip Joint anymore. I had a place off Madison Avenue that I liked just fine.

I would save that battle for later. Instead, I hugged Win back and told her I would see her later. I hoped Biggie had not noticed our sad faces, and I also hoped God would give me the right thing to say to Win before this weekend visit was over. I glanced over at Carter's house as I walked up the path; there were no cars in the driveway. While I knew I should stop in and visit with them before I left, I also wasn't sure what to say or do. So, I did nothing, keenly aware that doing nothing was just another way of putting off something that had the potential to blow up in my face.

"Agnes has fixed all your favorites for supper," Biggie said as I came down from putting my bag in my room.

I noticed that Biggie was moving slower than usual, each step requiring effort.

"I don't know, Biggie, I'd better check with Mama," I said. Poor Mama might have been cooking for days. I watched Biggie walk to her chair, almost collapsing into it from the brief walk.

While Biggie rested, I decided to walk to Mama's house, a few blocks north on Dexter Avenue. "Mama," I called, knocking on the door. Funny how I had a key to Biggie's house but not one for my own.

"Coming," she answered, and she let me in. If possible, Mama looked younger, happy, vital. Maybe having me gone lifted her load.

"Well, don't you look nice, Little Bit, especially your hair."

I grinned.

She smiled. "I'll make you some tea."

"You look nice, too, Mama." And she did.

"Blaine and I went to the matinee this afternoon."

"I'm glad that you and Avery's mom are spending more time together," I said, which probably seemed insensitive to Mama, since Blaine Mitchell was all my mother had left now that Miss Harriett and Virginia were gone. "Biggie wants me to have supper with her, but I told her I would have to check with you first."

"You go ahead and eat with your grandmother. I'm going to babysit for Addison and Haines. They're going to some Junior League dance tonight. I'm surprised that Win didn't mention it."

"Oh, she did," I lied. For once, my well-honed skill of prevarication had come in handy.

"What do you think about Win being president two years in a row?"

"I just hope the Junior League has its own version of the 22nd Amendment."

My mother laughed then. "I thought you would be regaling me all about Win and her antics. You two aren't on the outs, are you? You should try harder to understand her, Bit."

I looked at my mother. I wanted to tell her I was just now beginning to understand *her* and the closeness she'd shared with Miss Harriett and Virginia. But, if truth be told, I wouldn't really have a clue until many years later.

"No, we're not on the outs."

"Well, be prepared. She talked a lot about her trip up to see you and your friends," Mama said rather ominously. *What did that mean?*

"And Biggie was happy to hear you were coming home this weekend. Here, you made the paper," my mother said, tongue-in-cheek, as she handed me the society page of the *Erob Post*:

> *Miss Nina Barnes Enloe, "Bit," of New York, is visiting her mother, Mrs. Ben Enloe, and her grandmother, Mrs. H.B. Enloe, and her brother, Dr. Haines Enloe. Miss Enloe enjoys her busy work as an attorney at one of New York's oldest and finest law firms.*

It was a time warp here in Erob, Alabama. Nothing ever changed. News of any sort is hard to come by, so the editors of the *Erob Post* chronicle the comings and goings of Erob's "finest."

> *Mrs. Richard Montgomery, née Winifred Woodwiss Baxter, daughter of Mr. & Mrs. Robert Baxter, recently enjoyed a weekend in New York City where she visited Miss Nina Barnes Enloe. Miss Enloe and Mrs. Montgomery enjoyed seeing plays, musical theatre, and shopping.*

We saw no plays or musicals. However, we did shop.

Dr. & Mrs. Richard Montgomery and daughter, Winnie, named after Mrs. Montgomery's paternal grandmother, enjoyed time spent in San Francisco, where Dr. Montgomery was on a very successful lecture tour.

It was a pharmaceutical sales seminar, not really a lecture tour, mostly vacation. For years now, Judi Ann Miller had written the column under the guise "Society Editor-at-Large," as if there were several under her.

Every time someone so much as crossed the county line, they were on some very important business or very exclusive pleasure trip. It let folks know just how rich you were or if you married well, and being rich and marrying well were just the ultimate goal in Judi Ann's eyes. Judi Ann, to my knowledge, had never been out of the state of Alabama, except to go to Atlanta on a bus with the Baptists to see the Braves play ball.

The Watergate reporting of Woodward and Bernstein couldn't hold a candle to her crack investigative work. How she unearthed such useless information was a secret that only our society editor, at large, herself knew. Lots of run-on sentences, but you sure couldn't beat it for sheer information. I always marveled at Judi Ann and her seemingly unlimited supply of adjectives.

"Anyway, you'd better get back down to your grandmother's house. You know she hates to eat late. I guess after she goes to bed, you could come over to Haines's and keep me and Little Addie company. If you want to, of course."

That sounded good, albeit uncharacteristic of my mother to invite me to spend time with her. Addie would provide the buffer.

I left and walked back to Biggie's, and as Mama predicted, she was waiting for me, our plates served and ready on the table.

"I hope our food hasn't gotten cold," she announced as I walked into the dining room.

I wanted to say "you could have called me," or "you could have eaten," but Biggie loved being the martyr.

She had placed a pair of her favorite Meissen vases at my place. "What are these doing here?" I asked.

"I want you to have them to use in your apartment."

"I don't need them, Biggie," I began.

She pushed them toward me. "I'm quite certain your apartment could use them."

"Biggie, I don't want to take your favorite vases." As if Meissen alone could add some class to my small apartment, I thought.

"I want you to have them." Was she pleading?

"No."

"Then let me write you a check so you can get something you'd rather have."

"No. I don't need your money, Biggie!" I said for the first time, meaning it.

Biggie retreated, unrequited.

Only later did I realize that our conversation had nothing to do with money or Meissen vases.

The dance was a big success and raised lots of money for the Junior League charities, according to Addison when she and Haines got home later that evening.

"Win made a heartfelt speech, and everyone just bid higher and higher," Addison marveled.

"Now I'm just wondering how I'm gonna pay for it," Haines piped in, removing the tuxedo tie that Win had insisted he wear.

"What did you get, Haines?"

"A week in Gulf Shores." My brother, the exotic traveler. I wondered if anyone else donated enough money for a trip like that.

"Carter and Jenny got a romantic getaway to Atlanta," Haines said, as if reading my mind. "Jenny loves to shop and eat out, and I know Carter does what he can to make her happy."

How did she do it? How did Win emcee a festive gala when there was chaos inside no one knew about? I always felt Win would have come closer to confiding in either Haines or Carter before she confided in me.

"So, Miss Bit," my brother began, after Mama had gone home and Addison had gone to bed. "What brings you home on an unscheduled visit?" I hated when he addressed me this way. It sounded too close to "misfit," which, of course, I was.

"I better get back to Biggie's. It's late, Haines, and I'm tired."

He waited.

I perked up. "I do have a little scoop for you."

"Lay it on me." My brother, the gossip.

"Biggie," I said with great bravado, "tried to give me her Meissen vases."

"Those are her favorites!" Haines said incredulously. "I can't believe you, Bit. You have that woman—"

I interrupted. "And when I refused, she tried to write me a check. There's no telling how Win described my apartment to get Biggie to pony up like that."

"So how much did she give you?"

"It doesn't matter. I didn't take it or her Meissen vases."

"I guess you feel pretty good."

I did. At the time.

"Well, while Biggie is trying to give you her largesse, how about getting her to move downstairs?"

"I've noticed that she's having a lot of trouble getting around. What's up with that?" I asked my brother, the doctor.

"Like she would tell me. I have a feeling she didn't make as full a recovery as everyone thought from her stroke."

I said goodnight to Haines and told him I would talk to Biggie, but I knew that her will was stronger than any of her limbs appeared to be.

I snuck in her house like a teenager, but there was nothing wrong with Biggie's hearing.

"Bit."

"I'm home," I said, standing just outside the door of my pink room.

"Did you lock up?"

"Yes, ma'am." It had taken me an extra ten minutes to secure the umpteen locks Biggie had on her doors.

"Thank you, Bit." Biggie said. Then, "I'm glad you're here."

"Me, too, Biggie," I said.

Saturday morning, I woke up to the smells that conjured up memories. The redolent aroma that whispered with unshakable certainty, "Now *this* is the best part of your life." I slid out of bed and lifted the shade to see that the morning had gotten started way before I had. Biggie was already in her garden with her basket, picking flowers. Agnes's voice greeted me before I got to the kitchen.

"Well, good morning, Bit."

"Agnes!" I exclaimed, suddenly feeling like my trip was worth it. "What brings you here on a Saturday?"

"Your grandmother asked if I would come for a few hours to fix some of your favorites. She wanted your visit to be just right."

I poured my coffee, savoring the sights and smells coming from the stove. "Biggie had you come on a Saturday for me?" Before Agnes could answer, we heard a thud, thud, thud.

It's hard to say just what brought Carter Gideon over—the basketball hoop or the smell of Agnes's yeast rolls.

"Carter Gideon," came the voice from the garden. "It's still Saturday morning."

"Yes, ma'am." Carter stopped dribbling the basketball as I went out to say hello.

"Hi there. I heard a nasty rumor you were in town. Dressed for success, I see," he said, looking at my sweats and Duke T-shirt.

"Yes, but I'm not staying long. Just the weekend. Here are a few rolls for your trouble." I handed him a napkin that already had buttery imprints on it.

"Great. Come over if you can, and we'll catch up."

I felt guilty, but some moments can't be undone. I was still only available for polite chit-chat where Carter was concerned, and it seemed he was getting the hint. I hoped in the future I could be a better friend.

Biggie came inside and put the azaleas in a vase of fresh water. She placed them in the center of our table.

"Now we can have a civilized breakfast," she said, breathing harder than ever.

I agreed, and as I tried to pace myself by stuffing rolls into my mouth, I noticed the lavender azaleas. "All that teaching you did about azaleas finally paid off," I told Biggie.

She seemed genuinely amazed at my version of a compliment to her.

"Oh?"

I pointed to the lavender flower. "George Taber."

She nodded. "Very good, Bit."

"Would you believe, I actually met a man named George Taber in New York?"

I felt Agnes's presence in the doorway. The phrase *met a man* had grabbed her and automatically moved her to within good hearing distance.

"How odd," Biggie said, still focused on her flowers.

Agnes refused to budge until I offered her more.

"It's not like that, Agnes," I said, rolling my eyes.

"Like what?" Biggie asked, like my being involved with a Northerner was an absurd notion. Turns out, she had other things on her mind.

"Your brother feels I should move downstairs into the guest room. What do you say?"

I knew her legs were weak. I knew her breathing was labored. I knew it would be easier. I knew it was what Haines wanted, but I also knew a little something about this old woman's pride. After a long, deliberate silence weighing what I should say against my grandmother's dignity, I came up with, "You should do what you can manage."

She went into the kitchen so I couldn't see her face. It spared us both.

Win was cleaning out cabinets. The floor was covered in pots and pans. She looked exhausted and slightly crazy.

"Why are you going all Marie Kondo on your poor kitchen? What time did you get home?" She continued her tasks.

"About two o'clock or so." Still, she didn't stop what she was doing.

"Will you stop for a minute?" I asked. "Here, Agnes sent you some rolls. You still need to eat."

In true Win fashion, she opened the foil and daintily picked at a few pieces.

"Where are Rich and Winnie?"

"Winnie's at Mama's, and Rich is playing golf with Haines."

"Maybe you should take it easy."

"Spring cleaning." Again, we lapsed into silence.

I looked at my watch. "I have to take Biggie to Ukalene's. Her appointment is set in stone by Moses himself. I hate to go."

"Yeah, I know you're dying to organize these cabinets with me," Win said with a smile, knowing cleaning and organizing were definitely not my forte. Any closeness that had been forged between us was once again buried, our real feelings stashed in cabinets, hidden under the pots and pans of life.

I finally slipped over to see Carter and Jenny. Carter was mowing the grass, so I got a chance to visit with his wife.

"Thanks for the rolls."

"You mean Carter shared? He must really love you!"

She laughed.

"So, did you have fun last night?" I asked.

"It was fine, although those big parties aren't really my thing."

I knew I liked this girl.

"We missed you in New York," I said, thinking about Carter and Haines's recent visit.

"I guess you think I'm pretty weird, not flying," Jenny ventured.

"Absolutely not," I said emphatically. "Weirdness is what I look for most in a person." I smiled. "Besides, Jenny, if it weren't for my last name, nobody would give me the time of day. Surely you know by now that I'm a very black sheep around here."

"Then I think black sheep are chic."

I smiled and felt kindness around my heart.

I went to see Avery, and we took a walk. She met me on Magnolia Avenue at Biggie's.

"What did you think of the big dance?" I asked.

"It was so much fun," Avery said joyously.

"What did you bid on?" I asked.

"I know my name is mud with her." Avery said it like she had committed the gravest faux pas. "We didn't bid on anything. Everything was too expensive," Avery offered as a means of explanation.

"What did you wear?"

"A black sequined top and straight skirt. There was a real good sale at Wanda's."

I knew Wanda never had any "real good" sales. She must have seen Avery and made an adjustment to her prices, like Daddy and Haines did for medical services when people couldn't pay. This could still happen in a small town.

As I listened to Avery, I let my surroundings distract me from Win. How many problems had Avery, Win, and I solved by walking? If these sidewalks could talk. The sounds of the birds chirping, the smell of freshly cut grass, flowers, and fresh air swirled around us as we walked. Win had always walked ahead of us with her long legs. Was it always *this* green? The closest I got to nature in New York was seeing the sunrise after pulling an all-nighter.

I looked up and we were practically in town. I hadn't remembered the distance being that short. We had always rewarded ourselves after our "long" walks with a lemonade at Charlie's City Pharmacy. We still referred to it as Charlie's even though he had retired and his pharmacist daughters Joyce and Vanessa had taken it over.

"Hey, let's change it up today," Avery said abruptly. "Jimmy just recently opened the Coffee Bean Emporium. He and Trae bought that run-down house next to the Chicken Emporium and turned it into a coffee shop. Jimmy applied for a liquor license. Maybe I can work there making Sea Breezes. The coffee shop has sofas and chairs. It's so cozy! Let's go there!"

When we settled in our chairs with our steaming lattes, Jimmy walked over to speak.

"It's good to see you, Bit. You'll have to let me know if our humble beanery can compete with your big-city coffee shops. We can boast one thing they don't offer . . ." Avery and Jimmy exchanged looks and started laughing as Jimmy handed me a muffin. "Let me know what you think. You know the baker pretty well." I recognized the handwriting immediately.

"Win does your baking? When did she start baking? Is she here?" I about jumped out of the chair. Jimmy laughed.

"Noo . . . she bakes in her state-of-the-art kitchen and brings her goodies here. We have a pretty robust morning crowd."

"Our girl has become a real entrepreneur," Avery said. I shared the muffin with Avery.

As if on cue, Win happened to breeze in, carrying a picnic basket like Dorothy.

"Where's Toto?" I asked.

"I brought you a fresh batch of brownies, and I tried my hand at making scones. These are apple cinnamon. Let's call them 'apple pie' scones."

"Sounds delicious," Jimmy and Avery said in unison. Win reached in her basket and handed us each one.

"Sit down and visit," I said.

"I have to finish color coordinating my towels," Win said, and was gone.

"Where does she find that energy?" Avery asked.

I found myself not confiding in Avery for the first time in my life. I wanted to tell her about Win cleaning like a madwoman.

Her neatness and the valiant struggle for order made me know that this was more than wanting a clean house or the beginning of a nesting stage. Win Baxter Montgomery was scared. This was not a part of her life plan. It had been blown to smithereens.

It was a foregone conclusion that I would go to church. Biggie, for once, had full attendance on her pew. I was stuck between Biggie and Mama, then Haines and Addison.

The sermon was about God, Jesus, and the Holy Ghost, the usual suspects. Sermons are like soap operas—you can miss a few but pick right back up where you left off with the central characters.

We had Sunday lunch at Biggie's, where she held court. Haines was still a little miffed with me for not pushing harder for Biggie to move downstairs.

"You know how she gets," I said, feeling this was ample justification.

Like clockwork, Win arrived to take me to the airport, still in her Sunday best. Apparently even a trip to the airport required city clothes.

"Can I drive?" I asked, sensing Win's withdrawal. She looked exhausted and was disappearing right in front of me.

She handed me the keys to "Benzzie," her nickname for the car. On the highway and away from our respective lives, we slowly treaded into conversation. As we left the city limits, a beautiful rainbow emerged in the sky. I took it as a sign of hope. That everything would be fine. This was Win, after all.

"When will you know something for sure?"

"Tuesday or Wednesday."

"It takes a whole week to get results of a test this important?"

She nodded.

"That's outrageous that medical science can't come up with quicker test results when decisions have to be made," I said. Win seemed to enjoy my soapbox, because she smiled.

"They must be a bunch of men—not realizing the agony that this puts a woman through. I'll bet if it involved their prostate . . ." I was getting myself worked up. "Don't they know the test is for Win Baxter Montgomery?"

"Bit, I thought you rejected preferential treatment."

I guess my loyalty trumped equality in the eyes of the law. "I just think the results should come in quicker, that's all." Then I quickly added, "For everybody." We got stuck again in a snow-drift of silence.

"Well, at least you have the most organized kitchen in Erob," I said.

She smiled. "If only I could get my hands on that apartment of yours."

"Speaking of my apartment, Win, exactly what did you tell Biggie? Yesterday she tried to give me her favorite vases."

"I told her the truth. You do need a better apartment, Bit. Or at least something pretty for that drab place." The old Win returned with a jab of her own.

"I like my apartment just fine."

"What if you have friends over? I don't want you to be embarrassed."

"I'm always at the office. It suits me just fine."

Win pulled her seatbelt tighter around her and stared out the window. "It's not in a particularly desirable part of town. It needs a makeover in the worst way."

"It's fine," I snapped.

"You just need some help in getting it presentable. It's a bit of a mess, like that hair of yours. You need a haircut."

"Stop nagging the shit out of me." I stopped. I had gone too far. She pouted, and I fumed until we made it to the airport. Even in her grief, she somehow managed to inspire my anger rather than my sympathy.

She didn't thank me this time when we got to the airport, but what she did say remained with me for a long time.

"I'll call you." Her voice called out, "You're not like them, you know. You're the only one who didn't give me false hope."

I turned back around to look at her. There was something unfinished about her statement. I felt the air as people brushed passed me, rushing to check flight departures and gate numbers, but Win and I just stood there, letting our earlier exchange evaporate into the air, staring at each other, unhurried by the movements of others. I walked back to her.

"I'm keeping this baby," she said, finally pushing the hair out of her eyes. "I'll accept the news either way." And then she gave me a smile that was strong and unabbreviated.

fifteen

The following Tuesday I was at my desk, working on a document for Cy, wondering when, or if, Win would call with results from her tests.

"Planted any azaleas lately?" a voice asked. I didn't look up. I didn't need to. The voice was confident like my brother's, but unlike Haines's, it was devoid of any Southern accent.

I smiled. "Hi, George."

He stepped into my office. "Well?" he asked.

"Planted, no. But I did pick some."

"Want to go grab a sandwich, or do you already have lunch plans?"

"You wouldn't believe the men with flower names that have been beating my door down."

"I'll bet."

I hoped my self-effacing humor got me out of that one. "Sure," I said, glancing down at my cell phone once more. "Let me grab my jacket."

George Taber was taller than I first realized—at close to 6'4," he was over a foot taller than me. His black hair was combed back, a requirement for Goldman Sachs types, I supposed. But his hair wasn't slicked back with products in a deliberate fashion, nor did it, ugh, shine under bright lights. He wore a navy suit that hung perfectly across his broad shoulders. Under his jacket was an equally perfect blue shirt with white collar and cuffs, and he wore—be still my heart—cuff links. Most guys I knew only wore cuff links with tuxedos when they got married. He wore them just because it was a Tuesday. None of this seemed deliberate or self-serving, not even his stride as we made our way to the deli. He was easygoing, effortlessly catching my arm to cross the street. The easy manner he had with himself, his job, and me told me he was bemused at being compared to a lavender flower and confident enough in himself to handle it.

His hands were smooth; he had probably spent less time doing strenuous work and more time in the libraries of Williams College and Wharton, where he went to school. He caught me staring as we were eating our sandwiches.

"Do you enjoy studying people's fingers?"

"I'm sorry, it's a bad habit I developed when I was a child," I said, remembering days when I was transfixed on the coupling of Haines and Win and Carter and Avery. Staring and watching them do everything. Anything. Knowing even then that they were the central characters in my life's story.

"So, what's your question?" he asked me.

"Do you play the piano?"

He moved his fingers as if playing a scale. "As a matter of fact, I do. I was an only child, and I did sports and the piano. I hated it then, but now I use it for relaxation. I'll bet you're an only child too?" His blue eyes examined me.

"Why?"

"You just seem really independent and self-reliant."

"My older brother," I said with added emphasis, "would agree with your assessment."

"I'm usually good at picking onlies out. Is there a big difference in your ages?"

I wanted to say we were worlds and life experiences apart but instead said, "A mere three years."

The hour I stared at George Taber flew by, and as he walked me back to the office, I found myself wondering, *What if I had a whole lifetime with him?*

"I enjoyed lunch. Can I call you?" George asked, seeking my permission.

I was no dummy this time. I kept my answer short and to the point. "Yes."

The next day, I got two important phone calls. The first one came in the morning. It was Win, and when I answered, her voice was muffled.

"The test is positive. For Down syndrome," she said.

I closed my door and sank to the floor. My throat felt tight, and I was having trouble getting words out. "I'm sorry."

"Don't let them pity me, Bit," she said. We were quiet. It was as if she was mustering the energy to say what came next. I reached for the used Starbucks napkin to wipe my tears. I hadn't realized I had started crying. "It's a little boy. Rich and I have the means to take him to the best specialist if he needs heart surgery. We have the means to get him the best physical therapy and whatever else he needs. Don't ever let them call my child 'special.' His name will be Baxter. Don't let them pity me," she said again for emphasis, but this time she was having a hard time.

"Do you want me to call the others?" I asked.

"No. I need to do that. But, Bit, I just need a little time and space, okay? I would really appreciate it, if you tell them that." She severed our connection. In the months to come I occasionally would send her a text "just thinking about you." Most of the time she didn't reply, but sometimes she would.

I kept my door closed for the better part of the day. My heart felt watery, like the sky before the rains come. I saved Win some of the blogs I read. For when she was ready. Those that really talked about these extraordinary women. How their life had expanded not contracted. I wondered as I saved them not what God was going to teach Win but what he was trying to teach the rest of us. What, in fact, he was trying to teach me.

Later, George called to ask me for a Saturday night date. Again, I said yes, and then I called Wai.

"Can you believe it? George called me today to ask me out for Saturday!"

"Where is he taking you? You should meet him there. Take money to catch a cab in case you want to leave early. Take condoms. Take mace."

"Wai," I interrupted, "please don't get me too nervous. I don't think I'll need mace, or condoms." It was all a bit early for that, but it also felt like the beginning of something.

The rest of the afternoon I fielded calls from our group. Avery and Carter were the hardest. Carter was the last. He always forgot there was an hour time difference, so it was close to eleven o'clock. He told me Win had called him over.

"Where was Jenny?" Again I was struck by the oddness.

"Jenny and Win aren't the best of buds," Carter said. "Poor Rich. He is devastated. I've never seen Win like that. Just heart-broken." We lapsed into silence. "I'm thinking Baxter will need a pro to teach him the finer points of basketball," Carter said.

"Who do you have in mind, Gideon?"

"Very funny, Bit. I am a little bit jealous of Win. I know that's just terrible. How are you doing? Is this why you were home?" My tears came back from nowhere. In truth, I was mourning the loss of my friend. She would never be the same again. I was grateful for Carter. We stayed on the line, but our hearts were heavy with unfulfilled dreams and dreams that ended prematurely. I guess letting go of dreams is its own unique death.

There were three messages in my voicemail. All were from Avery. She never could decide whether to just go with the "call me" message or to elaborate—or a mixture of both, and with three kids now, she was constantly being interrupted.

"Hey, Nina. It's Avery. I know I'd better be quick. So . . . Kiran . . ." Click.

"It's me again. Leaving you another message. I'll be quick . . . I just wish you could come home more; we have so much to catch up on. Maybe I can get Win to drag you back here again . . ." Click.

"Okay. Here goes. Kiran's birthday party is three weeks from Saturday. Can you call that night and talk with her? I love you . . ." Click.

I laughed out loud. Avery never left me less than two messages at a time. But her *get Win to drag you back* comment left me uneasy.

Win and her blatant manipulation. God knew I'd had enough of that business from Biggie.

I dialed Avery's number. "To tell you the truth, I need a little break from Win," I said. "She's like a vulture swooping into my life, leaving behind bird droppings of bitter criticism."

Avery laughed.

"I'm serious. Would you believe she told Biggie that my apartment and my neighborhood were terrible?"

"I love your apartment," Avery interrupted.

"And there's no telling what she told Biggie about poor Wai."

"I like Wai."

Then I told her about George, and we agreed not to tell Win about him.

"But Win will know something's up," Avery said. "I don't know how she does it, but even as far away as you are, she'll be able to tell."

"I know," I said, turning my attention to Saturday night.

Because there are so many whackeroos in New York City, taking Wai's advice, I agreed to meet George at the restaurant for our first official date. He was already there when I walked in, wearing a smile that made me feel comfortable and welcome.

"George," I acknowledged. I returned his smile, and then I began worrying. "I hope you haven't been waiting too long."

"Oh, no, you're right on time." The hostess showed us to a table. George had chosen a perfect restaurant, the kind of place that's not so loud that you can't carry on a conversation but not so quiet that you're overheard. It was the kind of place that if our conversation stalled we could watch and listen to our surroundings. He was hedging his bets, I thought.

"Can I bring you something from the bar before I go over the menu with you?" the waiter asked precisely.

"Would you like to order a bottle of wine?" George offered as he studied the list.

"Sure," I said, adding, "you decide."

"Let's try your merlot," George suggested.

"Very good, sir," the waiter said, and then left us alone.

When he returned with George's selection, George raised his glass in a toast and said, "To Nina taking New York City!"

"What does that mean?" I asked, glass half-raised.

"Cy says you want to take over this town."

"Cy is full of it." As my first swallow went down, I took in George Taber again. Tonight he was wearing a tweed sports coat and gray slacks. His hair was combed back. His open-neck shirt was the color of café au lait. Even that color set off his blue eyes, and again, his clothes fit him impeccably.

"So, how do you know Cy anyway?" I finally asked, feeling myself staring again.

"My parents are friends with Cy and Olga. I went to school with their daughter, Robin."

"What was she like?" I asked.

"Get a mirror," George answered. "You bear more than a passing resemblance to her. Plus, she was smart like you too."

"Me? I'm not that smart."

"People are scared of you at the firm. Besides being incredibly smart, you've got Cy as a mentor. That's pretty lucky."

"Do you think Cy thinks of me that way? Like a daughter?"

"All I know is that when I told Cy and Olga I was going on a date with you, I got lectured by both of them about how I should treat you."

"Why?"

"Cy doesn't think of you as Robin, but he and Olga certainly do think a lot of you, Nina." He smiled. "And now I know why. It's not just your smarts, but it's the way you look at the world. Can I tell you that no one has ever told me my name is the same as a lavender flower?"

I smiled. "I thought it was a faux pas."

He smiled. "I thought it was memorable."

"Blame it on my grandmother," I said. "I think that 'Southern women have to garden' is one of the top ten commandments in the Southern women's handbook."

"What are some of the other rules?" George was curious.

"I didn't finish the book," I joked.

"C'mon."

"Okay. Funeral casseroles. Learn how to make them. And always know the books of the Bible by name whether you live by what they say or not. Always wear real pearls. If they're fake, it'll make people wonder what else is fake too." I patted Biggie's necklace, laughed, and drained my wineglass. "The final one is never move to New York City and drink too much merlot on a first date with a Northerner."

"Is there really a book like that?" George asked.

I replied. "Actually, I think it's something in the Southern DNA."

The rest of the night was like that, easy back and forth. But when it came time to go, we were headed in opposite directions. He to the Upper West Side and I to Murray Hill.

If Cy wanted to know about my date with George, he didn't let on. Despite what George had said, Cy and I didn't have that kind of relationship. He may have been protective, but I was also his workhorse.

"We've got a new deal," Cy said as he stuck his head into my office.

"When do they want to close?" I asked. I was busy working on another deal Cy had brought in the day before.

"In two weeks."

I looked up. Cy always brought me deals that needed to close in three days. "Why the advance notice?"

"I'm letting you drive it. If you need help, go to Orsen Burns."

Cy knew that I'd rather walk over hot coals than ask that pompous ass for help. I knew Wai and I would have to work around the clock.

"You wouldn't be trying to nip my personal life in the bud, now would you?"

"No, of course not. This just gives you a chance to shine in front of the partners."

So, Cy was giving me a real opportunity. A chance to be something other than his prodigy.

"Thanks, Cy," I said genuinely.

"You're welcome."

As he turned around to leave, I said, "In case Olga was wondering, I had a good time Saturday night."

"So did he." And Cy was gone.

Both Wai and I braced ourselves. We had both been part of deals that fell apart after one document round. We both wanted this to close, and we both wanted to look good doing it.

On Wednesday, almost like clockwork, George called to ask me out for the weekend. I told him the only way I could have dinner with him is if he brought it to me and we could have a nice romantic dinner in a conference room with Wai Wong. To my surprise, he agreed.

On Saturday night, George came bounding through the conference room door with Chinese takeout.

I introduced them. Unlike Wai and Win, they seemed to like each other.

"Here you go, Wai," George said, handing out plates and plasticware first to Wai, then me. "Here you go, Short Stop."

Wai interrupted, about to burst. "She's just a 'little bit'."

"Exactly," George said, not yet in on Wai's twisted joke. Wai was outing me in front of George on only our second date.

"Wai," I warned.

"Like I said, she's just a Little Bit."

I was shaking my head at Wai.

"What?" George asked.

"Meet Miss Little Bit Enloe." So much for my secret being safe with Wai Wong. "That's what her family calls Nina. Little Bit, because she's named after her grandmother, Nina Barnes Enloe, the big bitch. They call her Biggie, and Nina here is Little Bit. But, of course, in New York City, we call her Nina."

"Thank you, Wai," I said. "Now, why don't you go to the kitchen and get some napkins and something for us to drink."

"Little Bit," George said aloud. "I like it." He smiled at me. "But I think I'll stick with Nina. Or Shorty."

No matter how far you run, you can never run away from who you really are.

Miraculously, Wai and I got our deal closed on time. We took kudos from the partners and French champagne from the client. We drank it all and got a little tipsy.

"I hate not having a man around when I've got a nice buzz like this," Wai said as she drained her glass.

Avery Mitchell Fletcher could put on a child's birthday party as easy as Win decorated houses. I didn't know if it was that elementary education background of hers or if it was just inborn, but each year her ideas were something to behold. Piñatas, waterslides, and one year, she raided Sears for empty appliance boxes—washers, dryers, refrigerators, stoves, dishwashers. She had those boxes lined up in the backyard like a giant snake slithering in and out of the swing set and up close to the deck. She single-handedly decorated the inside of each box to look like everything from a scary cave to a jungle, from a haunted house to the slab that Cinderella slept on. After I saw it, I told her she ought to charge admission.

She could also be disorganized, like me, but when it came to her children's birthday parties, she couldn't be outdone.

I called just as Kiran's birthday party was ending. Courtney, the children's babysitter when she wasn't taking classes at the local junior college, answered the phone. "Hi, Bit. Arush is right here. Would you like to talk with him?"

"No, thanks, Courtney. Is Avery nearby?"

Before she could answer, another familiar voice came on the line and said, "Bit, couldn't you have made the trip down for the party? It's not the same without you here. I wanted to show you my new living room."

Win did have a beautiful home. Her "happy colors" were everywhere. Yellow and green in the kitchen, bright and sunny. According to Avery, Win's new living room was done in greens, apricot, golds, and lots of silk. A portrait of Win in white with pink and green hues hung over the mantle, and at the opposite end, the portrait of Winnie, commissioned just last year. Her house could have easily found its way into *Southern Accents*, with its custom molding and finery, but Win would deem such a thing ostentatious and T.T.F.W.—Too Tacky For Words. But she would love you forever if you merely suggested such a thing.

I could almost hear her gripping the phone.

"Hi, I couldn't make the trip right now. How are things with you? Are you okay?" I asked.

"Yes, but I feel like I weigh two tons. Nothing fits. It's awful."

Dead silence.

"Bit," she continued, my name sounding as frosty as a frozen daiquiri. I would have loved to have seen Avery's face watching this exchange in her kitchen.

"Win," I responded. "I'm surprised you're still there."

"Why?" she shot back. "Poor Avery needed help with

cleanup. That Courtney is no help, even when she's watching the kids."

I was quiet again, giving Win time to decide if she was going to be mean or cordial.

"So, Bit, is your cell phone broken or what?" Win asked, knowing she had left me six unreturned messages. Win didn't forget things like that, just like thank-you notes that were late and half-written, or never written at all.

"I've been really busy," I said.

"Really. Who's George?"

Damn Haines Enloe. He couldn't keep a secret to save his life. Whoever said women like to gossip never met my brother. Haines probably told Addison, and then Addison mentioned it to Win. Win was probably mad as hell at being left out of the loop.

"N.O.Y.D.B., Win," I said, flexing my own mnemonic Rolodex.

After going through her vast lexicon of Win-speak, she eventually gave up and asked, "What's that?"

"None Of Your Damn Business," I said jubilantly. "Now, can I speak with Avery?"

"Awkward," Avery said, taking the phone from Win. "You are such a coward, leaving me your little mess in addition to cleaning up at this party."

"I know," I said, "and I'm sorry."

"I'll never forgive you for this."

"Sure you will, because you're the best person I know."

"It's not that funny, Nina," Avery said. She told me about the party and about what a trooper Win had been—how, when Win thought no one was looking, Avery had caught her gripping the back of a chair just to hold herself upright. "You should be kinder to her. Our friends are like the solar system. Some always orbit on the inner ring. Others, for whatever reason, move to the outer ring.

Then just like that, they're back on the inner ring again. We need all of our friends no matter where they are. We don't kick them out of the galaxy. Win is just used to being in your inner orbit all the time."

"How can you trot out an Averyism just like that?" I asked. "Win is still a bitch who tries to control my life, even in Erob!"

"Yes, she is," Avery said, "but she's *our* bitch."

George and I had our third official date the following week. This time, he picked a cozy and romantic French restaurant.

"Do you like the opera?" he asked as we sat down.

"Only if it's in English, and only if it ends happily," I said as George laughed. Truth was, I had never been. Not much call for *Don Giovanni* in Erob, and Wai and I weren't "opera people."

"Would you like to go? I have season tickets."

If I'd needed confirmation George was erudite, here it was.

"I've never really been to the opera," I confessed, "but I'm open to trying it. Of course, that's what I had said about Long Island iced tea, too, and I got so drunk I spent most of the next day in bed."

George always knew how to order, and everything he chose was delicious, including the crème brûlée we shared. Normally it wasn't a favorite, but I devoured it.

The waiter said, "Maybe we should bring your wife her own dessert."

We smiled, letting the remark slide.

That's how it was with him, easy and comfortable. We enjoyed hearing each other's stories. His sounded exotic to me, and my stories sounded funny to his ears. Together we could fill up an evening with storytelling and laughter.

"So, opera this Friday, and on Saturday, we'll do something

you like to do. How would that be?" And just like that, our weekend was booked, and we became exclusive.

"Would you like to see my apartment?" George asked as we left the restaurant. Before this, we had left separately, and we still hadn't shared a goodnight kiss.

"I'd like that," I answered, and we headed up to the Upper West Side.

His apartment building had an awning. And a doorman. I noticed this because mine had neither. I also noticed the old molding and mirrors in the hallway. When we walked into George's apartment, I admired the many lamps, all with soft lighting. It would be perfect for any aging doyenne hosting a party, wanting to look younger. His color choice was neutral. But George's beiges and browns were rich and vibrant; there was a clear sense of style and confidence even under such mellow lighting.

"I'm doing it again, staring and not talking. I'm sorry, George. You have a nice apartment."

His apartment, like his clothes, fit him perfectly. It was also very neat and clean, almost as if he were expecting me. His bed was made. Wai says that most men don't care about their beds. They only care about getting you in them. My apartment seemed unsophisticated compared to his, like a cluttered English cottage, with my quilts and skirted furniture, so very unlike George's cosmopolitan bachelor pad. He had the Sunday *Times Book Review* and travel section tucked neatly under the pillow.

"This is so nice." Even I was underwhelmed by my inadequate vocabulary. Then, in the last room, off the kitchen, small with windows and a view, was the piano.

"My favorite room," George admitted. "Can I get you a nightcap?"

"No, thank you," I said, still trying to take it all in. And then he kissed me.

It was not a pushy kiss, but a kiss of introduction. A kiss that was gentle and curious. A kiss that lingered but left itself open to comparison . . . .

"I might need to get you home," George said, walking out of the piano room as if it held a curse or something unfinished.

"I can get myself there," I said independently.

"I'm not letting you take a cab alone at this hour."

So, we rode together, listening to the late-night talk radio in the cab.

"You want to come up and see my apartment?" I found myself asking, knowing I hadn't cleaned up like George and knowing it sounded like an invitation for more.

"Are you sure?" George asked.

"Sure," I said, mentally picking up clothes from my bedroom floor.

The apartment was dark, unlike George's. I quickly switched on a few lights and fluffed the pillows on my couch. Looking around to see if there were any stray coffee cups, I kicked day-old newspapers under a chair.

"I like it. It's like an English cottage in the Cotswolds," George said, admiring my apartment, the one Win had deemed unfit. "The plates on the mantle and the coffee cups are old," he guessed.

"Yes, some of Biggie's castoffs."

He smiled, and then he kissed me again, more generously this time.

"Cy would have a fit," I said. I could barely speak.

"Cy, who?" George asked distractedly, covering my face with more kisses.

Sunday morning my cell phone rang at an indecent 8:30 a.m. Red wine still lingered from the night before, and memories of George's mouth and me wanting him to stay, then needing him to leave, rushed back. He was ready, but I wasn't.

"Bit." The voice was unmistakable, the rise and fall of his drawl giving him away.

"Carter."

"Did I wake you? You're the first person I've called. Guess what?"

"What?" I asked, getting up and walking to the kitchen to get a glass of water.

"It took," he said, almost giddy.

"What took?" I asked.

"Jenny and I are having a baby!"

For a moment time stood still. Carter and Jenny having a baby. Carter would make the best daddy. Happy emotions unexpectedly stole the air from my throat and filled my eyes with appreciative tears. The silence got to him too. It was that way with us. Our emotions contagious to no one but each other.

"Wow, Carter, you and Win will have babies close to the same age! God help you! You'd better teach it to be tough so he or she won't get bossed around. Maybe that should be my job."

Carter laughed. It was easy to make him laugh.

"I'm so happy for you, Carter," I said.

"I know, Bit. Thanks."

Alone, I unwrapped the carefully preserved memory the way a mother might take her wedding dress out of storage for her daughter. No longer was there a need to keep this memory separated from the others. Surprisingly, even after all this time, the thought still sent a tingle through me, from my tonsils down to my toes. I started crying and tried to convince myself that they were happy tears.

The next day at work, Wai pumped me for information on my date with George. I told her about our plans for the upcoming weekend.

"And you haven't slept with him yet?" Wai asked suspiciously.

"No, Wai," I said. "I want to have a relationship with a bona fide grown-up, and I think I can have that with George."

Back in college, I'd been with boys who seemed glib and charming when inebriated who then turned dull in sober light. Except for one. Thomas Madden, a guy in my English Comp classes. When he read Browning or Tennyson, it was like some elevated form of foreplay. His hair was the color of chestnuts. He had a soft mound of hair beneath his lower lip, smooth as cashmere.

But it wasn't love—maybe desire or curiosity. The poor guy didn't own a Keurig, for God's sake. No caffeine in sight. Nothing. Nada. Zippo. Please.

Things were different now. I wanted, at least, to try.

"You know, a relationship where we get to know each other and feel comfortable and maybe even love each other a little first." Starting to sound sappy, I quickly added, "And then I can jump his bones."

"Your friend Avery was right when she said you wanted it all."

"Is it too much to ask for? A guy to truly love me—for me? And then to stay?"

"What do you mean, stay?"

Whispers of the past had crept out before I could stifle them.

On August 2nd, Richard Baxter Montgomery IV made his way into the world, all eight pounds of him screaming his head off. The nurses all exchanged glances and then gave Win sympathetic looks. She pulled me closer to her.

"If anyone in this hospital talks about Baxter being a blessing from God despite his handicap, at this particular moment, you have my permission to blow their heads off." I laughed in spite of myself. It sounded more like me than Win. But I also knew after months of being by herself, Win was going to be okay.

After two operas and seven dates, George and I finally made love. We had gone to dinner and then to a jazz cellar to listen to the music of an amazing vocalist who turned love and longing from Gershwin and Porter into an aphrodisiac. George held my hand and occasionally brushed the hair away from my face with his piano fingers. We didn't dance, which was good since I wasn't much of a dancer, but we sat close together with touches, smiles, and stares.

I don't remember how we got back to George's place. All I know is once the door closed, we were in unison, moving as one, and when we got to the threshold of his bedroom, I knew what it was to love and to be loved, to want and to be wanted.

"I love you, Nina."

I looked at him for just a second, wanting to take in this moment as the time in my life when I was sure of everything; sure of myself, of George and of life. For the first time, I was part of a couple. No one was more surprised than me to realize that I liked it.

I said it back, and then we began a slow exploration of terrain I was eager to discover. Afterward, I noticed George's body was as kind and graceful unclothed as it was fully dressed.

Three months later I was in my office when I got the call. It was Carter again, and I remember the sadness and the sudden stops and starts in our conversation. I didn't know whether to fill them or wait for him to continue. He was a brave man to personally deliver such unfathomable news.

Carter's baby would have been six months along that week, but the doctors said she was in trouble. That she didn't have a heartbeat. I couldn't believe that anything of Carter's didn't have a heart.

The doctors would induce labor, and the baby would come, stillborn. Unlike Win, unlike Avery, unlike Addison, there was no joy, no noise. Just silence and procedure.

Going home was a given. I wore my new brown suit.

"This year's black," Andrea had proclaimed, and I'd learned not to question anymore. Just pay and get it tailored properly.

There was a casket and there was a service. There were funeral casseroles, and there was even a name: Gladys Harriett Gideon.

Our small group gathered in a small circle for a small ceremony, looking at a small box buried in a small hole. I noticed Chewy and Jordan in the distance. Something in their unremarkable presence offered a simple, yet profound, validation. Only Carter spoke, and he read from *Charlotte's Web*, *Winnie-the-Pooh*, and Eugene Field. He didn't read any scripture, and I wondered if God had finally worn out his welcome with him.

"At least they're young," I whispered to Win as we were leaving the cemetery. "They can try again."

Win looked at me, an unspoken truth passing between us. "You and I both know that's not going to happen."

sixteen

I went straight to George's place when I got back to New York, and he took my clothes off as soon as I got in the door. Covering me with his body, he shielded me like he was protecting me from bullets, but it was only from the life I'd left behind. Afterward we lay in bed and drank a whole bottle of red wine. Grief sex and alcohol did little to blunt the sadness I felt for Carter and Jenny over a joy ending too prematurely.

Later that night I threw up all the wine I drank. The next morning, I woke up with a hangover, a headache, and an empty stomach. I put George's robe on and headed for the kitchen, where he was making coffee.

I smiled at him, and he returned it with a kiss on my cheek.

"Did you forget we have brunch with Cy and Olga today?" he asked as I inhaled my coffee. It would be the first outing the four of us would have together.

I just looked at him. "We can cancel," George offered.

No one, sober or otherwise, would dare change plans on a managing partner the morning of.

I dug into the robe's pockets to summon courage. What I found was a piece of paper that said "call Fran." I thought about it a minute and about its ramifications to me, to us.

"Who's Fran?" I asked matter-of-factly. I could see George pondering the question and pondering his answer. Finally, he said, "It's Frances Holbrook. Dr. Holbrook, Nina. She's a shrink. I go to her. Have for years. It's not a big deal. You know, everyone in

New York goes to one."

He must have sensed my confusion.

"I go when I get stressed at work."

"Why do you really go?" I asked.

"That's it, mostly. I see Fran about once every month or so. I get to unleash my parents on her," George smiled. I wanted more, and George gave it freely.

"I'm an only child, right? All of their attention is on me—good and bad. My parents wanted me to be head of my own investment house or something."

"But, George, you make a gazillion dollars doing what you do," I said, doing what I had always hated in others—oversimplifying a life.

"Everyone in my parents' circle does."

I thought about the Meissen vases again and all the pieces in Biggie's house.

"That's what's been great about you, Nina. You have money, but clearly you don't care much about it. You don't put on airs."

I barely have time to put on makeup in the morning, I thought. Besides, putting on airs can get quite heavy.

"My friend, Win, would get along fabulously well with your parents," I said. "Do you take anything? Any medication?"

"No," George said.

I realized my anxiety was irrational, but I felt the darkness. It was my own memories pushing into my skin like a cold, sharp knife. George was normal and evolved compared to me.

"My father committed suicide when I was thirteen. He was depressed, and he drank too much."

"Wow, Nina. I'm sorry. Really, I am. I know you never liked to talk about him, and I didn't want to push but . . . "

"There's not much to say, really."

George was quiet. "That must have been hard for you," he said.

"Yes, it was," I admitted, "and I blamed myself for his death for a long time. I think Mama blamed me too. Things were never the same between us after he died."

Besides Avery, George was the first person I'd ever voiced these secrets to. "It left a permanent stain on my heart."

"I guess he could have used a Dr. Holbrook," George offered. "Maybe you, also?"

"There's not exactly a shrink on every corner in Erob, Alabama. Then or now. Besides, you would be deemed really crazy by the good folks around there if you went to one."

"Better crazy than dead," George said. "It's just too bad he couldn't have gotten some help."

I managed to laugh. "Oh, he got help, all right. He cured himself," I said, "with a bottle of bourbon and a gun . . ."

Then abruptly I asked, "Should we get ready for brunch?"

Brunch went well, and Olga seemed happy. She said she was happy because I seemed happy with George. And I was. And work was going well too. A senior partner had recently given me a big client from Birmingham, Alabama.

"It's not like he needs me as a translator," I told Cy later, of Oliver Marshall. I guess Oliver thought Birmingham spoke an undecipherable language that only I had special skills to interpret.

"He needs you because you're good," Cy said, giving me encouragement.

Then, as luck would have it, a few days later Biggie fell and broke her hip. Haines said she was really in bad shape this time. I said I would come home the following weekend to help settle her into the downstairs bedroom. That would give me time to pull a few late nighters, close the deal, and release enough endorphins in George to tide him over until I got back.

I got to Biggie's after stopping by to check in on Mama. All the lights were off except over the stove, and it was just 7:00 p.m.

"Who's there?" came the voice. I walked to the downstairs guest room, now Biggie's room, and poked my head in.

"It's me, Biggie." After hearing no response, "It's me, Bit."

"Bit," she spoke softly. "What are you doing here?"

I was unaccustomed to her soft-spoken manner. To give this day some semblance of normalcy, I had counted on the gruff Biggie, but it was not to be.

"You broke your hip. And I'm here. To help."

Biggie pondered this. "I did? My hip? That's nonsense."

I was suddenly tired. Tired of sadness, tired of Biggie's confusion, and tired of death lording its power over us. Enough already.

"See you in the morning, Biggie," was all I could muster.

"Goodnight, darling." Sweetness from Biggie scared the shit out of me.

I wondered who that woman was in Biggie's bed, and I wondered if anyone would notice if I left right now and flew back to New York.

"Bit, quit sleeping the day away! Get down here." Biggie's voice, booming. It rattled me so much I about fell out of the bed. The clock said it was very early, but there was no way I could punch the snooze button on Biggie's demands. Yet as I started to wake up and moved to the top of the stairs, I knew I'd take *this* Biggie over the one I had encountered last night.

"We have a lot to do today," she announced.

She was waiting for me in a wheelchair. I rolled her into the breakfast room, as it was getting too chilly to enjoy breakfast on the screened porch. Agnes was in the kitchen, and she smiled and hugged me.

"You have to take me to get my hair done, and then we have to rearrange that wretched bedroom. Haines gave it a lick and a promise. He left all of my pictures upstairs and my jewelry. Who's ever heard of separating a woman from her good jewelry?"

Quietly, I mentioned how confused Biggie had been the night before.

"Yes, she's like that sometimes now," Agnes grudgingly admitted. "Only—"

I interrupted, "I know, I'm not here long enough to see it."

After the beauty shop and lunch, Agnes and I got busy. We took all of the framed pictures Biggie liked from upstairs and cleaned them with Windex. They looked like they had been taken yesterday, especially the ones of Haines and Win and Carter and me just before the Debutante Ball—it was hard to believe so many years had passed since then. I arranged them on the table so Biggie could see them from her bed. I got Agnes to help me move things around so Biggie could face the window and see her garden. I clipped some fresh blooms and put them on Biggie's bedside table, along with her pills and Bible.

We brought her jewelry box down and placed it on the dressing table near her bed. We put her favorite quilt at the end of her bed to keep her feet warm. A few days earlier, Haines had engaged Biggie's painter to widen the doorframe to accommodate the wheelchair. The house evolved again. I marveled at the flexibility of this old house. She could change effortlessly to accommodate her owner's needs.

Then I rolled Biggie in to have a look. It had rained all day, but now the sun shone outside the window, illuminating her garden with a perfect rainbow. She didn't say anything, not a word. She just looked around and then grabbed my hand.

"This is the best present anyone has ever given me, Bit," giving me what I believed to be an unencumbered smile. Was the rainbow a sign of Biggie's approval?

The day before I left to go back to New York, Biggie called me into her new bedroom. I noticed she had her jewelry box in her lap. "Bit," my grandmother began, "I'd like you to have my diamond watch."

"Biggie, I don't want your diamond watch," I said. "You keep it and enjoy it." We went through the list of her artillery, and to each thing my answer was the same: No.

"Bit, come over here. Get closer."

I feared being lulled into a trap, knowing that while her legs were no longer strong and her mind was sometimes confused, her ability to manipulate was still intact.

I came to the window where Biggie sat in her wheelchair. It felt like she was going to tell me some dark and threatening secret. She reached for the lowest compartment in her voluminous jewelry case, and I watched as she took out something small, wrapped in dark blue velvet.

"Your grandfather gave this to me on our first wedding anniversary."

It was a small ruby-encrusted pin. It was simple and understated, and Biggie had not worn such a thing in all her life; of this I was certain. She held it high, letting the rubies catch the light, showing off the small pin at its most favorable, like a salesclerk might do hoping to close the sale.

It was beautiful, unpretentious, and something that would go unnoticed to the ordinary eye. To me, it was gorgeous.

"This was never my taste," Biggie began. "I never wanted to hurt your grandfather's feelings." It surprised me that Biggie was ever concerned about someone else's feelings.

"Could you wear something like this on those suits at your office?" she offered, probably wondering how long it would take me to turn her down.

I surprised us both by asking, "May I have it?" as I pinned it on my navy blazer.

"Little Bit, it suits you. I'm glad." That glorious smile returned.

I was a little sorry that I'd never accepted any of Biggie's other offers. It clearly made her happy, and at that point in time, it seemed a minor sacrifice on my part.

Before leaving for the airport, I put Biggie to bed and made sure she was comfortable. She fell asleep quickly, her features relaxed, kinder, making her look younger and sweeter than she ever did when she was awake.

This went on for another year and a half, the back and forth. Haines summoning me to come home, Biggie threatening to die. And me, rearranging my work schedule, preferring weekend visits. George, wonderful George, forever patient even when I had to change our plans last-minute to fly home to Erob, which was often. Biggie came close to dying so many times I started to truly believe she would outlive us all—but then she'd always bounce back. Somehow, she always found a way to recover and make her way back to her beloved house.

And then, just like that, there was *the* call. Of course, I didn't know it at the time—how could I? Biggie was dying, for real this time, Haines said, and wants—no *needs*—to talk to you. But hadn't

I heard that a thousand times before?

Until she really did it. Died in her sleep. Peacefully. There was Biggie's list of instructions for me, the visitation and the funeral and the graveside burial and, of course, the casseroles. Everything carried out according to Biggie's instructions, down to the suit she would be buried in and the flowers that were to be displayed. She put me in charge, which was laughable, but with Win's help, everything came off without a hitch. Controlled perfection.

"Death always comes. He may ravage your body or rob you of your faculties first, but he always gets you. In a way, Biggie was lucky. She didn't have to pay too steep of a price," Win said at the time, throwing out another one of her cheery platitudes.

The chaos would come in the harsh aftermath. The reading of the will and that damn-it-to-hell codicil. Haines and Carter, especially Carter, and his sneaky legal maneuverings. Had Biggie been planning on telling me? Would it have mattered if I'd heard it all straight from her lips? I'd like to think I could have talked her out of it, but of course, I'll never know.

So, Biggie and I were *still* at war. Who says you can't have a second act even after you're gone?

part three

seventeen

My phone rang twice. No one spoke. It was Haines's number. It rang again.

"Haines?" I was back in New York. It was eleven o'clock, and I was still at the office. It had been three months since the codicil. Haines was having a hard time speaking.

"What is it?" His silence sent a chill up my spine. I tried to be patient, as if we had exchanged roles and I was the older sister trying to comfort him. But I was terrified.

"Carter." Nothing more. "He's been shot. They airlifted him to Birmingham. It doesn't look good." That was all my brother said. For once, he wasn't a doctor. He was a best friend. A million questions ricocheted in my mind. I let them keep bouncing around. I could tell my brother was in no shape to provide details.

"Haines, I am booking a flight to Birmingham. I'm coming home." That was the extent of our conversation. I was already punching in flights to Birmingham. How many times had Haines called me and wanted me to come home? We were the Fab Four: Haines, Carter, Win, and me—that is, until we added Avery and became the Fab Five. This time there was nothing. Just a man mourning his best friend. He was one of mine too. Carter Gideon.

I texted Cy and told him what I knew and that I needed to get home. He was gracious and told me to take the week off. I told him I would be taking my work with me, and that seemed to make him happy. Then I called George. It was my turn to fall apart.

"Nina, take your time. That kind of thing goes on in a small town? Do you want me to come with you?" My heart expanded for this man once again.

"No" was all I could get out.

"Nina, go home and pack and come over to my place. You don't need to be alone tonight."

"I love you," I said. And I meant it.

eighteen

On the airplane, I kept replaying the last time Carter and I were together. It was so ugly. I had said "get the hell out of my goddamn house." What if that was the last thing I ever said to Carter Gideon? Could our friendship be so elastic that it could stretch into eternity? He was still the best man I knew. My Carter. Even when he was getting into trouble with Biggie. I didn't have to dig deep in the reservoir of my memories.

"Carter Gideon, get over here. I mean it. Right now!" Biggie barked from her yard into the next. I sent a conspiratorial look at Haines. We had all been the recipients of Biggie's wrath, and it was never pretty. It didn't even matter that Carter was not her grandchild. She treated him like family, and that was quite unfortunate for Carter on this day.

Carter appeared from next door, trying desperately to tuck in his shirt. Hoping his good appearance would constitute leniency. We all knew Biggie was about to come down on Carter, and we all knew why.

My grandmother had never had grandchildren before Haines and I came on the scene. Our father was her only child. I think she believed grandchildren were tantamount to outdoor pets and must be fenced in. She was worried that somebody might snatch us. *In Erob, Alabama?* I'd always thought. *Please*. She hired a contractor who put in an expensive but beautiful wrought iron fence around her yard. I knew it was expensive because she got it from Charleston and did her best to bargain the manager down. She had to pay for shipping and installation and have it painted. Biggie never used bad words, but when she was writing that check I heard her mutter the words "damn fence. Those grandchildren better be worth it."

A mere twenty-four hours after having the fence installed, it happened. And I did my best to distance myself from what came next.

It was close to suppertime, so out Biggie came to lock the gate. She had Haines and me on our side of the fence and Carter on the other—or so she thought. Carter and Haines looked like preppy prisoners on that summer afternoon, each wearing their Izod shirts and seersucker shorts. Carter studied the fence a few minutes. He grinned from ear to ear and dubbed himself the great Houdini. I had seen that look before, and I was already backing off.

"All you have to do is turn sideways," Carter began, "and you can slide right through the bars. They're wide enough, and Biggie will never know." He demonstrated. He just turned sideways and slipped through the fence. It looked so simple. When Biggie came out, we all froze. She caught all three of us, on her side of the fence. Carter quickly slipped back through the fence slat like Fagin from *Oliver Twist,* hightailing it home.

Biggie was furious. "Carter Gideon, get back here!" He turned around, tucking his shirt in as he went. "You all think you're Huckleberry Finn. I'm only trying to keep you safe. I didn't want anyone to steal you," Biggie said, like she was talking about her favorite inanimate objects.

"I'm sorry, Biggie. I just thought it was funny," Carter said by way of explanation and apology. His contrition could use some work, in my estimation. She made us all promise that we would never slide through the slats. She even deducted a punishing amount from the allowance she gave us. She insisted Carter pay too. Each of our allowances for an entire month went into the collection plate at the First Methodist Church. What a waste.

The lesson I learned that day was if you were going to pull something over on the Big One, never, ever get caught.

Even now the memory made me smile. It was a rare occasion that it was Carter and not me that was in trouble with Biggie. But that wasn't the only time. I will never forget when she sat the four of us down for a lesson in accounting and accountability.

Biggie held what looked like a bill.

"Against my better judgment, because I wanted to teach you the value of money and give you a little freedom, I opened up an account, running a monthly tab, at the City Pharmacy. I have determined that was a bad idea, much like the bypass. This is my monthly statement from Mr. Charlie's pharmacy. It was through the roof! I've never been so shocked in my life! Bit, I see several charges for your lemonades and magazines, but you were always conscientious and told me when you bought a lemonade for yourself and for Win." Biggie paused. I recognized her game now. She was going to go down the row. For once, I was not in the deepest trouble, but I had a good idea where this was heading. I glanced down at Carter. I shook my head at him. He just grinned at me. It was about to get very ugly.

"Carter Gideon, do your parents have any idea how much candy, milkshakes, and other things you've charged to my account?" She waited, but not for long. "I made them a copy of this bill with all your charges, so they will have a pretty good idea of what you have been up to. How you've gone into that store every single day after school and charged a milkshake, a handful of candy, and Lord knows what to my account. Mr. Charlie blacked out the things that he didn't want me to see. I don't even want to guess what you boys have been up to. Certainly not in front of the girls." What could Mr. Charlie carry at his pharmacy that he wouldn't want Biggie to know? She glanced at Win and me as we glanced at each other. It dawned on Win and me about the same time. We put our hands over our mouths. My guess was that Haines had some nefarious part, but I couldn't be sure.

"Biggie, it can't be that much. I didn't do it to hurt you. It was just convenient. Haines said I could," Carter pleaded for clemency. Biggie was ready for that. This was a game Carter Gideon would never win. Even Win started laughing, and her composure was something to be admired. Biggie showed each of us the last page with the grand total. I noticed all the blacked-out expenditures.

"Wowza," I said. He got an eyeful of the bill with all the charges. He shot a look at my brother, and that's when I knew. Haines was pranking Carter. Carter just took it. He was just that good.

"I would've put it a little more artfully, Little Bit, but you are indeed correct. Now, how are the four of you going to pay my bill at Mr. Charlie's City Pharmacy?" I had shades of putting my allowance in the First Methodist Church collection plate again all because of Carter's sweet tooth and other things.

"I'm afraid you children have given me no choice but to close my account. We will all be on a cash basis from here on out. Carter, honestly, I don't know what form of punishment your parents have in mind, but I would suggest after all that candy that you better brush your teeth, or you will be in a dentist chair for the rest of your life." Biggie then gave the entire bill to Carter and left.

"Were you two B.Y.?" I asked. I didn't even try to hide my anger. Win smiled at me because I was using one of her little mnemonics. "Born yesterday," I said, exasperated.

Much later, I approached my grandmother. "Biggie, you know that most of the charges were Haines. He was probably just trying to play a joke on Carter. It's kind of funny."

"Little Bit, did you see that total? One never jokes about money. Never. Not even for one's amusement. Carter needs to learn to stand up to your brother."

"That's not Carter," I said.

"Don't worry. I fixed your brother too. Who do you think I have up at the church mowing the grass and picking the weeds?" A smile escaped her face. She met my eyes, and we both laughed.

nineteen

I walked into the hospital, not having a clue where I was going. Or what I might find. I saw the pitiful huddled mass that constituted everyone I loved most in this world in the waiting room. Win glanced up first. Then the rest glanced up at me like the wave at a sporting event. They looked at each other, determining who should be the spokesperson. It was usually Win, but she nodded at my doctor brother.

"Carter had surgery to remove the bullet near his heart, which had to come out. He lost a lot of blood. He's now in the ICU. The surgeon said it was still touch and go." I heard my brother's voice crack after delivering the news. I went over to him and hugged him. I looked at my brother. Stubble and worry covered him like a bad rash. He looked like he needed a blood transfusion. I wondered what this was doing to Haines, being a doctor himself and not being able to help his best friend.

"He is very weak. We can only go in one at a time and stay for just a minute. But he made it through this first surgery," Win said, as if to reassure herself.

"Barely," Haines said. "That damn case. No judge wanted it. Of course, Carter saw it as his civic duty to take it. Whoever said Southerners don't give a shit about social justice never met Carter Gideon."

Or you, I wanted to say. My brother practiced his own version of socialized medicine, taking vegetables for payment like Daddy had done. He was still the kind of doctor who treated everyone, no matter what form of "interesting" payment he received. Only in a small town would puppies like Bo-Bo ever constitute "currency." Carter had been judge ever since his dad died. In a small town it was less about prestige and more about who was willing to take it.

"What do you mean through this 'first surgery'?" I asked.

This time, Win took over. "There is another bullet lodged next to his spinal column. In his neck region. The bullet near his heart had to come out immediately because . . ." She paused. And she walked over to me and said the next part in barely a whisper.

"He was in danger of bleeding out. He did make it through this surgery. Unfortunately, he needs to have the second surgery as soon as possible. Probably the day after tomorrow. We've all given blood." Saying the truth had drained the color from Win's face.

"Should I give blood too?" I offered. I barely weighed a hundred pounds, but I would give it to Carter. Avery embraced me next. I didn't see Jenny anywhere.

"I don't think you weigh enough. But that's a generous offer," Haines said.

"Why don't you go in to see him? They will only let you in there for about a minute," Win suggested. She hugged me. "I think you need to see him, Bit. But he is in and out of consciousness, so I don't know how much sense he will make."

"I'll be quick," I said, and ducked into the room.

I wasn't even sure Carter was still alive. A chill traveled up and down my whole body. The machines. The packet of blood. The packet of fluids. It was all I could do not to throw up on him today. I didn't know how he could be alive. How could this be happening to Carter? And how could this be happening in Erob?

I took his hand in mine. It was so cold. I rubbed it between mine, trying to stimulate circulation. And life. Words.

Conversations. They all darted around in my brain. It was the simple ones that came out.

"I'm sorry," I said. Carter's eyes fluttered open. They focused on me.

"Get out," he whispered. I backed up and opened the door. I must've gone pale, because my brother came up to me.

"Are you okay?" he asked.

"He opened his eyes and told me to get out." I was shaking. I was so afraid. Full of regret.

"Well, that was the last thing you said to him. He probably is just remembering. He's in and out of consciousness, not making much sense," Haines offered.

I tried to find consolation in his statement. But what if Carter was having a rare moment of lucidity? What if that was the last thing we ever said to one another? Had I stretched the bonds of our friendship beyond endurance?

I looked at our little group, and I saw my emotions reflected back on every single face. Something caught my attention.

"Where's Jenny?" I asked. It was her husband, after all, that was on the verge of life and death. I saw a quick but meaningful glance exchanged between my brother and Win.

"She's resting," Win said, in a tone that meant "subject closed." I knew better than to pursue it.

"If I can't give blood, why don't I make a coffee run? I saw a Starbucks right near the hospital." I wanted to do something. Anything.

"That would be great," Win began. "Do you remember how I like my coffee?"

"Yes, Win. I remember all ten ingredients, including the one packet of Splenda," I said. Remembering how Win ordered her coffee, I always thought, *It's just coffee, not a damn nine-course tasting menu.*

"I switched to cashew milk," Win elaborated.

"Good to know. Avery can go with me."

On our way to get coffee, I stopped in at the chapel. Avery let me go inside alone. How many desperate prayers were made to God in this very room? Did my meager prayer have a chance at all?

"It's me. Don't hold that against Carter. His life has just started. He and Jenny want to have a family. Punish me." I sat there for a few minutes wondering if God would give me some ecclesiastical answer about Carter's prognosis. I was having trouble lighting a candle.

"Biggie, you don't need him. I do." And I said a quick prayer for the rest of us.

twenty

"Before we make our coffee run, tell me what is going on with Jenny. Don't say 'nothing,' because I caught the glance between Haines and Win." We sat down on the bench outside the chapel. I could tell Avery was debating what to tell me.

"Jenny has just been hysterical. Inconsolable. Win and Haines thought it best to let her rest at the hotel. She is so . . ." Avery searched for the right word. She looked at the chapel door as if God himself would deliver it to her, and then she said, "Fragile."

"Well, Avery, all that's missing from that statement is a 'bless her heart,'" I said.

"I thought about saying it, but Win does a much better job uttering those kinds of phrases than I do." It was true. Nobody could deliver a put-down so sweetly as Win could. I embraced her, and we almost laughed.

We settled into relaxed conversation. "I have so many regrets about that last conversation. Yes, I remember what you said about regret. 'A regret is like a potato chip. You usually don't just stop at one, and pretty soon the whole bag and your life are gone,'" I recited the Averyism from memory.

"Nina, I love it that you remember all my silly little sayings."

"The fact that I love you and remember all of your sayings may be the one thing that makes me redeemable." I began crying and couldn't stop. I fished around in my purse to get a tissue. Avery embraced me.

She was the person who would always side with me. "Let's cut Jenny some slack here. She's probably in shock. I feel sorry for her. I mean, what if it were your husband hovering between life and death?" I said, adding, "I'm worried about Haines. This must be so hard for him. Being a doctor and not be able to do a damn thing to help."

"I know. He and Win are trying to look after everyone." Suddenly, she started crying. The stress and strain of what was happening and what may happen was getting to her too. "What are we going to do without Carter? What kind of world is that?"

I didn't know the answer to that. Carter had been in my world and my life as long as I'd had a memory.

"You better look after Win. She will try to mother everyone and kill everybody with kindness." Avery was about to make a comment, but I interrupted. "If you tell Win I said this, I will deny it." And just like so many times before, Avery and I shared a laugh at Win's expense. But it felt normal. We were both looking for a sliver of normalcy. My world had always had them in it. They were the epicenter of goodness that made me a better person.

We handed out coffee when we returned, and when I got to Win, I gave her a look that said, "Don't even start with me if it's not right," which had been my cornerstone look our whole lives. I went to find a quiet corner to set up my laptop.

twenty-one

"Bit, wake up. It's morning. I told Avery I bet you dozed off with your computer open." It was Win. She hovered over me, looking concerned.

"How did you know where I was?" I asked, trying to come alive and work the kinks out of my neck and back.

"Because I know you," Win said, trying to comb my hair with her fingers.

Ordinarily, a statement like this from Win would have scared me shitless. But my "scared shitless" quota had already maxed out with Carter. We were not the kind of friends that read each other's thoughts and waxed poetic about finishing each other's sentences. Although we probably could.

"Carter?"

"He's still alive. They are assessing when they can go back in and remove the bullet near his spinal cord. Why don't we get some breakfast? Then we can go see Carter." Juggling everyone's worry is not as easy as it looks. For the first time, I looked at Win. She didn't even have on any lipstick. Her own hair looked like it could use a good brushing. No matter her age, Win Montgomery had always been in charge. Today, she actually looked weary.

"The surgeons have already warned us that spinal surgery will take a long time. Unless . . . but we won't think that way," she said, picking at her eggs. She had never been a fan of institutional cooking.

"Hey, I've been so worried about Carter, I still don't know what actually happened."

We both put our forks down and looked at each other a full minute. It dawned on me that Win and I had shared these sorts of serious conversations before, which had bonded us and made us reluctant adults together.

"Do you remember Ronnie Brown from our grade in school?"

"The cheater?" I started. "He sat behind me in almost every class and tried to cheat off my papers every chance he got. I will never understand how he even got through school. He probably plagiarized every single term paper. The biggest mystery is how he *ever* became bank president."

"Ronnie would've never even gotten to be janitor at Daddy's bank." Win smiled—a rare occurrence that morning.

"I was so glad Biggie didn't have her money there. He would've found a way to embezzle it. Didn't he get a lot of DUIs and lose the job at the bank?"

"That's just the beginning. Guess what his new enterprise was? Making meth in his garage and selling it to high school kids to get them hooked. That's how he got busted. And that's how he got Carter's court. He threw the book at Ronnie. And his redneck 'distribution partners' were so angry that Carter had put them out of business, they shot him in his front"—she paused—"I guess it's *your* front yard."

"Did they arrest these guys?"

"Not yet. They were driving a red pickup truck, and that doesn't exactly narrow it down in Erob. Unfortunately, you can't dress up a redneck." She paused, and we both looked at our plates of uneaten food. We got up to return to our hospital vigil. We embraced. Another rare occurrence between us. Was it I who was taking strength from her, or the other way around?

"Is he going to be okay?" She was confident about everything, and I was hoping even about Carter's fate.

She opened her mouth, and then she closed it. I recognized the look. The only other person in my life to be so confident but not have an answer had been Biggie. It was so long ago, but the memories were as fresh as this morning's coffee.

twenty-two

When Win and I returned from breakfast, they had taken Carter for tests, so I used that time to send work emails and talk to George. When I glanced up from my laptop, I saw Win and Haines huddled together.

Close to lunch time, I noticed Win had her cell phone out, and Haines was studying something on his iPad. To a bystander, Haines could've been Carter's doctor, and Win could've been Carter's wife. I saw Jenny standing alone in the corner. She had an almost ethereal quality to her because she was so pale. Her eyes darted around like a scared rabbit or a wounded deer. Whatever Haines and Win were up to, I knew enough to stay clear. I went over and embraced Jenny.

"I am so sorry, Jenny. You must still be in some kind of shock. I think we all are. You look like you could use some fresh air. Why don't we go on a food run?" I met her gaze and hoped I sounded reassuring.

"Thanks. I think you're the only one who understands."

I managed a smile for her. After we collected orders, and as we were leaving, I saw both Haines and Win glance up and mouth the words "thank you." Was it because I was being kind to Jenny? Or because I was getting her out of their hair so they could do whatever they were up to?

"Tell me what I can do for you. I know that's what Carter would want me to do," I said, as we entered the fast food drive-through lane. She still looked pale, but Jenny's eyes looked a little more alive and focused. "I know your friends think I'm nuts. But this is just crazy to me. I mean, when I moved to godforsaken Erob, I thought it would be boring. If I had wanted all of this, I could've just stayed in the big city and been happy." Ordinarily, a comment like this would be met with agreement from me, but I suppose hometowns are a lot like our mothers. You can complain and trash them all you want to, but once someone else decides to say something negative, you'll be the first one to defend her.

twenty-three

Everyone had their roles to play. I assumed mine was to distract Jenny so my brother and Win could do the serious business of looking after Carter. We went on a midafternoon coffee break, and when we returned, Haines and Win were huddled together with a new doctor. I heard the term "hospital privileges," but I didn't know what it meant. My brother looked up at me.

"Jenny, I would like you to meet someone. This is Dr. Tim Beeman, and he practices at Vanderbilt," Haines said, motioning for Jenny to come over. Once she did, the four of them were in a huddle, and I couldn't hear anything—not even with my finely honed eavesdropping skills that I had developed as a child. I went over and sat next to Avery.

"Any idea what that is all about?" I directed my gaze in their direction.

"Apparently this neurosurgeon is world-famous. Win called him to do Carter's surgery. His wife was a sorority sister of Win's. Dr. Beeman pioneered this new laparoscopic surgery where Carter's bullet is lodged. Haines had heard of him, but it was Win who got him here."

I was happy that she'd used her powers for good. She must've used her vast Rolodex of S.S.W.M.W.: Sorority Sisters Who Married Well.

"He wants to do the surgery in the morning," Avery said with no emotion.

"What? Carter is still so weak." My heart about jumped out of my chest. Just then, Jenny burst out crying.

"This doctor says the bullet has to come out, or Carter will be paralyzed."

"Better paralyzed than dead." I must've said it too loudly, because Jenny looked over at me. Haines gave me a look that said "shut up," and I realized they were trying to convince her.

I looked over at Jenny, and my heart just broke for her. I saw her nodding and then signing a paper. How would any of us act if the person we loved most in the world were fighting for their life?

twenty-four

It was early the next morning when they rolled Carter into surgery. I took one look at him and found my own heart becoming watery.

"C'mon, Bit. Let's go walk a few laps around the hospital," Win suggested. Great. Carter was in the fight for his life, and Win was worried about getting her ten thousand steps in.

"Go on," Avery advised. "The doctor said it could take all day."

Midmorning, Haines told us all he was going to see if he could observe the surgery. He was gone for hours. With each hour that passed, my anxiety grew. About three o'clock, I looked up and saw Haines coming toward us. He was pale and wearing a pained expression. I thought the worst. Win thought the best.

"Is it over?" Win asked.

He approached us slowly and chose his words carefully. He rubbed his hand over his chin back and forth, thinking. He did that during our childhood when there was unhappy news to deliver.

"Carter is still in surgery. The cardiologist had to be called. Dr. Beeman is finishing up."

"Why did the cardiologist have to be called?" I asked. Haines looked hacked. There was a long pause.

"Cardiac arrest," he said in a whisper. I knew better than to ask more. Besides, my eyes were stinging. Haines went back to the operation room.

We gathered around Jenny. An hour later, both Haines and Dr. Beeman returned. I noticed that Dr. Beeman's scrubs had sweat stains on the front.

"Your husband is in recovery. I was able to remove the bullet without invasion into the spinal cord. That simply means I don't think your husband will have any permanent damage. He's very weak. We will transfer him back to ICU in a little while. I know you all want to see him, but I think it's best to limit it to his wife tonight. He needs to rest. I will check on him in the morning. Haines, if you need me during the night, you know how to reach me." The two men shook hands, and then he disappeared.

My brother went over to Jenny and hugged her tightly. Genuinely. I observed him. The two people in the world who probably loved Carter best. Whatever differences they had were cast aside like discarded coffee cups. I got up and hugged my brother too.

"Why the cardiologist?" I asked.

"Carter flatlined twice." I had thought my brother was deaf. He was just having a hard time with the news.

We were each grappling with our own emotions. I heard someone walking toward us and looked up. In walked Addison, carrying a big cooler. When my brother saw her, his eyes brightened. His whole demeanor changed. You could just see the love between them. She set down the cooler and embraced my brother.

"Honey, you're a sight for sore eyes," Haines said.

"Just this once, I'm going to kiss you despite that wretched beard," Addison whispered in my brother's ear. When they finally broke apart, she announced, "I know you all haven't eaten a home-cooked meal in a couple days, so I brought a pork tenderloin and some green beans and baked a loaf of sourdough bread. I also made oatmeal raisin cookies, and I brought paper plates and silverware." She opened the cooler to show us the feast. "Arush has the kids."

I smiled at Addison. Oatmeal raisin cookies were my brother's favorite. She then went over to Win and Avery. They had an enthusiastic conversation about their children. I could tell that all three women enjoyed each other's company. I went over to Jenny and embraced her. They hadn't meant to exclude her, but surely she felt left out.

twenty-five

The next day, Carter was allowed visitors, even though he was still sedated. When it was my turn, the first thing I noticed when I approached his bed were Carter's lips. They were bluish gray. My index finger traced them. They felt dry. I didn't know if Chapstick was allowed, so I just leaned over and kissed them. Gently, not to disturb him. I noticed the oxygen tube in his nose. I looked around and saw all the trappings of a hospital room. The phone. The buzzer, Styrofoam cup and straw, and a box of Kleenex. I started crying. Unspoken apologies played out in my mind. I wiped my eyes and blew my nose and got up to leave. I leaned over and kissed him again. This time, his eyes fluttered. He looked directly at me as if I had gotten caught doing something I wasn't supposed to be doing. I held his gaze for a moment longer, and then he closed his eyes again. In another life I would've said to him, "We have to stop meeting like this."

After five days of Carter remaining stable in the ICU, Haines encouraged me to go back to New York.

"This could take a while. I'll keep you in the loop. I might need you to help me convince Carter to go to the rehab center," Haines told me.

"He's not going to the rehab center. It's out on the bypass."

"I know—that's why I will need your unique power of persuasion."

twenty-six

George met me at the door. He hugged me like I had been away in battle.

"I took the liberty of ordering Chinese takeout. Does that sound good to you?" I could smell sesame chicken and pork. Having dinner waiting on me, I embraced him fully.

"Would you like a glass of wine?" George asked.

"No offense, but do you have something stronger? I need something that's going to burn."

He got up, and I followed him to his little bar area.

"You're a Southern girl. You want a shot of bourbon?" He was already grabbing the bottle. It was something I had never heard of, Jefferson's.

"No thanks. Bourbon and I had a love affair once. It ended very badly. For me. Do you have scotch?" He took a beautiful bottle that had never been opened and freely poured me a shot. It tasted good. Just enough burn in my throat to make me feel alive. He poured another. I drank it like medicine.

"Nina, how does this kind of thing happen in a little town? Meth labs? One of your classmates?"

"I've decided small towns aren't much different from big cities. We don't have the number of murders, crimes, or scandals, but because we are a small town, everyone knows about it and talks about it the following day in the Piggly Wiggly or the Jitney Jungle. Ronnie—the guy who shot Carter—is what I like to call a bad seed. He was a cheater all during school. We were all surprised when he got to be bank president. There's a place for these bottom-dwellers in hell."

"Here's to Carter for making it through his second surgery," George said. I had switched to water by this point. We fell into bed, and I nestled myself into George, grateful for him. Lack of sleep, combined with no appetite and anxiousness, and I was already feeling the scotch. But what remained with me was the potent memory of bourbon and Carter's lap.

It was late again when my cell phone buzzed first, followed by my office phone. It was Win. It was clear to me that she had been elected spokesperson.

"I just wanted to tell you that they have moved Carter out of the ICU and into a private room. We will be able to watch over him better now." I smiled to myself. Clearly, Win thought she could look after Carter better than the entire UAB hospital staff. Maybe she could. I had seen her in action.

"I know you don't like to hear talk like this, but it's a miracle. God does answer our prayers. I don't think the doctors thought he would live through the first surgery, let alone the second. Carter has some kind of will to survive. Maybe he is waiting on you to forgive him. I shouldn't have said that last part. Don't jump all over me. I'm tired," she admitted.

"What about going home?" I reflected on the earnest but haphazard prayer I had made to God on the first day.

"He's a long way from that."

"Maybe Carter wants to stick around for Jenny."

"Maybe. I need to drive back to Erob to check on my children. They probably have forgotten what I look like. I just need to make sure Winnie and Baxter haven't set the house on fire and run off the babysitter."

I laughed. "No, they haven't. You know that road is bad. You probably should check into a hotel. That road is narrow and full of trucks," I said.

"Look at you. Caring about Carter and me. I'll keep you posted."

For the next several weeks, the date of Carter's discharge had been tabled. There were minor setbacks. After you had faced death, low oxygen levels and an irregular heartbeat seemed just par for the course. His cardiologist remained puzzled. Win, again, consulted her vast Rolodex of S.S.W.M.W. in the cardiology department and came up with another expert. It was someone Haines had gone to school with. He was brought in to consult. For the first time in the several weeks that I had been talking to Haines and Win daily, they appeared worried.

It concerned me that this would always be a health complication for Carter. The doctor wanted to do an exploratory operation to examine the structure and chambers of Carter's heart. I'm not sure if it was the uncertainty or the crack in Win's voice, but I scheduled a Saturday trip to Birmingham with a Sunday return.

Carter was still feeling the effects from the anesthesia when I went in to see him. He was asleep. I took his hand in mine, and it felt warm.

"I've been praying for you," I said, stroking his hand.

"I hope God doesn't hold that against me." His eyes were still closed. I started crying. And laughing. Like the rain and the sun competing for the sky's affection. I waited for him to say something else until Win poked her head in to make sure everything was all right. I needed a definition of all right.

The cardiologist could not find anything visibly wrong. He attributed it to scar tissue. He wanted Carter at Duke in six months for some follow-up tests just to make sure. He indicated that it would be Carter's stamina that took the brunt of the side effects. He seemed to be amused by Win.

"Tell Busy to email me, Gardner," Win said.

"Who the hell names their daughter Busy?" I asked.

"The kind of parents that know their daughter is going to grow up and be a doctor. A dermatologist. The kind of parents who nicknamed their daughter Bit," she said.

twenty-seven

George was out of town, and I was having a late dinner at home. I made my nightly call to Win. It was a horrible thing to think about, but in many ways, Carter's shooting had brought us closer. I called her every day to check in on him.

"The doctors think Carter will be able to be released in a few days, but Haines thought it was a good idea to order a hospital bed so he could stay downstairs. I've been on the phone with the hospital supply company and insurance. What a nightmare," she said.

"Where's Jenny?" I asked.

"No offense, but she is about as organized as you are about this stuff. Haines and I have been doing the heavy lifting, so to speak." She sounded tired.

"I guess the saying is true—if you want a job done right, hire the Junior League president."

"Carter is no more ready to leave the hospital than to fly to the moon. The doctors are still guarded about his long-term recovery. Haines is trying to get him to go to the rehab center out on the bypass. But that bypass is one place Carter Gideon won't go."

"If the doctors are still worried, why is he being released?"

"Insurance. And Carter hates us all having to commute to Birmingham. Carter would jeopardize his own health for the sake of our convenience." I recognized that tone. It was one of exasperation.

"You're doing a really good job, Win."

"Oh, dear Lord. It's the second coming. Bit Enloe just gave me a compliment. I want my children to learn to be kind. They love Carter. We've been planning meals for him when he gets home. They're so excited that he's leaving the hospital."

Again, I wanted to ask where Jenny was in all of this, but I knew better. "Just make sure you're looking after yourself. You sound tired."

"And now you're concerned. You *are* going soft. But speak of the second coming, guess who called me? Flo of the No-Notes. She wants to bring a casserole to Carter, and just guess what she said?" I waited.

"Florence said I didn't need to write a thank-you note! For the casserole! Can you believe her? Like I would ever take my etiquette cues from her."

I started laughing, and I couldn't stop.

twenty-eight

My phone rang at eight o'clock in the morning. I was just getting to the office.

"I was hoping it wouldn't come to this," Win began. I missed my elevator.

"What's wrong now?" I asked, dreading the answer.

"They will probably be discharging Carter on Monday. Bit, I have really worked on his house, but it is in no condition to welcome Carter home," Win said. "And who knows if that Jenny will even be there, she spends so much time in Charlotte."

My first thought was how Win referred to Jenny. My second thought was of Biggie's house. How it had expanded and accommodated her in every stage of life. I returned to the conversation.

"We've all been in to talk to him. Carter is adamant about not going to the rehab center out on the bypass. I know why he feels that way, but I am genuinely worried about him in his house. And I really don't trust Jenny to look after him . . ." Her voice trailed off.

"The way you can," I laughed.

"No," she countered. "I'm no nurse. He needs someone to check his oxygen levels still. And his blood pressure has been running so low, Bit." She paused. "I know it's Thursday. You probably have plans. I was hoping you could come home on Saturday and leave Sunday, like you do."

Had this behavior of mine become a thing? George was being patient, but I could tell he did not like this unwelcomed habit we had fallen into. "Wait. You want me to talk to Carter about going to the rehab center? Are you serious? You're Mother Theresa. I nominate you."

"I'm consulting the Saint of Last Resort," she chuckled. "Please. Do it for your brother. I'm worried about the strain on him." I was thinking about the strain it put between George and me.

"Shit."

"You can say all the bad words you want. Just come home."

"Fuck."

"Where on earth are you?"

"I am in the lobby of my office with thousands of people around me." I laughed, knowing no one cared what I said.

"I can pick you up at the Birmingham airport. Thanks, Bit."

twenty-nine

I walked into Carter's hospital room.

"Win must be pretty desperate to have called you. If you're here to persuade me to go to rehab, you can save your breath. But we both know I tend to do what you ask me to." He waited.

"Not every time, Carter."

"I don't need a trip down memory lane with you. What's your angle?"

"I'm not going to try and persuade you to go to the rehab center." I had his interest.

"What have you done with Bit?"

"Nothing. But I am here to negotiate with you."

"That doesn't surprise me. Negotiating with you is like negotiating with a terrorist. Just tell me what you want."

I really wanted to tell him to turn back time and not do the codicil.

"Here is what I'm proposing: You agree to either staying in Biggie's downstairs bedroom or having a hospital bed put in your sunroom. And you will hire a nurse to come in at least once a day and check your vitals. You have to do that. For them," I waved my arm toward the hallway, where Jenny, Haines, Win, and Avery were waiting. "They watched you almost die, and they're worried they're not going to be able to resuscitate you if something happens. Do you want that guilt on Haines's conscience?"

We held each other's gaze for a while.

"That's not such a bad compromise."

"Chalk one up for my Duke Law over your Duke Law. Or Biggie's training." It took him a few minutes, but he finally gave in and returned my smile.

I gave him a quick peck on the cheek, and I turned to leave. As I put my hand on the doorknob, Carter called out to me.

"You know, I remember," was all he said.

Remember what? Did he remember that we were still mad at each other, and this was just a temporary détente?

Or did he remember that I had kissed him? Not once, but twice. I had no business kissing a married man on the verge of death. Shame suffocated me until I couldn't breathe. I needed to get the hell out of there.

thirty

"Jenny's gone," Haines said. No one could say something so dramatic with so few words as my brother. He was the master.

"What do you mean 'gone'? Gone where?" I asked.

My brother's patience thinned. "Jenny left Carter. She's gone."

"When is she coming back?"

"She's not, Bit. She's filing for divorce."

It occurred to me that my brother was having a hard time putting all these words together in a complete sentence.

"Don't you think she'll be back? Carter's only been back at work for three months."

"No, she won't." Haines paused. "Carter still gets winded going up the stairs to his bedroom. I could strangle her."

"Haines, you *never* liked Jenny!"

"Well, I like her a hell of a lot less now. You need to come. Now."

It was my turn to pause. I wasn't ready to return to Erob, especially given my last encounter with Carter bearing down on me like a seaside destination preparing for a hurricane. Besides that, I was still mad at Carter. *And* Haines.

"Haines, it's just a divorce. It is not like a death. I have taken a lot of time off recently with Carter's accident. These partners were understanding up to a point. But now they want me back working."

Of all the statements I had ever made in my life, and grant it I had made some stupid ones, this was the one I wish I could take back the most. Angry or not, I had just done to Carter what Win had done to me all those years ago when Daddy died—minimized his pain. It would take me longer to realize divorce and suicide actually have much in common. Both leave you with a sense of abandonment. And neither has that odd thing called closure. We're left with words like "why" that seem as big as a whale's mouth and the feeling of not quite being "good enough."

"I'll get home when I can," I relented. "And tell Carter I'm thinking about him."

"Tell him yourself." And with that, my brother ended our conversation.

And I did. Albeit via the coward's way out: I texted Carter. I told him how busy I was at work, but that I was sorry. I should have just sent him wading boots to get through the pile of shit I was writing.

It took me another two months to get "un-busy" at work and spend enough "quality time" with George to feel I could get away. Haines met me at the airport. Even though it was late March and the weather was willing spring to come, it was a frosty ride in my brother's car.

His words were clipped, well-chosen, and full of disappointment.

"Bit, I know you're still sore about the whole Biggie thing, but at some point, you'd think you could put it aside for your friends. Win has been over every day to check on Carter. She's cooked meals for him. She's been a real trooper. Funny, I always thought you'd be the one to tend to him if anything happened."

"I get it, Haines. You're disappointed in me. You, Win, and Carter having some big 'kumbaya' moment."

"No, Little Bit, you don't get it. I have no idea about your relationship with this George, but this has been really hard on Carter. First, he almost died from that shooting, and then his wife has up and left him and nobody knows why."

We drove the rest of the way in complete silence. After we passed the "Alabama the Beautiful" landmark sign welcoming us into the state, I knew there was another dreadfully long eighteen miles until Erob. Which could be good, depending.

Finally, we made our way into town. Haines automatically drove us into Biggie's driveway. I looked at him curiously.

"What?" he said. "Like it or not, this is your house now. And it's the closest to Carter's. I'm not letting your sorry ass get away with anything else. Now get over there and see if you can apologize your way out of this one."

I found Carter sitting at the island in his kitchen, reading a paper. He motioned for me to come in. I surveyed the man who, despite everything, was still my friend. He looked the same, but when his eyes met mine, they were dull, not the vibrant blue I'd always known.

"Hi, Gideon." A casual approach.

"Bit, you came!" He said it as though he were surprised to see me.

"New York City's not a foreign country, you know." I had a long way to go to crawl my way back, and I wasn't doing myself any favors with clever comments.

He folded up the paper, quickly got to his feet, and then took off his glasses.

"Let's go sit in the den where we can be comfortable."

We made our way to our accustomed spots. I sat on the familiar sofa, grasping for words. I was at a loss, so I just kept looking around, as if the "right" words were tucked in the bookcases somewhere.

"I really am sorry, Carter," I said finally, my eyes making a 360-degree turn around the room. From where I sat, it didn't look like Jenny was gone at all. She could be at the grocery store. But as I looked closer, an eeriness settled in my bones. Nothing was out of place, at all. The house looked the same as it always had, even when Miss Harriet and the Judge lived here. I'd never noticed it before, but it was as if Jenny either liked everything Carter and his family had done to the place or knew all along she wouldn't be staying. As I was surveying the room, I noticed Carter surveying me. I had to come up with something.

"It wasn't your fault," I began.

"Damn. I expected more from you." His voice sounded odd, the tone slightly raised.

"I wasn't finished." My voice raised back. "If you'd let me speak and not interrupt . . ."

He nodded.

"I was going to say that maybe it wasn't you at all. Maybe it was this town. Maybe it was Erob. This town can be hard on a person. Think about me. I'm from here, and I don't want to live here. Maybe it just got too small and stifling for Jenny. Had you thought about that?" I remembered what Jenny had said about Erob, about staying in the big city if she wanted to be happy.

"So, why didn't she say anything?" he asked. "She could have changed things around. Are you saying she left because she didn't feel like she could redecorate? Good Lord, Bit."

"No, no." I felt like I was making things worse, not better. "Think about it. If you start to change things, that's making a commitment. Redecorating and putting your own touches into something means it's yours. You're putting your anchor down."

"Are you saying she never committed to me?"

I was beginning to think I shouldn't have come at all. Then Carter softened, and he was looking at me as if I had provided him some integral piece of the jigsaw puzzle. "I don't know. You might be right," he said. "We never argued. Hell, you and I have had more cross words than Jenny and I ever did."

"Maybe she was just unhappy here. She did go back home often. Maybe in Charlotte she was just happier. Stronger."

I was winging it now, throwing out theories and hoping one would stick and make sense. In truth, angry or not, watching poor Carter suffer made me sick. I should be the only one allowed to make him suffer.

"Maybe I just wasn't enough?" He locked his eyes on mine. Well, at least now we were in territory I understood.

For a while, I let the question sit between us like a drink that was too hot to even sip. Our silences have always been comfortable, and for that, I was grateful.

"I had the same feeling when Daddy died. If only I'd been good enough, I could have saved him, and he wouldn't have left." I paused again, realizing I'd just revealed something close to the bone about me when I was supposed to be here easing Carter's pain. Once again, silence exerted herself.

After a while I said, "I don't even know Jenny's favorite color."

"Yellow," Carter said, without hesitation.

We shifted positions, and I could hear him breathing. It seemed forced and ragged. He was hurting. I was glad the coffee table separated us. Finally, I managed to look at him, and only then did I see tears welling up. My first thought was to flee. Everything inside me felt uncertain and overwhelmed. Anger turned to guilt and formed the word *regret* around my heart.

"I'm sorry I didn't come home right away," I said quietly. "As soon as I heard."

"It's fine. I know you're probably still mad at me, but you're going to forgive me, right?"

I noticed the moon outside. It would provide enough light for me to get home unassisted by any flashlight.

"Bit?" The way he said my name filled the room like a distant echo.

The sound of the back door opening broke the spell.

"Carter? Dinner's ready. I hope you're hungry. Chicken casserole with artichokes and sun-dried tomatoes." Her voice, her actions were as familiar to me as anything else I knew by memory. "I even brought enough for you to have leftovers. How terrific am I? Of course, there's a honking spoonful missing because Baxter thought it was banana pudding. That the breadcrumbs were vanilla wafers. Imagine his surprise when he tasted an artichoke instead."

"You're the best. We're in here."

Win's determined footsteps grew closer.

Without realizing it, I had tears in my eyes. Win came straight over for a tentative hug when she saw me.

"Did I interrupt something?" She looked at us. "Bit, can you stay for dinner? It'll be nice."

The three of us walked into the kitchen as we had done so many times before. Win went to the silverware drawer and set the perfect place setting. She even managed to find festive placemats.

"I could go outside and clip some azaleas and daffodils so we can have a proper table . . ." She paused, waiting for a response. "Or, I could just go straight to the wine and pour us a glass."

"Just pour," Carter and I said in unison. It was the first time we had agreed upon anything in a long time. We met each other's gaze and smiled.

Win could adapt to any situation without a moment's hesitation. Just knowing she hadn't changed made me smile.

Somewhere between Rich's stomach and her Junior League duties, she had evolved into an amazing chef. I was in the process of pouring my third glass of wine when Win said, "Don't you think you've had enough? Or is that normal for you city folks?"

"No worries, Win. I'm on foot. Haven't you heard? I own the house next door." The truth was, I'd been drinking a little more than usual lately. It dulled the pain—blunted the confusion around Biggie's dying and the burden of Biggie's house, and it numbed the whole Carter situation. It also allowed me to continue keeping George in the dark. Just party, party, party, and everything is fine. He'd learned to leave me alone, saying only, "I'm here when you're ready to talk."

"So, Bit," Win continued, almost too casually, "what *are* you going to do about the house?"

If it was just the two of us, this sort of question delivered by Win would have provoked a snarky response from me, only to be one-upped by Win, and then we'd be at it for hours. But because Carter was sitting there, we played nicely with each other. That was the beauty of Carter.

"For starters, I plan on sleeping there tonight," I said, purposefully not giving her what she really wanted to know. Truth was, I wasn't entirely sure myself.

I woke the next morning and glanced at my watch. I had slept in way past late, like I had attended one of Cy and Olga's late-nighters. As I rolled over to reacquaint myself with my surroundings, I took a deep breath. I breathed in the smell of coffee, the smell of bacon, and the smell of spring. Much as I tried to deny it, all of the smells, when stirred together, spoke a single word: home.

As I walked into the kitchen, I threw my arms around Agnes. She released me and motioned to the breezeway, already occupied by Carter. Agnes and I glanced at each other, a covert conversation between us.

"Good morning, Carter," I said.

"Morning, sleepyhead. Can I get you some coffee? Or aspirin?"

I had to smile at this. After all, it was now my house, my food, and my coffee. But I saw how this was going. Win got custody of Carter for dinner, and apparently, he was my responsibility for breakfast. Leaving Avery out of the equation altogether was an act of charity for both Avery and Carter, since Avery couldn't cook her way out of a paper bag.

I went to my usual place at the table, leaving Biggie's chair unoccupied. Carter brought me a cup, and for the first time I noticed some thinness around his cheeks and his eyes. He had a long way to go from the surgeries and now this.

"I hope you two are hungry," Agnes said.

"We are," I said, "but I can fix my own plate, Agnes." I had lived on my own for too long to go back to being waited on.

Carter and I ate in silence. It was a little unnerving to me how bad he actually looked.

Finally, between bites, he asked, "Are you really still mad at me?"

Despite my sympathies toward his current circumstance, I was actually still angry. Furious. "Yes, Carter. I am."

"Is that why you've stayed away so long?"

"No, I'm busy. Busy at work."

"Biggie would have done it anyway. I told her you'd be upset. Even Agnes refused to be a witness."

"At least Agnes has good sense. It should have been anyone but you. You, of all people, knew how I felt."

"Well, nobody said you can't hold a grudge," he said, but there was a hint of a smile. "I just hope you don't. I'm running out of friends." He knew it was only a matter of time before I would forgive him. But not just yet.

As we continued our silent togetherness, the sound of a car engine and the screen door opening intruded. Win was back.

She grazed the top of my arm with her hand in a continuance of the good feeling that had been established last night over food and wine. Then she went to Carter. Behind him, she drew her whole arm around his shoulders, and it lingered there. It was a gesture reserved for long-marrieds and still-attentive spouses or devoted, loyal old friends. Win was not the touchy-feely sort; her lingering embrace seemed kind, and for some reason it settled and unsettled me at the same time.

"Sit down, Win. Have breakfast with us," I offered.

"Goodness, I ate ages ago. I just stopped by to see if you wanted to go for a walk." She looked at me. "That is, after you change your clothes."

Like clockwork. The familiar edge of disapproval in her voice. I had on a Duke T-shirt, no bra, and a pair of running shorts. Even Win drew the line.

"But I will have a cup of coffee and visit with Carter and Agnes while I wait." I hadn't even agreed to walk, but there it was. Decided for me.

"Wow. I didn't really notice last night how bad Carter looks," I began, as we made our way along the sidewalk. I noticed the tree-lined sidewalk. I heard the birds in their happy revelry and took in the unique smells of springtime.

"Believe it or not, he's looked worse. When Jenny first left, I made him go away for a week to the beach house. That helped some, but he's still got a ways to go."

"I can't imagine."

"I wish she just . . . died," Win said. "It would have been cleaner."

Win's words crawled around the two blocks it took to get to her house. I couldn't tell if it was the midmorning heat or the tone of her voice that seemed to strangle me.

"Not always, Win."

She reached into our collective well of memories. "Okay, maybe that was a little harsh. I'll give you that."

"If I wasn't already so mad at Carter, I'd turn it all on her."

"Well, Carter won't hear of it. He's warned us not to say anything bad against Jenny. He'll shut you down."

That would be Carter's attitude. Such a noble man. How could he be capable of such a kind gesture even in the midst of a cruel betrayal?

"It just seems to me it would be healthy for him to get angry. Pissed off, you know?"

"That would be you," Win said with a smile.

It occurred to me that, thus far, Win had been downright restrained in her inquisition about Biggie's house. Subtlety and restraint were not her friends. "You haven't pushed too much about me moving back here," I said. I looked her dead in the eye.

"You want me to?"

"Not really."

"Well, Carter warned us about that too."

Chalk another one up to nobility.

I had a long lunch with Avery. We ignored Carter's admonition regarding Jenny and dished about her shortcomings. It was very un-Avery-like, but also quite satisfying.

"I mean, Jenny was so brittle," Avery said. "But I guess even our little group needs a passive character."

I shared my thoughts about Jenny's lack of decorating the house. It was as if all at once, things that seemed so normal could now be viewed as telltale signs.

"Carter's taken several hits lately. Biggie dying, that wretched shooting, your pouting, and now this."

"Don't equate me to Jenny."

Avery was quiet. Uncharacteristically so.

"I think I need a strong cocktail after this weekend," I said, "or a Valium."

"Hearing about Jenny is tough."

I wasn't thinking at all about Jenny.

Avery understood, even better than me.

"You know, Nina, you've been with Carter in bad times before. What makes this so different?" I didn't have an answer.

I missed Biggie for her grand distractions and a place to put my blame. I missed Carter. He always had a hug waiting. Steady, even incorruptible in that steadiness. And Avery. She was always so straightforward. Not today. If Avery had her own answer, she wasn't sharing.

It occurred to me that friendship involved the kindness of overlooking. Overlooking how bad someone looks. Overlooking another's indifference to making a house her home, or overlooking another's inability to cook anything that wasn't Indian, or overlooking how another takes over with apparent ease despite her busy schedule, or finally, overlooking the most egregious infractions of them all: a friend who doesn't show up when it really counts.

thirty-one

When I got back to New York, I headed straight for George's apartment. He was waiting for me. It felt nice. To show my appreciation, I took him to bed. Not once, but twice. I'd been reminded that having someone is a blessing and that some loves have invisible expiration dates. And that some griefs don't rank up there with other griefs to receive the universal symbol of mourning, the funeral casserole, but are no less tragic.

After we were done, George laughed. "You should go home more often," he said. He kissed my cheek. He said the word "home" like a small prick, a topical graze. Nothing more. But for me, the word "home" required a full-fledged blood transfusion, and then some. It was not a simple act like Dorothy clicking her ruby slippers.

I finally got up the nerve to fill George in on my "inheritance."

"Does that mean you'll be taking me out to dinner tonight?" he ribbed as we went into the restaurant.

"Don't kid about it. I'm not touching her money. She can't manipulate me from the grave," I said. "Speaking of," I added in a more humorous way, "how do you feel about a summer house in Erob, Alabama?"

There was an hour wait, so we went and sat at the bar. We were happy to be together. I was happy to be in the anonymous frenzy that was New York City. No demands. We polished off our first quickly, the wine flowing through arteries and capillaries, replacing blood and feelings. The second glasses went almost as fast. We needed food, I thought, as we ordered our third glasses.

"So next week—*Madame Butterfly*," George said.

"George, can we take a pass, just this once? I don't think I can handle any more death for a while. Or you can go without me."

"I've been doing things without you since your grandmother broke her hip. You knew she wasn't going to live forever. Then Carter. And now you tell me you have this inheritance," George said.

Maybe that was it. I *had* thought Biggie was going to live forever, a permanent fixture in my life. She provided the perfect adversary—a perfect venue to vent my frustration, and now I had nothing to do with those feelings.

"I just need a break from those stupid death operas," I said louder, stupider.

"Are you telling me now you don't even like operas?" His voice matched mine in volume and stupidity.

I had never imagined myself to be the kind of person to get into a fight in public. I had certainly never imagined myself getting into a fight in public over something like opera. And I had definitely never imagined myself being the kind of person I would become by the end of the night.

"Maybe we should just take a break."

"Wait. How did taking a break from the opera get to be about us?" I was drunk and feeling nothing.

"I'm tired of being without you. We go days without talking," George said, jumping up from the barstool, ready to leave. "What the hell happened between you and Biggie? Forget it, you won't tell me anyway." He turned his back to me and threw two hundred dollar bills on the bar. More than ample to cover our wine, I thought, and he turned to go.

"Aren't you going to get your change?" I asked.

"Forget it," he said, disappearing into the crowd.

"George." I maneuvered myself around the bar patrons, misjudging the distance and falling into someone. I lost my balance again, and a nice guy helped me up. I think.

I woke up the next morning, badly hungover and naked, next to another naked body. His name was Ian maybe, or Evan. It had a lot of vowels in it, which is about as much as I remember. All I knew for sure was that "Vowel Guy" wasn't George.

I saw my clothes across the room. I searched my pockets. I had lost my keys. But that was the least of it. I'd lost a whole lot more. I'd lost myself.

There were five voicemails from George on my phone.

"I know you're just not answering your phone. I was wrong. I'm sorry. Please call me, Nina."

I peeled the guilt-ridden clothes off, wondering if I could ever wear the brown suit again.

I showered, changed, and turned my attention to food. I needed carbs. And protein. And Advil. The doorbell rang. I looked through the peephole.

"Nina, I know you're there," he said, staring back at me.

I opened the door to find George, with a bouquet of peach-colored roses. Beautiful roses.

"I'm sorry, Nina."

"I can't do this on an empty stomach," I said, letting him into my apartment. "Let's go get something to eat. No hour-long wait this time," I added.

"You got that right," George laughed. "I'm still hungover. Have you eaten at all?"

"Are you kidding? I passed out in bed," I said, lying as effortlessly as if I were ordering bacon and eggs. "Let's go."

"Done," George said. "And I hate arguing, Nina. Let's not argue again."

And we didn't.

"I can*not* believe it." Wai was surprised at my confession. "I, at least, knew their names," she admonished. The rule for one-night stands, I guess. Then she lightened up. "You're clearly not cut out to be a shacker. You'd better stick with George." And then, the unasked question passed between us.

"No, Wai, he doesn't know. And I'd like to keep it that way."

"Don't worry. Your secret is safe with me."

George would die if he knew what I'd done. I had never thought of myself as a shacker. When I'd gone back to George's apartment after breakfast to make up, I remember thinking *it's better this way*. At least for me. To remember, to know that feelings would be returned, for his smell to linger. Hermes cologne. No one wore it but him. His kisses, soft and still, like introductions. Even now.

Knowing that George loved me was better than being numb to all the emotions I needed to feel. The emotions were important.

Maybe it wasn't all so sinister. Biggie knew I loved her house, that I had always felt like it was home. Maybe she was just making it easier for me to visit. Maybe she did have my best interests at heart. Maybe this was all just unexpected grief for a woman I didn't expect to miss.

Damn Biggie and her precatory language. Damn her for leaving me like this. Her decaying body finally dragged her formidable will down with it. Damn her manipulation, and her generosity. I had always thought Win was a pro, controlling my life in

New York, but hell, she was just an amateur next to the Big One, who was still controlling me from the grave.

"What's wrong, Nina?" Cy asked one afternoon as we were reviewing a document.

He was right. I needed to talk. "This is one for Olga," I said.

"It's not George, is it?" Cy asked, backing away from anything that smacked of needing relationship advice.

"It's family stuff."

Cy seemed relieved, as if "family stuff" was an easier maze than "relationship stuff." He made a call, and Olga and I were on for an early dinner.

"You can come back to the office when you're done," Cy said, not wanting to take one of his highest-billable associates away from the office for too long.

When I arrived at the restaurant, Olga was already seated at a table, looking out into the room as if she ruled the domain. In a way, she did. She was drinking her red wine. I noticed because it just matched her lips. She had on one of her umpteen black suits and the large diamond broach in the shape of the eye of the hurricane pinned to her bosom. Then she smiled and became another person entirely.

I kissed her well-powdered cheek. "Nina, I'm so sorry about your grandmother," she said. "I haven't really had an opportunity to tell you in person."

"Thank you, Olga. And thank you for the flowers and note."

"You're welcome, darling. I am sorry about your friend's accident too. May I order you some wine?" I declined, mostly because of the other night, and my looming moral hangover. "I have to get back to work," I told her, and asked for water instead.

We ordered, and I began trying to unpack my emotional baggage that had been collecting dust for weeks.

"Biggie has gone and done it this time," I began. "She left me most of her money, and the worst thing is, she left me her damn house. Sorry, but I'm so damn mad at Biggie."

I wondered if she understood what I meant, yet assumed she understood the important parts. Olga was fluent in the language of grief.

Here we were—the emotional argument versus logic. Was there any logic to this decision? Does logic ever counsel the heart?

"What did her will say exactly, Nina?"

"Well, basically that it was Biggie's wish that I live in her house, love her house—which I do, by the way—get married and raise my children there. Oh, and to find happiness and peace along the way."

"Oh, my. I see."

I was going to say something funny like, *seeing as I have no children*, but Olga was not one to be toyed with.

"That was the last thing your grandmother wrote?" Olga asked, or pointed out.

"Yes."

"You must give her words grave consideration." And that was all she said. All she needed to say, really, and I was scared not to listen to her. I finally realized the secret of Olga and Cy's successful marriage, and it made me smile: Cy Weinberg was afraid of his wife.

This was not what I expected. I had hoped for more definitive advice.

"Well, Olga," I continued, after several moments. "What about George? Is he going to want to move to Erob? It isn't what one would call a hotbed of IPO activity."

Erob was no longer a place for me. It had nothing to offer. Wasn't that true?

"Family is everything, Nina," Olga said. Biggie's words, Olga's reminder—all telling me to at least think about moving back.

It was spring—the prettiest time, if there was one, in Erob. The pinks of azaleas, yellows of daffodils, and purples of hyacinths stroked the yards of Magnolia Avenue with the brush of an accomplished painter completing his most festive work of art.

The town, in all its perfect color, would gussy itself up for a very important visitor—one George Taber—if he would accompany me. I suddenly wanted him to see where I was from. I wanted him to meet the people in my life and see the house where I'd grown up. To see Biggie's house, the house that was now mine.

I wanted him to meet my family.

I didn't know what to expect from the visit. Nothing could have prepared me for what happened.

thirty-two

We arrived late on a Friday afternoon in May. Biggie's house looked the same as always. Well, almost.

I turned on the lamps in the den, in the living room, and on the desk in the breakfast room where the phone rested. Still, there was something missing. This house was missing its mistress; it was missing its soul. Her mighty personality had evaporated into thin air, and I couldn't figure out how to fill the void.

I asked George to put our luggage upstairs in my room, as if Biggie still occupied hers. He wanted to take a shower before we went to dinner at Mama's.

Then it hit me. There were no flowers. Springtime with no flowers in Biggie's house was a sin, so while George showered, I went out into the yard to get some azaleas and daffodils to turn her house—*my* house—back to the way it needed to be.

I was still putting together arrangements when George came down. The windows over the kitchen sink provided just enough light.

"It suits you," George said softly, pulling me into him.

"What does?"

"This. Arranging flowers, this sink, this kitchen."

I smelled him. "You smell better than the flowers," I said.

"Show me the azaleas," he said.

"Here. These are George Tabers."

"The biggest of all the flowers," he said in a manly voice, beating on his chest.

We laughed and kissed. Then we heard a hollow thud, quickly followed by some unfamiliar barking. We rounded the corner of the kitchen to the breezeway and there, shooting hoops, was Carter Gideon.

"Hey, neighbor," I shouted. "I'd like you to meet someone."

Carter put down the basketball and walked over. "George Taber, Carter Gideon."

The two men shook hands, and I saw Carter take in the fact that George was dressed for dinner and that his hair was slicked back. Carter was in an old pair of blue jeans and a worn golf shirt, still looking a little thin and ragged.

"I'm sorry about your wife," George offered. "And accident."

Carter's assessing eyes softened. "Thanks."

"I shoot a little. Nina didn't tell me she had a basketball court."

"Her brother and I keep it up for her."

"Gee, thanks, Carter."

"You know Win is planning on having a little something at her house for y'all tomorrow night."

"Goody, goody," I said.

George asked, "Is Win the friend who is . . ."

Before George could find the right word, Carter and I said in unison, "Yes."

We both figured Win was guilty of it, whatever it was.

"Who's this?" I asked, noticing a dog slipping through the gate and running toward us.

"That's Barney," Carter said. "Haines thought it might be a good idea for me to get a pet, and I found him at the pound a couple of weeks ago."

"Nice dog," George said.

I went to pet him, and he growled a little. "Maybe I should have named him Bit," Carter said, laughing.

"Very funny, Carter," I said.

"You want a beer?" Carter offered George.

"I don't have any beer," I intervened.

"Yes, you do," Carter countered. "Win and Agnes did some grocery shopping for you, and I told Win you needed beer. It's in the fridge."

"Is there anyone in this town who doesn't have a key to my house?"

"I heard they were giving them out at the courthouse," Carter said.

"I need to go up and get my sports coat if we're going to be on time for your mother's," George said, and vanished upstairs. Carter caught me looking at him.

"What? This is the nicest I've looked in months," he said, looking down at his grass-stained Levi's. "I shaved!"

I kicked off my heels, grabbed the ball from under Carter's arm, and ran to the hoop.

"That's a travel, Ref," Carter laughed. A laughter that sounded like it had been locked up for a while. And then it faded, as quickly as it had appeared, like a summer shower. I didn't realize how much I'd missed it. I wanted to be here when it came back.

We could have walked, so it didn't take us long to drive. "I'll say one thing about Erob. Everything is certainly close together," George said.

"Maybe too close," I said, reading his thoughts.

"People are friendly too," he said as people waved in passing. "Carter seems like a smart, nice guy."

"He is. He went to Duke and Duke Law. That good ole boy stuff is really an act. He's the best-read person I know. His father always quoted Shakespeare in his courtroom. Carter quotes all poets, Shakespeare, and the Bible."

"He's certainly protective of you." The way George said it sounded odd, unfamiliar, and his observation rattled me.

"Well, I grew up with him. He's like another brother, I guess."

Mama's house had never really been my house. In turn, I had never really belonged to her either.

Once inside, I introduced her to George, and I could tell she was quite taken with him, maybe even surprised that I had done so well.

"It's so nice to finally meet you, George. You're so tall. And handsome." She smiled at us, the smile she reserved for happy occasions. Then I smelled it. The smell that had held our kitchen hostage every Sunday. The smell that was our reward for going to both Sunday School and to church. The smells of pot roast, carrots, potatoes, and gravy.

"Goodness, I didn't think to ask, but you do eat meat, don't you, George?"

"Oh, yes," he said, but I noticed there was no "ma'am" at the end of it. I guess I didn't notice it in New York, but it stuck out here.

"For dessert I tried a new recipe I got from Win. It'll be in the next Junior League cookbook. She'll tell you all about that. I hope y'all like it. Pineapple casserole."

"You've got to realize something about the South, George. Everything, and I do mean everything—every fruit, every vegetable, every meat—gets relegated into casserole form sooner or later." I laughed, as did George. Mama, who by now was used to my negative but true comments about the South, just ignored me.

We heard the screen door slide open and then pop shut. It was my brother on his way home from the hospital.

"I just came to see what my sister brought home," Haines said, strolling into the kitchen.

"Haines!" I admonished him. Even Mama gave Haines that "behave" look, and right then I knew she liked George.

"Hi, I'm Haines Enloe, Bit's charming older brother. George, it's nice to meet you."

Both men shook hands.

"It's nice to meet you too, Haines," George said. Then I noticed it; inch for inch George and Haines were the same height. They had the same dark hair, and they were the same age, only Haines had green eyes to George's blue.

"Honey," my mother addressed her favorite child, "I wish you wouldn't work so hard. Are you taking care of yourself?"

"Ma, I'm a doctor," my brother answered. "Besides, I have to work for a living, not like my richy-toes sister here."

I rolled my eyes. Haines could poor mouth better than anyone I knew.

"Hey, George, don't you find Erob a friendly little hamlet?"

"Yes, people are friendly," George said, clearly amused by my brother.

"That's because you were in the local rag."

"Oh, Lord, who told Judi Ann?" I asked, shooting an accusatory look at Haines, who never kept a decent secret in his whole life. "Do you want to scare him off right away?" I thumbed through the paper to find the latest society column:

> *Mr. George Taber of New York and Goldman Sachs is visiting with Miss Nina Barnes Enloe, also of New York, her mother, Mrs. Benjamin Enloe, and her brother, Dr. Haines Enloe and his family.*

"I can't believe this stuff really goes on." I couldn't tell whether George was charmed or horrified.

Hurricane Haines was getting ready to leave. "Gotta get home to the wife and kid. You'll meet Addison tomorrow night at Win's. You're gonna love her."

Then he kissed Mama's cheek and left.

I saw it then—the ease, the familiarity. Haines belonged to her. His upbeat attitude chased her sadness away.

The meal that night was as good as expected, and Mama's pineapple casserole was a hit.

As George and I were leaving, Mama seemed to be both happy and relieved. "I'm so glad you came, George."

"Me too, Mrs. Enloe. Thank you for a wonderful dinner."

"Frances, please."

It seemed odd to hear my mother introduce herself as Frances.

"And George, beware of Bit and Haines's friends. You're in for an interesting time tomorrow night," Mama said knowingly.

"So I'm told," George said, and then we went home.

My nose was the first to notice. I breathed in the smell of the heat and butter dancing together down below and exhaled, a cleansing breath for all my yoga friends, and then breathed it in again. Once was not enough. Yeast rolls. Then, as though vying for attention, I smelled the greasy Saturday morning smell of bacon cooking. Agnes, bless her, was here.

"Who's here?" George asked, as if his own nose was nudging him awake.

"Agnes," I said, turning myself over to get up.

"Everyone does have a key, huh?" George asked sleepily.

"Seems like it," I said, and got out of bed. I pulled a pair of sweats on under the T-shirt I had slept in.

"What am I going to wear?" George asked, looking at my getup. "I only brought dress pants."

George, in his effort to impress my family, had brought his best clothes.

"They'll do fine. You get changed, and I'll go and check on Agnes."

I bounded into the kitchen to see her at the stove fixing a third plate.

"Morning, Agnes. It's great to see you. What are you doing here on a Saturday?" I hugged her fully.

"I'm your grandmother now. I wanted to meet George. I've been hearing all about him." Then Agnes motioned to the breezeway where Carter sat, reading a newspaper.

"Are we feeding him too?"

"Carter says you can afford it, that's why you have that big tab at the Red & White."

I shook my head. God only knew who else I was feeding.

"Just Elrod," Agnes answered, as if she knew my every thought. "Take this out to him, will you, Bit?" she said, handing me a steaming plate.

"So how did you and Slick sleep?" Carter asked, taking his plate and not even glancing up from his paper. Before I could answer, Agnes was standing there. Apparently she wanted to know the answer to that one too.

"Don't call him that, Carter."

"You two just behave. Miss Nina, God rest her soul." Agnes went back into the kitchen and almost bumped into George.

"You must be Agnes," he said.

"And you must be George. I hope you know how special that one is," she said, looking at me.

"I do. I also know Nina loves you," George answered, garnering an approving nod.

"Your breakfast will be ready in a second." She herded George out of her kitchen and onto the breezeway.

"Carter?" George seemed surprised to see Carter turn up again.

"I always shoot hoops on Saturday morning. Biggie said I could only shoot after nine o'clock. I'm trying to get Bit to lift that ban. What do you think, George? Can you convince her?"

"Let's go for it," George said. "I win, Nina decides; you win, she lifts the ban."

I watched the two men playfully go at it, dueling over the ball—dueling for bragging rights. To this day, that ban is still in place. Poor Carter. Can't catch a break.

Dinner at Win's on Saturday night was an event, to say the least. We were the last to arrive, except for Avery and Arush, who were always late. Habits, even bad ones, seem to grow comfortable with years and, in a way, are almost expected.

"George, this is Win and her husband, Rich."

"And that he is," chimed in my brother, who now was as rich as Rich.

"Behave," Addison admonished, and Carter laughed.

"And this poor, long-suffering woman is my sister-in-law, Addison," I said, pointing out Haines's wife.

"And you must be Avery," George said, taking her hand and covering it with both of his. It pleased me to see him holding it so carefully.

"And her husband, Arush," I finished the introduction.

"You are in for a treat tonight," Win began, getting everyone's attention. "Everything we're having tonight is from recipes in the new Junior League cookbook, and we have the wines to go with each course."

I laughed at vintage Win. "In other words, this is not a party for George and me at all. We're just here to be guinea pigs for your recipes."

But Win went on, unwavering. "We have duck confit salad for starters, lamb with greens and artichoke ragout, potato and leek sacks, and a flourless white chocolate cake for dessert."

"You really outdid yourself," Avery said.

"But Win, since when did the good folks of Erob start liking duck confit?" I asked, thinking that was terribly sophisticated for our town.

"You'll see," Win promised.

"My money is still on Agnes or anything from the *Half-Baked Harvest* cookbook."

"Do you follow her? I think she is amazing." Avery said.

"I didn't think you even owned a cookbook, Bit," Win countered.

"Wine anyone?" Rich interrupted, no doubt tired of the talk of cookbooks and exotic recipes.

We all picked Avery to deliver the toast. She had a way of recalling happy times in our lives and mixing that with one part blessing. All the while it reduced her to tears and got her all choked up. Avery, like Carter, was not only content with life but appreciated every minute of every day.

Carter said, "I've got my stopwatch going," as if he were timing her to see how long it took her to get emotional.

"I'll be good." She knew we'd all be disappointed if she didn't cry.

"Okay, let's see," she began. "We are so happy to have Nina back home again and to have George here with us. We hope you feel warm and welcome with us, George, because we want you to be." She smiled in his direction. "And we are glad this is a happy occasion for us to come together because we are so blessed to have each other, and Carter is . . . here." She met Carter's eyes and fumbled. I wondered if she were about to say "alive." I knew Haines still worried about him.

"And we are blessed that Win has cooked this wonderful meal for us." Only Avery could make *that* sound sincere.

Glasses clinked all around. The wine and food combinations were indeed outstanding, albeit a bit highfalutin for Erob, Alabama. I decided white chocolate cake didn't need flour after all. Everyone had George's attention, especially Win, who seemed totally smitten. I could tell they all liked him and probably wondered how I could get such a man. I was secretly glad Win had put on the display of finely culled sophistication to offset the homespun charm of the rest of the visit.

After dinner, we moved to the den for more conversation. That's when I noticed it. For the first time in our history together, I was not alone. I was part of a couple. I had someone. I would no longer be banished to Biggie's staircase or sent to the single daybed in Win's beach house, watching the rest of them.

But my happiness was short-lived. There, alone on the ottoman, sat Carter. The sadness moved back over my heart and ruined it for me. That was my role, fifth wheel. Carter didn't know how to handle this, not like me. After years of being alone, I was the one with all the experience.

I got up, leaving George's side, and went over and sat in the chair that was paired with the ottoman as if to shield Carter from the cold loneliness that was palpable. I patted his shoulder, but I knew it would take more than a noble gesture to stop that kind of draft.

Win's house had not one but two staircases—a formal one in the foyer for company and then the back staircase, the one that the kids used. Avery and I always used the back staircase.

So, while George talked about himself and Goldman Sachs, and Win took kudos for her cooking prowess, Avery and I snuck up the back staircase to Win's room for a private visit. It was as if the room was expecting us. The lamps were all on, and the pillows were fluffed on the love seat. A vase of azaleas sat perked atop a table, waiting for the conversation we would bring.

"Well," I said to Avery as we plopped down in our customary places. "What do you think?"

"He's terrific, Nina," Avery gushed. "And I can tell he really likes you."

"George is special. I like him a lot."

"Do you think you will get married?"

"Married?" I asked. We hadn't talked about it, but we certainly hadn't ruled it out either. "I don't know, Avery. It's gotten complicated. Damn Biggie. Damn her and damn her house." Even now I felt the gravitational pull. A spell. Why else had I still not put a "For Sale" sign out in the front yard? Because there was a big difference between saying *damn old house* and letting go of that damn old house forever.

"Nina, stop that. Don't speak ill of Biggie. She's gone now, and she loved you. What would she think about you fornicating with a Yankee in her house?"

Biggie's displeasure still could bring me joy.

"What would she hate worse, the fornicating part or the Yankee part?"

"The Yankee part for sure," I said.

"Maybe George will want to leave the rat race behind and move to Erob. You never know."

I wasn't sure I wanted to leave the rat race.

"Give him a chance," she urged.

"What do you mean?"

"You close down. You said he loves you."

"What are you talking about? I'm an open book of emotions." I hadn't really thought about my life without him either.

"Maybe. Are you going to go to church and show George off?"

"Hard no! We will probably just grab an early lunch at the Chicken Emporium and head to the airport," I said. "Let's change the subject. How are things with you and Arush?" I asked, putting Avery in the hot seat.

"Not great, but better. He's still not making a lot of money, but he's agreed to pay Courtney, the babysitter, two Saturdays a month for us to go out alone, and the kids love her. You know, Nina," Avery continued, "marriage is hard. But you know what it really is?" I let Avery talk, sensing this had been pent up, and she needed to get it out.

"No, Avery, what is it?" I asked.

"It's a collection of memories," she said, "that two people share, that bind them together more than any ceremony ever could. A collective history. I mean, who else but Arush can share the birth of my children? The moment Dhillon came out and we knew that we had a son, or when Kiran lost her first tooth, and the joys of our unexpected child, Ruhi? Who else could I share that with? For better or for worse, it's Arush. I want us to attend their milestones together, as a family. I know that's a choice, but when I see their faces, I know it's the right one for me. A lot of memories have happened in my house, humble as it is." She paused. "Do you remember the first time you and I met?"

"I do," I said. "It was at Biggie's house. When my daddy died." She nodded and patted my hand.

"Yes, you looked lost and sad and so little."

"God, Avery, I even remember what you were wearing. That smock top with the embroidery on it and those red shorts. You were the best friend I'd always wanted . . ."

"Lord, Nina," Avery said. "I don't remember what you were wearing, but I do remember that top. It was my favorite, and I think those shorts were always a little snug." We laughed.

"It's not some Hallmark movie, you know," Avery said, softer now. "It's about . . . about finding your other mitten. You know, when it's winter, and it's cold, and you're digging through that box of scarves and hats and gloves that's been up on the top shelf of the closet, and you wonder if it's there, and then you find that match."

An Averyism. One I wouldn't soon forget.

"You and George make a good couple," Avery finished.

"Well, he sure has Win eating out of his hand. But I think friendship is a collection of memories too." We hugged.

"He may have an easy time with the Queen Bee, but I feel for him with Haines and Carter," she observed.

"How's Carter doing, anyway?" I asked.

"Really"—she paused, as we went from shallow to serious in a heartbeat—"not so good, Nina. The puppy has been a big help, though."

"Yes. I've met Barney. He's cute. So are you saying that Carter is one of those men who just needs a wife?" I asked.

"I wouldn't say that necessarily. He could use someone to spice up his life."

"What do you mean? I sense insider information. Or you're just being plain passive-aggressive."

Avery quickly changed the subject. "Nina, go save George. Between Haines and Carter—"

"—And Win!" I quipped, as we folded our secrets up and

put them safely away in the most private compartments of our hearts.

I woke up early, and when I couldn't go back to sleep, I threw on my sweatpants and headed downstairs to sit on the breezeway.

I loved this time of day, although I rarely got up in time to enjoy it in the city. Spring had settled into Erob, and there was a newness in the air. A cleanliness. I breathed in deep and let it linger inside my body, connecting me to the day. It was quiet now. Uncluttered. Thoughts could scamper around like the squirrels in the grass, not having to meet expectations.

The sun was just beginning to climb into the sky, bringing light and warmth. The flowers were waking up, smells popping up from their leaves all around me. They could be savored now, before car fumes and noise beat them down. It was like so many springs and summers for me, here, far away from the sadness in Mama's house after Daddy died. This was where the happy smells always were. Here were *my* happy colors.

I remembered days when Win, Avery, and I sat on the breezeway having our tea parties, with the real tea that Win insisted upon and Agnes so graciously delivered. How we must have gotten on her last nerve with our childish demands for perfect parties. How we had rolled our eyes when the sound of that basketball intruded. How, we wondered, could Haines and Carter play together for hours on end? I'm sure they wondered the same about us.

Biggie's house had always given me shelter when I felt sad. When I needed to get away from Mama. Like a friend, it had provided a barrier from judging eyes. A safe harbor. Like Avery and even Win, this house was home.

But I had escaped, left for New York. It was what I'd always wanted. To be Nina Enloe, and not Bit. To live in New York City, not Erob.

And I was successful. Very. I was happy too. Wasn't I?

I had it all. I loved my work. I was on the verge of making junior partner. Making partner at any level had always been my dream. I loved Cy and Olga. And George. At thirty-one, I didn't want to be alone anymore. That's one thing to be said about Biggie. With H.B., she'd experienced the love of a good man. But if I moved back here, I would have to start my own practice and work my ass off. For what? Would I even have a practice? And my love life? Chances were, I wouldn't have George any longer, and I sure as hell had no prospects here. Unless you counted the twice-divorced Buck, who owned the tire store.

I didn't want to end up like those nameless old women in my Murray Hill neighborhood, bundled up in hats and scarves, their faces barely discernable, with their little sacks of groceries, tottering slowly home alone.

Bit, never make a decision out of fear. My daddy said that to me. He'd said it when I was afraid to ride my bike without training wheels, because I was scared I was going to fall on Biggie's driveway and hurt myself.

I made that promise. To him. But now, what was I afraid of? Dusting off that old, pesky memory. God knows, falling off a bike resulted in only superficial bruises. Moving back here, right next door to Carter, could cause a blow far more fatal and permanent. I thought about Erob and New York as vying suitors and had to laugh. It seemed an unlikely rivalry. Lopsided, amusing even, but scary?

"What are you doing?" George asked, coming through the breezeway door, wearing the crumpled-up pants he'd worn the day before. "It's so early."

Neatness, I decided, became him. In rumpled dress pants, he was just another messy investment banker.

"I'm waiting," I said, still lost in thought. The word drifted up into the air and hung between us.

"Waiting?" he asked. "Waiting for what?"

I sat a minute before coming up with an answer. "I'm waiting for Biggie's newspaper."

"Didn't you cancel that when she died?" George asked logically.

"That's right, I did," I said, getting up to make coffee, encapsulating that damn memory. One life barging in on the other once again, ruining a perfect moment. Would it really be so hard to live two lives, equally separate and fulfilling? Or if I had to choose, which one could I not live without? It was then that I knew I had my answer, as my heart had already dropped anchor.

That night, our last night in Erob, George and I ate at home by ourselves with food Agnes had fixed for us, despite her obvious disapproval of our sleeping arrangements.

I used some of Biggie's good china. It seemed celebratory, in a way, since we had survived the weekend of overt scrutiny. We lit candles and had wine and music.

"This house suits you, Nina," George told me for a second time, and I wondered if it suited him too.

"How so?"

"It's beautiful, but in a quiet sort of way. All these nice things stacked here and kind of scattered maybe, but if you look close enough, you'll see a collection of rare things. The house is weathered, but at the same time gracious and open and welcoming. Not pretentious or on display like it could be. It blends. It could be showy, but that's not in its nature. It has 'good bones,' as they say."

I wondered if he was still talking about the house.

"And now that I've come here, I've decided that the name Bit suits you too," he said as if putting a punctuation mark on something.

"I thought you liked Nina."

He smiled. The smile you see in a dream that gets further away before fading and then eventually disappearing into the horizon.

"Nina," George began, trying to find words that were as difficult for him to say as they would be for me to hear. "I love you. But what am I going to do? Get a job as a loan officer at the Citizens Bank on Main? Come home at five o'clock every night and wait for you? Join the Erob Rotary Club?"

I had to laugh. Erob didn't even have a Rotary Club.

"I don't have to move back," I said heavily, as unexpected tears welled up in my eyes and started to spill over. "In fact, I don't even have to keep the house. I can call a realtor and have a sign up in the front yard next week."

Then I said it without any thought or restraint. "But if I did move home, we could still see each other. I could come up, and you could come down. On weekends. Long distance, with a twist. Celebrities do it all the time."

But it was too late. I had said the word: *Home*.

"I don't want that kind of a half-hearted relationship. Do you, Nina?" George asked.

"Maybe."

I got up and took our plates into the kitchen. Through the window and across the yard, I saw Carter's upstairs lights turn on.

I thought about them. Avery, Win, Haines, and Carter. Did I really want to continue a half-hearted relationship with them too? Did I want to have a half-hearted relationship with their children?

They represented the best part of me. They knew me. They understood me, accepted me, and loved me, even with all the crap I brought into this town each time I visited.

I was quiet in this realization when I came out of the kitchen, only to discover that George had disappeared. I hadn't thought about him once during this equation.

I went to the bottom of the stairs and heard the floor creak with activity. I walked up to find George beginning to pack. Did I want to find him like this every Sunday night, packing to fly back to his life in New York?

I tried to make deciding go away. I tried to make what had been said disappear.

"Well, I certainly don't have to make any decisions tonight," I said.

He, in turn, waited a long time to say anything, our love comforting us through the silence, our love making it harder to find the right words to say. "Nina," he began, folding a shirt. "You do have a decision to make." He hugged me, his chin resting on top of my head. The blue of his sweater scratching my cheek, the scent of his Hermes cologne filling my nose.

Back in New York we didn't speak of George's visit to Erob. Nor did we speak of "For Sale" signs.

Two weeks later, he and I broke up in a most peculiar way. He asked me to marry him. He was just too late. Why hadn't we talked about this before now? Why hadn't we talked of marriage at all? Instead, he just blurted out, "Nina, let's get married."

"What? George, are you serious?" I asked, willing to accept a somewhat convincing answer.

"I don't want you to leave," he said simply.

"Who's to say I'm moving back to Erob?"

"C'mon. You're in denial."

We were silent. Unexpected tears burned in my throat.

"This is killing me." He got up and started gathering his clothes before getting dressed.

"What are you doing?"

He sat back down on the bed. He slumped over and put his head between his hands. I reached over to hug him.

"George?"

"Your life's waiting for you, Bit."

That was the first time he called me Bit. And the last.

I watched him go, fade, and disappear. Another man I loved, leaving.

Despite the breakup, it took another six months for my heart to arm-wrestle with my head and let go of my dream of making partner. I put on a smile through my lingering misgivings, unsure I would ever find a job I liked as much as this one. I would move back to Erob after Thanksgiving. I figured that the flurry of Christmas shopping and cards and decorating that followed would take my mind off the life in New York I was leaving behind.

The office threw me a goodbye party. I watched the eager associates, who were bidding for my cubicle, trying to one-up each other for attention from the managing partners. It was nice to let go of that pressure, and I was proud of the "big shoes to fill" reputation I was leaving at the firm. Funny, they could take my office, but they could never take Cy and Olga away from me.

Olga came to the office toward the end of the party. What the office didn't know was that we were going to have dinner together afterward, and our little trio was more my style—familial and comfortable.

"This must tear you out of the frame," I said to Cy, "to come late and miss the early-bird special." He smiled.

"I would pay full price anytime to have dinner with my two favorite girls," Cy said, patting Olga's hand and then mine.

I felt pressure behind my eyes and knew tears weren't far behind.

"I have lost good lawyers to babies, other firms, and in-house counsels, but I have never lost one to a state and a city without an airport. I must be losing *my* touch."

"You'll never get rid of me, Cy," I said.

"You promise?"

"Promise."

"Well, this isn't from the office, but from Olga and me. We love you."

"I love you too," I said, knowing Wai Wong and this old man and his beautiful wife were the best things I was leaving from my life in the city.

I opened the turquoise box with white ribbon. It held a key and a sterling silver necklace with a dangling heart.

"The key is the key to our house if you ever need us." He paused. "And the heart may be dangling from the necklace, but it stays connected to the key." Then his eyes welled up.

"Your Jewish parents love you very much," Olga said, because Cy couldn't. "And you can always come back."

I wanted what they had together. A history. Memories. Jokes. Bonded by both happy and sad times.

thirty-three

Maybe Thomas Wolfe had a point when he said, "You can't go home again."

On my first day back in Erob, I couldn't get any fresh arugula, and the beef people at the Winn-Dixie had never heard of tofu. Ricky Lee Traylor back in the meat department said he could try and get it for me, but first he needed me to spell it for him.

Carter's law office was vacant now that he was a judge, so I rented it from him for my office. The same day I got my first client: the bank. Being right next door helped. That and knowing the bank's owners. I had my house, I had an office, and I had my first client. I vowed to be patient and sort out the rest of my life one day at a time.

On my first night back in Erob, I went to bed with the smell of Agnes's famous yeast rolls, the sound of the thud of a basketball, and the dueling voices swirling in my head that both bossed me around and comforted me. I knew things would be different; I just wasn't sure if I was ready.

I gave in and let Carter help me put up a Christmas tree. It's a good thing we don't know what the future holds, or we'd just stand frozen in place. A year ago, I never would have believed that so much would have changed; that I would live in Erob, the mistress of Biggie's domain. How much else was I willing to give her?

There was no debate over where to put the tree. Even if I wanted to do things differently, according to Carter, it was

S.O.P.—Standard Operating Procedure—meaning the front bay window where Biggie had always placed it. His heart seemed lighter. Almost jolly. In keeping with the season, I put on some Christmas music and handed him lights and ornaments. I even donned a Santa hat, which made him laugh. It made me happy that I could still do that.

Agnes was leaving as Carter finished stringing the lights.

"There's a pot roast and some vegetables on the stove for supper."

"Thanks, Agnes," I said, grateful for her help.

"Let's open some wine first," Carter said. He seemed to be moving around easier.

Carter and I ate on trays. It was cozy. It was nice.

"I never put up a Christmas tree in New York," I admitted, feeling nostalgic.

"Seriously?" Carter asked.

"Seriously."

"So, how do things stand between you and Slick?" he asked.

"George," I corrected one more time. I paused before answering. In truth, George was a good man, and he had been good to me. Good for me. And even though we'd been broken up for months, I still missed him. I knew I had a chance of being with him right now if I'd stayed in New York. But an "if only" can ruin your life just as surely as its sister "regret" can. Since I'd decided to move back to Erob, "if only" had crept into my sentences so many times. It sounded like Avery and me singing Taylor Swift over and over. Lyrics not required.

George Taber deserved to be judged in full, not just by his clumsy marriage proposal. George had given me confidence in myself. While Avery had always allowed me to be me, George was a sophisticated stranger who had found my quirkiness charming.

What he did remained with me, and I would appreciate George for that forever.

"George and I have decided that a long-distance romance won't work very well for us," I said slowly.

"I'm sorry."

I looked at him and realized how close we were sitting. I jumped up.

"How about some eggnog?" I needed something harder than wine. I handed Carter a Christmas glass of eggnog.

"This is tasty. Does this have any nog in it?" He smiled. "This definitely isn't bourbon."

"Oh nooooooo. Brandy. I've sworn off that devil's brew."

"You haven't said anything about Win's upcoming Christmas party," he said, changing the subject into more comfortable territory. "Aren't you glad you moved back home now?" He grinned. I grinned back and changed the subject once more.

"So, I'm thinking about doing some renovations around here."

"Like what?"

"Nothing major." Taking a gulp of holiday cheer, I said, "Maybe sprucing Biggie's room up and moving into her bedroom, since it's bigger and connects to its own bathroom. Knocking out a wall or two to enlarge the closets. Update the bathrooms." I paused. I waited for his opinion. I had already hired a contractor to look at it and draw up plans. I was amazed and proud that Biggie's house, now my house, could accommodate a new owner so easily without changing the true character of our house. "Well?" I asked. I was suddenly feeling strangely anxious. "What do you think?"

Carter exhaled as if he had been holding his breath for a long time. He nodded. "I thought you said 'nothing major.' I guess you decided to tap into Biggie's money." He smiled. "It sounds good. I think Biggie would approve. This really is a great house."

"I have an early Christmas present for you," I said, looking directly at Carter.

"I don't see any presents under the tree."

"It's not that kind of present." I still hadn't broken our gaze. I needed to get this right. For Carter. For me. For us. "I'm sorry, Carter," I said as unexpected tears filled my eyes.

"So how far back does this apology go?"

"To the beginning."

Where memories begin, I thought. "Seeing you near death, well . . . and the codicil and hearing you tell me to get out of your hospital room . . ."

"What do you mean?"

"I rushed home to see you and you told me to get out. I was afraid that it would be the last thing you ever said to me." This moment was *too* heavy. I finished my eggnog in one big gulp.

We were silent for a while. After a time, Carter spoke.

"Go easy, girl. You're gonna have to swear off brandy too. You do remember I was high on painkillers. I don't remember you even being in my room that day." Carter got up and leaned down and kissed my forehead. I followed him into the kitchen.

He walked to the door and turned around. "Thank you, Bit." He opened the door and left me. Tears welled up in my eyes again.

As I went to bed, I was grateful. When we offer someone our forgiveness, we are the ones who truly receive the gift.

This is how it works in a small town. I walked into the Peoples Bank of Erob. I walked straight to Ramona Walker's office, stopping briefly to speak to Ruby, the teller who had been there since I was a little girl, and sat down.

"I want to close all of the accounts. The ones in both my name and Biggie's," I said to Ramona, "and I want to open up a savings account in just my name."

Ramona proceeded to pull out a form that I signed, and then she transferred $275,489. Just like that. On a random Tuesday, with no driver's license on me or death certificate or account number in hand. And wearing dirty tennis shoes. Can you imagine trying to move even seventy-five cents in New York City with only a smile and some lighthearted banter?

"Do you know your mom still comes over?" I asked.

Ramona smiled. "You know Mama," she said. Tantamount to *yes*. In the South, why use one word when you can use three? Ironically, I had drawn up divorce papers for Agnes's latest no-count husband.

My first full week as Erob's first woman lawyer was less than intellectually compelling. After I'd reviewed my biggest client's (the bank) documents, I did a title search for Martha Crawford, which Stacy Abernathy at the courthouse practically did *for* me. So, I threw in drawing up Martha's will for no extra charge. My hourly fee in New York had been whittled down to whatever the client could pay. For Martha, because she was such an excellent baker, fresh sourdough bread seemed a fair price, especially since she was going through such a hard time and didn't have any money. I also appeared in Carter's courtroom. In a small town, there's no such word as "recusal." My client, Elrod, was charged with disorderly conduct and public drunkenness. We pleaded guilty, remorsefully, and Judge Gideon sentenced Elrod to a few days in jail in lieu of a fine, which he didn't have the money to pay. So much for getting my painting done.

All that happened on a Monday. After my bank visit, Tuesday morning was spent buying magazines for the waiting room, and Tuesday afternoon was spent reading the magazines, cover to cover. I was beginning to think I had made a huge mistake.

Wednesday, I called Wai. She really didn't have time for me. She had gotten in a new IPO from Cy, but she did stay on the phone long enough to tell me the hot gossip about Charles Burns getting caught cheating on his wife with another associate. Charles was asked to resign. I would have given anything to have seen that pompous ass pack up his desk. I would have surely made partner with him gone.

When Wai and I got off the phone, I realized I would never do an IPO again. I would never pull another all-nighter, or work past 5:00 p.m. What the hell am I supposed to do between 5:00 and midnight? Watch *Wheel of Fortune*? I hated that show. I missed my noon lattes and caffeinated afternoons, adrenaline and deal closures. Damn you, Biggie, how could you rob me of sleep deprivation in exchange for a personal life? I took Wednesday afternoon off. It wasn't a big deal. All the banks closed on Wednesday afternoons, and some businesses too. I guess I could subscribe to Netflix and binge the shows I missed while I was being a productive member of society.

I decided to do the one thing I enjoyed most. I went to see Avery. She and Ruhi were playing in the den. I went to the refrigerator and poured myself a glass of iced tea.

"We're in here," Avery said, and I plopped myself on the floor.

"Hey, Aunt Bit, I'm Cinderella," Ruru said to me. Avery may call me Nina, but her children, influenced by Haines and Win, called me Bit.

"Did you take off work early?" Avery asked.

"As if I have work to take off from," I began. "Remind me again why I moved back, and is it too early to start drinking?"

"Because your family and your friends are here, and I need you to help raise these children. And I need someone to brag on my tea. And my Sea Breezes."

"I'll do that!"

"Besides, God has a plan for you," Avery said.

"So I've heard, but I'm starting to wonder if this is His idea of a cruel, sick joke."

"You'll see," Avery said positively.

"Keep reminding me, okay?" I asked, still not sure at all. "So, what are you wearing to Win's Christmas party?"

"My usual: black skirt and a Christmas sweater," Avery said. "Don't even tell me what you're wearing."

"Why?" I asked.

"Because you'll probably wear some sophisticated something," Avery said, and laughed. "With a designer label."

"New York really helped me in that department, I'll give it that."

"You look great," she said.

"I'm not going to change my haircut or my makeup or give away my designer clothes just because I'm back in Erob."

"You certainly look better than you ever have."

"You think? Maybe I should think about buying some tires from ole Buck."

"Don't you dare!" Avery admonished. "If I have to see his crack peeking out from his jeans one more time . . ."

"How's Arush?" I asked, escaping that mental image.

Avery sighed. "His business has done really well since he opened his online store. People here in Erob, well, you know, they still want to touch and feel things and know what they're getting, but the rest of the country? It's all online. And he and I? We just keep rocking on." I could see pride mixed with sadness on her face.

Ruhi and Avery walked me to my new car, an old Volvo sedan in mint condition. The sun was going down but was still out just enough to have it streaming through the tree limbs and glistening down in long gold-and-dust-filled tendrils. I picked up Ruru and hugged her tight.

"Look, Ruru," I began. "See those long rays of sun stretching down to the ground?"

She nodded as we all focused on the veins of light.

"Those are God's fingers, and they're reaching down from heaven to always protect you."

Ruru smiled as Avery said, "You remember."

"Of course," I said. "I remember all the Averyisms." I turned to go, suddenly feeling better about everything.

Agnes was waiting on me. "She's *your* friend," she said.

"What do you mean?" I asked, walking into the kitchen. I couldn't believe what I saw. Win was in the middle of my kitchen with every cabinet door open, rearranging everything.

"Why did you let her in?" I asked Agnes. She shrugged and then asked, "How am I going to find anything?"

"Agnes," Win said, turning, "you are not going to believe how efficient your life is going to be from now on."

"I wasn't aware it wasn't," Agnes said. She wasn't afraid of any of us, least of all Win.

"I can't tell you how long I've been waiting to get my hands on these cabinets," Win said with glee. But it troubled me, as I had vivid memories of the last time I saw her do this.

I walked closer to her and whispered, "Are you pregnant?"

"No, silly. But listen up. Agnes, come over here and I'll show you what I've done." Win got up, ready to make her presentation. "You too, Little Bit. You'll need to know this."

"All I need to know is where my coffee and coffee cups are."

"Y'all are just going to love this," Win exclaimed, highly pleased with herself.

"Thirty years," Agnes said as she tried to take it all in, surely hating this new arrangement as much as I did. "Thirty years." Some things bear repeating.

"Win, you're not going in my underwear drawers next, are you?" I asked.

"She should have started up there rather than in the kitchen," Agnes said. "I'm telling you . . ."

"I would start by throwing out all those wretched T-shirts you sleep in," Win said.

"Those T-shirts all have sentimental value," I began. "I love the one you brought me from San Francisco and, of course, all my beloved UNC ones. Do *not* go near those drawers. I mean it, Win." And I did, and she knew it.

"I just wish you had some pretty nightgowns."

"What for? In case George comes back? I have a news flash for you. He didn't want to live in Podunkville, and at this moment, neither do I!" I grabbed a bottle of wine and a glass, stormed upstairs, and slammed my bedroom door.

Too bad I didn't get the complete tour, because in the morning I couldn't find where Win had put the coffee in my new, efficient kitchen. I ended up going to the Coffee Emporium, vowing to change the locks on all the doors and maybe even install an alarm system, complete with a motion detector, just to keep Win away.

"In the freezer," Win began logically, meeting me at home the next day after work. "I saw on Pinterest that the freezer keeps coffee fresher."

"So, the coffee is *not* placed near the cups. Is that what you're saying? That's not very efficient," I was giving her the hard time she deserved. "You want a glass of wine? I want a glass of wine. But let's see, where are those wineglasses?" I asked, throwing up my hands and feigning confusion.

"They are all up on the top shelf, of course."

"Very efficient for someone who is five-foot-one, Win," I said.

"Well, that was Agnes's idea. To put the wineglasses on the top shelf."

"I see. More like Agnes's way of trying to curb alcohol consumption."

"That's what kitchen ladders are for," she said, pulling a small step stool out like a magician from behind the pantry door. Win was nothing if not enterprising.

I got two wineglasses down and had Win do the honors of opening the bottle.

"To being together again," she said, raising her glass in a toast.

"How about we drink to healthy boundaries, if you know what one is," I said. She'd typed up a list of commonly used items and where they'd been placed. When she was finished, much as I hated to admit it, the kitchen was, in general, more efficient, and Win's "cheat sheet" was a stroke of genius.

We went and sat in the living room with the Christmas tree, and I made a fire.

"When did you learn to make fires?"

"There's a lot you don't know about me, Win."

"I see. Well, then, how about this? I really can't believe I'm asking you, but you have lived in New York and all . . ." Win's version of a compliment. "Do you think you could help me pick out an outfit that is sophisticated and will look good on me? One that will look good on TV?"

"So, you think I have sophisticated taste now?" I asked, wanting to hear Win say it again.

"Yes" was all I got, and in my own desperate attempt to wrangle a compliment out of her, I had overlooked Win's comment. "Wait. What do you mean, an outfit 'that will look good on TV'?"

"I've been nominated for the Woman Entrepreneur of the Year for the tri-county region. They want me to be on the *Patsy and Doug Show*," Win said calmly, but her excitement betrayed her until she almost squealed.

"You mean that cable show that our moms used to watch? Are those people still alive?"

"Well, can you help me shop? We can go to Atlanta and check out Neiman's and Saks, and we can have lunch at the Zodiac Room," she said, adding, "to prepare me for stardom."

I was getting a vision of it now. Us in our good clothes, high heels, and, of course, dining on chicken walnut salad with shopping bags gathered around our feet. And Win still going strong.

"I'll have to check my calendar."

"Avery told me you're not that busy." Win sighed. "Well, when will you be joining Erob's Junior League? That way you can be a part of all of this all the time."

"Hell, no," I said emphatically. Why would I belong to a club to hear Win drone on and on when she droned on and on in my kitchen every day?

"Avery likes it," Win said, but I still refused.

"Avery likes anything you do," I said. "Don't start with me, Win."

And for the second night in a row, I locked myself away in my bedroom and wondered if I would ever have privacy in my own house and why I'd ever come back here.

thirty-four

Win had more than mastered the art of cooking; at her annual Christmas get-together, it was entertainment on steroids. A highlight was her homemade eggnog, or "mocha-nog"—served up in her silver punch bowl alongside accompanying silver punch cups. With plenty of brandy.

She dished it up and made a toast.

"To Patsy and Doug!" she said, as she and Rich clinked their cups together.

I watched the ease Win had with Rich and the ease she had with my brother and Addison. And Carter. It would be hard for a stranger to really tell who belonged with whom. It was as if the group was a single entity.

As everyone was putting the food on the buffet table, I felt a little like that stranger, or maybe more like an interested observer. Especially without George. They had done this every year for years, and usually without me. Just before the meal, I followed Win into the kitchen as she finished lighting the candelabras and was about to turn the kitchen overhead light off.

"Win, I'm impressed. Very Edith Wharton," I said. She smiled, and then something caught my eye on her desk. I went over for a closer look. It looked like a rainbow on paper—lines in pink, green, orange, and blue. All neon colors and then a little yellow mixed in.

"What's all of this?" I asked, holding the calendar up for Win to explain.

"That's my new calendar. The children have their own colors, and Rich and I have ours. Winnie's activities are pink, Baxter's activities are in green. He's by far the busiest." I could hear the pride in her voice.

I flipped the pages, truly amazed. "You mean to tell me your children have this many activities?" Every day was like a color splash of "oh the places to go" and "fun to be had," complete with color-coordinated incentives and rewards for good behavior.

"Lord, these children are busier than I am," I said, looking at dance rehearsals, playdates, and Bible school. They were definitely busier than Win and I were when we were children. All we ever did was have tea parties. "I was going to ask you to help decorate my upstairs, but it looks like you're too busy for one more thing."

"Of course I'll help you, Bit. Looking at swatches is fun."

"I'm glad you think so."

It was time for dinner, and it began with another one of Avery's teary toasts.

"All is right with the world. Nina is finally home, and we are so happy. She's where she belongs and where she is loved. And we are glad"—Avery paused as the tears filled up each eye—"that Carter is doing so much better." She sat down abruptly, and Carter reached over for a hug. I felt my own eyes filling up as I watched the two of them together. "Friends and family are everything," she finished, and after a moment, I added, "I wish you would toast to a prosperous law practice, because all I've done is read all the magazines in my waiting room."

"Here, here," they all said, and glasses clinked again.

I smiled, but in truth, I had hoped that my being Erob's first "lady attorney"—as Martha Crawford referred to me—wouldn't be this hard.

Win had prepared grilled lamb chops, asparagus and capers, Yukon gold potatoes, and portabella mushrooms au gratin. After a dessert of a delicious hot cranberry bread pudding with a white sauce, Avery and I escaped up the back stairs and settled into our usual positions in Win's bedroom.

"Hey, do you think we can stand her upcoming brush with fame?" I asked, referring to Win's much-anticipated TV gig.

"I can handle it," Avery answered. "But can you?"

We walked back down to the kitchen just as Rich and Haines started drying the first of the Lenox holiday dishes that Carter had washed. Arush was keeping them company.

"Perfect timing," Haines said. "Bit always did have a knack for knowing how to get out of doing the dishes."

"You got that right," I said.

The night ended with laughter brought on by familiarity. Everyone hugged and kissed, although we would probably see each other the next day. Win, I knew, would come by tomorrow for a play-by-play recap of the evening.

As Carter and I rode home together, I mentioned my fascinating discovery of Win's color-coded life. "Have you ever seen it?" I asked him, still oddly amazed by such organization. It explained a lot, actually.

"Not only have I seen it," he said, "I've been in it."

"What color were you?"

"Yellow." I remembered seeing the yellow on the calendar. "Right after Jenny left, Win got ahold of my court schedule. On days I had early court, she would call me to make sure I was up. Most mornings she'd come over and have coffee with me." Typical

Win, getting into everyone's business, but taking Carter's court schedule? That took gall.

"Didn't that just drive you crazy?" I asked, knowing it would me, but Carter, like Avery, was too nice and could handle Win's interference.

"Well, sometimes, Bit, it was nice to hear a woman's voice in the morning, you know?" He paused. "Even Win's."

I noticed it when Carter walked me to the door. I opened the door and turned on the lights. He grimaced. I grabbed him by the forearm.

"Are you okay? Does it still hurt you sometimes?"

"Why, Bit Enloe, I never took you for the kind of person who actually cared."

"Well, I never took you for the kind of friend that would just up and die on me," I responded, turning on lights. This time, he took my arm.

"I know all your secrets. How every day you called either Win, Avery, or Haines to check on me. I don't need you hovering over me." He went to my refrigerator and grabbed a beer.

"Do I need to call Haines?" I asked, studying him as he closed the refrigerator.

"Hell and *no*. He has been the worst of all."

"Aw, c'mon! You're his best friend. Cut him some slack. He knows what your body has been through. Maybe we should just check with him." I started grabbing my phone. He stopped me.

"Don't. My doctor said it's just back spasms. I just need to do some stretching. But I appreciate your concern." He laughed. "You didn't really have any of it right after Biggie died."

"I worry."

His expression softened. "I know. I'll just take the beer to go." I watched him leave. Watched his lights turn on at his house and then turn off finally. I wrestled with my own feelings, to call my brother or to honor my friend. I turned out the lights without calling my brother.

I was still at the office late on Christmas Eve. That, in and of itself, was a bit of a Christmas miracle. I heard a rap on my door. I was expecting Avery and Win later for our gift exchange when I'd heard the knocking.

"Merry Christmas!" Now you wouldn't exactly hear *that* on the streets of New York City. It was Martha Crawford. She was bearing gifts.

"Martha, did we have an appointment? Merry Christmas to you too!"

"Aren't you the silly one. This is your Christmas present. Some of my sourdough rolls. I'm guessing you're going to have your family over to Ms. Nina's—I mean *your* house—for Christmas lunch, and I thought you could use them." She smiled and sat down.

I was perplexed. In all my years in New York City, no one had ever given me homemade goodies.

"Martha, let me pay for the rolls."

"Bit, I'm not taking your money." She was on the verge of being insulted. "Just wanted to remember you and your kindness at Christmas. Surely you remember what small town life is like. It's in your blood. Your DNA."

Maybe I had forgotten. Last Christmas I ordered Chinese takeout. "Merry Christmas. Thank you for the homemade sourdough and cinnamon bread. You'll make my family happy campers." That was the thing about the good people of Erob. If they wanted to show their gratitude, there was no stopping them.

Win and Avery came together for our gift exchange and some Christmas cheer. They had pooled resources and given me a Yeti thermos and a membership to the yoga and Pilates studio. It was owned by Trae, Jimmy's boyfriend, whom we credit for the "modernization of Erob"—with their Coffee Bean Emporium (now complete with wine) and yoga establishment. We went through two bottles of wine, exchanging more laughter than gifts. I don't remember a time when we'd been so relaxed with each other.

I gave Avery a new Christmas sweater, and for Win, labels for her baking enterprise that said "Whisked by Win" in green cursive behind magnolias. Win squealed. Avery gave Win pottery. I loved Avery to pieces, but her gift-giving left room for improvement. Win looked up, smiled, and said, "I don't have this size!" I was always amazed by Win's ability to lie behind a compliment.

If it weren't for the hammering upstairs, coupled by the occasional rumble of a ladder being dragged across the floor, the ambiance would have been truly festive. "When is it going to get finished?" Avery asked, looking up to the ceiling.

"Well, I decided to hire that contractor, Craig Willingham, to come in and knock a few walls down to make the bedroom, bathroom, and closet areas larger. And add new cabinets in all the bathrooms and closets. It's going to take a little longer than originally planned," I explained.

"Are you sure you're not going to just knock Biggie's entire house down for revenge?" Win asked, laughing at her idea.

"You wouldn't be the first person to think that."

"Craig is supposed to be really cute," Avery chimed in.

"And single," Win added.

"He is on both counts. He's spent so much time in my bedroom, what's a little overnighter?" I winked, clearly feeling no pain.

"You're bad," Avery sighed.

"He's expensive," Win continued, bringing an end to our frivolity. "By the way, Bit, have you paid Elrod yet?"

"Only half so far. He'll get the rest when he finishes, but when he leaves today, he isn't getting so much as a 'Season's Greetings' from me, lest he spend it on whiskey."

"Now if that wasn't a Biggie comment, I don't know what is," Win snickered.

All three of us started laughing and giggling until Elrod himself came down to see what all the commotion was about. He took one look at us and grabbed the third bottle of wine off the coffee table, went into the kitchen, and poured the remainder down the sink drain.

"Hey, Elrod, that's a little bit like the pot calling the kettle black, don't you think?" I called out.

"Win, give me your keys," Elrod said. "I'll drive you and Avery home."

Elrod, sober as a judge, driving Win and Avery home. A Christmas miracle indeed.

I woke, like the man in Clement C. Moore's poem, to the sound of "such a clatter" that I did indeed rise from my bed to see what was the matter. I ran downstairs in nothing but my special Christmas "Bah Humbug" T-shirt, and standing there in the kitchen was somebody better than St. Nick himself. Agnes, dressed in festive attire—bright red pants and a sparkly Christmas sweater—was wrestling with a very large turkey.

"Agnes, what are you doing?"

"I got to worrying about you managing the big Christmas turkey, so I just stopped in to help. It won't take me but half a jiffy. Besides, it needs to go in right now to be ready for lunch." She went to her task, and soon the bird was in the oven.

"You want to join me for a cup of coffee?" I offered, seeing she had also started a pot brewing.

"Well, that is our Christmas tradition. Nina and I would have coffee together on Christmas morning." I realized Agnes had her own memories, and they brought her here. I rarely heard Agnes call my grandmother Nina.

"Just a minute," Agnes said. She took her cell phone out of her back pocket and dialed a number. "Carter, you need to come over here around noon and take this bird out of the oven."

"You know, Agnes, I can get a turkey out of the oven myself."

"It will be nice for Carter to get out of that house." It was then that I recognized Agnes's own compassionate brand of manipulation. I poured us each a cup of coffee.

"Oh, I almost forgot." I went over to the desk and picked up two envelopes. I held them out to her.

"You've already given me my presents," Agnes protested, putting her hands up. I had given her some money and the cookbook *Half-Baked Harvest*.

In truth, when I first moved back to Erob, I wanted to eat foods that I enjoyed in New York. Agnes was game to experiment. We nudged butter to the background and added olive oil to our repertoire. We roasted vegetables like kale, sunchokes, and Brussels sprouts. Haines and Carter made fun of me, but they came around when Win started serving them. Agnes thought she had won the lottery when I introduced her to balsamic vinegar. I realized that cooking, like Erob itself, could be modernized.

"This isn't really from me. It's from Biggie," I lied. She looked at the official document.

"What is it?"

"Biggie never got around to doing these for you those last couple of years," I said, opening the larger envelope and unfolding the papers. "It's the Social Security you've earned. I've updated the forms and made the payments, and when you want, you can even retire."

"I could retire, and you could hire Win! She knows her way around this kitchen, seeing that she organized it."

"Hard pass, Agnes."

"Thanks, Bit." She laughed so it would cover up her emotion. She and Biggie had that in common.

I discovered that generosity, like forgiveness, means more to the giver than the receiver.

I went upstairs and showered. I looked past my yoga pants and pulled out a skirt that I'd gotten on sale at Bergdorf's. My "skirt of many colors," I called it. Blue, citron, orange, gold, and black, with an embroidered overlay. I threw on a black biker jacket and pulled my hair into a ponytail.

Memory, it seems, has a mind of its own. Whether it was the house's memory or mine, it was hard to know which took over. I set the table, placed the Spode Christmas dishes out, and arranged some flowers—unlike Biggie's elaborate arrangements, just a few camellias and red berries would have to do.

"Are you happy now, Biggie?" I asked out loud, as if she were standing on the threshold of the dining room, beaming. I smiled, and for the first time, I felt a sense of warmth toward my grandmother, along with something a little scary. Kinship. We both loved this place. "I got it right, Biggie," I said to the house.

But of course, Biggie would be Biggie. Most likely spirits don't change their true personalities in the afterlife.

"Okay," I said. "I'll put out the salt cellars and spoons," as if The Big One herself had ordered me to do so. "Don't press your luck. You know Little Addie will have a field day with them." There would be salt all over the place.

As I walked downstairs, I heard the oven door open and then close. I looked at my watch. It was noon.

"Ho, ho, ho, Carter!" I said as I entered the kitchen.

He was putting the remaining casseroles in the oven. He was pensive, thoughtful. It had been some time, but after all, this was the first Christmas without Jenny. That's where he and I differed. Death, or separation, had almost helped my relationship with Biggie. I missed her at times like these, but routine and tradition were comforting. I'd just had a reasonable conversation with a chair about salt cellars. It felt real, and my grief was eased by talking to her.

"You don't have to stay if you don't want to."

I think he must have been ashamed. I had caught him with his guard down.

"I didn't want to burn myself."

As he was taking his presents to the living room, we met each other's gaze, and for a moment, neither of us said anything.

"That's how you used to wear your hair."

I looked at Carter, in his freshly pressed button-down shirt and khakis, though they were still baggy.

"You clean up nice, Gideon. Would you like a mimosa?"

He followed me into the kitchen to make the drinks. When we came back through the dining room, Carter noticed the four place cards left on the sideboard. I knew his eyes had rested on Jenny's.

"Biggie used to say, 'if we keep their place cards, it's like they're still with us.' See, I still have Biggie's!"

He fingered Jenny's a moment more and then said, "Maybe this year we can get rid of that one."

I found myself reluctant to do so and tucked it away out of sight instead.

We heard a ring at the back door. It was Mama, and her hands were full. She was carrying ambrosia—nectar of the gods. In the other arm she had made her delicious cranberry relish, which would make even the driest of birds tasty.

Mama had also brought in a container of toasted pecans. I'm sure she got the nuts from Jimmy's. Aside from being Erob's hipster proprietor, Jimmy also sold fresh-shelled pecans during the holidays, and during the summer months, homegrown tomatoes and fresh Silver Queen corn. We ate dinner efficiently and moved on to dessert.

My mother sliced the cake and filled Biggie's good sherbets with ambrosia.

I went back into the living room with coffee. I noticed both Carter and Haines had almost wolfed their dessert down without waiting for it to brew.

"That's a crime."

"Some of us like sleep more than we like caffeine," Haines replied. "Hey, I heard you're Jimmy's best customer, buying those overpriced lattes with fake milk."

"I prefer fancy coffee to fancy cars." Haines had just bought himself a little Christmas "toy"—a new green Jaguar.

"Lucky for you guys, I prefer both," Carter said. They could talk about Alabama football, Duke basketball, garden gadgets, cars, and religion in no particular order.

It was fun to watch Addie run around the living room. A teacup tilted over in its stand but didn't break. She'd adjusted it upright and kept on running. How many times had her father and I done the same thing? Haines had noticed it as well, smiling across the room at me. He, too, remembering that even at our most rambunctious, none of Biggie's finery was ever broken. Where did we get the radar that told us just how close we could get to something important without breaking it?

Christmas weather in Alabama is highly unpredictable. Sometimes it's bitterly cold, with winds so strong they can pick you up and carry you to your next destination. Other Christmases have been so mild that it's easy to test out your new bike, new football, or walk off Christmas dinner with a stroll around the block.

This year happened to be mild, so I walked to Avery's house to see what Santa Claus had brought the children. When I got back home, it was almost dark. I saw the floodlight on in the back, and I heard the sounds of two aging warriors grunting and sighing, dribbling the basketball.

"I thought the two of you had gone home a long time ago. Don't you take a break for Christmas Day?" I asked.

"Nope. Not one of Biggie's rules. Sorry," Carter said, and kept on playing. Then he looked at me. "You *are* going to let us play, aren't you, Bit?"

"Well, I have to now so you can get even with Haines."

"Thanks, Bit," Carter said.

I watched them go at it. It made me happy, especially after Carter's year. Both were thirty-five years old, but they still looked young to me, like the boys who had claimed this spot as their own so many years ago.

Haines was tall and still thin, his dark hair only edged with gray. His clean face showed signs of a five o'clock shadow. His long legs and torso still stretched effortlessly like a rubber band until his hand and the ball connected to the net. His eyes hadn't lost their spark or their conviction and confidence.

Carter, too, had dodged the clock of time, although maybe not as well as Haines.

But his compassion and the story his eyes told made up for any physical shortcomings. His sandy hair was all but gone, but that didn't seem to matter much because it only showcased the boldness and the blueness of his eyes. They could still grab you and make you laugh or cry with them. I should know.

I listened to them play until there were more sighs and groans than the sound of the ball going into the basket.

"Okay, time!" I shouted from the breezeway. They almost looked relieved.

"I'd better get home."

"You think?" I admonished him. "It is a family holiday, after all." Haines was doing what he thought was best for his friend, and I knew Addison understood, but it was getting late. I went up to my brother, feigning a hug. I mentioned Carter's back spasms.

"You need any help cleaning up?" Carter asked.

I looked around. "It looks like Mama and Addison did a stellar job. I have some scraps for Barney for you to take home." I walked over to grab them.

"Barney will love it. Thank you for the Duke basketball tickets. I can't believe you didn't buy a ticket for yourself."

"Well, they were pretty expensive. I am still paying for all the renovations. Besides, I wanted you and Haines to be able to just get away. Like you used to. Just be friends."

"You mean before he became a nervous Nellie around me? Between the shooting and the divorce, I don't need him making house calls. Today was a good day. I actually got tired all on my own. What were you whispering to Haines about?"

"Haines left one of Addie's Santa presents over here."

"I thought you were a better liar." He thought for another moment. And smiled. "Thank you for the tickets. Sometimes you just shock the hell out of me." He hugged me.

"Don't forget your scraps," I said, extricating myself from his embrace. He picked up Barney's treats and headed home. I heard the wrought iron gate close, heard Barney barking, and smiled. I started turning my own lights out.

The dishes and kitchen were cleaned, and the tablecloths and linens had been whisked off to the laundry room. The place cards were stacked neatly on the sideboard. Mine caught my attention. Three little letters. Social Security would be hard-pressed to find me someday. The nickname I'd been given had remained and survived, even when the namesake hadn't. I ran my fingers over the card, like I was reading braille. B-I-T. Sometimes relics and memories tell us all we really need to know about ourselves.

thirty-five

The next morning, at eight o'clock sharp, Elrod arrived at the breezeway door. On foot, his usual mode of transportation, unless someone drove him when his license was not in use. Turns out Elrod had spent Christmas Day in jail but had been released on his own reconnaissance, as it would never occur to Elrod to run. Where would he go?

"Why didn't you call me, Elrod?" I asked. "I'm your lawyer."

"I didn't want to bother you, it being Christmas and all. I figured you'd find out soon enough."

"Well, how about some breakfast anyway? I was just about to eat."

"Thanks. How was your Christmas?"

"Good, Elrod. It doesn't sound like yours was very nice. You should stop drinking that stuff. What would I do without you?"

"It's a curse. I just hope you're not like your daddy, and you don't let it get a hold on you like it done him . . . and me."

"No, Elrod. I'm not going to let it get a hold on me," I said.

"Good. I wouldn't want that for one of my kids." He ate his breakfast and then headed upstairs, his work ethic still intact.

I was surprised, in a way, that Elrod considered me one of his. He at least had the ability to raise two fine children, which is more than some completely sober parents can say. His son, Elrod Jr., was a doctor, and his daughter, Viola, a stockbroker in Atlanta.

"But don't you go getting any ideas about taking me on as a project," he called out from upstairs. "Your grandmother and Win have already tried."

Elrod couldn't have been much over fifty. I found his words and his resignation of life unsettling. It reminded me of Mama before and after Daddy died, and a sense of sadness unexpectedly crept up around me. Elrod was smart. He could do anything he wanted.

But the thought of my changing him had never occurred to me.

The legal business in Erob after Christmas was slow. Slower than usual, so I decided to take a few days off and go to New York to make good on my promise to visit Cy and Olga. I was struck the moment I got there how, in just a few short months, my life had changed—it wasn't long ago that I could claim residency here and only visitorship in Erob.

"You know, Olga, Alabama does have a few grocery stores." While I had been in her kitchen, I had scarfed up her tuna salad and blueberry muffins. I reminded her as she prepared a care package for my trip back home.

"I like doing this for you, darling," she said. I felt our mutual need for each other, a need that distance hadn't diminished.

"How's George doing?" I had to ask.

"I must tell you, Nina. He's dating someone."

For a moment I pondered this and then said, "Lucky girl."

Win's appearance on the *Patsy and Doug Show* was such a success they wanted her to come back on a regular basis for cooking segments. Who else had the time to go on every week?

Avery and I wondered how we would put up with Win's "celebrity."

Arush and Avery were going away, and I was excited to stay with the children. Avery had given me doctors' numbers, their complete itinerary, and a million instructions. Nothing like Win, of course, but still, lots of organized information.

"You can take the kids out for a Happy Meal one night, and the other you can fix the chicken casserole and vegetables I left in the fridge."

"Just go and have a good time," I said. I hoped it would be a second honeymoon for them. I hoped it would remind them of why they were together.

"I married with my heart," Avery had said only yesterday.

"The other mitten?"

"Exactly," she answered. "Win, on the other hand, married mostly with her head—logic, organization, what looks good on paper."

With that argument, Avery had not sold me on the idea of the heart.

"You, Bit," Avery began, "will marry with both because you want too much."

"That's a big 'if,' Avery. Not even Buck has been interested," I said, and we laughed.

Baths, story time, and bedtime went fast, and Ruru ended up sleeping with me. Nobody ever told me that a toddler would have enough strength and size to hog both the covers and the bed.

Breakfast was pancakes with chocolate chips.

When dinner rolled around, I was already hearing rumblings of a revolt against the chicken casserole. Blessedly, the back doorbell rang, and it was Carter, bearing pizza.

"Pizza!" they shouted.

He and I were poised in a perfect "good cop, bad cop" position, until I rolled my eyes and gave in.

At bedtime, I had to admit, two sets of hands were better than one, and Carter and I got the job done quickly. When we were able to sit down on the sofa, our bodies, but not our emotions, were finally in repose.

"What's on Netflix?" Carter said. "We can pick one of those indie films you like."

"What were you up to last night?" I asked, excited to watch something else after a day of nonstop Disney animation. "I figured you would have stopped by before now."

"I had a date, Bit."

He didn't say it smugly or like it was big news. He just said it. But it sat between us like a hot coal of information that I was afraid to touch. There had been moments like this between us before, and they always left me wanting to say something important. Something right.

I guess it made sense that Carter would have a date. Why wouldn't he? It had been over a year since Jenny left, and his divorce was finalized. Of all the people I knew, Carter deserved another chance.

"Bit," he said quietly. It didn't look like our movie would get watched tonight, but it kept rolling. "It wasn't a date really. Stacy and I just grabbed some dinner at the City Café, and I didn't want you to hear about it from someone else."

"Stacy from the courthouse?" I asked, as if I needed clarification.

"Yes. She's nice."

"She can run a title search like nobody's business," I said. She was also cute, young, and blonde. So much for my big pontification moment. That coal was indeed too hot for me to touch.

"Do you think you'll see her again?" I tried to sound casual. "How did it go?"

"It went fine."

"I think it's a good thing, Carter," I said. "I do." If wishes came true, that would sound honest.

"Well, we'll see," he said. He seemed to want more from me. Or was it just my imagination?

"Carter, you have to make yourself happy," I said, knowing I should take my own advice. Carter noticed too.

"Did that just come out of Bit Enloe's mouth?"

"No, she's been taken hostage by three children," I said. "But if you go and ruin the best title researcher at the courthouse, I'll have to hurt you, Carter Gideon."

He smiled, and the ease that had been ours throughout the years came back.

The Every Day Café was not as fancy as the City Café, but the food and the prices couldn't be beat. It only served breakfast and lunch before it closed at 2:00 p.m., and it's kid-friendly; one of the only establishments not owned by Jimmy. The café had a black-and-white tile floor and a chalkboard with all the sandwiches, soups, and salads available. There are no surprises at the Every Day. Monday's special is always Monday's special. The cash register and the ordering are done at the same place. There's a counter and stools to sit on if you're a businessman in a hurry or if you don't want to get caught up in the throng of babies and mothers. There are tables and chairs in the back, and they shout out your number when your food is ready. Cindy and Sam Mantanopolis are the owners, and are, to my knowledge, the only Greeks in town.

They make the best grilled pimento cheese sandwiches in the state. Martha Crawford bakes all the bread for the café, including her cranberry nut and savory rosemary sourdough. Pair it with a scoop of chicken salad heavy on the Hellmann's mayonnaise and it's a mighty fine lunch. I typically opted for turkey on toasted rye with an artichoke spread or grilled chicken salad with homemade Thousand Island dressing, a recipe that Sam shared with no one but his son Chris. It's the kind of place where you need lots of napkins. Not very health-conscious; Wai would have loved it.

As I waited on Avery and Win, I noticed Joyce and Vanessa Weathers at the counter. I spoke to "the twins," Susan and Dusty Peterson, who were my age and our hometown CPAs. I never understood how siblings work together.

"Pull in your powerhouse. It's going to rain this afternoon." It was Laney Lynch, our Pilates instructor. I attended her class with Elaine Bonner, who owned the feed store, and Susan after work. Elaine had also inherited her grandmother's house and lived across the street from Haines. That's what you do in the South. Inherent houses. Most people do not have the emotional hangover I had over Biggie's house. We were an eclectic little crowd but enthusiastic nonetheless. I rolled my eyes.

"Yup, they're saying it'll be pouring later," Laney, our resident weather nerd, continued as Avery came in. "When you come to Pilates later, we'll have one of our rainy day 'pajama days.'" Avery and I agreed and took our tea, still waiting on Win.

I turned to Avery. "Details! How was your weekend?" I asked, seeing the muscles ease in her face. "Did you make any memories?"

"Oh, Nina. I wish Arush and I could do that more often. He's a different person. I'm a different person. We walked and hiked and talked," she said wistfully.

"You can go anytime you like," I said. "I offer free babysitting."

"Thank you, Nina. The kids had a great time."

"Can I ask you something, Avery?" I asked.

"Ask away."

"How's Carter doing?" I started, but before I could ask what I really wanted, a look of consternation registered on Avery's face. "I mean, do you think he has recovered from the gunshots? I'm worried. Is he still lonely?" Based on his recent admission about Stacy, I really wanted to know.

"Lonely? I hardly think so," Avery said, making no attempt to hide her displeasure.

"What do you mean?"

"Let's just say that sometimes Carter doesn't like the truth," Avery said.

Before I could get an explanation from her, Cindy shouted from up front, "You girls gotta come see this!"

It was Win. She was in a new car, and it looked like a tank heading toward us down Main Street. Leave it to Win to have the first Hummer in Erob.

"Good Lord, what is that?" Avery asked, as Win stepped down from the driver's seat.

"Expecting a bomb attack?" I asked.

"No, Bit. I got it to lug all the baked items, silly."

"Those are some well-guarded muffins," I said under my breath.

We waited as Win ordered her usual half salad, no cucumbers, no bell peppers, and chicken noodle soup without the noodles. Then she pulled out that calendar of hers with all the colors and social engagements.

"Well, ladies, I can stay till one o'clock today," she said, as she checked her book. "Not a moment longer."

"I should do that," Avery murmured.

"I brought my calendar for a reason. I've been thinking," Win said. "With Bit back home, we can now have two tables of bridge again. Rich and me, Haines and Addison, Avery and Arush, Carter and Bit. Eight. We can have supper and play bridge. Should we start next Friday?"

"We can't do it that weekend because I gave Haines and Carter tickets to the Duke game."

"You sure gave Carter an extravagant Christmas present," Avery said, looking at me.

"I think that's nice. Carter almost died, and he's still not out of the woods." What was happening here? Win defending me? I changed the subject by grabbing Win's calendar. Of course, she had already penciled bridge in. At her house.

"Can't we play something more, I don't know, current? I have Cards Against Humanity."

"That sounds dreadful, and I don't want it in my house. We'll help you with bridge. It will all come back, you'll see." Win was always more confident in my abilities than I was. "Let's say seven o'clock, and I'll serve supper. Avery, do you think you can get Courtney to watch your children?"

"I'll call her."

"Good. Oh, by the way, did you and Arush have a good time this weekend?"

Avery would never discuss her marriage with Win.

"We had a marvelous time. Nina looked after the kids."

"So I heard," Win said. "Along with Carter?" she asked, turning to look at me.

"Yes, he brought over pizza Saturday night," I said.

"Well, that boy stays pretty busy, doesn't he?" Win said in a cryptic tone.

"What do you mean?" Avery asked.

"Somebody saw him having dinner with Stacy from the courthouse at the City Café," Win offered.

"Win," I said, hoping to stop her.

"He shouldn't be dating her," Avery said. "She's got a reputation."

"Avery's being passive-aggressive again," I said. "They were just eating together." But I felt the hot coal back at my feet. "Besides, Avery, it's been a while since the divorce became final."

"Now *children*," Win jokingly admonished.

I was surprised by Avery's attitude. She had always been so careful, so solicitous of Carter. There wasn't this much drama between Carter and Avery when they broke up. It left me confused. My loyalties teetering between them.

Judi Ann Miller, our beloved society editor, died of a massive heart attack in her sleep. We heard the news as we were leaving the Every Day. Who needed social media or the local newspaper when you had the Piggly Wiggly, the City Café, or the Baptist church news blast? The visitation was going to be from five to seven, which meant no pajama Pilates.

Here's the thing about visitations in the South. You want to get there early to beat the crowd; lines start forming early. Like the opening of a *Star Wars* movie. Or the C and E'ers for a Christmas or Easter service. I picked Avery up at 4:45. There was already a line when we got there!

After we spoke to everyone, including the grieving family, it was about six o'clock when we left. On our way out, we ran into Buck.

"Hey Bit, I've been meaning to call you. We should get together for coffee. Did you know the Coffee Bean Emporium changes over to the Wine Emporium at five o'clock? Jim is working on a liquor license. You know what they say—liquor is quicker! That may suit a lady such as yourself." He winked and said “lady” like “lay-dee.” Making it sound just disgusting.

When we got to the car, I turned to Avery.

“Did I just get picked up at a funeral visitation?”

“I think that tells you all you need to know about Buck Whaley,” Avery said in summation.

“Maybe I should tell Buck that a woman such as myself does not like to be called . . . Lady.”

thirty-six

Since moving back to Erob, the only house that I'd not gone to visit was His house. I'd told Mama up front that I wasn't going to be a regular churchgoer. I wasn't going to play the part of a hypocrite. It wasn't that I had divorced God, but we were, to say the very least, estranged.

I gave in one Sunday and quickly found Mama on one side of me and Carter on the other. There was no escaping God in that sandwich.

The hymns were slow and seemed to go on forever. After the sermon, Carter had the thankless job of going up to the pulpit and announcing that there was a $9,000 shortfall in last year's budget that needed to be made up as soon as possible. Now it was the rest of the congregation's turn to tune someone out. I saw Avery across the church with her kids. She caught my eye and smiled.

After church, Mama wanted me to speak to the preacher, but I didn't want to give him the impression that I was going to follow in the footsteps of Biggie, Mama, my brother, or Carter. No use getting the man's hopes up.

On the last day of March, exactly three months behind schedule, Elrod finished painting Biggie's room. In all my life I had not slept there. Even when I was a baby, Biggie banned me to my own room. If I were afraid, I would take my pillow and blanket and sleep on the floor outside Haines's door, but I never dreamed of going into Biggie's domain.

But now, it was all *mine*. Gone were Biggie's beiges and creams, the elegant landscape of a woman in repose. Now pink and green frolicked up the walls. The wooden headboard had been covered in soft fabric, and Biggie's chair was replaced by mine, the one I'd had in New York, so Avery or Win could plop down in it and talk to me. The fabrics were as expensive, I imagined, as Biggie's, but the room, my room, was more welcoming.

I had arranged the pictures on the dressing table. Some were Biggie's, but most were mine. I placed the Debutante Ball photo of Win, Avery, and me in the center. There was a picture of Haines, tired and unshaven, in his green scrubs holding Addie. Another of Mama, Daddy, and me and Haines on our last Christmas together before the life I knew ended. And finally, Biggie's picture that Win had taken of just Carter and me at the Debutante Ball. It had always been the picture closest to Biggie's bed and her favorite one of me. Naturally, I was doing what she wanted. Carter was smiling—his eyes happy before grief changed him. I thought of Stacy, our title searcher, and I wondered what she would do to ease Carter's pain.

The room seemed to welcome the paint, the color changes, and me. In fact, the whole house had seemed agreeable to all my changes. I offered Biggie a spot on my new pink and green chair. She, in turn, offered me peace and a good night's rest.

After a long day at the office, I brought some work home, and I had it strewn all over the breakfast room table. This in and of itself would have caused Biggie great consternation. She hated eating at the same table where one was toiling away.

Martha Crawford had spread the word about my being an "excellent lady lawyer" and about my adjusting payment plan. It was almost April, and I now had enough work that I often had to bring it home.

I had just gotten into things when I heard a knuckled rap on the pane of my back door. It was constant and unobtrusive, and I knew it was Carter.

"I brought this." He held up a sack. "I know you've had a hard day."

"How did you know?" I asked him as my cell phone rang.

"Because of that." He pointed to the phone just before I answered it.

"Oh no. Elrod again?" Turns out, Elrod had been picked up on another DUI. I didn't even know how many this one made. But I was instantly sad as time was clearly running out on him. "Okay, Elrod, I'll see you tomorrow," I said, then I hung up.

Suddenly I was glad Carter was there.

"I found out a little while ago. That's why I thought you could use this," he said.

"What is it?"

"Inside this bag is dinner made especially for you by Mr. Red White," Carter announced proudly. Red White owned the City Café, and I had been pestering him to get some more exotic choices on his menu. Red's real name was William, but when he was a little boy he had a head full of red hair, and thus the nickname was born. His hair was all white now, but calling him William just wouldn't do.

"Thank you so much! Did you get something for yourself? Sit down and eat with me," I said, making room for the both of us at the table.

"I know the first of the month is hard on you. Is all that bank stuff?"

I nodded.

"I don't envy you, that's for sure," he said. "I remember it too well."

"April Fool's Day takes on added meaning," I said, surveying all the documents. "And I think I'm the fool."

He nodded knowingly and laughed.

"And what's with all the divorces? Ever since Christmas I've had folks coming out of the woodwork wanting to split." I was instantly sorry I'd brought it up.

"People never divorce at Christmas in Erob, Bit." He spoke quietly and authoritatively. "Too hard on the kids and families, but you hit a wave just after. A third of those will reconcile, and another third will realize they are pregnant and stay together. It always happens that way."

"How about a piece of pecan pie for dessert?" I asked, changing the subject.

"If you insist." Carter smiled. His smile was easy, more willing to travel across his face than it had been in a while. His mood seemed lighter, as though he had been away on a much-needed vacation.

It had been a while since we'd been this lighthearted with one another, and yet we slipped into these roles as if we were understudies in a play, anxious but eager for the chance.

"Since you're here," I said, "I have something for you." I was feeling happy, knowing my surprise would make him smile. "Here," I said, handing him an envelope.

It was a check made out for $9,000. Carter looked at it and said, without missing a beat, "I don't know what takeout costs in New York, but this . . ." he stopped. "What's it for, Bit?"

"You're in charge of the budget at church."

"And?"

"Well, it's for the church budget shortfall. I made it out to you," I said. "I have one stipulation. They can't know it's from me. I don't want a bunch of vultures on my trail. I can't think of anything worse than folks on the stewardship committee thinking I might be generous, and a Christian."

Carter not only smiled, but he also laughed.

"Biggie has rubbed off on you after all," he said. "You are so like your grandmother and her demands."

"Go to hell, Carter. It's from her account."

Carter gave me a bemused look. "What am I gonna tell the teller down at the bank?"

"Oh, I don't know. Tell her it's for services rendered," I laughed, stuffing my mouth with a big bite of pie.

"Think somebody would pay that?" Carter said.

"Stacy might," I said slyly, looking away, missing his full expression. "How are you and she anyway?" I asked.

"Fine," he said.

"I'm glad, Carter." And then, more seriously than I intended, "Are you happy?"

My gaze had been hard to pin down, but his eyes caught mine and held them for a time.

"I'm all right, Bit," he admitted. "Let's drop it." His words stung. We had always been willing and able to discuss anything, and I felt he was cutting me off.

"Avery seems—"

"This doesn't concern her," he said.

"We just want you to be happy," I said, wondering what Avery had said to him.

"I know." His eyes softened toward me. "Listen, I'd better let you get back to work. Bit, thank you for this money. I can't tell you what it means for the church."

He got up to leave and waved the check at me. "And I hope it was as good for you as it was for me."

I surprised myself by blushing. I had planned on showing Carter my new bedroom, but somehow it just didn't seem like the right time.

The following Tuesday I was at the threshold of Carter's chambers after Elrod's hearing when I felt it. I thought I might have the stomach bug, but I would be wrong. Really wrong.

"So, Miss Enloe," Carter began, "Are you mad that I ruled against you and Elrod?" he asked, as he took off his glasses and nibbled slightly on one end. Like he had done a hundred times before.

"Nah," I said. Another DUI for Elrod, and Carter was legally bound to take away his license for another year. "You know Elrod. He gets by on foot most of the time anyway."

"I guess so," Carter said, and he leaned in, both elbows on his desk, still biting his glasses. I could almost hear the crunch of wire rim. His blue eyes were unencumbered, and he was staring straight at me. It hit me so hard I had to lean against the door-frame for support. My stomach collapsed and my insides were flipping and fluttering. Butterflies. Nerves, I hoped, but I couldn't take my eyes off him. Good Lord, it was just Carter.

"Bit, are you okay?" He put his glasses back on to take a better look at me. Spell broken.

The intensity of my emotions surprised me. But I fought the feelings and pushed them back down so I could make a clean getaway. *We were in the back seat of his car; I was just sixteen . . .*

"I'm fine, Carter," I said, glad I wasn't hooked up to a lie detector.

But I wasn't fine. He gave me a funny look.

As I left, I looked back at him before we were on opposite sides of the door. I wondered if he felt it too.

After work, I went to see Avery. I had mentioned to her that I wasn't feeling great, but whatever feeling I'd had earlier in the day had passed. All that remained was the knowledge that it had happened, and I wasn't all that sure how to talk about it.

She was out back planning another birthday party, no doubt taking a risk with an outside event, since April could go either way in Erob. It could be warm or it could be cold and rainy. Weather, as Chewy and Jordan would tell you, can be such a curious thing.

"Boy, I sure hope it doesn't rain," she said, coming into the house. "Fifteen children. If they have to come inside, I don't know if I could stand it!"

"Of course you can. You're a saint," I declared. "Besides, rainy days allow us to pause and recalibrate."

"The exception to that rule is birthday parties! Are you feeling better, Nina?"

"I'm happy to report I am fine," I said.

"So, what kind of bug do you think it was?" Avery asked directly.

"What are you really asking—you're being passive-aggressive again," I said.

"I know what I know . . ."

The clock read 7:27 a.m. when I woke up to a noise. I got out of bed and looked out the window to see Win's Hummer in the driveway. There was no way in hell that I was going to walk this early—not on a Saturday. I didn't even bother to put on my sweats under my T-shirt. She wouldn't be staying.

I came into the breakfast room, and Win didn't say a word, but when she met my gaze I could see that her eyes were lined with traces of red. She stared at me in my too-short T-shirt.

"You really need to start sleeping in a decent nightgown," Win whispered. That was the beginning of the conversation. It seems so out of place now, so unimportant, so disconnected. But it's that statement that remains with me to this day.

"I've made you some coffee. You'll need coffee."

"What's going on?" I asked.

"Sit down," she said, and I sat at my place. Win grabbed a chair and moved close. Leave it to Win to invade my personal space.

It was then that I noticed her face. It was red and blotchy like a sweater that had been stretched and had lost its shape. Win had a problem. It wasn't often that she came to me, but she sometimes cried to gain my sympathy.

"Have you exceeded your allowance again, Win?" I asked. Maybe Rich had stepped in with a plan. Just the word *budget* could send Win into schisms.

"Yes. I mean, no." Win seemed uncertain of the words coming out of her mouth. "That's not why I'm here."

"Well, what is it, then?" I asked.

"You know today is Ruru's birthday, and Avery would do anything for those kids."

It was a statement, not a question, and I nodded.

"Well, Ruru wanted pancakes, and Avery was out of chocolate chips."

"Chocolate chips are Ruru's special birthday treat," I added.

Win nodded. "So, Avery went to the Winn-Dixie out on the bypass to get some."

So like Avery. Always doing what pleased her children.

"When Avery was pulling out, she was hit by an eighteen-wheeler."

Silence.

"Bit." Win paused. The cadence of her voice seemed off. "She was killed instantly." Then Win grabbed my hand and squeezed it as if she could squeeze the pain away. I remember this, too, because it was so deliberate, but I felt nothing. Like a thunderstorm that suddenly comes up out of nowhere and pummels the ground, her words hit me hard but made no sense.

"She died instantly, Bit." I noticed that I could see the white of my underwear through my T-shirt. Win was right—it was too threadbare and way too short.

"Avery didn't suffer," I heard from somewhere.

"What's that supposed to do for me, Win?" I hissed with a rage I didn't even know I possessed. Her eyes filled with tears as if I'd slapped her.

We had never been good in moments like these, and this was no exception. We usually tried to grope for words, but today, we didn't even muster a pretense.

"What can I do for you?" she said.

"What you'll never be able to do for me. Just leave me the hell alone!" the voice raged. Still Win sat there, unflinching. Was it shock, dignity, or kindness? I don't know, but I remember her demeanor was open and receptive to feelings that spilled out of every pore. We were connected to one another at that moment and forced to face uncomfortable emotions that sprang out of our bodies like uncontrollable leaks.

My brain finally made contact with my mouth, and I looked at Win and asked, "Did Ruru get her chocolate chips?"

She didn't answer me. It was a stupid question. But grief nullifies everything we know to be true, to be logical. The whole purpose of the trip, unfulfilled, seemed like an unnecessary addition to the pain. I noticed Win's blue eyes, and I thought of my Mama's eyes when Virginia died and how they looked like wells about to overflow. Win's eyes were like that now, full of tears, close to spilling over. I felt sorry for her as I sat still and dry-eyed, but the news of Avery's death had transported me into a place where there was no emotion or truth.

The silence seemed more tolerant than our flimsy attempts at conversation. Words collapsed and became the first casualty, but after a while, I was able to ask, "Where's Haines?" He should be here with me.

This question must have hit Win hard because the tears fell down her cheeks. Her voice was quiet, and I had trouble hearing her at first.

"He's with Avery."

"What?"

"Haines is with her."

Win was left with it. Not only was she the one to deliver the news, but also to fill in the details. Win paused as if it were important to get this right. She was now speaking slowly, as if I were deaf, trying to read her lips. "He didn't want her to be alone." Win stopped. "She's donating, well . . . he just didn't want her to be alone."

My chin began to quiver in acquiescence to grief and death. My brother would see Avery's heart. A heart I had seen many times myself.

These details gave this awful truth life.

Birthdays, chocolate chips, organ donation. Those words didn't belong together.

Win got up. "Somebody needs to check on Carter," she said. Carter. Why would she need to see him? But even in my haze I was reminded that the bypass had exacted its vengeance next door at another point in time, and old wounds would open up again. "But I will stay with you for as long as you want me to."

"I want you to leave."

As her hand reached for the doorknob, she turned back. She must have read my mind because she looked embarrassed and disappeared without another word.

We both knew I wished it had been her instead.

Alone, I wandered around the breakfast room, living room, and dining room like a stranger in a foreign land trying to get my bearings. I ended up in front of the cabinet where I stashed the liquor. I pulled out a bottle of scotch and instinctively took a swig. It burned all the way down, the first real sensation I'd felt since Win came over. I took another. Then another. Then another, until I was only mildly aware of the burning in my stomach. This might work, I thought. I might actually be able to float through the next few days. I took another gulp for insurance.

Someone knocked on the door. I vaguely remember putting the bottle down and seeing it was Carter. He had come. I let him in. Seeing him standing there in his suit looking back at me, I realized I hadn't had enough. He embraced me but then quickly broke us apart.

"How much have you been drinking?" he asked. "You need to put on some clothes."

I allowed myself to look at Carter. He had never interrupted our embrace so abruptly, and for a moment I was hurt. Where was my warm and fuzzy Carter? But seeing his eyes close like this, I could see in his what I felt. His blue eyes were splattered with red, and he looked horrible. I was not ready for this.

"I'm not drunk," I said, but I had become unsteady, both on my feet and in my head.

He put his arms on my shoulders and spoke decisively.

"Listen, Bit, you need to get upstairs now, take a shower, put on a nice dress and jewelry, and show the kind of respect your best friend deserves."

"Get your hands off me. You're just like Win." I offered him my best put-down.

"You get upstairs right now, or I'll throw you in the cold water myself."

I believed him. He followed me up the stairs. I went into the bathroom and took a long, hot shower, steam and tears mixing to form moisture on the mirrors. I wrapped myself in a towel and realized for the first time that there was no one left here to call me Nina.

I began to cry loudly now, from deep inside, from one of those secret compartments in my heart that only Avery knew about. I slid down against the door; my bottom hit the cold tile. The next thing I knew, Carter was on the other side, crying with me. It reminded me of another time, and another door, and again, of that same goddamned bypass. I put my head deep into my towel and let it absorb the downpour.

I don't know how long we stayed there, but eventually I heard Carter get up. I only remember I wasn't ready to leave yet. My feelings were safe here. He knocked on the door, and I knew it was time.

"I need to get dressed," I said, "and I can't do that with you in here." Then "Don't go." I knew that of anyone, Carter would be tolerant of my mixed messages.

He left but didn't go far. He sat on the top stair close to my bedroom. I went to my closet, passed over the gray, brown, and navy suits, and got out my black dress. Black. Avery deserved the real thing.

Before I put it on, I went back into the bathroom and threw up.

Finally, I came out dressed, with my hand full of Biggie's double strand of pearls. I sat down next to Carter on the steps and handed them to him. He hooked the pearls around my neck and then his arm came around my shoulders, this time sweetly. With just the two of us sitting quietly at the top of the staircase, the house suddenly seemed very big. I could feel his full body tremble against mine.

"You look nice, Bit. Avery would be proud of you," he whispered, wiping his eyes with his handkerchief.

And then we walked downstairs together to go and do the hard part.

We got to Avery's, and I immediately took inventory of the cars: Mama's, Win's, Agnes's, and Avery's mother's.

We went in through the garage, through the small utility room. I saw the birthday balloons hiding behind the washer and party hats crouching in the corner like they were embarrassed.

Walking into the kitchen, I noticed a flat row of casseroles lining the counter—like a tornado had leveled a neighborhood of cheaply constructed ranch houses. I turned to leave, but Carter blocked my escape.

Win was in the kitchen, businesslike now. "Courtney has Kiran and Dhillon. Ruru is running around here somewhere. Arush is in the bedroom. He's not in very good shape, but he wants to see you both," Win said.

At that moment, Ruru came barreling into the kitchen.

"Aunt Bit, Aunt Bit, Aunt Bit!" Ruru always said my name three times. I picked her up and realized Avery would have had a fit. Arush had her dressed in a pink dress with red tights. Avery was adamant about few things, but she had a rule: white tights except for Christmas and Valentine's Day. I took Ruru into her bedroom to the chest that housed all her clothes. There were three drawers full of white tights.

I didn't see another pair of red tights anywhere.

"What are you doing?" It was Carter. He had followed me.

"I'm dressing Miss Ruru here," I said, trying to hold her still to peel one pair off and put the other pair on.

"What's wrong with the red ones?"

I shook my head at Carter. Please, not now.

"I just saw Arush."

"I'm going. Stay with her," I said, passing off Ruhi like an Olympic torch.

Ruru interrupted, "Did you know that today is my birthday? We're going to have a party."

Precious Ruru. Would she blame herself for her mother's death? I knew all too well the burden of guilt I had carried about my daddy. It had changed me forever.

If only I hadn't started Mama and Daddy's fight. If only Ruru had not wanted chocolate chips. If only. I would not let it destroy my darling Ruhi. I would not let that kind of baggage attach itself to her. This time, it would be different.

Arush looked up as I came in, and his whole body collapsed into the bed.

"Arush," I got out. We had never been close, but here we were, feeling the exact same thing and knowing at this moment that we shared an understanding of pain.

"Bit." My name came out through threads of sobs. "God, she loved you. She worried about you," he said. My knees were showing signs of deserting me. "Can you help me? She wanted to be buried here. I don't know anything about funerals or plots in Erob."

I looked at him for maybe the first time ever. I felt instant shame. I had never had a conversation with him about his beliefs or practices. I always focused on myself being an outsider. Here was Arush, a true "outsider." I had never given any thought to his particular customs after the wedding.

"If you're talking about a cemetery plot and a casket, don't worry about that, Win and I will take care of it. We would be honored. We'll go to Featheringill's Funeral Home right now."

"Bit. There's something else." I looked up, and his eyes reminded me of an old woman's.

"Yes."

"Avery told me that she wanted you to read something at her funeral."

I felt myself getting smaller. "What? Arush, I can't do it." I heard the words squeak out of me.

"Avery wanted you to read. She used to mention it to me. 'If anything ever happens to me,' she'd say, 'I want Nina to read.' It would please her."

My insides lurched.

Finally, I said, "Okay," from a place inside of me clearly on autopilot. "On one condition. I get to go first, before the preacher and before the music. I won't be able to do it after that."

"Okay. Thank you, Bit."

I heard Win's footsteps in the hallway. Was she checking on me or making sure Avery's conditions were honored?

thirty-seven

I don't remember much about the days leading up to the funeral. Everything was a blur. Win and I decided on a plot that was of equal distance between the Gideon and Enloe plots. I floated through those minutes and those hours until it was time to do my reading. My version of a funeral casserole.

"My reading is from *The Little Prince*, by Antoine de Saint-Exupéry," I said.

In one of the stars I shall be living.
In one of them I shall be laughing, And
so it will be as if all the stars were laughing,
when you look at the sky at night. . . .
You—only you—will have stars that can laugh!
And when your sorrow is comforted
(time soothes all sorrow) you will be content
that you have known me. You will
always be my friend. You will want
to laugh with me. And you will sometimes
open your window, so, for that pleasure . . . .

I couldn't look at anyone when I read. When I was finished I sat down. I was glad I was first because when the music started, the tears flowed. Carter embraced me, slipping me his handkerchief.

After the service, we went to the cemetery. I stood away from everyone else, close to Jordan and Chewy. I breathed in the warm, spring air. The first real breath I had taken in days.

"It sure smells like it's going to rain soon. Avery is going home," Jordan said.

"Yep, smells like rain," Chewy added. "The sky smells heavy. Sure does. Do you think that windbag of a minister will finish before the skies open up and ruin my new sport coat?"

It hurt me to hear their small talk. But it was better than looking into that deep, dark hole in the ground.

I thought about the question I posed after Carter's shooting. *Could the bonds of friendship be so elastic they could stretch into eternity?* I looked at that wretched hole and sent a silent prayer that it could.

After the graveside service, it began raining. Carter, I noticed, wandered over to his own family plot. Win and I just stood there watching the dirt turn into mud. I wondered who would protect Avery from the rain. She loved the rain—it was "cozy," one of her favorite words. She called rainy days "pajama days," and she and the children would stay that way all day. "The rain brings good luck and messages from heaven. You'll see, Nina." What sort of message could come from today? Win and I held the flimsy umbrella, staring at the mud trickling away. I turned to her.

"You've got mascara running down your cheeks," I said.

"It's just the rain," Win said, wiping away the mascara. Later, Win brought me home. I was worn out. Elisabeth Kübler-Ross gypped us by omitting the stage of exhaustion in her stages of grief. "I brought you a plate of food," Win said, handing it to me before I went inside.

Then it occurred to me why people make funeral casseroles. It wasn't so much for the first days when nobody feels like eating, but more for now, after the service is over and the visitors are gone. When you come home and open the refrigerator and there's nothing to eat. All that remains is the cold, cheap light bulb.

Not much later, I heard a knock at the back door. I figured it was Win. It was Jimmy.

"I liked Avery a lot. She was nice to me and Trae when we moved home. I brought you a plate of chicken and your favorite latte. Don't tell anybody, but in the bag is a bottle of the Pinot Grigio you two always ordered, in case you need something stronger." I hugged Jimmy. He had paid attention to our orders. I realized it was his version of a funeral casserole. I drank the latte first and found it very satisfying.

After Avery's funeral, the world began again. Without me. People made their way to work. Birds chirped. I wondered how everything could be so unchanged. How could people go on when I felt suspended in time, unable to move?

It was still raining, and I had taken the week off from work. These rainy days had given me permission to stay in bed. Avery would approve of my "rainy day policy." Pajamas on rainy days was her idea, after all. Avery would never be at my wedding. Tick. She would never see me become a bride. Tick. She would never see her children get married.

The ticking crept in when I wasn't even looking for it. Avery would never be a grandmother.

Somewhere in the middle of the morning I heard a knock on the door. It was Win.

"I brought us a couple of sandwiches from the Every Day."

Avery would never eat with us at the Every Day again. Tick.

"Is it lunchtime?" I asked, having forgotten breakfast.

"Just about." Win tried to look unconcerned, but her voice always got higher and faster when she was, making it easy to tell. "It cleared up enough to eat on the breezeway. Do you have any iced tea made?" Win kept on.

Avery would never make iced tea again. I should have learned how she made hers, but I never did. Tick.

"I don't have any tea made, Win."

"I can make it real fast," Win said, as she filled the teapot with water.

The teapot went off, interrupting the silence between us.

"Fill the glasses with ice, Bit," Win said, as she let the tea steep.

We were much more effective at completing tasks than we were at offering each other comfort.

"Does your glass need any more ice?" I asked, prolonging my job.

"No, you know I don't like much ice."

"But the tea will be hot," I protested.

"That's okay," Win said.

"If you're sure," I said.

"I am." Win ended my job.

"Sit, " Win said as she brought the tea out to the breezeway. We sat together like a tripod, missing a leg.

I took a sip, and the sugary, mellow taste touched every taste bud as it went down.

"I can't do this, Win," I said, leaving my half-eaten sandwich and running inside my house.

In the late afternoon, she was back again.

"Just sit here for a minute," Win said, motioning me out to the breezeway.

"It's too nice outside," I complained. I didn't want any part of it.

"Five minutes."

Win and I sat exactly five minutes on the breezeway in total silence. Then she left, without saying goodbye or telling me when she would return.

I felt sick, like I had the flu. I ached all over. Other days, I felt like a walking, talking, gaping wound that needed stitches.

Then there were times it felt like a full-blown amputation. Not just of Avery, but of those desires, wishes, and wants surrounding our friendship. I mentioned this to Haines. He called them "phantom pains" and talked about "spirit limbs" like soldiers hurting. Could I have a "spirit" heart in place of the heart Avery took with her? "Haines, could you shoot a few baskets?" I asked my brother as he was leaving, longing for something familiar.

He shot a few balls alone. My brother, a good man. I hadn't become obsessed with Avery's last seconds yet, but I knew when I did, I would bombard him with morbid questions. I ached to have all of my questions answered. I smothered him with questions about life in heaven.

I heard the wrought iron gate open when Carter came over to join Haines. They played in total silence, except for the sound of the bouncing ball and the swoosh of the net. Watching Carter, I could tell his stamina hadn't returned, and then I worried about him awhile.

Then Win came through the gate. Still not talking, each of us mesmerized by our common bond of memory. The sun called it quits long before we did. All of us needing each other and searching for something to make us normal again.

I couldn't stop dreaming about her. In one dream, I ran into her by chance at the Winn-Dixie, and her cart was filled with groceries and umpteen bottles of Gatorade. I woke up determined to ask her about all this the next time I saw her. Avery didn't even like Gatorade. Then I realized she was gone.

In another dream, we were sipping tea on her deck, watching Ruhi dash around in the sprinkler, and we were talking about Arush. Somewhere in the secret compartments of my brain, the message entered, saying, "Don't worry about Avery and Arush getting a divorce. Avery's dead." But my dream played out even so, and when I woke, for a moment, I worried about their marriage.

In still another, Avery, Win, and I were having lunch at the Every Day, and George Taber was eating a sandwich at the counter. We wondered if we should invite him to sit with us. Then I woke up and realized with relief that I was not going to run into George at the Every Day anytime soon, but I also wouldn't be eating with Avery there ever again either.

Dreams became both a comfort and a cruelty . . .

After thinking about only myself for a month, I woke up one morning wondering about the children. It had been a while since I'd seen them, so I got myself together for a visit. Arush met me at the door. There was hollowness behind his eyes; the light had vanished from them. He looked like a jack-o'-lantern without the candle.

"Arush," I said, "I'd like to take the kids out for ice cream, if that's okay with you."

"Sure," he said. "They'd like that."

We drove down to the local ice cream parlor. Dhillon was distant, and Kiran seemed withdrawn. Ruhi focused on the ice cream and the party-like atmosphere in the place, but when we got home, she clung to me, begging me not to go.

Promising to return again soon, I went home and sat in my car in the garage, feeling the amputation of unfinished conversation. I hadn't felt cheated as much as I felt tricked. Tricked into thinking there would be more. More of everything.

Well, God, you must really be laughing, I thought. *We never saw this one coming.* It was one thing to swindle me, but for those three little children, it was beyond my understanding.

Avery would never have ice cream again. Tick. When I stopped crying, I got out of the car and went into the house. Right away I saw it, on the wrought iron coffee table on the breezeway; the little blue paperback book. *A Grief Observed* by C.S. Lewis. I didn't have to look inside the front cover to know my mother had been there. If anyone should know about grief, it was Mama.

Just then I heard the almost melancholy strains of the gate opening and closing, followed by Barney barking. Carter took his customary stance as a generous barricade up against my screen door.

"You're home," he said through the screen. I was suddenly aware of his passage into manhood.

"You can come in, Carter. Keeping tabs on me?" I asked, needing to sit down.

"Feeling any better, Bit?" We were good at reading each other's eyes.

"I didn't think I could feel worse, you know. But today I took Avery's children out for ice cream. You should see them. How can your God do this to them?"

I could see his eyes darting around, having a private conversation with himself, trying to pick the best advice for me. "I hate to say it, but 'time heals' is a crock."

I had waited for Carter to say something eloquent and beautiful. But what he offered was something else. The truth.

"This stinks," he finished.

It was uncharacteristic of him to be so blunt. It sounded more like me than Carter. But take all the poetry and platitudes away and boil it down to its simplest form, and he was right. Grief did stink. The invisible pain that wouldn't go away.

"Bit, you can't get over something like this quickly." He paused. "Maybe never. You just learn to live with it. You really won't move on until you accept that." He stopped. It was like he was remembering all the times, like now, he was asked to accept loss. Accept grief? Had he even really done the same himself?

But looking again at Carter, it was as if he had just absorbed it somehow. Maybe that was how he did it. He had just made grief a part of his life to coexist with the happy times.

"I just keep thinking about our last day. It looked just like an ordinary day to me." I paused. "I mean, Avery was blowing up balloons, Ruru was dancing around, I was drinking tea, and we were just talking about the weekend."

"You're lucky," Carter said. "You and Avery had a regular day just like so many others you've had." He paused. "That's a wonderful thing."

"But she didn't give me any warning. She didn't offer me anything profound about my life."

"Profound doesn't mean intellectually arresting, Bit. The moments you just described were everything in Avery's life she valued most. People often miss the most important moments because they're looking for something earth-shattering to happen."

An Averyism from Carter.

I took an easy breath in, and it wafted through me as if filled with healing salve.

"Avery and I argued the last time I saw her," Carter said.

"Please, Carter. You two never had a disagreement. What was it about?"

"Nothing much." Carter looked at me and then away. "Only . . . she was right."

"Well," I said, trying to return the favor. "She probably knew that *you* knew she was right, and that had to give her enormous satisfaction."

"It would indeed." Carter got up to leave.

He came close and then reached out to hug me. I could hear his heartbeat in my ears. Strong and steady. A chute of gratitude bloomed around my heart. That his life had been spared. Tears welled up. I felt the stubble on his chin against my cheek. I looked up at him to see the sadness again in his eyes.

Finally, I let him go. The day had worn me out.

The only reason I even looked at the book Mama brought me was because it was short. I read the entire thing, cover to cover, and even found portions comforting. C.S. Lewis never doubted God's existence, only why he did terrible things. I figured C.S. Lewis had the bar raised too high for God in the first place.

I hadn't seen Mama since the funeral, so I drove over to return the book to her. I found her in the kitchen, cooking. Even if it was only for herself, Mama cooked a full-course meal just about every day.

"I got your calling card," I said, holding up the book. My voice was edgy.

"Would you like some coffee?" she asked, turning the stove off but keeping her back to me. It occurred to me that most of the deep conversations I had with Mama had been with her back.

"Sure, Mama, thanks," I said, sitting down at the table.

"Did you read it?" she asked, joining me. Facing me this time.

"Yes. Surprised?"

"No." She ignored the blades of my growing irritation.

"How did you do it, Mama? Virginia and Harriett?" I asked.

She took a long sip of her coffee, as if she were about to tell a stranger the story of her life.

"They were very different, you know," she began. "Virginia was sick for so long that it was inevitable. So, her illness brought Harriett and me closer. We began confiding in each other about Virginia and other things. Harriett, of course, knew all about your father." As if an afterthought, she added, "Harriett had a keen insight into my children. Harriett's death was the real blow in my life."

I was surprised; I'd always thought it had been Virginia.

"She knew everything about me, so a word could act as a whole conversation, or a joke," Mama continued.

"You lost a good friend when you lost her." Her blue eyes met my brown. "She loved you, Bit. She knew you were an emotional child, a sensitive child. She had one of her own, you know."

Mama was talking about Carter, but there was something in me that wouldn't touch it, like picking a flower that wasn't quite ready to bloom. Instead, I asked, voice raising, "Did it ever occur to you, Mama, that I knew that about myself and it scared me? The only person I ever knew in my family who was emotional put a gun in his mouth."

"Your emotions scared me too, Bit," Mama confessed. "Harriett told me to let you be, but you were so like Ben." She let the obvious rest between us awhile. "I did what I thought best, by letting Biggie and Agnes take you on."

"Now *that* was a good idea," I said, and managed a laugh.

"Well, parents don't always have the right answers. We're just older versions of you," Mama said.

"But you never once offered to comfort me," I shot back. "You always seemed so mad with me. And Daddy."

That one hurt. I could see it in the way Mama flinched. "There are things that are hard for you to understand, Bit. I was in pain with your daddy. When he was alive *and* after he died. I was glad for you and Haines to stay at Biggie's so much. I didn't want you to suffer like I did."

And I'd just thought my mother was disinterested.

"Bit, I wasn't stoic with Harriet," she continued. "But along the way, I have given myself the freedom to remember the fun and happy times, and good Lord, Bit, I have so many good memories." Mama smiled the smile that stole her face far too infrequently.

She stopped talking then, and I looked away, both of us comforted by memories. This was much like a conversation with Avery or Carter, but unchartered territory for Mama and me.

"Mama, do you think Daddy went to heaven?"

She was quiet. "Your daddy helped the sick, the poor, and all of the people others rejected. He had depression, and he started drinking. I don't think God holds one bad act against you."

Friendship, it seems, is immune to the generation gap. It survives even when our friends don't. I would never understand her kind of faith or conviction, nor would she ever understand my emotional outbursts of doubt. My way seemed more natural, but her way seemed easier.

thirty-eight

It had been nine weeks since Avery died when I got a call from Carter at my office.

"Listen, Bit, I don't think I'll make it to our meeting this afternoon. I've got to finish writing an opinion. Can we just grab dinner and go over things then instead?"

I didn't think Carter and I had made plans, although since Avery had died, I didn't trust my brain to remember things. But a meeting? With Carter? Surely I would have remembered that.

"Carter, it must have been somebody else. We didn't have a meeting today."

There was a long pause. "Sure we did. It's on my calendar."

"No. I don't have anything for today," I said. But something was dawning on me. The word *calendar*.

"Well, do you want to do dinner or not?" Carter asked evasively.

"Carter, what's going on? And keep in mind that you're not a good liar."

"Nothing, Bit. Dinner or not?" Carter prodded.

It occurred to me that I had seen Carter, Haines, or Win almost every day since Avery died. I then saw in my mind Win's rainbow datebook and the yellow highlighter. I had this vision of Win scheduling me, my dinners, my late afternoons with each of them, scheduling my life. Doing the things she was good at. My apathy played well for her. It was clear I was being managed.

"I get it, Carter. You've got Thursdays. Is that it?" I said finally.

"No, Bit."

"You're such a bad liar," I said, hanging up the phone and going home early.

I half-expected Win to be sitting in the breezeway, flipping and popping her sandal nonchalantly. She wasn't, but it didn't take her long to show up.

I was waiting for her as she shot in, her speech prepared.

"Now, Bit, before you get mad and say, 'Don't start with me, Win,' let me just say a few things first."

She began, "I did arrange for Carter, Haines, Addison, and me to come by. It's hard, Bit. Everyone wants to do it for you. For us."

Win continued. "We all know how you are, so we did this. We know you're hurting. We know you're sad. Avery would want us to take care of you. This is the only way we know how. The only way *I* know how." Win paused, as if losing her balance and then regaining it. "I know you have something to say, so just say it."

I sat there for a long time, letting the past wounds between us retreat. In truth, I had needed each of them, each of those days.

And so I said what I needed to say. "Thank you, Win."

It threw her off guard. Kindness from me usually did. Then I got up and went over and hugged her bony chest close to mine.

We had hobbled through another day.

I was getting through my morning when I came face to face with them in the Winn-Dixie. All I could see was Avery's face. Those fucking murderous chocolate morsels. They killed my Avery. I picked up a bag and whacked all the other bags until the whole display was lying in a semi-circle in the aisle around my feet. Thank God there was nothing breakable. Unless you counted my heart.

Chad Leverett, the stock boy, stood out of my way, petrified he might get plummeted and buried under bags of chocolate pieces.

After I desecrated the whole display, I stepped over the carnage on my way out of the store, leaving it all for him to clean up. I could see the headlines tomorrow: "Death by Chocolate Befalls Local Stock Boy."

Grief is such a different emotion than love. Love is like gliding, floating on top of the water, or skipping down a path lined with flowers. But grief is like one slow slog through something thick. Love may be messy, but grief is like stumbling through a stubborn maze, and when you get to the end, there's no prize—just a bland acceptance.

Close to August, and my birthday, I heard rumblings from Win about parties, presents, and balloons. I told them each individually and collectively that I wanted nothing of the sort. Just dinner, if they just *had* to do something, and I hoped they would listen to me.

On my birthday, I woke with a hodgepodge of feelings. There was no order or logic, but after months of living like this, grief had no desire to be logical, fair, or relenting. It was a sunny day, yet I prayed it would be raining. The secret of rainy days is that they expect so much less of us. Cozy days. "Pajama days." The secret of rainy days is they allow me to blame my tears on them.

Things hadn't gotten better. If anything, they had gotten worse. In the beginning, I rationalized that Avery wasn't really gone; she was just *busy* or *on vacation*. Now the truth was settling.

I had thought that when I crossed further into a new decade that *I* would be somehow different. More together. Wiser. More "adult-ish." Instead, I felt like the same old me, but frayed around the edges. I thought after another trip around the sun I would have all these brilliant lightbulb moments of clarity. I still felt like the same hot mess I always was.

I went upstairs after I ate my breakfast to take a shower. Soon it would be time to play the part of "birthday girl." Grief had taught me to be a good actor. I could get dressed, put on my happy face and the smile that pinched me on the inside, and when people asked me how I was, I could say, "Fine," and make them believe it.

I had to work, but I was taking Mama to lunch at the Every Day because on your birthday, you get a free sandwich and cookie. When I got home, I dove into the couch to sleep, or hide. I couldn't decide which.

Before long, I heard the wrought iron gate open and shut, and I knew it was Carter coming over to take me to Win's. I was exhausted and didn't want to go. He and I went out on the breezeway and sat together on Biggie's love seat, so close our knees were touching.

"I went to work, Carter," I said, as if that was plenty to ask me to do for one day. It seemed a whole lot easier than facing them.

Carter put his arm around me as if that was conversation enough to begin with. He seemed to know how being around people I loved so dearly would remind me of the one I missed so much.

"Bit," he said, "if you want to cry through dinner, it's okay." He paused. "It's your party, and you can cry if you—"

"I get the picture, Carter," I interjected. Even his stupid joke made me sad. Because he was trying so hard, I hugged him for his efforts. I found myself fitting nicely next to his heart as his arms came up to cover me.

"You have my word, Bit."

Despite my initial misgivings, I trusted him.

We got to Win's house, and surprisingly, there were no banners, balloons, or props, and no birthday cake in sight. Even the celebratory excitement had been sucked out of the atmosphere by a thunderstorm that seemed to come out of nowhere to pour buckets of rain as we ran into the house from the car. Where was a rain burst at the beginning of the day?

It didn't seem festive, nor did it quite seem maudlin, but it didn't seem casual either. There was a certain deliberate attempt to not be anything.

"Something smells good, Win," Carter said.

"That's squash casserole, and we have pork tenderloin in a honey and soy glaze, and spinach salad." She had poor Rich getting the pork off the grill in the downpour.

In place of festive champagne, Win served wine. As the wine got poured, there was an awkward moment that couldn't be ignored. Avery would never offer up another toast. It was just another reminder of the amputation of milestones. And celebrations.

Win stumbled to her feet, gathering herself to do what was necessary as she always did. "Well, this is not the kind of birthday we planned for you, Bit. But . . . well . . ." She cleared her throat and tried again. In a doomed attempt to be funny, she added, "it sure beats the alternative!" leaving us all in unfortunate silence.

No one moved. Tears sprung to life in Win's eyes and her lower lip trembled. In any other circumstance, I would have cheered the fact that perfect Win had made a clumsy faux pas, but I showed restraint.

Rich stood up, covered his wife's hand with his own and said, as if nothing had happened, "To Bit." Even after they sat down, he held his wife's hand. Then he clinked his glass to hers. Then everyone reluctantly clinked their glasses and started eating.

After dinner and before dessert, which was one of Agnes's caramel pound cakes that didn't say "Happy Birthday" anywhere,

Win announced, "We have something for you, Bit. I know you said that you didn't want a fuss, but I hope you don't mind." Haines and Carter looked at each other while Rich and Addison looked away.

Haines got up to bring me a wrapped present.

"You didn't listen to me," I said. "I didn't want any presents." Emotions started bubbling to the surface.

"It's okay. Open it," Carter said in a reassuring voice; a voice I could trust in moments like this. A voice I could trust with my life.

I opened it, almost dreading what I would find. It was a tightly bound piece of parchment paper. Unrolling it, I found what looked to be an architect's handwritten plans. I tried to make sense of this gift and what it was exactly. There seemed to be a grassy courtyard with wrought iron benches, a bird fountain, different plants that attracted butterflies and hummingbirds, a statue of St. Francis of Assisi, and a sandbox for children. It was attached, it said, to the church, with a handwritten notation that explained it as "A place to come and pray or just to be." At the top of the drawing, the title: "AVERY'S GARDEN."

My throat gave way, and I closed my eyes, trying to keep the tears from coming, but it was no use. My sadness mixed with their thoughtfulness overwhelmed me and was so unexpected my tears broke free in confirmation.

I looked down at the drawing again. My eyes roamed over every detail, even where they had drawn in the butterflies and hummingbirds. Then I saw the notation in the corner, "Given by Avery's friends." Friendship memorialized.

Turning quickly, I ran up the back stairs to Win's bedroom. In happier times, Avery would have been with me, sharing secrets here on Win's green love seat, plush with pillows. There was a vase of hydrangeas and gardenias greeting me, and I composed myself by thinking of catty remarks I might say to Avery about Win, but all I could think of was that damn parchment paper.

Win appeared in the doorway, waiting to be welcomed into her bedroom. *Play nice, Nina,* something inside me said. Surely it was the sliver of goodness that was Avery that remained with me.

"May I?" Win asked.

"It's your room," I said, waving her in.

"I'm sorry, Bit," she said, sitting down next to me. "We hoped you would like it."

"I do, Win," I said, looking at her. She was clearly not comfortable in this space, with me, with this silence. Emotions spilling out all over the place. It would've been better if the vase of flowers had tumbled over, water gushing everywhere. At least that would have given us something to focus on rather than our feelings.

"So, Bit," she asked, "What did you and Avery talk about in here?"

"Mostly you," I answered.

She was quiet. Then said, "I knew it."

We sat there again in silence, and when we finally made our way downstairs, the dishes had been done—a trick Avery and I had mastered.

To the group still gathered in the living room, I said, "I'm sorry to have to run. I appreciate the gift, really." I was still overwhelmed by their planning. "I guess it's a good thing that it's not inside the church. Better chance of me actually visiting, right?" and everyone laughed.

Carter drove me home in silence. He waited until I unlocked the door and turned on the lights and the floodlights before he left. I noticed it for the first time as he was walking away. I called him back.

"Carter, come here a second." He turned and joined me on the breezeway.

"What's wrong, Bit?"

"Look out at the courtyard . . . yours and Haines's basketball court." He waited and looked. "Now, put grass instead of brick, a fountain, and a couple of wrought iron benches here." I let it dawn on him.

Whether they had known it or not, their subconscious memories had found an outlet in an architect's pen. Their inspiration had come from a spot where we had all spent our childhood together.

I went to bed. They hadn't exactly listened to me, but they had listened to Avery. Listening, the most underrated and rudimentary form of love.

I thought Win's black-and-white Christmas picture was perfect that year. Eight months after Avery's death, it was still hard, and black-and-white seemed to reflect the colorless world I was in. Arush and Courtney took the children to get their pictures made, and on December 31st, Win had a supper to celebrate this dreadful year coming to an end. Good riddance.

Before the party, she stopped by my house. Her blonde hair was scattered uncharacteristically about her face, matching her flustered facial expression. Win never got nervous over a party. I attributed this state to something rare and maybe sinister. After all, unwelcome visits by Win in such a state were reminders of that day.

She came into the kitchen, bringing a burst of cold wind in behind her.

"Bit, I need to talk to you. It's important." She led me into the breakfast room, and we assumed our places.

"No, Win, I can't take any more." I dangled so precariously now. One more thing could annihilate the tenuous coping strategy I had in place. "Please, Win." Begging her to keep me ignorant.

"Bit, you need to hear this from me. Arush is engaged."

Win had done it. She had killed Avery a second time, and this time it hurt just as bad.

I moved away from her and into another room. When she followed me, I asked, "Who?"

"Courtney."

"The babysitter?"

"Yes."

My mind went to places it shouldn't have gone. Courtney worked for Avery and Arush long before Avery was dead. I wondered how long it had been going on. Win stood silent.

"Well, you're the one that's such a stickler for protocol and all. You're the one who gets bent out of shape when folks wear white after Labor Day. And don't write thank-you notes. What's your take on all this? It hasn't even been a year, Win. Eight months!"

Knowing Win, I could predict her response, but I was wrong.

"Bit, you should see those children. They miss their mother. They love Courtney, and she really loves them. Do you really think Avery wants her children not to have someone who will love them and give them plenty of hugs?"

Damn Win. When she's right, she's right.

"How come Arush can move on, and I can't?"

Win smiled. "Because sometimes our friends mean as much as our spouses do to us, or more." An Averyism coming out of Win.

My friends had given me room to grieve these many, many months. By doing so, they had given me the chance to begin to love Avery again. In place of nothingness, my heart felt the regeneration of happy memories.

The next day, Arush appeared at my door. I invited him in.

"I'm sure you know about me and Courtney." It felt awkward without Avery. I nodded. He continued, "I hope you'll understand, but we are moving back home. To Ohio. My parents are there, my friends, my life. I hope you won't see this as me taking the children away from you . . ." He stopped.

I remembered the day that Avery died. He looked so unmoored. Alone. Avery had been his home. They had created memories and their family here, but without Avery . . . We had never excluded him, but had we done enough to include him? I felt instant shame. I walked him out. I saw the shafts of sunlight stretching out through the tree branches. C'mon, Avery. Overkill, don't you think? I hugged Arush, thinking about my own move back to Erob.

"I do understand. I did the same thing."

Win always said that months that were cold and dreary like January and February were tailor-made for card games, so on a Friday night that threatened snow, we assembled in her living room. I was rusty, and bridge, even a good hand, didn't hold the prominence in my life it once had, but I lasted two rounds. Win and I were partners, and Win's no trumps clobbered Haines and Carter. Then Carter and I paired off against Addison and Haines. Carter and I didn't make very good partners. My lack of concentration about what had been played combined with his hoarding of aces until they were ineffective proved disastrous. But I had fun.

On the way home, Carter was quiet.

"You seem particularly contemplative tonight," I said. I felt the need to fill the car up with big words and small talk.

"Does it bother you?"

"Not particularly. You often keep your cards close to the vest."

"Are you still talking bridge?" he asked.

"Well, yes," I said, sensing a mood as we got to my house, "and no."

He walked me inside, and I started turning lights on, and then I went into the butler's pantry between the kitchen and breakfast room, where I dropped my keys into the wooden fruit bowl on the dryer.

"If you had just played those aces earlier," I said, turning around.

Carter was so close that I could feel his breath waft over my entire face. The line had never been clear or certain, but he was stepping over some kind of boundary. The air became frail and delicate between us. Or maybe it was my legs. There was a sudden stillness as we both stood there, waiting to see if a trap would ensnare us. When nothing happened, his eyes locked onto mine.

"Dammit, you talk too much," he said, and then Carter Gideon kissed me, against the dryer. Once, twice, and then, well, I lost count.

Those kisses did not pussyfoot around. They went way past the introduction stage like George's kisses. Carter's kisses were that and then some, hot chocolate with foam and marshmallows after sledding in snow.

Then he looked me in the eyes and said easily, "I love you, Bit." It was as if he'd been carrying it around awhile, comfortable with it, like one carries a sentimental old relic in one's pocket. Then he kissed me again, and this time, I kissed him back. Meeting Carter's enthusiasm, I felt everything, even the cold dryer handle against the back of my leg. My heart was responding to something other than grief—something long buried, or something I felt unworthy to receive. I felt his arms wrap around me as if to prop me up so I could feel the depth of what it was, but it was all so fast, it would be easy to lose control.

Then my head caught up, and it dawned on me that I was out of breath. I was overcome with emotions. What was Carter doing to me? The memory that had been sealed for so long sliced wide open inside my heart. This was not a tipsy, childhood kiss. This was sober. Grown-up and real.

"Stop it!" I said, breaking free and running to the safety of the dining room. Standing at one end of Biggie's long table, I motioned for Carter to stay on the other. I needed the thick mahogany and glass between us.

"No, Carter," I said, breathing heavy now and wiping tears from my eyes. It was his natural response to come and comfort me, but I wanted him to stay put. "We can't," I said.

I felt like something had been broken, coming apart into little pieces. Something fine. Cherished. Priceless. Like Biggie's Meissen vases. There wasn't a sound except for Carter and me, our torn breaths loud and unregulated.

"Bit," Carter said, offering to help, but he couldn't, since he helped break it.

I worked up the courage.

"No, Carter," I said again, as if it were all my decision. "We can't. I push and hurt people I love. Push them away. George. Daddy. Even Avery. Regardless of what 'we' are, I can't bear losing you too." His hospital stay was too fresh.

The statement was, by its own admission, one of love and need. I was unaware of where it came from, but I was fully aware of its accuracy. What should produce joy was producing sorrow.

But that was the way it has always been with Carter and me. Love and loss—equal tributaries flowing into a river of mutual feelings.

Coming home had been the easy part. Remodeling Biggie's house had been emotionally un-invasive. But standing here with Carter and all the ghosts filled me with fear. Being with Carter could be the best thing that ever happened to me, unless I ruined it. Because I knew how much I loved this man. Loved him enough to walk away.

"I won't leave you."

"Don't make promises you can't keep, Carter."

And then he clarified it. "I'll never leave you the way your daddy did," he said.

"I can't . . . can't do this," I managed, remembering Cy and Olga's offer to come back to New York any time I needed. "I need to get away."

"I'll go with you."

I shook my head; I needed to do this alone.

Ghosts from the past were calling, and I needed to get far, far away.

The next day, everything on the surface looked the same as it had the previous day. Only my insides felt the shift.

I drove to my office and put up a note saying I'd be out of town for a while. I sent emails to my clients explaining that I was taking a brief hiatus, and then I called Win. "You know, Bit, you can always use our beach house," she said.

"Thank you, Win," I said, "but I'm going to visit Cy and Olga for a couple of weeks. You know, get my roots done."

"Well, your roots *could* use some attention," she said.

That's when I heard it. Something I hadn't heard in Win's voice: fear and vulnerability, all at the same time.

"You *are* coming back, aren't you?" she asked.

This weakness in Win surprised me. At times in our friendship, I would have given anything to hear something close to vulnerability, but now it made me sad, and it made me think of Avery. Now what remained was only Win and me and whatever it was that we had together.

"Where else would I go, Win?" I asked.

thirty-nine

Olga and I settled into a comfortable routine. Our choices were simple and exactly what I needed. Retail therapy or attending an "under the radar" play. I relished eating Olga's tuna salad again. Dining in or out. On the fourth day, I had my roots done and had a long, inebriated dinner with Wai, like we used to. The next afternoon, we were having a cup of tea when the doorman buzzed. Olga unfolded her legs from beneath her and moved toward the foyer. She launched into a conversation with the doorman and then her unexpected guest. When she returned, she gathered up her shoes and announced, "You have company. Your divorcé is here."

I was about to correct her, as I didn't have "a divorcé," when I saw him at the threshold of the living room. I never thought of him any other way except who he was: just Carter.

Carter stood there, not budging. Fear bubbled to a slow boil in my throat. "I don't know where Nina's Southern manners are. I hope you will join us for dinner." Carter accepted. "Then I need to get to the market if we're going to have company tonight." She excused herself.

My thoughts were swirling around like falling leaves.

"Bit . . ."

"How'd you find me?" Carter had only been to New York once, and this city was a lot more difficult to maneuver than Erob. "Never mind. This has Win's fingerprints all over it."

"Win doesn't even know I'm here."

"But here you stand."

"George helped me," he confessed. "Haines still had his number."

"You called George?" Men! And yet. I felt a small hiccup in my heart.

"Can I at least stay for dinner?"

I nodded, not sure if I had a greater fear of Olga or my own feelings. "Yes, you can stay for dinner. I told you I needed time. I needed to get away. From Erob. From you. What are you doing here?"

"Making my case," he said.

"There's no need for that. I don't want to be your consolation prize."

There was a brief pause. "You are definitely not that, Bit. If I wanted something easy, believe me, it wouldn't be you."

I managed to smile. "Easy? I'm the cliché. I'm the girl next door."

"And why is that a problem?"

Now I was feeling exasperated. "Because I'm not a happy-endings kind of girl, Carter. I'm not your type." I was trying everything I could think of.

"I don't have a type."

"Yes. Yes, you do."

Now he waited for me to make my case. Just like the judge he was.

"Look at Jenny," I said. "Stacy. Or any girl you've ever been with. All of them sweet. Nice. And Christian."

"Do I have to remind you how those relationships turned out?" Carter asked.

His manner irritated me. He seemed so comfortable with this information, and it was like a torpedo to me.

"I love you, Bit." There it was again, and he just wouldn't stop. "I've loved you since you got drunk on bourbon and threw up all over me. I loved you when we fought about you wearing a goddamned corsage to that Debutante Ball. I loved you when . . ."

It did touch me that his repository of memories was as deep as mine. A collective history. But it was too much.

"Stop, Carter," I interrupted. "What happens if I wreck us? Our friendship?"

"I'll give you custody of Win." A purloined smile appeared from nowhere. I wished my damn confidence was as contagious as his damn confidence. "I need to check into the hotel and change for dinner."

When Carter arrived for dinner, he was wearing a new sport coat and bearing a bottle of wine. He handed it to Olga, and she nodded in appreciation.

"Aren't you enterprising? How did you know this is my favorite?"

"The doorman suggested it."

During dinner, Carter regaled Cy and Olga with stories of our growing up. He made them sound charming and funny, and I couldn't help but laugh at our adventures. It was amazing to me, even after all these years, that so many of my fondest memories contained him. He had woven together a beautiful tapestry of memories. Our memories.

"So, Carter, how are you feeling?" Cy asked. He remembered all the times I was frantically making phone calls to check on Carter.

"I am feeling good now. I was lucky. Thank you for asking." I noticed how my two worlds had blended together so seamlessly. I could tell Carter enjoyed their company and they his. It was clear—they were defecting to team Carter.

After dinner, Carter extended his appreciation and said his goodbyes. I walked him to the door.

"Bit, are you coming home soon?"

"I just need time to process."

He nodded. "Process this." He proceeded to kiss me. As far as closing arguments go, it was compelling. He put his hand on the doorknob and turned around to look at me.

"Maybe I'm the one who's the consolation prize," he said, leaving us on opposite sides of the door. Yet again.

"No, Carter," I whispered into the emptiness of the foyer. "You're the fucking jackpot."

Olga appeared in the doorway. "I didn't know we were harboring a fugitive." She went to the kitchen to prepare us both a cup of tea. We sipped our respective teas, and after a while she asked, "Did I ever tell you how Cy and I got engaged? After the war, after everything, after seeing my mother lose her husband, I decided I did not want to marry. I didn't want to put myself through that heartache. But Cy persevered. He had to come all the way to where we were—by ferry. Did you know Cy is deathly afraid of boats and gets horrible bouts of seasickness . . . ?" Her voice trailed off.

"Cy is the other side to my heart," she said.

I met her eyes. "The other mitten," I murmured.

I slept fitfully that night, thinking about my roots. And it had nothing to do with my new highlights.

As our ritual, Olga and I were fixing hot tea before bed. I had been there for two weeks now, and even I was starting to worry about my shopping bills.

"Olga, I've decided it's time for me to go. I can't thank you enough for your hospitality. I still don't have closure on some things, but I'm feeling much, much better."

Olga placed her teacup and saucer on the table. It bobbled, making a deliberate noise as if her hand had gone frail. She breathed in—slowly, quietly—twice.

"There is no such thing as closure, my dear," she said. "Closure is a big-city word, coined by Park Avenue therapists to line their pockets. One does not get closure from tragedy, death, or premature abandonment. The best we can do is allow it to sit with us, accept it, and maybe enclose it, if you will, into our lives."

She paused. "Your brother, your friend, and your divorcé seem fine to let those collective memories just be, and they seem to accept you. Maybe it's time for you to let them in. Maybe it's time for you to give that sweet man a chance."

I left with promises to return, but I wasn't ready to go back to Erob yet, so I took Win up on her offer and headed south to the beach house.

There's something magical about waking up at the beach, no matter what time you get in and no matter what your reason is for visiting.

I was a little surprised that Win hadn't assumed I would come here and stocked the fridge for me. It was empty and untouched, and I went to the market to get a few supplies.

Her "happy beach house colors" welcomed me back, and I ate my way through the first five days. On the morning of the sixth day, I decided to listen to one of her voicemails.

"Hey, Bit, if you're at the beach house and want a good restaurant, Frank's has a great special on crab cakes on Saturdays." *Was today Saturday?*

Here I was, on the verge of a nervous breakdown, and Win was touting the virtues of local crab cakes.

Forgoing Franks's, I did takeout at a local dive with a questionable sanitation grade. I had fried shrimp, hush puppies, and fries. If I was going to die, I would die greased-up and well-fed.

Early Sunday morning, I took a walk on the beach. As I was walking back, I saw them from a distance. Those legs. I'd know them anywhere.

"Well, it didn't take you long to find me," I said, as the legs got closer. "I hope you brought some of your muffins."

"Whisked by Win." Then, "I was always better at hide and seek than you."

"You were always better at everything, Win," I returned.

"Don't start with me, please," she asked.

"That's my line."

"I know." She paused. "How are you?"

"A little better, but pretty much the same."

"Well, we can hope. I picked up some groceries on my way in, and I thought I'd cook for us."

"I've already been into Rich's wine. I hope that's okay."

We ate lunch and returned to the beach. I don't think either one of us said a word all day until we came back to the house for dinner.

"Guess what I have?" Win asked, producing a small can of Coco López, piña colada mix, and vanilla ice cream, Avery's secret ingredient.

"I'm not in the mood, Win," I said.

"Sure you are, Bit." She went to the blender. Win took piña colada–making very seriously. Her custom was to blend the ingredients together with the perfect sort of crushed ice.

She poured our drinks into glasses, and we took them out onto the porch. It was dark, and the only sounds were of the ocean and of the sea animals that claimed it. The ceiling fan provided a backdrop with its rhythmic, whirring hum.

"To Avery," Win declared, raising her glass high.

"To Avery," I agreed.

The darkness allowed us to be alone in our thoughts. I heard Win breathing softly from time to time.

"Hey, Win," I said, feeling safe in the darkness. "I've always wanted to know something."

"What?"

"Why did you tell me about Baxter?"

She began, "Rich was completely devastated. I was pretty close to losing it. I needed someone that wasn't going to give me a bunch of happy talk. I needed your ambivalence. I needed your ability to tap into your own anger with God."

"I'm your go-to girl for all of that," I said.

"Hey, you did come through," Win said.

I laughed. "I'll give you this, you played the hand you were dealt like it was the hand you chose all along." I could feel her smile. Perhaps the darkness does reveal more than it hides.

"I read all those blogs you sent me. They were right, I can't imagine my world without Baxter in it. If I didn't have Baxter, I would really be a number one bitch."

"Baxter did make you a better hugger. Don't worry. You managed just fine in the bitch department." I laughed and gave her a hug.

"I'm still me."

The next morning, we settled into a routine that would define our next week together. Win would get up first and make coffee and cook. I would drag myself out of bed and have a cup.

Avery and I never could touch Win in the kitchen, especially at the beach, what with fresh sea bass and salmon at her disposal.

"I'm glad I went to Cy and Olga's," I told her on one of our walks.

"They love you," Win said.

"Olga and I did plenty of shopping," I said, knowing that would keep Win interested.

"You were in New York City, my dear," she responded.

"I bought some new . . . sleeping attire," I added.

"It's about time," Win said, but she didn't ask why.

On our walk the next day, she asked me why I seemed closer to Cy and Olga than my own mother.

"They accepted me," I said. It sounded easy.

"Your mama gave you space," Win reminded.

"So did Daddy. I mean, he checked out early and gave me nothing but a big, blank canvas."

Win stopped abruptly, looked at me. "Your father was fucked up, Bit," and then she turned and moved on down the beach. "Not everything is about you, you know."

I stared at the back of Win's head. *What was going on? This is how she tells me she cares?*

"Well, I just can't wait to tell Haines and Carter you said the F-word, Win," I called after her.

"Like they would ever believe you," Win shouted back as she kept walking. "On second thought . . ."

When we got back, Win fixed us a piña colada and proceeded to tell me the deets, the treasure chest of her secrets.

"So I was in the pharmacy drive-through getting a refill for my sedative—"

"Sedative?" I interrupted.

"Yes, I was a hot mess." She took a sip of her colada. "I was in the drive-through, I couldn't find my prescription, the woman behind me started laying on her horn. I got out of my car, in my pajamas, walked to her window, and I screamed, 'If you fucking blow that horn one more fucking time, I'm going to blow your fucking head off.'"

I blushed. "Who was in the car?"

"Berma Ellen Woods from church."

We both laughed.

"Carter was across the street. He had to come over for some . . . legal intervention."

"What did Berma do?"

"Put me on the prayer list of course." Win was on a roll. "Then, there was the time that a speech pathologist showed up on my doorstep three weeks after Baxter was born. I was in my four-day-old pajamas, and I told her to fuck off and slammed the door. Poor Carter had to deal with that one too. He's hung out with Rich in his man cave while Rich smoked cigars and gave me space. Baxter adores him. You think I fought so hard to save Carter for the rest of you. I did it because I needed him."

"I would've paid good money to see you take down Berma."

It was our last night when I asked her.

"Why are we friends, Win?" I asked. It fell in the same category as all the big questions of life: What is love? What is God?

"Good Lord, Bit. We are not going to do this for the remaining time, are we? I don't have to slice and dice my feelings all up to know things. I know that you know the real me, even better than Rich or even my mother ever could."

"Really?"

"Sure. You're here at my beach house, with me," she said. "And," she added, "I know you too."

Years ago, this would have scared the living hell out of me, but I just sat there, with nothing to say, because I knew it was true.

forty

I got home late on a Thursday night, almost a month after my journey began. My mental holiday. As I unpacked, there were no souvenirs. That damn emotional baggage took up all the space. I noticed the lights were on at Carter's. When I turned on my lamp, I noticed his went out, the way a parent may wait up for a child after a date or coming in past curfew. It was enough for me to know he was there. It was enough to be home.

I ended up staying at the office late the next night, figuring it would be easier to catch up on work there rather than trying to lug it all home. I heard a rap on my office door, and I recognized it easily.

I unlocked the door, and his eyes met mine. Time had done nothing to diminish my feelings for him.

"Hi."

He came in, and I went and sat behind my desk.

"I figured you might be hungry. I brought you a burger from Red's." He smiled.

"I'm swamped, Carter." It sounded like an apology.

"I know." He paused. "It's okay." He got up to leave. As he stood in my doorway, in front of the frosted glass door that said in black "Bit Enloe, Attorney-at-Law," he asked, "Are you all right, Bit?" It was not a casual question.

"Yeah, Carter," I said. "I am."

He turned to leave, lingering a moment, his shadow silhouetted on the other side of the door. I ate my burger, but it left me wanting more.

Another week passed, and Win had bridge. I didn't think Carter and I could take being partners again, but we were, and we actually won a game.

When we got back to my house, he came in and began turning on lights.

"Bit?"

"Yes," I said, turning to face him.

"What do I have to do to stay longer? Ask to borrow a cup of sugar?" He stopped. And then, "I don't care if it bothers you to hear me say it. I love you."

He said it just like that, *I love you,* like he had grown so accustomed to the words that to him, there was no longer a need for formality between us.

I smiled, and for once, it came out easily. "I love you, Carter."

We embraced. I disengaged myself from him to lock the door, locking us both in on my side for the first time, and turned out the lights.

We walked upstairs with our arms about each other as if we had done it this way for all our lives. It seemed already a habit, but there was something in me that was undeniably giddy.

When we got up to my bedroom, I sat on the edge of the bed and waited. Then I remembered and jumped up, grabbing the Bergdorf's bag from New York from the closet. I pulled out a nightgown with the price tags still attached.

"I bought this," I began, undoing the blue silk nightgown from tissue paper, "for you."

Carter sent me back over to the edge of the bed and untangled the gown. He looked at it approvingly and smiled. And then he folded it back up again and laid it on the chair.

"I like you just the way you are," he said. Then he started undressing me. He took each piece of clothing off me, one at a time, and folded them neatly and put them on the chair. He went slowly, deliberately, until I was sitting before him for the first time in my life, naked. Unburdened. Finally free to receive all the love Carter poured on me. He took his time, every movement having its own relevance, every moment its own significance. After, silence and darkness covered us in its large embrace, and I wasn't at all surprised that we fit together so completely.

I was vaguely aware that this had been a man I had known all my life. Nonetheless, I was stunned by all the amazing things Carter Gideon had just done to me. Later, we repeated our lovemaking, slowly like before, as if cementing our feelings. And once more, that time fast and demanding; we were making up for lost time. Somewhere in the night we lay still, my back nestled in his chest like two of Biggie's sterling silver spoons resting safely and protectively inside the velvet-lined silver chest. I turned and traced the outlines of the scars from his surgeries. I was so profoundly grateful that his life had been spared and he had forgiven me.

"Are you okay?" I asked.

"Why wouldn't I be? You're home."

I heard the key turn before I actually woke up.

"Who's that?" Carter asked.

"It's Win," I mumbled. "I've really got to get the locks changed." I was exhausted. Deliriously so. "She's making coffee and getting the bagels. She'll give me five or ten minutes. She knows where everything is. She arranged it herself." I got out of bed. "Don't worry, I'll get rid of her."

I put on my walking shorts and shirt. I turned around to tell Carter I wouldn't be long and saw him propped up on one elbow, watching me. Now, I had seen Carter Gideon's bare, naked chest plenty of times, but I had never seen Carter Gideon's bare, naked chest propped up in my bed before. I smiled and stored the memory up like a keepsake.

"What?" he asked.

"You've got to be pretty proud of yourself. But are you okay—I mean your heart—after last night?"

I watched his little mind working.

"I dare you to trot over to your doctor brother and tell him what we did last night and how many times. What would he say?"

"That you were lucky?"

Then Carter Gideon laughed. The one that was loud and uninhibited. It had been the soundtrack of my childhood. My memories. It had been in hibernation for so long, and now it was back. And I was home to hear it. I ran back and gave him a quick kiss.

"What?" he asked. "Just think how I could perform for you if you took me to see Duke play each year." Then he laughed again.

"All right, Gideon. I'll be back."

When I got down to the kitchen, Win was taking our bagels out to the breezeway.

"Hi, Win. I can't walk today. I've got Carter upstairs fixing my leaking sink."

Damn. That was so lame since Carter was our most un-mechanical wonder. But now I knew in which areas he did excel.

To her credit, Win didn't even raise an eyebrow. She just began pouring coffee.

From the staircase came his voice, saying, "I'll take a cup," and then Carter appeared in the kitchen wearing the same clothes he'd worn the night before and carrying absolutely no tools. Still, Win didn't look askance.

We sat down as Win handed Carter his coffee.

"Well, Carter, if I had known you'd be here, I'd have brought you a bagel."

"That's all right, I'll just have a bite of Bit's," and with that, Carter took a big, possessive bite of my still untouched bagel. "You girls have a good walk." And then he left. I must have turned ten shades of mortification.

We watched him walk away. The sun was already out. I noticed the long, outstretched tendrils of sunlight extending through the trees lengthwise, out like a hand on the courtyard. I saw God's fingers, and I hoped Avery was right in that God's hand would indeed protect me and this kind, good, wonderful man. I watched him disappear on the other side of the wrought iron gate.

"So, Bit," Win said when it was just us, "did Carter fix everything?"

"Yes, Win," I answered, "he did."

As we walked, I held my secret. It was still too new and too fresh to share. I could still smell Carter on me—the citrus smell of fresh oranges. I knew if I had been walking with Avery, I would have spilled it before we were off the breezeway. But with Win, I needed more time. I would tell her soon.

The next Saturday when Win showed up, she was carrying three bagels. Carter had left five minutes before she got there, and I was making coffee.

"Three bagels, Win? You've never brought three bagels before. Ever."

"Well, you may want it later, or you can feed it to the birds."

"You are a lot of things, Win, but not too subtle. Carter isn't here," I said playfully.

She looked dejected. I waited, before adding, "But he was."

That prompted an expression from Win, but she was too smart to ask questions. She had learned that lesson painfully in our childhood. We began our walk.

In truth, our walks had come to mean more than physical exercise. We had gotten to know each other again, gotten to like each other again. We would talk about the serious and the ridiculous. Always starting with local gossip and then talking about our families, our disappointments, or my escapades in New York—my one-night stand with vowel guy. To my surprise, she nudged me in the ribs and said, "You were a shacker." I laughed. I didn't even know Win knew such a word. And I'd learned that even with lucky dust, it took a great deal for Win to keep up appearances, and her marriage to Rich wasn't as easy as it looked.

"So, do you want to hear about Carter or not?"

"What do you think?"

"It all started with a crappy hand of bridge," I began, although it had started a lifetime ago.

"At my house," Win interjected, giving herself much of the credit.

"That's right."

"Does this have anything to do with your trip to New York and the beach?" Win asked seriously.

"Yes, it does. I needed to get away. I needed to give Carter a better version of myself. He deserved that."

In the middle of the sidewalk, in public, for all to see, Win hugged me, and I welcomed her flat chest.

"I'm sorry, Bit. Are you better now?"

"Yes. I am."

"And this thing with Carter. Are you getting married soon?"

"Win!" I exclaimed. Win was steamrolling me. We were back to our regular, crazy normal. "You are way ahead of yourself. That, I don't know."

"'The Honorable and Mrs. Carter Gideon'," Win said. Marrying well was an art form for Win, and she had perfected it. She loved titles: doctors, judges, generals. Now, here I was in her mind: marrying a judge. Never mind that it was judge of circuit court in Podunkville, but it would suffice for addressing and prestige purposes.

"You finally did it, Bit. You got the best one too."

Win was right. Maybe I did have lucky dust.

"Listen, Win, Haines doesn't even know. Please keep this a secret."

"You told me first."

"Well duh, Win."

"Does Agnes know?"

"You know Agnes. Yesterday she said she washed a pair of Carter's white socks and a golf shirt. She said to me, 'I suspect you'll see Carter soon to give these to him, won't you?' and then she gave me that look of hers."

"She knows," Win said. "She's probably ecstatic."

We were quiet for a while.

"I've got something to ask you, Bit," Win said. "I've been thinking about it for some time now."

"What is it?" I was getting alarmed. Win seemed serious.

"I want to be buried in a pink St. John's suit."

"Win, I'm not listening to this," I said, not wanting to think about death anymore. Not even hers.

"Pink is my color, you know. When I go, I want you to march

right up to Atlanta and get me a pink St. John suit immediately. And—"

I hated this. "The heels to match, I know," I cut her off, almost involuntarily, knowing how Win's accessorizing mind worked.

"If it's spring and the suits have those flowers attached, you can leave it on. Use your discretion about that."

"Okay, Win."

"But this is the important part," Win said earnestly. "Before they lower me into the ground, just snatch that suit off me and save it for Winnie and sorority rush or for her trousseau. No use letting a perfectly good St. John suit go to waste," she finished.

Practical Win.

If I had not known she was perfectly serious, I would still be laughing. Win worried more about looking good than any damn hymn or reading. Who knew a St. John suit could take the sting out of death?

After Win had wrangled a promise from me about the St. John suit, I went over to my brother's house. I knew he loved me, and I knew he loved Carter, but I didn't know how he would feel about his best friend being tangled up with his crazy sister.

Addie met me at the door.

"Aunt Bit!"

"Addie, hi!" I said.

"My Aunt Bit, she's Little Bit," Addie returned, laughing.

"Where's your daddy?" I asked her.

"He's in his office," Addie said. That meant he was dictating letters to his patients and their files.

"Is he in a good mood?" I asked, hoping.

"I don't know," Addie said, leading me through the living room. She stood on the edge of the threshold of Haines's office door. Haines and Addison's house had a room right off the living room that they'd turned into Haines's office, closed off by two French doors.

"Well, look who's here!" Haines said, waving me in.

"Can I have a word in private with you?" I said, closing the French doors, shutting Addie out, and sitting down on the other side of the desk.

"What's up?" my brother said, looking like a doctor hearing about his patient's symptoms.

"Haines," I began. "I don't know where to begin."

He sat there patiently.

"Haines," I said again, "this is hard."

I paused and then spit it out. "This is about Carter and me."

And he smiled. He knew.

"I know, Little Bit. Carter has already asked me if he can marry you. I told him you give your own damn permission," Haines said.

"What?" I asked, shocked. "What do you mean about getting married? Oh shit. What was Carter thinking telling you a secret like that?"

My brother smiled his broad, easy smile, the one that made him look both handsome and dangerous.

"How much is it going to cost me to buy your silence? Carter has always loved you. Even when he knew you were going to move to New York. Even when you put him through that shit about Biggie's will."

I interrupted. "And . . . *that* secret you could keep?"

"Well, there was Jenny, and you weren't . . ."

I finished, "I wasn't ready for him yet."

I hugged my brother a long time, and I could tell he was happy for us.

"I love you both," he said. "I just wish you didn't have to go through all of it just to get to this place."

I broke away from Haines, startled by my own realization. "Haines, I had exactly the life I was supposed to. Without all that other stuff, I would never have been in a place to appreciate Carter. Or Win. Or a perfect brother. Death hasn't compromised my love for Avery at all, although I do wish Avery could see this now."

"Don't you think she does?" he asked easily. "Heaven is just a change of address." I saw my brother's faith as clearly as I saw his desk, his eyes, his love.

"Thank you, Haines."

I left my brother's to head toward Dexter Avenue and Mama. She was in her usual spot, back toward me, standing at the stove, when I walked into her kitchen.

"Hi, Mama," I said. "Do you want to go to the Every Day for lunch?"

"That would be nice, Bit, but I'm going to the movies with Blaine."

"Some other time, then. Mama, I need to tell you something."

"What is it, Bit?" she asked, still not turning around.

"Do you know already?"

"Know what, Bit?"

If she knew, she wasn't letting on. She could keep a secret better than Haines.

"Mama, please turn around and look at me," I said. And she did. "Carter and I are seeing each other."

She smiled, longer than necessary.

"Are you happy, Bit?"

"Yes, ma'am."

"Good. Then I'm happy for you." No hug, no prying.

"Did you know?" I asked.

"Know what?" Mama asked, still telling no tales.

It was at church the next day that Carter and I had our first outing. He had a budget report, and I figured he could use my support. As promised, my attendance at church did cause something of a commotion, especially when I bypassed Mama's pew and went past her to sit with Carter in his.

Berma Ellen Woods came up to me, wearing her snootiness like a corsage. "Well, Little Bit, are you gonna tithe now?"

I left church without even speaking to the preacher. Baby steps.

Three weeks after going public, I came home from work, and Agnes was there. Win's Hummer was in the driveway.

"Why are you still here?" I asked Agnes, who still came over some afternoons, not always to cook, but to watch Netflix. In truth, Agnes had spent many a late afternoon with me, eating dinner and, of course, binging Netflix together.

"Ask Win."

Win came from the direction of the living room to the breezeway and held a "thumbs-up" sign to Carter, who was standing on his side of the wrought iron gate.

"What's going on?" I asked Win, as Agnes went into the living room to see, keeping me on the breezeway.

"Ask Carter."

Carter walked through the gate and onto the breezeway, still dressed in his suit and tie from court. He looked distinguished and handsome, and I wondered if my heart would ever not be affected by his presence.

"Carter, what's going on?" I asked as Carter, Win, Agnes, and I formed a single caravan and moved into the living room.

What I experienced was a scene from a movie. There, in the middle of Biggie's living room, was a small round table covered in gold taffeta, draped over in green silks tied on the side with two silk knots.

"Happy colors," Win said.

The room was lit by candles and nothing else. Win—and Biggie—furnished the candelabras, and the room was filled with the smell of lilies and gardenias. My mind drifted to Avery, but I smiled. The table was set for two with all silver finery, including Biggie's best bone china. Win just looked proudly at her handiwork, but maybe it was something more.

Of course. This was it.

I leaned over to Carter, "This seduction scene isn't necessary. I'm going to say 'yes.'"

He turned to me as if we were all alone. "You're worth it, Bit," he said, and I kissed him right there in front of Win and Agnes.

"That's our cue." Win nudged Agnes. "Just let me get dinner, and we'll be off."

"You cooked, Win?" I asked, and hugged her for her effort.

"I did, and not from the Junior League cookbook either. But I think you'll be pleased." I recognized it immediately. The smells were unmistakable.

"Chicken biryani?" She nodded. Carter's eyes fogged over.

"This is really nice, Carter," I managed.

"It was all Win's idea. Her creation." The way he said it prompted my next question.

"This looks like quite the elaborate production. Did she drive you crazy?"

"In a word, yes. She came by the courthouse with a bunch of swatches and draped them right over the opinions I was writing. She wouldn't budge until I picked one."

I looked down at the two layers of fabric covering the table and knew Carter had patience that no one else did.

"She brought you swatches?"

"That's Win."

Carter jumped up and went in the kitchen. He came back with champagne and a book.

"I'm sure you recognize your growing-up manual."

"Gideon? Is this your idea of foreplay? You know Dr. Seuss is one of my love languages."

He cleared his throat.

Oh the places you'll go
With your head full of brains and your shoes full of feet
You're too smart to go down any not-so-good street
And you may not find any you'll want to go down
In that case, of course, you'll head straight out of town.
He made eye contact.
I'm afraid that sometimes you'll play lonely games too
Games you can't win
'cause you will play against you.
So be sure when you step,
step with care and great tact
and remember that life's
a great balancing act."

I smiled. Then he took some license with Dr. Seuss, but I don't think Teddy would mind.

We're off to great places, today is the day
our mountain is waiting
let's be on our way.

He blew out the one candle on Biggie's secretary and took the candle out. There were two rings resting comfortably on the edge of the rim. He took the rings, got down on one knee, and looking up at me, said solemnly, "Nina, will you marry me?"

"Carter," then opting not to say something funny, I said simply, "Yes."

He showed me the rings, but I knew them already. His mother's engagement and wedding rings. Redesigned especially for me much in the same way that Miss Harriet herself had fashioned my debutante corsage.

"I think she'd like to be represented on your hand."

He slid the rings on my finger. He turned the diamond around and kissed it tenderly.

"I love you, Carter."

"I love you, too, Bit."

Later I wore my new blue nightgown, as we commemorated the evening. Win was right. A nightgown made me feel pretty. Afterward, we were lying there, but still awake.

"So where are we going to live?" Carter asked. "You do know my house has the swimming pool?"

I smiled. "If you don't move over here—the basketball hoop, well, it's coming down." Thanks, Biggie, I thought, for being ahead of your time.

"Damn, you play hardball," Carter said.

"It wasn't the sound of you and Haines swimming laps that brought me home, you know."

Carter smiled. He liked my answer.

"What do you want to do with all the bedrooms?" I asked.

His answer was swift. "Fill 'em up." I kissed him, and he fell asleep.

I glanced at his scars before getting up. They looked painful. Curved. But they had brought us together. Sometime after midnight, Carter appeared in the living room beside me.

"Sometimes I have terrible insomnia. Just one of many things you'll have to get used to with me," I said.

He sat down.

"You mentioned once that the last conversation you had with Avery was an argument," I continued. "What was it about?"

"You."

"Me?"

"She said that I'd have to make the first move. That you would never do it. Jesus, was she right."

"Avery wanted us together?" I asked. That was her insider information?

Carter laughed. "She did. Her matchmaking skills were better than yours."

With that, Carter took his cue to leave me with my thoughts, but not before turning and saying, "You know, Bit. You can always talk to me. Even when you wear those wretched Carolina T-shirts."

I knew his love had given me great latitude in which I could be the me I really was. It would take a while for me to become Bit Gideon, and Carter accepted that. I was just becoming Bit Enloe and getting comfortable in *her* shoes.

But it was in my power to fulfill my dream of an Avery Gideon. My version of clicking the ruby slippers. Not in the way I had initially planned, but with the children I could have with Carter.

epilogue

My name is Nina Barnes Enloe. Most people call me Bit. Maybe this story does end the way it begins. With Haines and Carter playing basketball, albeit with a little tulle draped along the court, and Win still bossing everyone around. I heard her yell at them from the breezeway.

"Just once, would it be too much to ask for you to take one day off? You're going to be all hot and sweaty, and you're ruining my decorations. This girl doesn't get married every day, you know. Don't you have more respect for your sister, Haines, and your soon-to-be wife, Carter?"

Wife. I wondered if that word affected Carter the way it did me. I briefly glanced over at my bouquet that Cy and Olga gifted me—gardenias, lilies of the valley, and forget-me-nots. I was sitting at the dressing table getting ready.

What say you about your only granddaughter marrying Carter Gideon? I thought. *Well, we are certainly fulfilling your last request, in spades. 'Til death us do part.* I paused in my thoughts. *If you can hear me, I didn't make a decision out of fear, and just look who I got.*

Biggie, Avery, Agnes, Mama, Cy, Olga, Wai, and Win. They all had loved me differently, but Avery had always been my steadying force. People are not always going to love us in the same way, but that should not diminish their love. In the end, it's only important that we are loved.

Carter and I decided to get married the week after July 4th. Cy and Olga flew in with a care package: tuna salad. "In case you want a little nibble, darling." Win wanted me to get married in June. Can you imagine me, a June bride? I had only one attendant, Win, of course, but I had two flower girls—Winnie and Addie. I had invited Arush and Courtney, but they couldn't come. It would be too hard, he said, and for me as well.

I looked in the mirror. I barely saw my reflection. What I saw were all the pictures I had stuck so haphazardly along the edges. Some were so old and had been there so long that the ends were curling up. Just like that, the past and the present folding into one. Avery, Win, and me in so many; the stories those pictures could tell.

They are happy stories and sad ones. They are buttery and warm to the touch, smelling of yeast. They make a thudding noise, but only after 9:00 a.m. on Saturdays. They come in the form of early-bird specials, citrus, and gardenias, and in happy colors. They can also be filled with sadness and terrible piercing sounds. They are our memories.

Friendships, in turn, can be as elastic as good houses. They can expand beyond this world, and they can bloom into something unexpected and deeper.

I thought about the word "home." It can be messy. Complicated. Subjective. Like love itself. It can retain dual citizenship. It can change over time.

It can be a location. A brick-and-mortar structure.

An assortment of foods.

A collection of feelings.

A repository of memories multiplied over time and experience.

Or . . . is it where we find our best selves? Where we are happiest? Strongest?

Is it a group of people? Our village? Our squad? "Our roots," reminding us who we are?

Can it change over time . . . ?

Home is an alchemy of all those things. Maybe the word "home" is as flexible as the word "house," changing and morphing over time and circumstance.

I briefly thought of Arush going "home" to Ohio. And Jenny. I thought of Chewy and Jordan saying Avery was going home. They are merely changing addresses, but they reside quite comfortably in our hearts.

Tears began to flow as Win appeared at the door. Her mascara was running.

"Are you crying?"

"It's just the rain, silly. It's coming."

I smiled. "Win, it's a good thing we're friends."

"It's your wedding day, for goodness' sake. Get it together," she added, humoring me. Then she grew serious. "Avery saw the best of things for you, Bit." Then she hugged me tight, trying to fill her quota and Avery's too.

"I love you, Win," I said, finally meaning it.

"Let me go check on those boys," she said, glancing at her reflection in the mirror. "I just know they are ruining the tulle I had placed on the hoop . . ."

Win ran downstairs, but I realized she was crying. The day was getting to us all, and it was almost time. Almost time to turn the basketball court into a place for sacred marriage rituals.

"Bit! Bit!" I came running down the stairs, clutching at my robe. "Take a look," Win said, pointing to the sky that had started to gray over. I breathed it in.

"It smells like rain too," Win said. I didn't hear her voice at all but Chewy's voice from another day, the day we buried Avery.

I looked up again and took in the moisture-filled atmosphere just as seemingly thousands of sunlit tendrils of light pushed through the gathering clouds. I knew in that moment that everyone I had ever loved was here, and I smiled up to the heavens.

I ran upstairs, yelling out to her something old, made new, "When you're right, Win, you're right!"

acknowledgments

I suppose one wonders who is left to acknowledge when I dedicated the book to my beloved village. Some members of this village need singling out.

Melissa Walker is always my first reader. I don't think I have ever sent out a book that has not had her stamp of approval. She has a keen eye that I respect. The other who made *Rainy Days* exceptionally better is Lew Burdette. He is usually my second reader. He gave me wonderful suggestions to think about especially the day that Bit meets Avery. Your suggestions improved those scenes. And thank you for being my partner in crime during childhood.

Special thanks go out to Samantha Bradshaw for discussing the sensitive topic of Down syndrome with me. You were open, receptive and generous with your thoughts. Much love to you. And Susan Lancaster for exploring the terrain with me and letting me work through the grief. I guess I owe a big thanks to Kaitlin Ciarmiello who said "if Leslie is open to it . . ." Well I never had a chance. I always respond to a writing dare!

Big thanks go to my patient and empathetic editor Ezra Fitz who understood how hard this was for me and when it was done uttered the famous line "Sometimes you take a book where you want it to go, and sometimes the book takes you, doesn't it?" Each novel my characters tend to be much smarter than I am and I am at my best when I shut up and allow them to TELL me what to do.

Many thanks to Jas Dillard for helping me navigate Arush's culture and background and giving me some delicious dishes. I can't wait to taste them IRL. You are so kind my friend.

Big thanks go to Kevin Wilson, Patti Callahan, Kristy Harvey, Lisa Barr, Colleen Oakley, Amy Greene and the indefatigable Jill McCorkle who shakes her pom-poms. These PEOPLE. These BUSY people have kept me afloat with emails and beautiful blurbs. I love you all and most days I keep my jealousy of your wicked talent at bay. Ha ha!

There are just some people that have made this publishing gig easier. I appreciate you Lisa Harrison, Francene Katzen and Brenda Gardner. Either you guys were publicists in another life or you should be in this life. Thank you for publicizing my books. And special thanks to Amelia Keesler for helping me edit, drink coffee and for adoring Taylor Swift as much as I do. To Sally Brewster at Park Road Books and the War Eagle team at Auburn Oil Booksellers who suggested BAE time and time again. Thank you for embracing BAE and Me.

The group who saved my books from obscurity are the bloggers. I'm not going to name them all because YOU know who you are. I hope you do anyway. You have single-handedly rescued my books and I am in debt to you. Please know I could not do this without you.

And thank you to those well-meaning friends that called up their bookstores and said "please carry this book." I know who you are too.

I bow down to all the people at Turner. You guys are simply the BEST. Todd, for discovering me on a walk back at Sewanee. Stephanie, no one works as hard as you and is as conscientious as you; you pushed me to turn out the best product. The crazy-talented

Emily Mahon for, I think, the prettiest cover yet! And to Lauren. Bless you Lauren for putting up with all my crazy questions and treating me with such care and patience. And thanks to Josh and Carey. You truly make up the best part of Leslie Inc.

So, it really does take a village to publish a book and one village idiot to write the book. I know my part and I play it well.

book club discussion questions

1. How does your book club community fulfill you in ways other groups may not?
2. Bit wants to leave Erob for the Big Apple. Have you ever wanted to move to a place "where people don't know who you are?" Why or why not? What does each place mean for Bit, and how is she defined in each place?
3. Win seems to have all the "lucky dust." Do you believe in luck? Why or why not? Do you have friends who have "lucky dust"? Do you?
4. Why do you think Win and Bit remained friends in spite of their differences and disagreements? What holds their friendship together over the long haul?
5. Avery is a peacemaker. Which relationships call on you to be a peacemaker? What sacrifices are required?
6. Erob is a quintessential southern town. What are the benefits and challenges of living in a small, tight-knit community?
7. Bit says she hopes the bonds of friendship are so elastic that they can stretch into eternity. Do you think this is true?
8. Of the three friends, Bit, Win, and Avery, with whom do you identify most, and why?
9. All three girls have childhood dreams that ultimately turn out differently from the way they envisioned. What are some of your childhood dreams, and how have you seen them play out?
10. Funeral casseroles serve to acknowledge grief. What examples of compassion have been most meaningful to you?
11. Bit's journey has been all about finding home—in places, in relationships, in herself. What does home mean to you?

about the author

Leslie Hooton is many things: a fabulous friend, a powerful speaker, a flower enthusiast, and a lover of language. You don't want to miss her beloved novels, *Before Anyone Else* and *The Secret of Rainy Days.*

Growing up in a small Alabama town, Leslie went on to earn her B.A. and M.A. from Auburn University and J.D. from Samford University. She became intrigued by people and discovered everyone has their own unique stories. She attended the Sewanee Writer's Conference, and studied with Alice McDermott, Jill McCorkle, and Richard Bausch. Leslie resides and writes in Charlotte, North Carolina. Follow Leslie on Instagram, and Facebook. Go to Lesliehooton.com for book clubs or speaking engagement contact information.